MW00613655

the Trust

A BO MARTIN THRILLER

Scott M. Colton

Copyright @ 2018 by Scott Colton

This book is a work of fiction. Names, characters, places, and incidents
are either part of the author's imagination or are used fictionally, and any
resemblance to actual persons, living or dead, business establishments, events, or
locales is entirely coincidental.

To my wife and children,
for being there in good times and bad.

If things go wrong, don't go with them.
—Roger Babson

Cast of
Characters

Bo Martin	Attorney
Ruby Martin	His wife
Bella and Max	(Their prized dogs)
Bye Martin	Father
Teresa Martin	Mother
Ms. Everett	Secretary
Hank Miles	Best friend
Burt & Sophia Milner	Neighbors
Bart Sinclair	Jeweler
Dana Sinclair	His wife
Joe Marx	Jeweler
Philip Houseman	British attorney
Paul Schwartz, Esq.	Attorney
Ross Brown	Accountant
Harrison Frazar	Bahamian banker
Victor Butin	Russian mob leader
Igor and Ivan	Russian goons
Milton Rogers	Rich tycoon
Brenda Rogers	Tycoon's wife
Lee	The Rogers's four children
Lance	
Lawrence	
Luke	

Brad Penny	Diamond maker
Jim McDonald	Civil attorney
Steve Fleishman	U.S. Attorney
Nick Long	U.S. Attorney
Mae McReynolds	*Palm Beach Times* reporter
Jean Valhomme	Belgian entrepreneur

Chapter
One

It was nearly 2:00 a.m., and Bo Martin, Esq., still was unable to fall asleep. Although Bo was a marathon runner with a normal resting pulse rate under thirty-five, his heart was pounding as if he were in the middle of a race.

Bo crawled out of bed trying not to disturb his lovely wife, Ruby, and their two energetic prized Vizslas. The dogs—also referred to as the "red dogs"—Bella and Max, were their children. They were treated with so much love and attention that they became spoiled rotten. Bella and Max remained motionless in their designated places on the king-sized bed. Max continued his loud snoring, but other than that, the house was silent except for the slight purr of the ceiling fans.

Bo quietly put on his beach shorts and t-shirt and crept across the wooden floor to the hallway. He gently closed the bedroom door behind him and walked through the living room and outside through the French doors. Bo shivered as the cool ocean breeze swept over his body. He remarked to himself how beautiful and peaceful the pool looked with the reflection of the moon shining down on the rippled water.

Unfortunately, Bo's idyllic moment was shattered by the dread that surrounded and consumed his thoughts. He felt the weight of the world on his broad shoulders.

Even in normal times, Bo's legal practice weighed heavily on his mind. The nonstop demands and needs of his various clients and the everyday administration of running a law firm in the competitive market of Palm Beach,

Florida, commanded most of Bo's attention. But now, Bo was faced with a huge dilemma. He thought, *Do I continue to trust my client and adhere to the sacred and paramount attorney-client privilege, or do I look after myself and spill the beans?* Bo sighed again and stared out in the distance at the small ocean waves that crashed upon the sandy beach. *How did I get into this mess, and more importantly, how do I get out of this troubling situation?* Bo ran his fingers through his hair and scratched his head, which was a nervous trait.

After about thirty minutes of deep thought, Bo's shoulders sank, as he dejectedly walked back into the safe confines of his lovely home and attempted to force himself back to sleep. At exactly 5:00 a.m. the alarm sounded, and Bo rose again and brushed his teeth. The dogs quickly bounded off the bed when Bo silently motioned for them to join him on his daily ritual run, along one of the most famous beaches on the Atlantic Ocean. To Bo and the dogs, it was just a soft place to run, undisturbed by the general public.

Bo and Ruby's house was situated on the north end of the island of Palm Beach, Florida. At first sight several years earlier, they fell in love with their small cottage-styled Bermudian home. Rather than continue the trend of the new-money society that bulldozed the older homes on the island and replaced them with giant concrete mansions, the Martins lovingly and painstakingly restored their "ocean shack," as they commonly referred to it. The house was painted a beautiful yellowish crème egg color, which blended well with the bright glossy white shutters and white roof. The Martins' cottage sat on almost one-half acre of prime oceanfront. Bo and Ruby, singlehandedly preserved all of the native vegetation to create their own personal utopia. The bougainvillea, impatiens, coconut palm trees, and huge ficus hedge shielded their house from the public eye. Bo slaved over the manicured lawn and landscape. He also toiled with the sprinkler system on a weekly basis, usually cussing profusely to himself, the red dogs, the neighbors, and anyone else who might happen to overhear.

The only invasion to their privacy came from the surfers who walked across their yard to reach the infamous Reef Road. To those in the know, Reef Road is a surfer's Mecca. Whenever there is a northern cold front, the wind and storm surge cause unbelievable sets of swells. The sandy bottom off Reef Road forces the waves to pop up and create an awesome eight-to-ten-foot tubular wave. It is not uncommon to see fifty to sixty surfers riding waves at daybreak on a windy winter's morning.

Fortunately for Bo, there were no waves this morning and therefore no surfers, just Bo, Bella, and Max running quickly in the morning darkness. Bella and Max ran further ahead, chasing the baby finches that dug in the sand at the fringes of the surf, looking for small crustaceans. Bo was so consumed with his personal dilemma that he did not notice the two men dressed in black, eyeing his every movement. At 6:00 a.m. after a quick six-mile run, thoroughly drenched by the hot and humid south Florida weather, Bo returned to the cottage for his cool-down swim in the pool with Bella and Max. The pool guy always wondered why there was so much sand in the pool, and Bo didn't have the heart to tell him that the dogs and he traipsed it into the pool from the ocean every day. After a quick shower and shave, Bo was ready for work. He walked over to the king-sized bed and bent over to kiss Ruby goodbye. Ruby immensely enjoyed her morning sleep after Bo and the dogs left for their 5:00 a.m. run. Bo's sense of dread started to weigh heavily on him again, and Ruby sensed his somber reflection, asking him what was wrong.

"Honey, you look as though the world is on your shoulders. What's wrong? Are you feeling okay? Are the dogs all right?"

Bo answered with his usual line: "Everything is fine; I just have a lot of stuff going on at the office. The dogs and I had great time at the beach as usual, and don't you worry about a thing! Go back to sleep, and I'll call you later this morning."

Ruby accepted his answer and proceeded to fall back to sleep with the two tired and slightly wet Vizslas, snuggling beside her.

Bo slowly backed his BMW along the white picket fence and out of the Chicago brick driveway that he and Ruby had installed brick by brick. He looked admiringly at his small home and then proceeded along the two-lane ocean road toward his Worth Avenue office. With his thoughts primarily on his dilemma, Bo entirely missed the black Cadillac STS that loomed behind him. Suddenly the car collided into him from behind, causing Bo to swerve and almost lose control of his vehicle. Bo quickly pulled over and watched with his mouth agape as the black car continued to speed down the road, as if nothing had happened. Bo attempted to get the license number, but there was no plate. *Was this some kind of threat, or was the driver just another elderly millionaire in a hurry to get to breakfast*, thought Bo. *More likely the latter*, thought Bo nonchalantly and continued along to work. He didn't even look at the back end of his car when he arrived at the office. What was the point? The damage was done, and along with that came the hefty bill from the BMW dealership. It was just one less thing, he wanted to think about today.

The office of Martin and Martin, P.A., was located at the far eastern end of the famous Worth Avenue. Worth Avenue is one of the premier shopping avenues in the entire world. Gucci, Tiffany, Rolex, and many other upscale stores draw thousands of shoppers annually. The shoppers were hoping to rub elbows with the rich and famous and also just to stroll down the elegant street. In the winter social season, it is the place to see and be seen. As Bo's father liked to say, "The rich have the same problems as everyone else, except that money is not one of them."

Fortunately for Bo, his father bye, purchased the stoic two-story building in the 1950s and continued to hold on to it, despite some outrageous purchase offers of late. Rent on Worth Avenue was up to nearly $150 a square foot, excluding CAM, and increasing substantially each year. The elder Martin had retired from the practice of law and was enjoying his days at the Martin family summer home in Nantucket, Massachusetts. Bo drifted off for a few moments, smiled, and wished that he, Ruby, and the dogs were in Nantucket, or anywhere else in the world, but not here.

Bo was usually the first to arrive and open up the office. Bo thoroughly enjoyed being the only person in the office. He often was able to get an hour or more of solid work in before his secretary, the elderly Ms. Everett, showed up and began her incessant mothering: "Did you have breakfast?" "Are you going to court this morning?" "Have you reviewed your calendar?" "How is Ruby?" and "Why don't you slow down? You are working too hard." She was definitely a nag, but she had a mind like a trapdoor. There was never a name or a face that she couldn't recall, and she was absolutely fantastic with Bo's mostly elderly clientele. She also loved Bo to death!

Bo was dressed in his usual attire—khaki pants, blue shirt, Gucci shoes, alligator belt, and silk amoeba tie. He totally abhorred suits. A Brooks Brothers navy-blue blazer was a permanent fixture on the door hanger, ready for any court appearance or social occasion. His short brown hair was always neatly trimmed, and his year-round tan complemented his intense green eyes. Bo was just shy of six feet and appeared muscular despite his lean runner's frame.

Chapter
Two

o was the only child of Bye and Teresa Martin and enjoyed the family trappings of wealth. Bo excelled early on in academics, and found his true calling in middle-distance running. From the age of twelve, Bo ran competitively. Bo knew, virtually, every crack of every sidewalk and road in Palm Beach. It was not uncommon of him to run upwards of one hundred miles per week.

By the time Bo reached the age of sixteen, he was a high school All-American. He was recruited by all the major universities and finally chose the University of Florida in order to remain relatively close to home. At UF, Bo majored in accounting and excelled in the five-thousand- and ten-thousand-meter races, earning All-American honors each year. In 1984, his senior year of college, Bo was considered a favorite to represent the United States at the Olympic Games in Los Angeles. Unfortunately, a torn hamstring impeded his training efforts, causing him to finish fourth at the trials. He missed qualifying for the Olympics by a few hundredths of a second. It was a devastating loss.

However, Bo turned a negative into a positive by using his newfound free time to apply for law school and study for the law school entrance exam. Bo aced his exam and shortly thereafter was accepted and continued his law school education at the University of Florida. Bo's first semester was absolutely terrible. He hated his classes and the Socratic method of teaching. *Why do I care what my fellow students think about a case or the legal statute?* thought Bo. All I want to know is what the teacher believes is the correct answer. If Bo's father had not been an attorney, Bo most certainly would have finished his law career after one semester.

Bo, nevertheless, continued to stick it out and eventually found tax and probate law to be his only real legal interest. Bo always returned home to his family's homestead each summer in Palm Beach for necessary R & R. His mom, Teresa, was one of the most caring, giving, and energetic individuals he had ever met. She was also his biggest supporter, and he learned compassion and charitable philanthropy from her.

Bye on the other hand, was the epitome of the traditional attorney. He was one of the most respected and honorable attorneys in all of Florida. Bo respected his father immensely, and worked hard to earn his father's praise. Bo was blessed with wonderful parents, and he acquired the best traits from each.

The three years of law school passed quickly for Bo. Although he did not graduate in the upper 10 percent of his class, he did shine in the tax-related classes. Bo interviewed at several of the area's top law firms, much to his father's chagrin, who would have preferred Bo to immediately practice with him. Bo worried that nepotism would detrimentally affect his legal career if he went straight to work with his father, so instead he went to work for the largest firm in Palm Beach County. Bo soon hated every minute of big-firm life!

In all big law firms, associates are generally required to bill over two thousand hours a year. That equates to forty hours a week for fifty weeks or eight hours per weekday. However in order to accomplish actual billable hours, an associate must work ten to twelve hours to legitimately bill eight hours. Bo abhorred billing and the daily time sheets that went along with them. Each minute of the day had to be accounted for. Bo could never understand billable hours. Why would any attorney agree to settle a legal matter if the attorney continuously gets paid until it is settled? "Never settle" was the mantra of most large law firms. Furthermore, Bo questioned, why do clients agree to give blank checks to attorneys? No wonder the proliferation of lawyer jokes and attorney bashing! With billable hours, the only winner is the law firm. Maybe that is why people say, "What do you throw an attorney who is drowning? His or her partner!"

Bo suffered through five long miserable years learning the ropes and making acquaintances before leaving to join his father and create an estate planning/probate practice. Bo immediately eliminated billable hours and instead created a fixed fee for estate planning and a percentage rate charge for handling estate administration. It did not take long before Bo's own legal practice with his fair and modest billing practices mushroomed. Bo enjoyed the success and the freedom.

Fortunately for Bo, the next best thing that happened to him was meeting his southern belle, Ruby. Ruby was raised in Charleston, South Carolina. She was tall and strikingly beautiful with long blonde hair and brilliant blue eyes. It was love at first sight for Bo when one day he saw her walking along the Palm Beach bike trail. The infamous bike trail meandered between the beautiful stately mansions and the Intracoastal Waterway. The trail was comprised of asphalt rather than concrete. Asphalt, which tends to be more forgiving on the knees and other joints, is why Bo ran there, as often as he could. Bo had never seen this beauty on the trail before, so he figured she must be vacationing and he would never run into her again, or so he thought.

As luck would have it, Bo's mother, Teresa, had also noticed Ruby at Ruby's Healthy Café. The café was a breakfast and lunch eatery, nestled a block north of Worth Avenue. Teresa, and her tennis partners all loved the food, but Teresa also knew that she had found the gem for her Bo. It wasn't until weeks later that Teresa was able to play matchmaker and convince Bo to join her for lunch at Ruby's Café. With just one smile and a gentle handshake, Bo's heart melted. The courtship lasted only several months because both Ruby and Bo knew they had found their perfect mate. Very shortly thereafter, Bo and Ruby were married at the Martin family home in Nantucket. The two of them had never been happier. Bo's practice was a success, the firm of Martin & Martin, P.A. was thriving, and Ruby worked busily at her café.

Unfortunately, Bo's idyllic life was changed when Bye Martin abruptly announced his retirement. That left Bo as the managing partner in charge of handling a fifteen-person law firm in the highly competitive market of Palm Beach. Bo tended to his legal career and practice while Ruby juggled the home remodeling and her restaurant.

The ever increasingly difficult area of estate tax law and estate planning consumed more and more of Bo's already limited time. It was becoming almost impossible for Bo to keep abreast of the law while handling his clients with the undivided personal attention they demanded and that Bo had previously provided.

It was at these most hectic times when Bo wished he and Ruby would just sell everything and move to Nantucket. They both could open a small restaurant and live the simple life. Bo was certain that Bella and Max would be happy anywhere. But Bo continued to persevere. What would happen to his employees if he were to simply close up shop? He also couldn't bear the thought of telling Ms. Everett that the firm was going to close and she would be without a job, or for that matter, a life. No, the law firm of Martin and Martin, P.A., would carry on. There were simply too many good people to take care of properly.

Bo's mind was deeply engrossed in a challenging estate planning scenario when Ms. Everett slipped into his office with a worried look on her face. "Bo, what happened to your car?" she asked.

Bo hunched his shoulders and replied, "It's just a fender bender. Some old guy in a hurry banged into me this morning on the way to work."

"Well, you better have it fixed and at the same time have your neck examined. My dear friend Mitzie suffered whiplash eight months ago in a simple fender bender, and she is still not right," said Ms. Everett with a look of deep concern.

Bo responded by saying that he would go for a swim later in the evening to get the kinks out. "I'm okay. I'll be just fine." Ms. Everett shuffled out of the office, leaving Bo alone in his thoughts.

When Ms. Everett was finally gone, Bo picked up the phone and called his best friend, Hank Miles, a private insurance investigator. Hank and Bo had been close friends for as long as Bo could remember. They had been running buddies for years and almost never missed their Thursday night bridge run where each pushed the other to run faster. Hank and Bo also were the coaches for the local charity, Team in Training. They helped raise funds for leukemia cancer research and trained participants to run in a marathon. In the six years that they had been coaches, the two had traveled to marathons all over the world. Their animated, and often much embellished stories, continued to enthrall their wives, who let the boys have their time together. Ruby was certain that half of what they bragged about was complete and utter nonsense.

Hank knew, immediately that Bo was concerned by the tone of his voice. Hank put his investigative mind on full alert, as Bo proceeded to tell him about the black Cadillac and the resulting fender bender. Hank listened intently and realized that the accident certainly seemed suspicious. Hank asked, "Is there anything else that you are not telling me? Don't leave anything out. Any disappointed clients or disgruntled heirs out there that are mad at you?" Hank chuckled, trying to make light of the situation and trying not to remember what happened a few short months ago. Bo thought about it for a second, trying to figure out if any one of his numerous clients was upset with him or caused him concern. He also desperately tried to fight back the vivid thoughts of what had happened to Bo and Hank not too long ago. Finally, Bo answered "No," but he said it rather unconvincingly. The dead silence on the phone left each man considering the impossible. No, it couldn't be, but unfortunately there was *one* special client. Just the thought of his name, caused Bo to feel a sense of dread again. *Bart of Diamonds! Bart Sinclair.*

Chapter
Three

*I*t all had transpired almost a year earlier, Bo reflected, trying to remember the sequence of events. Bo and Ruby were blessed with excellent neighbors. Although most of Palm Beach was littered with older multimillionaires, the north end of the island did have some younger couples and children. In fact, Ruby's best friend lived right next door. Sophia and Burt Milner had purchased their home at around the same time as Bo and Ruby. Both couples even used the same general contractor to redo their homes. The girls became inseparable, and Bo and Burt were happy that they had each other. The Martins and Milners frequently dined together, and the girls spent most of their free time in each other's company.

However, it was the neighbor at the end of the road who was causing Bo's dread. "Bart of Diamonds," as he was nicknamed, lived in the largest home on the north end of the island. His mansion was at least eighteen thousand square feet, and he recently purchased the adjacent lot to install a grass tennis court and a putting green. Bart had several children and was on either his third or fourth wife. His parking garage contained a Ferrari, a Jaguar, a Porsche, and several Ford Explorers. Behind his house was a sixty-five-foot Viking Sportfisherman. Also a smaller thirty-four-foot Venture with triple 300 horsepower Yamaha engines, a twenty-foot Boston Whaler, and several wave runners. He was known for spending money like water. Bart of Diamonds was in the high-end jewelry business, and his jewelry store was located in the heart of Palm Beach toward the western end of Worth Avenue.

Several years earlier, Bart came to Bo to get assistance with his estate planning matters. At that time Bart was worth in excess of one hundred million dollars. Bo created an elaborate estate plan to minimize inheritance taxes while maximizing the amount of money passing in trust for his children. An additional trust was created for Dana, his latest and much younger trophy wife, upon his death. Bo was extremely familiar with creating complicated estate plans for wealthy older men with children from previous marriages who married much younger women. The goal was always to protect the children, as well as the surviving younger spouse while minimizing the amount passing to the IRS. It was difficult and somewhat treacherous to achieve a nice balance one that would fend off litigation and the universal fight for a bigger piece of the pie. Nevertheless, it was what Bo enjoyed the most, and it definitely paid the bills.

It was Bo's belief that most clients were unfamiliar with the idea of inheritance taxes. Many incorrectly believed that upon death, the assets went untaxed to the deceased's heirs. In 1986, the IRS amended the tax code to allow a spouse to pass an unlimited amount of assets at death to the surviving spouse. Any assets passing to non-spouses, were subject to the substantial inheritance tax. Bo's expertise was in minimizing that tax.

For example, if a man died with ten million dollars in assets and devised all of his assets to his children, the federal inheritance tax would impose a 35 percent tax on everything above $5,400,000. Within nine months of the man's death, the IRS would be owed approximately $1,610,000. However, through the use of advanced estate planning techniques, Bo often created GRITs, GRATs, GRUTs, Q-PRITS, family limited partnerships, and irrevocable trusts to help minimize the impact of estate taxes. Bo's clients were mostly wealthy winter residents of the island, and Bo was delighted to help a family achieve its goals while also minimizing the amount of money passing to the IRS. Bo was definitely not fond of the IRS or its nitpicking lawyers because he believed it was unfair that the IRS taxed assets upon death and created double taxation.

Bo had implemented a sophisticated estate plan to achieve Bart of Diamonds' goals. Yet, Bo secretly wondered how Bart had gotten so wealthy selling jewelry. When Bo had purchased his engagement ring for Ruby from Tiffany's, he knew there was a huge markup. But he had no idea how large the typical jewelry markup actually was. Bart had informed Bo that the markup was in excess of 100 percent. When he dealt with a wealthy client, a two-million-dollar diamond sale resulted in a profit to him in excess of one million dollars. Bo realized he most definitely was in the wrong line of work!

Almost one year ago to the day, Bart of Diamonds and a hunchbacked elderly man had met with Bo to create an irrevocable trust. The elderly man stated that his name was Joe Marx and that he had acquired a considerably large diamond collection during his lifetime. He also declared to Bo that he had no family and that he desired to leave his entire estate in trust to Bart and Bart's children.

Bo instantly, felt that something was fishy. It sounded too good to be true. However, Bart was an excellent client, and the ever increasing cost of running a law practice convinced Bo to take the case. *What could be the harm?* thought Bo. To make matters even more unlikely, the elderly man wanted Bo to serve as the sole trusteeover his trust. Naturally, Bo would be entitled to a trustee fee on an annual basis for managing the trust's assets. It was all so enticing to Bo that he couldn't bring himself to say no.

As was customary in his practice, Bo requested detailed personal information from Mr. Marx. Unfortunately, Mr. Marx wished to maintain his private identity and disclosed no information. He did state that Bart of Diamonds would act as his liaison, and all drafts and documents would go to Bart. This was so peculiar and weird that Bo should have declined the legal representation in spite of the potential yearly large trustee fees. Against Bo's better judgement and gut instinct, he relented and agreed to prepare the trust. The lure of relatively easy money was simply too great to pass up!

About one week later, the Marx Irrevocable Trust was finished. Bo called Bart to arrange another meeting. Bo should have, again, heard voices of concern when Bart replied, "I'll pick up the trust; just leave the date and the year blank." The voices in Bo's head were now screaming, but the allure of easy money, was too great to overcome. Two days later the fully executed trust, predated five years earlier, was returned to Bo with a set of instructions attached.

Bo was directed to obtain a federal tax ID number and to create a bank account. It typically took around a week or more to obtain a federal identification number from the IRS. Bo called Bart of Diamonds on his cell phone to inform him that it could be a lengthy process. Bart had no problem with the delay and thanked Bo for his hard work on his behalf, and most importantly on behalf of his family.

Several weeks later, as Bo was finishing his morning run, Bart of Diamonds came out of his mansion and yelled out to Bo, "Can I talk to you for a moment if you've got the time?"

Bo jogged over to him and said, "Sure; what's up?"

"Mr. Marx would like you to contact his London-based attorneyabout the sale of one of his corporations to me. His attorney's name, phone number, and the name of the company are all in this envelope. Mr. Marx would also appreciate it if you would contact him today."

Bo reached for the envelope and said, "I have a conference call at nine, and as soon as I finish up there, I will give him a call."

"Sounds good," said Bart, "but just remember that London is five hours ahead of us."

"Yeah, I got it. Thanks, Bart. See you later," then he gave a slight wave, turned, and jogged home, trying to keep the sweat from dripping on the envelope and ruining the ink.

Later that morning after finishing up his conference call, Bo reached inside his desk and pulled out the envelope Bart of Diamonds had given him. Bo, with the assistance of his ever faithful Ms. Everett, placed the overseas call and immediately was transferred to Philip Houseman, solicitor. Bo informed the British solicitor that he was an attorney in Palm Beach, Florida, and was calling on behalf of one of his clients desiring to purchase a corporation called A Trading Co. He was somewhat difficult to understand because of his heavy British accent, and Bo did his best to listen carefully. Phillip confirmed that he did indeed represent Mr. Marx and that Mr. Marx had informed him that he would be hearing from Bo. Philip Houseman also readdressed his client's desire to remain as private as possible and that he had been given total authority to negotiate the sale of his company.

Bo, at a loss for words, stammered on about his role as trustee of the irrevocable trust and his client's desire to purchase A Trading Co. Bo couldn't help but think that the purchase price would likely be in the millions of dollars. When Phillip finally got around to the purchase price, Bo's jaw almost hit the floor. The total purchase price was a paltry twenty thousand dollars. Bo quipped to himself, "Only twenty thousand dollars? Why such a small deal? My fees will exceed that insignificant sum!" There was no further discussion regarding the price, and after getting Phillip's fax number and direct phone line, Bo said he would be in touch shortly.

Bo immediately proceeded to type up an email to Philip Houseman, confirming the terms of the purchase, the parties involved, and where and by what method the funds would be transferred. Bo then called Bart of Diamonds to discuss his phone call with Philip. Bo also questioned Bart about how he planned to purchase the corporation. What Bo wanted to ask, however, remained lodged in his own mind. Finally, Bo just had to ask, "So Bart only twenty thousand dollars? What are you buying for that meager sum?" Bart seemed rather distant and preoccupied and told Bo to get whatever further information he needed from Bart's own personal attorney, the infamous Paul Schwartz.

Bo was well aware of Paul Schwartz, as were most Palm Beach attorneys. Paul was a rather seedy character to which his looks matched quite well. He was not a good-looking man to say the least. He was overweight with a jaundiced look to him. His hair, what was left of it, was greasy, and to make matters worse, he attempted to comb it over his head to hopefully give the appearance of a somewhat full head of hair. It didn't work! However, Paul's looks did not interfere with his popularity as a high-powered attorney. He had a skillful knack of representing clients in highly publicized cases. Paul was a criminal law specialist who served as the personal attorney to some of the wealthiest families on the island. In the winter season, Paul was a fixture on the social scene and often rubbed elbows with the richest of rich in the hope of acquiring another well-paying family. For thousands of dollars, Paul would render all sorts of legal advice—both criminal and civil—and made himself available twenty-four hours a day. Paul was extremely effective in helping distraught families when their children or guests were arrested for DUI or disturbing the peace after a lively night of frolicking. It was widely rumored that Paul paid off the police to watch certain in-bars where the kids of these wealthy families were known to hang out. AuBar, was a nightclub that tripped up the Kennedy clan on numerous occasions. It was easy after that for the police to catch them on a DUI. Once arrested, Paul wouldof course, be available to help, thereby enabling him to receive exorbitant fees in a time of crisis.

Paul also represented noted drug smugglers, embezzlers, murderers, and tax cheats. His hourly rate was approaching eight hundred dollars. Paul's recent highly publicized divorce from his third wife and carefree lifestyle undoubtedly put quite a strain on his personal finances.

Bo was very concerned that Paul was Bart of Diamonds' personal attorney but kept it to himself while he placed the personal call to Paul. When Paul came to the phone, Bo was somewhat flattered—either Bo was important in his own right, or Bart of Diamonds was real important. Bo's ego was instantly deflated when Paul said, "I spoke with Bart this morning and was expecting your call. You know with Bart, I am always available. He is one of my best clients and has been for over ten years." Bo's self-image was then completely shattered when Paul said that he had not recommended Bo to assist with Bart's estate planning matters a few years ago. His ego perked up a little when Paul said that he suggested Bo for the irrevocable trust matter.

Bo was somewhat relieved when Paul mentioned the trust. Bo thought to himself, *This means that Paul knows Mr. Marx, and that he found him to be competent.* Bo was also toying with the idea of exactly who he represented.

In most trust situations, the attorney represents the settlor or creator of the trust. As trustee, Bo also had a fiduciary duty to the beneficiary, Bart of Diamonds and his family. So, Bo was torn between his legal representation of the settlor, Mr. Marx, and his fiduciary representation to Bart Sinclair and his family.

Paul, most importantly, confirmed the existence of Mr. Marx and reiterated to Bo that Mr. Marx was a widower with no family. Bart of Diamonds, and his parents had done business with Mr. Marx in the past, and everything was completely legitimate. Bo was still greatly troubled by the predating of the trust document itself but let it slide as he listened to Paul run on about his close relationship with Bart of Diamonds. By the time Paul had finished talking, Bo felt betterabout everything.

Later that same day, Bo was able to speak directly with Bart, who was out on his yacht with his wife and several of his children. Bart was pleased that Bo had spoken with both Philip Houseman and Paul Schwartz. Bart explained to Bo that the twenty thousand dollars was just a token of his good faith to buy A Trading Co. In a very short time, the trust would be funded with millions of dollars from the sale of diamonds. Bart led Bo to believe that business was booming, and that he couldn't keep up with his clients' demands for larger and more beautiful diamond and jewelry ensembles. Before hanging up to catch some more tuna and dolphin, Bart gave Bo the name and number of his accountant. Ross Brown, would be able to assist Bo with the wire transfer of the twenty thousand dollars. Bo was pleased to have most of his questions answered. However, the feeling in the pit of his stomach, did not go away.

Bo telephoned Ross Brown's office and was informed that Mr. Brown was with clients and that he had meetings all day. Before hanging up, Bo stated that he was calling on behalf of Bart of Diamonds, and left his number. Less than fifteen minutes later, the smooth deep voice of Ross Brown, was on the line. Ross bragged about being Bart of Diamonds' personal accountant, and how they often yachted together. Bo thought that Ross lived in West Palm Beach, not Palm Beach, and branded him a wannabe and a name dropper. In fact in all of Bo's years as a trust and estate attorney, he had never had one client utilize the accounting services of Ross Brown. Bo thought that to be somewhat odd.

After listening patiently to Mr. Brown's rendition of self-importance, Bo had heard enough. Bo cut Ross short by getting right to the point of the matter and informed Ross that "Bart Sinclair had engaged Bo to represent his family in the purchase of an offshore company. The initial amount that he will need wired overseas is twenty thousand dollars. Does Bart have a sufficient amount of cash to effectuate the transfer?"

Ross replied, rather indignantly, "Bart has several million dollars in liquid available cash. Virtually all of his money, can be transferred at my sole discretion."

"Good; then," Bo contended, "I will need your email, address, and account information to conclude the purchase of A Trading Co." Bo was relieved that a West Palm Beach accountant handled Bart's finances and tax returns. Bo, personally, was not impressed in the least by Ross Brown.

Bo still had many concerns regarding Bart Sinclair, but each time he spoke with one of Bart's representatives, his questions were answered. For the rest of the afternoon, Bo returned numerous telephone messages and emails, dictated several letters, and completed a complicated estate plan. He also attempted to leave the office before seven for once. Just as he was leaving, Ruby called on his private line (of which only his beautiful wife, his mother, Teresa, and his buddy, Hank Miles, had the number). Bo naturally carried a cell phone, but like his father, abhorred the thought of being tethered to a phone. Ruby conveyed that they were having dinner at the neighbors' house, and Hank was available for a late run. Bo was pleased that he could shoot the breeze with his buddy Hank and hopefully release some of his stress.

Halfway during their up-tempo run, Bo asked Hank for a huge favor. As an investigator for a large insurance company, Hank had unlimited access to highly classified information regarding individuals and corporations. Bo asked Hank to search the background of Bart Sinclair and his assorted corporations. Hank naturally jumped at the opportunity to help his best friend, and upon the conclusion of their run, jotted down all the personal information necessary to conduct his search. As Hank was leaving the Martin residence, he gazed at the gigantic mansion of Bart Sinclair and wondered how does someone make so much money? Hank proceeded down the island in his two-hundred-thousand-mile beat-up Volvo, oblivious to the surroundings of the rich and famous.

Bo, dripping in sweat from his invigorating run with Hank took his traditional cool down in the pool and was immediately joined by Bella and Max. After rinsing off the chlorine, all three proceeded to visit the neighbors, Sophia and Todd Milner and their champion bred poodles. At any given time, it was not unusual for the Milners to have upwards of ten prized poodles on their property. Fortunately for Bella and Max, the Milners' dogs were not snobs, and they welcomed the big red dogs into their domain. Bo could smell the aroma of another fresh homemade pasta dish and couldn't wait to taste it. Between Ruby and Sophia todd and Bo often chuckled how lucky they were to have such beautiful wives and excellent cooks.

Later that night after some delightful lovemaking, Bo reflected on the day's events, and before falling asleep, considered it a successful one.

Chapter
Four

Bart of Diamonds was rasised as the only child of Jack and Dorothy Sinclair and certainly enjoyed the finer things in life. To say he was raised with a silver spoon was an understatement because Jack Sinclair owned one of the largest jewelry stores in New York City. Jack and Dorothy Sinclair were generous supporters of the arts and traveled in the city's most exclusive circles. They were an engaging couple that, unfortunately, was often too busy, personally and professionally, to take care of their only child. Bart, therefore, was basically cared for by several nannies and upon reaching the age of thirteen was sent away to boarding school. He bounced around from school to school for a multitude of reasons, but mainly for his lying and unscrupulous behavior. Bart also was a prankster who often acted before thinking, and seemingly innocent jokes usually ended up with someone getting hurt.

Bart later attempted college and almost succeeded before succumbing to the lure of women and booze—Bart's Achilles heel. Eventually, he settled back in New York City and began learning the jewelry business. Bart concentrated primarily on diamonds under his father's watchful eye. Jack was known as a "strict disciplinarian" within his company, and this somewhat helped control and curb Bart's wild ways. Bart was fascinated with diamonds and within a few years had learned the diamond business inside and out. He was quite anxious to exert his control over the company, maybe a little too anxious!

Jack and Dorothy Sinclair met with an all to sudden death. They were involved in a one-car auto accident coming home from the symphony when Bart was only twenty-five years old. During the probate of their estates, it was noted by some legal professionals in the community that Jack and Dorothy Sinclair, the owners of one of New York's finest jewelry stores, owned not one piece of expensive jewelry. Young Bart was indeed one clever son! The federal estate taxes on the "nonexistent jewelry," would have been in the tens of millions of dollars. Within two years of the Sinclairs' death, their once extremely profitable jewelry store was liquidated, and Bart was living in Palm Beach, Florida.

Bart married Mandy Resnick at the age of twenty-eight and promptly had three children in less than four years. At the ripe old age of thirty-two, Bart opened Diamond and Sons on Worth Avenue and began catering to the rich and famous. Numerous affairs later, Bart became a widower when Mandy unfortunately met the same fate as his parents and died in a one-car accident on the way home from a girls' night out. Less than one year later, Bart married Martha Bie, an older wealthy marketing entrepreneur. During Bart's second marriage, the jewelry store prospered, primarily through the marketing skills of his wife and Bart's dealing in diamonds. While Martha toiled endlessly at the store, Bart enjoyed the finer things that Palm Beach had to offer.

Bart became a highly accomplished marlin fisherman and traveled all over the world attempting to land the next big one. At one time, he even possessed the world record for the largest white marlin ever caught on a fifty-pound test line. Bart was also well known as an extremely generous tipper who loved his women and his drink. The former being one that he could never get enough of, and the latter being one that he got too much of. Bart's exploits landed him in serious hot water at times, and hence, his legal relationship with the infamous Paul Schwartz flourished.

Once again tragedy struck when Martha died unexpectedly in a scuba diving accident while vacationing in the Cayman Islands with Bart. Even though Bart and Martha had access to the best diving guides the island had to offer, Bart suggested they go solo in an attempt to spend some alone time together on the reef. Martha jumped at the chance to be alone with her husband, and since they were both accomplished divers, thought nothing of it. Back on shore after the accident, Bart explained to the Cayman police officers that he did not know why Martha's regulator malfunctioned at a depth of 100 feet. Bart made sure to mention that he was several hundred feet away from her when he noticed her in distress. By the time he got to her, it was too late.

A widower for the second time, Bart wasted little time in finding wife number three. He married his trophy wife, Dana White at the age of thirty-eight. Four years ago on their wedding day, Dana was twenty-three years of age and six months pregnant.

Four years later, Bart of Diamonds had purchased the lakefront Palm Beach mansion, a ski home in Vail, Colorado, a small island in the Bahamas, and continued to run his lucrative Worth Avenue boutique. Bart further extended his brood by having a second child with Dana.

Chapter
Five

It took Hank a few days to uncover the personal and financial information requested by Bo regarding Bart. What information he did find, unfortunately, did not dispel Bo's concerns. Hank was also able to provide Bo with an outline of Bart's history of companies. Bo already knew that Bart was worth in excess of one hundred million dollars when he assisted with Bart's estate planning matters. Based on Hank's investigation, Bo was relieved to learn that Bart had no prior criminal felonies or outstanding warrants. Personally, Bart was also judgment free and was not presently involved in any personal litigation.

Corporately and civilly, Bart had been sued several times. All the lawsuits were followed by countersuits of slander by Bart's trusted legal advisor, Paul Schwartz. It was interesting to note that all the lawsuits were settled and the settlement agreements sealed by the circuit court. There were no current lawsuits pending.

Diamond and Sons was the personal holding company owned solely by Bart of Diamonds. Underneath this umbrella was Diamond Shipping LLC, Diamond Buying LLC, Diamond Sales LLC, and Diamond Manufacturing LLC. Each company controlled millions of dollars and dealt with overseas corporations. Officers of these companies included Paul Schwartz, Esq., and Ross Brown, CPA.

The State of Florida was presently auditing the corporate records, but nothing appeared out of the ordinary, and no enforcement action was undertaken by the Florida Department of Revenue.

Thank goodness, thought Bo as he finished reading Hanks rather extensive background summary investigation into the infamous Bart of Diamonds. *My mind should be at ease, but why is it not?* thought Bo to himself.

Several days later Bo received an email, followed by a fax from Philip Houseman, solicitor informing him that A Trading Co. was available to be purchased at a price of twenty thousand dollars and included the necessary wire transfer information. One aspect of the email was quite troubling and sent chills up Bo's spine. A Trading Co. was not a London or British Company but rather an Isle of Man corporation. What little Bo knew of offshore companies caused him serious concern. Bo had attended several seminars over the years regarding offshore accounts and was well aware that the Isle of Man was a country off the coast of Great Britain that catered to drug smugglers and money launderers. All Isle of Man corporations were sealed with a shroud of secrecy, and little if any information was ever forthcoming. Bo also thought it odd that Philip Houseman was representing the seller of A Trading Co. and also Bo Martin, trustee, as the buyer. In America, there would be a serious conflict of interest for the attorney to represent both sides of a deal. Philip was evidently unfazed by any sense of potential conflict.

Later that same morning, Bo called Philip to discuss the email. During the course of the conversation, Bo attempted to pry a little more information out of him. *Talking to Philip was like talking to a brick wall*, thought Bo. Philip with his British accent, spoke very eloquently and paid little if any attention to Bo's questions and concerns. To get right to the point, Bo finally asked Philip if A Trading Co. was a legitimate company and whether Philip's client sold jewelry. "Tell me, Mr. Houseman, is our mutual client legitimate?"

Philip replied indignantly, "I personally profess to you that my client is a legitimate businessman engaged in the jewelry import and export business. If you are concerned with purchasing the company, maybe your client, Mr. Sinclair, should get a new, more experienced attorney. As soon as the money is wired, I will give you the name of the banker in the Grand Cayman Islands for you to transfer ownership of the sole banking account for A Trading Co. Now, I am pressed for time and late for another appointment. I shall expect the wire transfer no later than noon tomorrow!" With that, Bo listened to the click of the line and the resulting dial tone. The Isle of Man and the Grand Cayman were two banking offshore havens that Bo did not want to ever deal with.

Bo muttered to himself, "How did Philip learn the name of Bart Sinclair? I distinctly don't recall ever providing him with the name of Bart Sinclair. So how did he get that information?" Bo felt numb all over.

Bo immediately proceeded to call Paul Schwartz and ask him what he knew. Paul accepted Bo's call and within minutes was trying to comfort and address Bo's concerns. Paul began by saying, "Yes, Bart did ask me to call Philip Houseman, and yes, I must have mentioned Bart's name to him."

Bo shot back, "If you are calling Philip, why am I even involved? Bart doesn't need me when he has you. Why don't you just handle the purchase? What does he need me for?"

Paul responded curtly, "Bart trusts you and knows your honesty is beyond reproach." Bo was silent for a moment before asking, "Did you know that A Trading Co. is an Isle of Man corporation?" Paul said no, but added that it was not uncommon for an overseas jeweler to seek privacy. Bo shouted back, "It is not uncommon for an overseas drug smuggler, but not a jeweler? Why don't you tell me the truth, Paul?"

Paul responded, "Bo, I'm sorry, I have an important call that I must take. Just retitle the account in the Cayman Islands and do as you are instructed. Goodbye."

Another click and Bo was once again listening to a dial tone and wondering what really was going on. Bo's gut was definitely telling him to run, don't walk, and ditch Bart of Diamonds. As Bo listened to the dial tone, another question arose in his already aching head: how did Paul know about the Grand Cayman account?

Bo next proceeded to call Bart on his private cell phone number. Bart picked up, and Bo could hear the roar of the boat engines in the background. *Bart must be hard at work again on his customized fishing boat*, thought Bo. Bart asked Bo to hold on for a second, and three minutes later he was back. "Sorry for the wait. That was Paul on the line, and we had some business to discuss."

Bo responded angrily, "Bart, what is going on? Why are you even using me when you have Paul?"

Bart immediately countered, "Paul is my personal attorney, but I wouldn't trust him with a dime of my money. Yes, he is a good friend, but I just don't know how good! Everyone knows Paul is a shark when it comes to money, but he is also a damn-good attorney, and he has gotten me out of a jam once or twice.

Bart continued, "Either you agree to be my trustee and look after me and my family and stop questioning matters, or I will leave and take my business elsewhere. But, Bo, I honestly trust you and know that if anything happens to me, you will look after my wife and children. You will do the right thing!"

Bo felt a slight confidence boost and asked Bart why Joe chose the Cayman Islands. Bart responded, "Why not? It is close to a house of mine in the Bahamas, and I buy and sell a ton of jewelry there. Plus, I have fond memories there."

Bo felt a chill come over his body as he recalled that Bart's second wife's death was suspicious and occurred while diving off one of the Islands reefs. How on earth could this man have fond memories of that?

Bart concluded the conversation by telling Bo to call his accountant so that the wire could be sent early the next morning. Bart's final words were, "Trust me, there is nothing illegal going on. Goodbye!" Bo thought, *Famous last words*, as he listened to yet another dial tone.

Bo's final call was to Ross Brown, who confirmed the wiring instructions and sent an email acknowledging receipt.

Lastly, Bo hand typed his personal acknowledgment to Philip Houseman that evening so that the deal would be concluded prior to noon of the following day, as requested. Bo timidly emailed the correspondence sheet out to Philip and finished his business concerning Bart.

By the end of the day and after signing off on his computer, Bo called it quits and left the office.

Bo took considerable delight in seeing his two red dogs and Ruby outside in the yard anxiously awaiting his return. The two dogs jumped and licked Bo incessantly and attempted to impede Bo and Ruby's own hugs and kisses. When asked how his day went, Bo responded, "Pretty good." It was made even better when he stepped inside the house and smelled the aroma of rigatoni a la vodka one of his favorite dishes. "Ruby, you can read my mind; how did you know I was hoping for Italian tonight? Thank you."

Ruby responded by telling Bo, "You know, honey, you really do work too hard. How about we go away for a mini vacation soon? We both could use some time away. The Milners can watch the red dogs. Oh, please, we haven't been on a vacation in such a long time!"

Bo proceeded to change into his Bermuda shorts and white polo shirt, as if he hadn't heard her request for a romantic getaway. When he could sense that Ruby was getting somewhat upset by his lack of attention to her, he said, "Hey, honey, how about we go to the Grand Cayman Islands? There will be a little business to take care of, but I certainly will make time for a lot of pleasure and relaxation!"

Ruby was so excited that she screamed, "Of course that sounds great. When? Oh, can we really?"

Bo waited for a few seconds before saying, "How about a week from Wednesday?" Ruby screamed again, "Yes" and then showered him with playful kisses.

Even Bo thought it would be wonderful to relax in the sun and dive on the Cayman's spectacular reef walls. "I guess I better get my wallet out," Bo said with a bit of sarcasm. Bo absolutely knew that Ruby would have to go shopping, as she couldn't be seen in last year's resort wear!

The following morning Ross Brown successfully wired the twenty thousand dollars to the Isle of Man account. Bo also had Ross wire transfer the sum of five thousand dollars to Bo's trust account for spending expenses and the upcoming trip to Grand Cayman. Bo was very relieved when he received the wire transfer confirmation and therefore proceeded to catch up on his numerous phone calls and ever-demanding clients. A few days later, Philip Houseman delivered by Federal Express the outstanding shares, corporate seal bylaws, and articles of incorporation for A Trading Co. He also included the name, address, and account representative of the Bank of Grand Cayman to assist Bo with re-titling the overseas account for A Trading Co.

Bo next proceeded to have Ms. Everett complete the corporate kit by naming the Marx Irrevocable Trust as the sole shareholder of A Trading Co., Bo Martin, Trustee. By this time, she had also received the federal tax ID number for the trust and was ready to complete the corporate kit. Ms. Everett was so highly qualified and competent that she had virtually completed the task before Bo even thought of asking.

She informed Bo that everything was in order and ready for his trip to the Bank of Grand Cayman. Ms. Everett knew in her heart that Bo and Ruby could definitely use a getaway. Further, the only remaining item that the corporation needed was money. Bo figured he could take care of that with one phone call.

Bart of Diamonds was working for a change at his Worth Avenue store when Bo called with the good news. Bo informed him that he would be traveling to the Caymans to personally re-title the account and that all he needed was a small cashier's check to deposit into the corporate account. When Bart asked if one hundred thousand dollars was sufficient, Bo said it was more than enough. Bart said, "The check will be in my mailbox this evening. Come by and pick it up."

When Bart coyly asked whether Bo would be traveling alone, he was pleased to learn that Ruby would be accompanying him. "Good. I hope you and Ruby will be able to relax a little bit while you are down there. I'll have Dana put something in the box for Ruby as well," he snickered.

Later that evening when Bo and Hank were returning home from their weekly training session, Bo stopped at the Sinclair mailbox and retrieved the package marked "Have Fun." Inside was the one-hundred-thousand-dollar cashier's check, a thong bikini, and twenty-five hundred dollars in cash. Bo concurred that Bart sure did know how to spend money. Hank on the other hand, promised that he would investigate A Trading Co. on his firm's new high speed computer. Maybe he would find something useful. After all these years of friendship, he knew that his buddy was worried about Bart of Diamonds and thought that Bo's naivety could lead him into serious trouble. Hank vowed to make sure his best friend was okay and left later that evening with more determination than ever to get more answers and information on Bart of Diamonds, Joseph Marx, and A Trading Co.

Chapter
Six

With their bags packed, Bo took one last look around their beautiful home, sadly said goodbye to Bella and Max, and exuberantly stepped into the BMW to see Ruby's radiant smile. Bo remembered how much he loved to see her smile and vowed to make efforts to keep it that way. They both turned around to wave goodbye to the red dogs and knew the Milners would take great care of them. Bo's mind was racing. Thinking about the past few weeks, Bart of Diamonds, Paul Schwartz, Philip Houseman, the Isle of Man, and everything else almost caused him to miss the terminal exit to drop Ruby off to check the luggage. It always amazed Bo how quickly the West Palm Beach area was growing. It was not long ago that the West Palm Beach Airport was a small-town facility with outside-only disembarkment from planes. The explosive population growth of the West Palm Beach area, not only fueled the drastic price increase in the value of homes on Palm Beach, but the crime rate as well. Bo parked the car in long-term parking and caught the bus to the terminal. Bo could have parked in the garage parking, but it was double the cost, and although Bo was raised with a silver spoon, he was downright frugal at times.

After the grinding one-hour delay at the airport check-in and TSA screening, Bo and Ruby soon found themselves comfortably settled into their seats on Air Bahamas for the hour-and-a-half flight. The plane was a single prop plane, and Ruby never stopped squeezing Bo's arm in fear that they would crash into the midnight blue ocean. Deep down Ruby was mortified of flying, but she wouldn't ever pass up a trip with her beloved Bo. For as much as Bo was devoted to Ruby, she in turn was devoted to him. Ruby often reflected how lucky she was and how happy and almost complete her life truly was. Only a child could complete the fairy tale. Bo and Ruby had been trying for several years to have a child and had even been to fertilization specialists in the hope of bringing another Martin into the world. Bo's parents bye and Teresa, were always pressing the child issue and nothing would have pleased them more than discovering Ruby was pregnant. Bo knew that a child was always on Ruby's mind and prayed each evening that the good Lord would bless them.

Fortunately, the plane trip was uneventful, and they were soon taxing to the exclusive Grand Cayman Hotel. The hotel was situated on the south end of the island where it enjoyed the wonderful cool ocean breezes. The landscaping was luscious, and the Jack Nicklaus–designed golf course further captured the beauty. Bo had heard through the grapevine that the hotel and grounds were purchased with illegal drug money and that the grand architect had unlimited funds to create this utopia. Bo reflected that it was certainly money well spent.

Bo and Ruby's room was on the third floor and overlooked the beautiful Atlantic Ocean on one side, and the golf course on the other. The ocean breeze swept through the room as Ruby opened the French doors leading out to their own private balcony. The extreme beauty of the Cayman Islands quickly found Bo and Ruby in each other's arms. Soon thereafter, the Martins showered and dressed for a candlelight dinner at the exclusive and notorious Cayman Pearl Inn. As expected, the dinner was absolutely delicious, and Ruby and Bo walked off their dinner with a romantic stroll on the beach under the starlit skies.

Bo asked Ruby, "Honey, are you glad we're here?"

"Of course," responded Ruby, "but I do have one question: what type of business do you have over here?"

Bo, thinking quickly, said that a recent client of his created a trust account with a local trust company. Bo was meeting with the trust officer to assure his client that the money was invested properly.

Ruby sensed there was significantly more to the story but left all legal matters to Bo's discretion. Ruby knew that Bo was a man who often kept matters to himself. Plus, Ruby was not interested in taxes and death and really didn't understand most of it. All she knew—and wanted to know—was that Bo handled all of her café's bookkeeping and tax records. Before Bo reluctantly agreed to take over Ruby's books, her records were in such shambles that he could hardly make heads or tails out of them. It was a good thing Bo came around when he did because another few months, and the precious Ruby's Café would have gone under. Bo paid off her debts, gave her money to revamp the decor, and straightened out the books.

Ruby also learned that simply having blank checks does not ensure there are funds in the bank account. Bo knew that Ruby's idea of balancing the books, or her own personal checking account for that matter, was simply making sure she had a sufficient number of checks. Ruby never worried about the money aspect, as she knew Bo would always provide for her.

Ruby decided that the following morning she would do some shopping while Bo met with the trust officer. Bo had no idea how long it would take to re-title the account, but they made tentative plans to meet together for lunch, pool side at one o'clock. Later that night, Bo and Ruby made love while the ocean breezes helped cool their overheated bodies. It wasn't until the next morning that Bo realized he did not have his cell phone. The only thing he could think of was that it must have fallen out of his pocket while he and Ruby were down on the beach. He did not have time to go looking for it now, and was hoping that someone else would find it and return it to the hotel lobby.

While Bo and Ruby were enjoying their little getaway, Hank Miles had finished his extensive and complete investigation of A Trading Co. The results caused him serious concern. Hank made several attempts to contact Bo on his cell phone to no avail. He left a message with the front desk to have Bo call him immediately. All Hank could do now was wait to hear from Bo, and he hoped it would be soon, so he could warn him about his findings.

Hank made one final phone call before completely satisfying his curiosity. From what Hank had discovered, there was nothing regarding A Trading Co. or even A. Trading Co. for that matter. However, there was an *A Trading Company*, and Joseph Marx was the director. A Trading Co., was a shell corporation created in 1963 in the Isle of Man. For a pricey fifty-thousand-dollar fee, various London attorneys created shell corporations that satisfied all corporate filings in the Isle of Man but in actuality were merely fronts for illegal operations—namely, drug and money laundering. A few Isle of Man corporations maintained accounts in the hundreds of millions of dollars while others were merely intermediaries. Money was wired one day into the shell corporation, and the very next day it was wired elsewhere. Of course, the Isle of Man banks charged excessive fees for their services. However, the biggest service they provided, was one of non-reporting and secrecy.

For example, Isle of Man corporations file nondescript annual reports, which do not disclose any information. The Isle of Man banks are able to keep these accounts and transactions private, and no US civil proceeding can force them to disclose any information regarding the corporate accounts. In essence, the Isle of Man financial institutions, provide the same form of security that the infamous Swiss banks were known for.

From what Hank was able to ascertain, significant funds came from Palm Beach and were thereafter deposited into A Trading Co. Due to the security protection, he couldn't determine where if anywhere, the funds went after hitting the bank in the Isle of Man. Hank was also able to locate a phone number to A Trading Co., Hank called the number from his home phone right before five o'clock and was immediately placed in computer mode as an operator answered, "A Trading Co. Presently all our lines are busy. Please leave your name and number, and we will call you as soon as possible. Have a nice day!"

Hank did not leave a number and made a mental note to call again in the morning. Little did he realize that in a small internal office in West Palm Beach, a man speaking in Russian hollered at another Russian informing him of Hank's name and phone number. After a few keystrokes on the computer, the two large Russians were in a dark Crown Victoria, proceeding toward Hank's home residence.

The Russians were the size of NFL linemen. Six foot four, three hundred pounds of solid muscle, and not a sense of humor amongst them. Their size-sixty jackets failed to conceal the semi-automatic weapons lying close to their bulging pectoral muscles.

The Russians, Igor and Ivan, barely spoke during their twenty-mile drive north along Interstate 95. They disembarked at the exit to Jupiter, Florida where Hank, his wife, and young son resided. The Russians soon found the correct street and were looking for the house number when they spotted the old Volvo in the driveway. The Miles's residence was one of several hundred homes in the manicured community of Abacoa. Most families had several young children, and the dark Crown Victoria with blacked-out windows was somewhat out of place in this friendly, new, and vibrant community.

After circling the street two times and being careful to avoid any further suspicion, the Russians parked in an empty lot, four houses down from the Miles's, and waited. They must have consumed a half dozen protein bars during their wait.

With pinpoint timing, Igor exited the car moments after watching Hank open his front door to retrieve the morning newspaper. Running extremely fast for a 300-pound man, he was able to arrive at the driveway entrance just as Hank bent down to pick up the paper. Hank never even saw or heard him coming until he felt a crushing blow at the base of his neck. Igor picked up Hank's limp body and carried him to the car like a loaf of bread. Ivan had already opened the back door and Igor hurled the inert body into the back seat and immediately closed the door. Seconds later, the Russians drove away, as if nothing happened.

Hank awoke to a staggering and relentless pain behind his neck, causing him dizziness and nausea. He managed to regain some of his senses and realized that he was in a moving car. He tried with all his strength to sit up. Unfortunately, Igor heard Hank stirring in the back seat, and responded with a swift fist to the jaw, causing Hank to lose consciousness once again.

Upon reaching their destination, Igor and Ivan carried Hank into the West Palm Beach warehouse and abruptly shut the door behind them. The warehouse was dark and dreary, and they left Hank lying on the cold cement floor as they went into the office to wait for a call. Thirty minutes later, Ivan was spewing Russian into the phone and making animated gestures while yelling in his deep voice.

Hank awoke to the sound of shouting voices but had no clue what they were saying. In addition to his neck pain, his jaw was definitely swollen and hopefully, not broken. He was scared and trembling when the two huge Russians exited the office and helped him to his feet.

Hank spoke first, "What the hell is going on? Who are you?" Igor then answered in his best English, "Why did you call A Trading Co.?"

Hank passed Igor a questioning look and said, "I have no idea what you are taking about." His response elicited a swift blow to his abdomen, causing him to drop to his knees in intense pain.

Again, Hank answered, "I don't know what you are talking about."

Ivan spoke next, "You placed a call from your home phone to A Trading Co.. We are just trying to find out why you called the company."

Hank hesitated before answering. "I called a wrong number earlier this evening when I was trying to call a catering company." Hank made up a fake number and changed the last two digits around from the number of A Trading Co.. He further responded, "As soon as I got an answer message, I knew I had the wrong number, so I hung up."

The two Russians looked pensively at each other before both in a simultaneous action, plunged their fists into Hank's stomach. Hank writhed in pain and fell heavily to the ground with a thud. He knew he couldn't take much more punishment, but he was damned if he was going to mention Bo.

Hank weakly cried out again to the Russians, pleading for their mercy and contending complete innocence. "You have the wrong guy. I do not know what you want, or what I did wrong. Please, I have a wife and son, why would I jeopardize anything? You have the wrong guy."

After only a few short grunts, the two Russians went back into the office, leaving Hank alone on the cold floor. Hank knew he could never win a verbal argument with the two goons, so with every ounce of his energy, managed to rise and actually stand. He then proceeded to limp out of the warehouse. The two Russians never expected Hank to be able to rise on his own, much less leave the warehouse. Once outside, Hank staggered and dragged himself as fast as his legs could take him before miraculously finding a trucker getting ready to climb into his rig. The trucker took mercy on the battered and bruised man and helped Hank into his cab, and off they went.

After a few deliveries, the trucker dropped Hank off at his home. To show his sincere appreciation and gratitude toward the trucker, Hank gingerly and slowly went inside to get his wallet and handed the guy a one-hundred-dollar bill. Hank had never been so happy to be home, and alive! After a quick shower, he was off to the emergency room to check on his right jaw, which was swollen the size of a grapefruit. His burning ribs also concerned him.

Chapter
Seven

B o had taken the ten-minute taxi ride to the Bank of Grand
Cayman. It was a large building, prominently situated in the heart
of downtown and was painted a light pink and white. He patiently
waited for Mr. Harrison Frazar, the assistant VP in the bank lobby, and kindly
declined the offer of coffee or tea. He passed the time by admiring the tropical
decor to the bank. The woodwork was deep cherry and featured rattan style
furniture with tropical pictures and paintings. The ceilings were at least twenty
feet high, creating the illusion of a much greater space. The lush carpeting was
a forest green with red flecks, almost like coconuts. There were four tellers
and three assistants in the main lobby. The trust and banking offshore services
department where Bo was sitting, consisted of several offices. The telephones
were ringing frequently, and the bank was similar to any of those found in
Palm Beach. Bo could sense the presence of money, but more importantly,
secrecy.

Harrison exited from his office moments later and extended his hand
and apologized to Bo. "Sorry for the wait. Pleased to meet you, Mr. Martin. Is
there anything I can get you? Water? Coffee?"

Bo kindly declined and shook Mr. Frazar's soft and clammy hand.
"Beautiful bank you have here!" said Bo. "We like to think so," answered Mr.
Frazar. "Come, come into my office, please."

Bo followed Mr. Frazar into the generously sized office and listened
patiently to him explain the history of the bank, his important position, and the
services his bank had to offer. While he was talking, Bo gazed around the office,

trying to gain some additional insight into the banker. There were pictures of what appeared to be his wife and two children prominently displayed.

After a few minutes of small talk, Mr. Frazar asked to be called by his first name. Then Bo got right down to business, regarding the re-titling of the bank account.

Bo figured he would need to sign numerous forms and affidavits and provide documentary proof of the validity of A Trading Co. with stock certificates evidencing his ownership of the company as trustee.

Bo was floored when Harrison said the paperwork was already processed.

"Complete? How do you figure?" questioned Bo.

"Well, Mr. Martin," explained Harrison, "A Trading Co. has been a significant client of the bank since 1985. Since we deal in secrecy, we unfortunately cannot reveal any further information to you. Simply sign this signature card, and you will have sole and total control of the account."

"For further privacy purposes, enclosed is a list of the names of ten fish found in the Atlantic Ocean. When requesting a transfer of funds for wiring purposes, simply include the name of one of these fish in your request for funds. This featured protection will enable us to act on your request. We will need no other information. And please, do not reveal this information to anyone."

Bo sat silently, thinking for several moments, letting all this information sink in. He then asked, "Is this all that I need? You mean to tell me that you will transfer any amount of money I desire, simply by including the name of a fish?"

"Correct," nodded Harrison.

"What about a tax ID number? What about voice authorization? Is any of that necessary?"

"No, no, and no," said Harrison in response to all those questions. "All that we request is a written confirmation signed by you!"

Bo inquired further, "What if someone forges my name?"

Harrison responded immediately by saying, "The risk is all yours. The bank is not liable or responsible for any forgeries on your behalf."

"Don't ask, don't tell!" responded Bo.

"Correct," answered a smiling Harrison.

For the next ten minutes, Bo sat and attentively listened to Harrison explain the fees charged by the bank. Bo was shocked by the outrageous fees, but since it was not his money, he didn't care too much. When Harrison finished speaking, Bo presented him with the one-hundred-thousand-dollar cashier's check and waited for Harrison's assistant to provide him with a receipt. The receipt acknowledged the deposit and displayed the new account value.

To Bo's astonishment what he read nearly took his breath away. He could have fainted. There was already fifty million dollars in the bank account. Quickly calculating his fee in his head, Bo figured that an annual trustee fee of one percent would be $500,000. Not bad for so little work. *Pinch me, I must be dreaming!* Bo thought he was on cloud nine before reality sunk in and spoiled his glee.

Harrison presented Bo with his business card and private number and then escorted him out of the bank. Bo's mind was still swirling with questions as he left the bank, feeling a little dumbfounded. *What the heck is going on here,* he asked himself and not for the first time.

Bo couldn't stop thinking, *Who in the world would pay twenty thousand dollars for a company that already had fifty million dollars in liquid funds? Something smells fishy.* Bo could name ten possible reasons, and more than likely, Bart of Diamonds, Paul Schwartz, and Ross Brown were definitely not innocent bystanders. *The big question,* thought Bo, *is why am I even involved?* Bo struggled with this question as he walked back down Main Street toward his hotel.

Ruby was sunbathing at pool side when Bo stepped out of the hotel after stopping off at the room to change. Ruby was clearly the most beautiful woman on the pool deck, and her radiant smile helped to allay Bo's nagging concerns. Ruby was enjoying a tropical drink with a pink umbrella, and she was happy to see Bo attired in his swim trunks. The two made quite an exquisite sight.

Ruby asked, "Darling, I'm so happy you were not tied up too long. Did you get everything taken care of?"

Bo quickly replied, "It was an easy job. I just had to sign a few routine forms—nothing out of the ordinary, and certainly nothing for you to worry about."

They soon ordered lunch salads and spent the rest of the day soaking in the sunshine and enjoying the beautiful surroundings.

Since they were leaving the next morning, the Martins decided to stroll along the store fronts together to see if anything interested them. Ruby had been in and out of several of those same stores earlier in the day. The Cayman Islands were loaded with jewelry shops, and Ruby made sure they walked past all of them. Despite their wealth and social prominence, Bo and Ruby preferred the simpler things in life. However, Ruby did love jewelry, especially the items that came from her husband. These trinkets included a Cartier watch, a two-and-a-half-carat diamond-and-emerald studded wedding ring, dazzling diamond earrings, and a signet ring. Ruby was hoping that the next loving item would be a diamond encrusted tennis bracelet that she spotted earlier in the day. They finished the evening at a famous local hangout, enjoying fresh fruits, fish, rice, and beer. Bo enjoyed his time away with Ruby, and tonight he was not going to let today's affairs interfere with their evening. He ordered another round of beers.

Later that night after a moonlit walk along the beach and some more wonderful lovemaking, Bo couldn't sleep a wink. He dreaded going back home to face Bart of Diamonds. He sure hoped that Hank had found out more information.

As they were leaving the hotel for the airport the next morning, the concierge clerk called after him, "Mr. Martin, we have something here of yours." It was his cell phone, a little sandy and scratched but still working. He noticed there were numerous missed calls from his buddy, but they were in a rush to catch their plane. They had overslept, or rather just stayed in bed a little bit longer than they should have, so he didn't have time to call Hank back until he got back to the States.

Chapter
Eight

H ank had a difficult night sleeping. He was black and blue and sore all over with several cracked ribs, but fortunately his jaw was not broken. The pain medication failed to numb all of his senses. His right hand clutched the .38 handgun under his pillow, just in case the two thugs made another surprise visit. Hank was clearly frightened for his and his family's welfare, but he also worried about Bo. Hank also was upset that his running schedule would be interrupted because of his injured ribs. He had several local races coming up including a marathon, and he definitely did not want his running schedule to be cancelled.

Bo and Ruby had a smooth flight home, even though Ruby was sure the plane was going to crash with the slightest bit of turbulence. Bo was glad to find their car safe and sound, and in no time at all, the Martins were back at home with their extremely excited red dogs.

Bo had barely unpacked before heading to the office. Ruby caught him just before he left.

"Bo, why can't you just call the office to see how everything is? Stay here with us," pleaded Ruby.

"Honey, you know how much I want to stay here with you and the dogs, but I won't be more than an hour, two hours tops. You never know who may have died these past two days."

Much to Ruby's chagrin, Bo wasn't to be denied, and Ruby begrudgingly kissed Bo and went to the bedroom to unpack and unwind with the dogs in tow. "At least bring your cell phone and don't lose it this time!" she yelled.

"Yes dear," replied Bo, as he headed out the door with his cell phone in hand. As much as Bo loved technological advances, he hated being available by a cell phone, twenty-four hours a day. However, due to his business and the type of clientele he represented, it was definitely a necessity for him to be available anytime.

during the short drive to Worth Avenue, Bo couldn't stop asking why or how someone could possibly purchase a company for twenty thousand dollars when it already had fifty million dollars in its bank account. Bo's gut was burning, and he didn't really know where to turn. He was hoping that Hank would have found something, and later he planned on paying a personal visit to Bart of Diamonds. At around six thirty in the evening, Bo pulled into his designated parking space at the office. The office was deserted, as everyone had left for the weekend. On Fridays, Bo usually let the staff leave by four o'clock.

Bo spent about thirty minutes checking his messages. Ms. Everett had sorted them into three piles: urgent, Monday, and sometime in the future. There were several urgent messages from Hank, and at that instant Bo realized he never listened to his cell phone messages. He immediately dialed Hank's number. The moment he heard his friend's voice, the lights and electricity went out, leaving Bo all alone in the dark. He told Hank about the lights and told him he would call right back. Hank tried to catch Bo and warn him of the potential danger, but Bo had already hung up. Bo sat in the dark and waited for what seemed like an eternity for the electricity to come back on. Minutes later, the two Russian giants, Igor and Ivan, accompanied by a small bespectacled elderly gentleman barged into his office, shining a ray of blinding light, directly into Bo's eyes. Fear instantly gripped Bo, and he tried gallantly to keep his wits.

"Who are you, and what do you want?" shouted Bo, trying his hardest to appear tough and unafraid.

"Sit down now," said the bespectacled gentleman with a Russian accent.

Bo did as he was told while trying desperately to get a better glimpse of the short man. Bo did not even want to look at the two giant bookends and their oversized muscles. Even in the dark, they looked immense.

"What do you want?" Bo demanded again.

"Mr. Martin, my name is Marty," said the small man with the deep Russian accent, "and these are my assistants. If you do everything I ask, then I won't need their services. We are businessmen of a client of yours. We go way back."

Bo replied, "Funny, I've never heard of you before. What type of business are you in?"

No sooner had he finished speaking when Bo felt a swift blow to his right jaw, knocking him out of his chair. He saw nothing but stars and wondered where it came from. The big goons couldn't possibly move that fast, or could they? As he sat trying to clear the cobwebs, his jaw felt like it was on fire. Bo could taste the blood inside his mouth, and he was truly frightened.

"What business do you have with A Trading Co.?" asked the little man.

Bo replied, "I have no idea what you are talking about." This time another blow came from the left side and was lower and resulted in at least one cracked rib, maybe more. The swift blow also knocked Bo out of his chair, and he crumbled to the floor.

It took several seconds for Bo to get back in his seat and the constant beam of the flashlight continued to impede Bo's sight. Fear and rage were boiling up inside him. "Stay calm and find out what's going on," he muttered to himself.

The man again asked Bo what he knew about A Trading Co. Bo said nothing and braced himself for another strike. Fortunately, none came.

Bo was deeply concerned that the men would search his old tattered briefcase underneath his desk and find the Bank of Cayman records, checking account, stock certificates, and word list. The two big goons began searching Bo's desk, drawers, and cabinets for information with their own personal flashlights.

Within five minutes the big men had completely trashed Bo's office, but had somehow overlooked the old briefcase at his feet. Finding nothing, Bo was whacked from behind, causing him to sprawl out onto the floor and nearly lose consciousness.

The small gentleman called off the big goons and approached Bo. "We will be watching you. We know where you live, and we adore that beautiful wife of yours," were the last words Bo heard, as he watched the three men's feet exit from his darkened office. For several minutes Bo just lay there on the floor thinking. Finally, Bo struggled to his feet, shuffled downstairs to locate the electrical panel, and flipped the switch. The electricity shot back on, and Bo had just enough time to catch a glimpse of a dark STS Cadillac, pulling out onto Worth Avenue.

Bo gingerly walked into the bathroom and took one look at his enlarged right cheek, which was already turning a dark shade of blue and lightly touched his left-side ribs. He was still very frightened. *Who were those men?* thought Bo as he reached for the telephone.

Bo quickly dialed Hank, and this time there were no interruptions.

"Jesus Christ," screamed Hank. "What happened? What took so long to call me back? Are you okay?"

"Hi," replied Bo as he grimaced in pain. "Hank, I've just gotten beaten up, I have no idea who they were, but they were interested in the A Trading Co."

"Well that makes two of us. Join the club, buddy."

"What?" asked Bo, nervously.

"While you were away in Grand Cayman enjoying yourself, I was kidnapped, beaten, and left to die," shouted Hank.

"You've got to be kidding me!"

"Well, I wish I was, but I am not. They were wondering why I tried to contact A Trading Co., and when I wouldn't tell them what they wanted to hear, they nearly broke my jaw and fractured a bunch of ribs. I won't be able to run this week," stated Hank, rather upset.

"Well, it was obviously the same guys I just met."

"Are they still there?" Hank asked, nervously.

"No, they just tore my office apart, and when they couldn't find anything, they left with some pretty nasty threats."

"Are you okay?" asked Hank.

"I'll be alright. I think I can drive home. Ruby is going to be frantic with worry, and is going to want to know what is going on!"

"Of course she will be, but try not to think about that right now. What did they want from you, Bo?"

"They wanted to know what I knew about A Trading Co. Of course, I told them nothing, but I think they knew better. At least they certainly believed I should know more."

Hank remained silent for a moment and then said, "What's going on here, Bo? Level with me."

Bo said, "I'd love to, but not on this phone. Let's meet tomorrow afternoon for lunch. I will call you on my way home." A few moments later, Bo and Hank agreed to meet at Chuck and Harold's at noon. "See you tomorrow," said Bo, "and let's hope that both of us have a safe night!"

"Great; same here. See you there," said Hank.

It took Bo what seemed like forever to walk down the stairs to his car. The pain was barely tolerable, but he was able to drive home nonetheless. As he passed the Milners residence, he thought he saw a car that looked remarkably similar to the one driven by the incredible hulks parked in the driveway behind the daunting iron gates.

When Bo opened the front door, the red dogs exuberantly greeted him. Their front legs landed on his injured left side and brought immediate tears of pain to his eyes. Ruby took one look at her poor husband and called the dogs off.

"What happened to you? Are you okay? Oh my God!"

Bo, seeing Ruby's beautiful eyes fill with fear and concern for her husband, said that he was fine. "All I need is some Advil."

"Advil? What you need is an ambulance. Get back in the car, I am going to call the Milners, and we are going to take you to the hospital."

Minutes later, both couples were at Good Samaritan Hospital's emergency room. Through his family connections, Bo was admitted immediately, much to the displeasure of the numerous waiting patients.

Thank goodness, the jaw was not broken, and only two ribs were fractured. The knot on his head would go away, and he only suffered a mild concussion. The doctor instructed them that Bo was to take it very easy for the next couple of day, and that he should probably remain in bed for the entire weekend. He also prescribed some pain medication to help Bo sleep.

On the way home, Bo was grilled by Burt and Sophia, but he played it all down and said he was muggeds getting into his car. *Funny*, thought Burt, *how come they didn't take your wallet, watch, or wedding ring?* Burt couldn't contain himself and asked, "I'm sure that you had that old brief case with you, since you brought it here to the hospital with you, and kept it close to your side. Must be something pretty important in there"!

"I don't really know," exclaimed Bo. "Lucky, I guess." They laid Bo to rest on the couch in front of the wide-screen television, and after the Sinclairs left, Ruby demanded to know the truth. She knew when Bo was fibbing, as he tended to do on some small issues, but this was no small matter, and she stood firm with her hands on her hips, glaring down at Bo.

"Honey, I swear to you. I really don't know." Internally, Bo shouted to himself, *Please don't call Hank. Please don't call Hank!*

"I don't know why you keep secrets from me. I am not going to break, you know! Does this have anything to do with our trip?" asked Ruby.

"Now, why would you say that?" groaned Bo.

"It's just that you were very secretive about Grand Cayman, and for some reason, I just believe the two things are related."

"Honey, believe me, I don't know what to say to you. All I know is that I'm in pain, and I would like to get some rest. We'll talk about it tomorrow, okay?"

"You bet we will," muttered Ruby, as she turned to let the red dogs out the back door. Bo knew he would not be sleeping in their king-sized bed tonight. Not only was Ruby angry with him, but he also knew he would not have been able to drag his sore, swollen body from the couch all the way into the bedroom. Even though he was not next to Ruby, it did not take long for Bo to fall asleep with Max snuggled at his feet.

Chapter
Nine

Bo awoke the following morning with Bella pressed up against his back. He felt a little better and was able to brush his teeth, which, although painful, made him feel almost human. However, his ribs made it difficult for him to breathe deeply, but otherwise, he figured, he would be fine. The knot on his head was also smaller.

Moments later, both red dogs were up and eagerly awaiting their morning run. Bo dressed gingerly and knowing he was not going to be able to run, tried unsuccessfully to tell the dogs that they would have to settle for just a nice walk on the beach, as they watched the sunrise come up over the ocean. The walking helped to loosen up his body a bit. Ruby was waiting for them as they all washed off the sand in the swimming pool.

"Sweetheart, you really had me worried. I don't know what I would do if anything ever happened to you. Please be more careful and honest with me. Now level with me. Do you know who did this to you?"

Bo looked into those baby blues and said, "I have no idea, but believe me, I will get to the bottom of it." Ruby quickly shot Bo a look of disbelief. "Trust me, honey, I will do nothing stupid, okay? As a matter of fact, I plan on meeting Hank for lunch today to see if he knows anything." Ruby was somewhat relieved, but not completely convinced, and kissed Bo lightly on his good cheek before going to make breakfast.

The morning passed quickly, and before he knew it, lunch time had crept up on him. He rushed off to the restaurant at the pace of an elderly man. Hank and Bo looked like *Rocky* castoffs as they arrived moments apart and gingerly hobbled from their cars to the outdoor restaurant in the heart of Palm Beach. Both attempted to laugh at each other's predicament, but their fractured ribs limited their heckling.

They mustered fear-filled smiles.

After they exchanged stories, Bo came clean about his involvement with the Bart of Diamonds and apologized profusely for causing Hank any pain.

"What are friends for?" exclaimed Hank.

"Well, good buddy, I never imagined A Trading Co. would be such a wild card."

Both agreed that Bo needed to meet with Bart Sinclair personally and get to the bottom of this. They also decided not to involve the authorities. "The last thing we need is for the Town of Palm Beach police to get involved," said Bo.

"Are you worried about the police, Bo?"

"I'm worried about the FBI. This is much bigger than a local police matter. Get serious. This is an international matter that will get ugly!"

As they left the restaurant, they made plans to walk on Thursday evening. Running was definitely out of the question for the time being.

Bo called Bart of Diamonds on his cell phone after leaving the restaurant. Fortunately, Bart was home and agreed to meet with him immediately.

As Bo entered the Sinclair private driveway, he wondered what he was going to say and how he was going to find the elusive Joe Marx.

Bart met Bo at the door and led him into the mansion. Bo had never set foot in the residence and was immediately awestruck by its extravagance and opulence. The house had twenty-foot-high ceilings, marble floors, antique furniture, costly paintings, and the latest, and most expensive technology, money could buy. Bo was certainly impressed.

Bart led Bo into his magnificent study and closed the doors behind them. He opened a box filled with the finest Cuban cigars, and selected a Cubano. He made a slight gesture with the box toward Bo, but Bart knew he didn't smoke. Bo declined immediately before slowly settling into a chair behind the mammoth Louis XIV desk. Bo was afraid to put his hands on the desk in front of him since it was so beautiful and ornate. He didn't dare ask if it was an original.

Bo was in no mood to beat around the bush, so he spoke first. "Bart, there is a serious problem. My friend Hank and I were beaten up because of A Trading Co. What is it where is it, and why the hell am I involved?"

"Slow down," replied Bart. "Take it easy."

"No, you take it easy," snapped Bo, who was starting to lose his composure after all of the eventsover the last several days. "You and your friends have not been beaten up, and I bet your wife has not been threatened either! This is getting to be more than I ever expected, and I want answers, and I want them now!" demanded Bo.

"Okay, okay, but let me tell you first that Joe Marx is dead."

"Dead? Joe Marx is dead. How? When?" asked a numb Bo.

"Two days ago. Heart attack. No foul play," said Bart.

"Let me see the autopsy report," retorted Bo.

"There was none. Like I said, there was no evidence of foul play, and it was what he wanted," answered Bart, curtly.

"Bullshit" screamed Bo. "A Trading Co. has over fifty million dollars in it, and you bought it for twenty thousand dollars. I was born in the day, but not yesterday."

"Listen to me. There is nothing illegal going on. Ask Paul Schwartz or ask Ross Brown. They will tell you."

"No, Bart, I want you to tell me. I don't want to hear it secondhand. Tell me the truth, and tell it to me now!"

"Okay, all right. This is covered by the attorney-client relationship, right?"

"Exactly," said Bo. "I'm listening."

"Joe Marx was my supplier of diamonds. He worked with my father years ago and continued to work with me. He was the primary reason for my success, and he personally taught me how to survive and prosper in the jewelry business. He had no family except for me. Everything of his is now mine."

Bo interrupted, "Bart, have you ever heard of inheritance taxes, probate, or do you not remember all the estate planning work I did for you."

Bart replied, "I handled my parents' estates just fine, and I have already taken care of Joe's."

"In what, two days?" Bo exclaimed.

"I have my ways," said Bart, sporting a cunning and devious smile while rolling his cigar through his fat fingers.

"I'm sure you do. I'm sure you do," uttered Bo in complete disbelief.

Bo rose to leave, but Bart pleaded with him to stay.

"Let me begin by telling you that Joe Marx acquired his diamonds from Russian suppliers. The guys that you met recently work for a bad dude named Victor Butin. His family is part of the Russian Mafia. I am sure you have seen mafia movies before, but let me tell you that those Italian guys are nothing compared to these Russians. They are ruthless."

"However, Joe made them lots and lots of money. Millions upon millions of dollarsover the past thirty or so years, I would imagine. The only problem that I can figure out is that somewhere Joe must have lost a shipment—a very big shipment. I presume they are just trying to locate its whereabouts."

"Is that it, is that all?" inquired Bo.

"Not quite. You see, Joe Marx was also skimming from me. That's how I got him to sign the trust, and that's how I was able to buy A Trading Co."

"Are you telling me that Joe Marx was the client of Philip Houseman, and that Joe Marx was also my client? Bo asked incredulously.

"Yes," replied Bart. "You see, Joe got into the jewelry business years ago. He was first introduced into it by his father. Later he provided diamonds to my father, and then, ultimately, to me."

"Okay," answered Bo, trying to wrap his brain around these family relationships that went back many years. "But what else?"

"What else? There is nothing else. The trust that you created for me, which you called the Joe Marx Irrevocable Trust, is the one hundred percent owner of A Trading Co. You are the sole trustee, and you must manage the money for the benefit of me and my family. It's as simple as that! But, let me tell you under *no* circumstance are you to disclose any of this information to anyone, ever! You got that, Bo? Never!"

"Not so fast, Bart," Bo replied. "These Russian thugs are after anyone who inquires into A Trading Co. They will stop at nothing. If I was a betting man, I would say that your friend Joe owed them lots of money, and they aim to collect. I don't know what sort of scam you two were playing, but I am out. I quit as trustee." With that, Bo slowly rose from the magnificent leather chair.

"Okay, fine. Just walk away. You are such a weakling. I now know why people say you aren't half the man your father is. You have no spine, Bo Martin."

"Shut up," screamed Bo, who by this time was now totally enraged and trying his best to stand up. All his life he had tried to emulate his respected father, and now this man was attacking Bo's self-esteem. It hurt his ego, and he was hot under the collar to say the least.

"Bart, all I've ever asked of you is simply the truth. I am not spineless, and all I want you to do is level with me. Are there drugs involved?"

"Hell, no," replied Bart. "I've got five kids. Do you think I'd ever get involved in drugs?"

Bo's mind was now working overtime. How he wished he had paid more attention years ago in his criminal law classes. Bo vaguely remembered reading about money laundering and conspiracy, but he recalled that you had to have knowledge and intent. Bo possessed neither, or so he thought.

"Tell you what, Bart. Call Paul Schwartz right now, and get him on the phone."

"Now, Bo? I don't want to bother Paul at this hour."

"Do it now, Bart!" The tone of Bo's authoritative voice prompted Bart to take action.

Bart slid the cell phone out of his shirt pocket, and proceeded to call Paul. "Paul, this is Bart. How are you? Fine, fine. Could you talk to young Bo Martin right now? I think he's got some questions for you. Okay. Hold on; let me give him my phone."

Bo grabbed the phone from Bart. "Paul, it's Bo. I know you're a busy man, and I know that you represent Bart, and so, speaking lawyer to lawyer on Bart's behalf, I need to know if there is anything illegal going on with Bart. Drugs or anything else that he's possibly involved in?"

Paul waited several seconds before slowly responding in his most eloquent, condescending voice, "Now Bo, would I represent Bart for over ten years now if I thought for even one second that he had done anything illegal? Of course not! Bart is a genuine businessman. He buys jewels at a discount and sells them at a higher price. It's as simple as that. As his accountant will attest, Bart also reports and pays all his taxes. Now if you don't mind, I'm very busy."

Bo paused before asking one last question. "Did you know that Joe Marx is dead?"

"Well, yes," said Paul. "It was quite a shock receiving a certified death certificate about your client!"

"My client?" said Bo pensively.

"Why, yes. Joe Marx was your client. I sure hope you did a background check on him before agreeing to serve as his attorney. I've heard he has Russian ties."

"What exactly do you mean by that, Paul?"

"Oh, nothing, except that if he was involved in anything with the Russian Mafia, you had better worry about your own life. The criminal conspiracy and money laundering charges are the least of your worries," chided Paul.

"Conspiracy?" questioned Bo, now almost screaming into the phone. "What conspiracy? I only met the man once, and I did it for Bart. Hell, I don't even know where he lived or what exactly he did for a living!"

"Now, Bo, calm down. What is the chance that the FBI wants you? Relax, I know the name of a great criminal attorney if it ever comes to that," said Paul, as he laughed, uncontrollably into his cell phone.

"Comes to what?" shouted Bo. "I haven't done anything wrong."

"Oh, really," said Paul. "Rumor has it you are the trustee over a large sum of money, my friend. As a trustee, you have a fiduciary duty to the beneficiary of that trust, and as Bart's attorney, I will be watching you like a hawk to make sure that you do your job." So just do your job, and remember that I will be watching every move you make. And be assured if anything is out of the ordinary, I will sue you in an instant. Gotta run. Bye."

Bo listened to the dial tone and he was visibly shaking. His mind was reeling. Conspiracy, money laundering? Who exactly was Joe Marx, and where did he make his money? These questions and more were turning his stomach into knots.

Bart of Diamonds was studying Bo intently. He was observing how shaken Bo was after his talk with Paul. Earlier that day, Bart had spoken with Paul, and together they had prepared for this inevitable confrontation. In fact, they had planned on it.

"Bo," said Bart, "are you okay? Can I get you anything?"

"Uh, no. I'm fine; just sorting things out in my mind that's all."

"Well, good, 'cause I've got a little bad news for you."

What else would go wrong, thought Bo?

"In light of this matter and Joe's death, I think that I may need a new lawyer—one without so many possible conflicts. If Joe was into anything illegal, then I don't want you, as his attorney to bring any trouble on me or my family. I really hope you don't mind, and that you understand."

Bo's head was definitely spinning now. I'm being fired by Bart of Diamonds. This asshole has hung me out to dry!

Bo was so upset that he was now completely at a loss for words.

Bart, sensing Bo's frustration, rose from the chair and announced, "I've got to leave now. I hope you don't mind. I'll see you around," as he reached out to shake Bo's hand and usher him out of his office and toward the massive front doors of the mansion.

"Take care, Bo. Remember that as my trustee, you have a duty to me and my family. You better use the trust proceeds solely for me and my family, and you better keep excellent records, as I will definitely be watching everything you do."

Outside, the cool, fresh salty air felt refreshing on Bo's overheated and shaking body. He was panicked and fearful. Things had happened too fast. Much too fast!

Bo proceeded to get into his car and drive the few houses home. His fractured ribs were the least of his worries now. *The Russian Mob. Holy shit!* he thought.

Chapter
Ten

B o was happy to see Ruby's beautiful face as he walked into the cottage. Gosh, she was gorgeous, thought Bo. Before he could reach her, the two red dogs intercepted him and proceeded to lick him profusely. Only after he had lovingly pet both dogs could he finally kiss his wife's sweet lips. Immediately Ruby sensed Bo's fear, and she held him tight. "Honey, what is it? Did you and Hank figure things out?"

"Oh, Ruby if it were only that simple. It appears that the client who created a trust for Bart Sinclair and his family is now dead. Supposedly he did business with the Russian Mafia and they now want their money back." Bo said it so quickly that Ruby couldn't comprehend exactly what he was saying.

"Excuse me," asked Ruby. "What trust and which client?"

"Just a relatively new client," replied Bo.

"Well if he's dead, what's the matter?" questioned Ruby. "They didn't kill him, did they? Oh my God, they killed him! Oh no, oh no! Are they going to come after us?" Tears were streaming down Ruby's face. She had never been more frightened.

"Hold your horses. We are perfectly safe," explained Bo, trying his best to console his wife. Ruby suddenly pulled away from her husband and with a gasp said, "That is why you got beaten up!" She then turned and rushed to find her cell phone.

Ruby proceeded to pick up the phone to call 911 when she felt Bo's hand grab the phone. "Who are you calling?" questioned Bo.

"The police, who else?" answered Ruby.

"Well, hold on just one minute. Let's think this through first."

"Dear, you have cracked ribs, your client is dead, and the Russian Mafia most likely killed him, and now they are after you. You just returned from the Cayman Islands where you did business with a bank, and I presume there was enough money involved for you to take two full days out of your hectic work schedule and . . . and your best friend was also beaten up and kidnapped! Which by the way, you conveniently forgot to tell me! Is there anything, anything else that I perhaps omitted? Am I forgetting anything, Bo? Am I?"

Bo didn't have the heart to tell her that he was also just fired by Bart Sinclair. However, he wasn't going to resign as trustee. Not just yet! His annual fee alone was worth five hundred thousand dollars. He would have to prepare over five hundred estate plans for that kind of a fee. No, it was best to sit tight and wait.

"Honey, don't worry. As long as I am in control of the trust assets, we will be just fine. Trust me."

Funny, thought Ruby. "Trust you? I seriously doubt it!"

Later that evening, Bo tossed and turned over and over until even the red dogs were awakened. Bo put on his khaki shorts and stepped outside and listened to the ocean waves beat down on the sand and was joined by Max and Bella. Eventually, even Ruby stepped outside to console him. The whole family felt Bo's heavy burden, and huddled together, trying to comfort him.

Bo spoke, breaking the silence. "If Joe is really dead, then under Florida law, his creditors must seek claims against his probate estate. That means the Russians would have to file claims for recovery of their damages in a court of law. They also would be required to prove the merits of their claims. If anything was illegal, their claims would naturally be stricken. Further under Florida Law, creditors have only ninety days to file claims after the first publication of the notice of administration." The wheels were spinning in his mind as he continued speaking out loud.

"In order to preclude their claims, I would have to open a probate estate. To do that I need more information, and I would need a certified death certificate. If I am successful, the Russians would conceivably be legally out of luck if they failed to timely file a valid claim with merit. As the personal representative of his estate, I could object to any bogus or unsubstantiated claim." *For a layman*, Ruby thought, *what Bo was saying seemed reasonable.*

Bo next discussed the irrevocable trust itself. Florida has a fraudulent conveyance statute that allows creditors or the IRS to attach proceeds if they were fraudulently transferred to another party, prior to a lawsuit, or prior to death. However to prevail, a creditor must first uncover the transfer and then later attempt to set it aside. Since Bo had no idea where the source of the trust money actually came from, (presumably from sales of diamonds), the possibility of a fraudulent conveyance lawsuit was slight. Bo was starting to like his odds. Further, Bo concluded, the irrevocable trust was unknown to the world except for Bart of Diamonds, Paul Schwartz, Joe Marx, and Philip Houseman. Also, Harrison Frazar, the Bahamian banker, knew that the trust owned A Trading Co. Bo hoped there were no others.

Bo realized that his next step was to confirm the death of Joe Marx. *That shouldn't be much of a problem*, thought Bo. A valid death certificate should suffice.

Ruby along with the red dogs and Bo quietly returned to the warm inviting comfort of their king-sized bed, but no one fell fast asleep. Ruby had promised Bo that she would not to do anything until he could do more research into matters. Out of her love and trust for Bo, Ruby reluctantly agreed not to contact the police, but she was still gravely concerned about everything.

The first thing Bo did Monday morning was phone Florida's Health and Rehabilitative Services (HRS) and attempted to locate a death certificate for Joe Marx. He called the Palm Beach County morgue and various local mortuaries that Bo had done business with. Funny thing, nobody had any knowledge of the death of Joe Marx. In fact, there was not even an unclaimed unidentified body. It was as if Joe Marx had never existed.

Bo then proceeded to call Paul Schwartz. Paul answered his cell phone on the second ring.

"Paul, this is Bo. How are you today?"

"I am fine. How can I help you?" said Paul, rather coldly.

"You mentioned to me that you were aware of Joe's death. I was just wondering how you knew or where you heard it."

"Now, Bo, I told you that I received a certified death certificate."

"That is really weird, Paul because I've read all the papers, contacted HRS, and have even called all the local mortuaries. It's funny, but not one organization has ever heard of Joe Marx."

"You don't say. That is strange. But guess what, Bo. He died in Hungary," uttered Paul, rather smugly.

"Hungary? And I presume you read the Hungarian newspapers as well," mocked Bo. "I'm beginning to wonder about you, Paul, and, I'm thinking of going to the FBI this afternoon. I'm sure they would love to hear about how you became informed of Joe's alleged death in Hungary."

"Now hold on, just a minute, Bo. Are you threatening me? If you are, you had better prepare yourself for war because I would make mincemeat out of you," retorted Paul, sharply. "Don't be stupid and do something you will later regret; think everything through, Bo, and I will call you later."

Bo knew that he had frightened Paul, and now he was left with a rather large dilemma. *What do I do next?*

Later that day, and just before turning off the office lights, Bo was startled by a surprise visit from Bart of Diamonds. Bart was in his usual attire, Sperry Top-Siders, Sportif shorts, and a flowered Tommy Bahama shirt.

"Got a minute?" asked Bart.

"Sure," said Bo.

"First, let me apologize. I want you to know that I am still your client, and you are still my lawyer, right?"

"If that's what you want!" said Bo.

"Good, I was worried that you wouldn't want to have anything to do with me. I need you and your legal mind. You are the only person I really trust, and I know you will look after my kids if anything were to happen to me."

I wanted you to have the Last Will and Testament of Joe Marx," said Bart as he handed Bo the document. It's a simple will that leaves everything to my kids." Bo proceeded to read the three-page original document.

Bo noted that Joe proclaimed to be a Hungarian citizen residing in Palm Beach County. He named Bart as his Personal Representative and left his entire estate to Bart's children in equal shares, per stirpes. It was properly signed and dated. Bo realized at once that the notary was none other than Paul Schwartz, and the witnesses were Ross Brown and his wife, Giselle. The Will was also dated with the same date as the predated Irrevocable Trust.

How convenient, thought Bo. *What a coincidence.* This was all sounding much too neat.

Bo spoke first. "What other assets did Joe have?"

Bart responded, "Well he lived at a condo of mine in Old Port Cove, and he drove a car owned by Diamond Trading Co., as he primarily only dealt in cash."

Funny, thought Bo. *Then how in the world did he accumulate fifty million dollars?* "Bart, a man of his means must have had numerous accounts with millions and millions of dollars. Where are the accounts, and where is Joe? Level with me for once, please? I can't help you if I'm left in the dark. I believe you need my help, Bart."

"Okay, sit down, and let me tell you what I know," said Bart, sounding almost human. "I can't tell you much because there is still a lot that even I don't know, but I will tell you this, it's all legitimate," professed Bart. "There is no doubt in my mind that Joe is definitely dead, as this certified death certificate clearly proves." Bart handed the official-looking document with a raised seal to Bo. Bo looked it over completely. Naturally, it was written in Hungarian, but he could decipher the name, Joseph Marx, and the date of death. At least that much was clear.

Chapter
Eleven

art began by explaining to Bo all about the mining of diamonds in South Africa, the DeBeers family, and how the price of diamonds was determined according to the four Cs—color, cut, carat, and clarity. He also delved into the fact that the two largest diamond companies controlled virtually all the diamond sales in the world. It is strictly a matter of supply and demand, and by keeping the supply low, the demand stays high, which artificially inflates prices and creates a stable market for diamonds.

From there Bart chronicled in detail, the wholesale, retail, and distribution scheme of the diamond trade.

After what seemed like an hour or so, Bart finally came to Joe Marx and his relationship with Bart's father.

Joe Marx was born in Russia and immigrated to Germany at an early age. He was half Jewish and during World War II, served as a spy for Russia. When the Allies overthrew Germany, Joe worked in the German black market. He was so adept at this business that he very shortly amassed a small fortune. It was during this prosperous time that he befriended the Butin family. The Butins rose to prominence making their money in loan sharking, gambling tobacco, liquor, prostitution, and blackmail. "Anything illegal or immoral" was their motto. However, what truly made the Butin family so powerful was their reputation as being the meanest, cruelest, and most ruthless enforcers around. Death and pain went hand in hand, and the Butins developed a reputation of sheer terror if you unfortunately happened to cross their path.

Victor Butin one of the Butin family sons, was a bit short of stature, but his enormous good looks, great personality, and impeccable taste in clothes, more than made up for his lack of height. Originally Victor did not really care for the harsh tactics his family was notorious for. Victor's real passion came in the form of weight lifting, which he excelled at during his youth. Since Victor showed so much promise at such a young age, the government sent him to a school where the emphasis was on training. Because Victor showed such promise for the Russian athletic program, the government overlooked his family connections. Victor trained hard, and soon he was good enough to compete on the national and international level. For a boy so short in stature he became a giant in the sport of weightlifting, quickly reaching Olympic caliber. The Russian government proclaimed Victor one of their elite athletes and promoted his weight-lifting prowess throughout the world. It was at one of his competitions in South Africa that he met, fell in love, and later married one of the young daughters of the DeBeers family.

The DeBeers family took a quick liking to Victor, not only because of his athletic success but also because of his intelligence and his devotion to his new bride. With his family's urging, Victor soon gained access to the DeBeers' inner sanction and its mining operations and the diamond-producing dynasty. Unfortunately, the love of his life fell in love with someone else. Victor actually caught his new wife and lover together in his own bed when he came home a day earlier than expected from a competition. This betrayal tore him apart and hardened his heart. Even though their marriage was over, he quickly used the Butin family criminal methods to blackmail his ex-wife into allowing Victor continued access to the DeBeers diamonds.

Victor developed a simple ingenious way to smuggle the diamonds into Russia and other parts of the world. As an elite weight lifter for the Soviet Union, he traveled the world. Airport security was always lax for the Soviet weight lifting contingent, and Victor smuggled the diamonds in an ice packet pouch that he carried with him wherever he went.

Victor was always complaining of some sort of weight-lifting injury, and hence, the ice pack became his crutch and his best defense. The numerous diamonds were always placed inside a plastic bag and then surrounded by ice. Victor repeatedly filled the bag with ice, thereby continually hiding the jewels located therein.

Once the jewels were safely smuggled into the country, Victor engaged Joe Marx to sell them on the black market. With Joe's numerous contacts, the diamonds were quickly sold for significant prices. The Butin family prospered, and Victor quietly expanded his power and influence.

When Victor's Olympic career ended, he continued the smuggling operation by employing the new younger Russian weight lifters. They carried the diamonds in their ice packs while he, as an assistant Olympic coach, watched their every move. He paid the weight lifters well and used his family's influence to continue the extremely profitable enterprise.

As the United States rose to economic prominence, Americans desire for more and more expensive diamonds and jewelry grew insatiable. Victor realized that the USA was an untapped market.

Unfortunately, Joe Marx had grown rather complacent and was content living in Eastern Europe. He had even settled down, married, and had a daughter. When Joe wanted no part of Victor's ambitious expansion plans and refused to work for the Butin family, tragedy suddenly struck the Marx family. One night when Joe was away on business, a mysterious fire destroyed his home, killing his wife and young daughter.

With no living family members and his world totally shattered, Joe reluctantly agreed to travel to America and help sell the smuggled diamonds. Joe's first contact was Jack Sinclair. Jack had grown tired of dealing with the Hasidic Jews as middlemen and was looking for a way to eliminate them and their 40 percent cut from his ultimate profit. Joe was in the right place at the right time, and soon Jack Sinclair, Joe, and Victor Butin became partners. Jack's business flourished, and everyone became immensely wealthy. This prosperous relationship continued until the untimely death of Jack and Dorothy Sinclair.

What Victor failed to completely realize was that Joe had vowed to bring down Victor Butin, no matter how long it took. He would avenge the death of his family. He could never ever forget or forgive. His sole purpose in life became the immense desire to get revenge on the Butins. He just had to wait for the right time, and he knew it would come sooner or later.

Joe had no family to support, no close friends, not even a pet. He drank to drown his sorrows and gave away the bulk of his money to local children's charities. He no longer possessed any desire to obtain material goods. He was headed on a downward spiral when in the midst of his sorrows, Joe came up with an idea. He realized that the only real way to hurt Victor and the Butin family was in their pocketbook. Joe was the point man, and Victor Butin was in desperate need of a new buyer for his smuggled diamonds. Joe realized that violence against the Butins was suicide, but at this point, he did not care. He also knew that this plan would most likely take several years to play out. Joe didn't care how long it took, as long as he made Victor pay. The first step in Joe's plan was to travel to Palm Beach in an attempt to rekindle his remote relationship with Bart Sinclair. Frankly what he knew and remembered of Bart was very little.

At this point in their uninterrupted discussion, Bart asked Bo, "Can we take a little break?"

"Sure," replied Bo.

Bo hurriedly called Ruby at home and informed her that he was working late on a new estate and was presently in a meeting with the family members. "Go ahead and eat without me. This is going to take longer than I had anticipated. I'll see you later. Love you."

While Bo waited patiently for Bart to return to the office, his mind was working overtime trying to digest all the information. Most of it made sense and was somewhat believable. After about a ten-minute break, Bart returned to the office where Bo sat eagerly waiting to hear the rest of the story. "Okay where did I leave off?" asked Bart while sitting down and propping his Sperry Top-Siders on Bo's cluttered desk.

Bo replied, "At the time you met up with Joe Marx."

"Oh, yeah. Well, I had just opened my Palm Beach store, and things were not taking off like I had planned. Even with margins of one hundred percent, I was saddled with a nagging wife and three kids to provide for. Plus, living the Palm Beach lifestyle is awfully expensive."

"Don't I know that," joined Bo.

"Even though it appeared that I was doing well, the only way I kept afloat was by selling off my father's jewelry collection, which I had inherited. Try as I may, I still couldn't make enough money to continue the lifestyle my family and I wanted to live. I couldn't understand how my father had acquired such wealth. Then, miraculously, just as I thought I might lose my business, Joe Marx appeared at my store."

"Joe had aged considerably since I last saw him, and he certainly didn't seem like a happy guy. Yet Joe was an answer to my prayers! His diamonds were spectacular, the best I had ever seen, and he offered them to me on consignment. More importantly, his diamonds were relatively cheap. I was able to begin undercutting my competitors at Mayors, Hamilton, and even Tiffany's while still maintaining profit margins of over one hundred and fifty percent."

"After the death of my first wife, Mandy, I relied on Joe to assist with my marketing and advertisement efforts. Since I sell exclusively to the rich and famous, Joe suggested that I promote myself as being fabulously rich and famous as well."

"Soon I was mingling in the same social circles as my parents had during their lifetimes, except that I was in the unbelievably extravagant world of Palm Beach. Most importantly, my store was flourishing."

"I met my second wife, Martha on the Palm Beach social scene. Both Joe and I realized that she was my entry to the super wealthy, as she had inherited over one billion dollars. Unfortunately for me, it was all tied up in trusts and generation skipping vehicles that did not include me. So I married her. All was fairly good for several years. While I was out pursuing Marlin, Martha was promoting my store to her fabulously wealthy friends. She was brilliant, and together we really prospered. The diamonds from Joe kept coming, and through our social connections, I was able to sell numerous multimillion dollar jewelry ensembles. Life was good on the business end."

"However, as you probably guessed, my marriage was not picture-perfect. I must tell you, not that you haven't guessed already, but the only reason I married Martha was for her money and the fact that I knew she would have great success with the store. It is not as bad as it sounds—I really did try to make a real marriage out of it, but to tell you the truth, I was not sexually attracted to her, and she hated my children. So naturally, I began—or should I say, continued—having affairs and drinking too much. I became aware that Martha might uncover the fact that Joe Marx and his company, A Trading Co. was not a middleman. I knew it was only a matter of time before she would have figured out everything including the Butin family. There was no way I could ask her for a divorce. Paul had informed me that if I attempted to divorce her, I would have to give her half of everything, and she would keep everything she had. Funny thing how that works, isn't it, since she had ten times as much money as I! If I asked her to stop putting so much time into the business, it would be like a siren going off. She definitely would know that something was going on. I also knew there was no way in hell she would not go to the authorities with what she was about to find out! It was at this time I suggested we go down to the islands for a while for some R&R, but also so I could get her away from the business for a few days while I tried to figure out what to do. I certainly was in a bind, and I didn't know how to fix the situation. That is when tragedy struck, and Martha accidently died while we were out on a dive."

"How convenient for you," interrupted Bo.

"Whatever," said Bart as he continued with his story. It was clear that her death did not disturb him one tiny bit. Bo couldn't imagine his life without Ruby.

"Right after her death, I landed the big one."

"The big one?" queried Bo.

"Yes, the big one in a million. A guy with more money than sense! This man, Milton Rogers, became my meal ticket." Bo had never heard of Milton Rogers.

"I had previously sold him and his wife over a million dollars' worth of jewelry. The Rogers live in an oceanfront mansion in the middle of Palm Beach, just south of the Breakers. He was some sort of a publishing tycoon, who had just sold a huge chunk of his empire. His four sons were too lazy to continue running the company, and rather than watch it go down the tubes under the children's mismanagement, he had simply sold out.

"Shortly after his $1.5 billion windfall, he started coming around the store, measuring diamonds, asking questions inspecting jewelry, and being a rather big annoyance. Since he was a good customer, I let him do his thing, hoping that he would spend some more of his fortune at my store. It seemed like he was coming around every day just looking around, asking questions, but never buying anything. My staff and I were literally getting quite tired of seeing him. One day he came up to me and said he wanted to buy one hundred million dollars' worth of diamonds.

"I couldn't believe what I was hearing. I was shocked but also very excited! After picking my jaw up off the ground, I asked, 'A hundred million dollars?'

'Yes,' Milton replied, 'a hundred million dollars.' I was going to make a $50 million profit. I was on top of the world, man."

"Then what?" asked Bo.

"Well, Milton wanted to spend fifty million dollars in year one, and fifty million dollars the following year. He advised me that these purchases coincided with future installments from the sale of his business."

"That sounds incredible. Did you ever investigate Milton Rogers?" interrupted Bo.

"Well, no, not really. I contacted my attorney, Paul, and notified him of my potentially huge client, but I didn't do any background study on Milton if that is what you are asking. I didn't feel it was necessary."

"I immediately called Joe, who was quietly living in my condo in Old Port Cove and keeping an extremely low profile. I often wondered why he wasn't living luxuriously with all his money, but he would only reply by telling me that money was not his motivation. But I told him money was truly my motivation!" laughed Bart.

At this point, Bart received and answered an emergency call from Paul Schwartz. Bo excused himself from his own office to give Bart some private time. As much as he wanted to listen in on their conversation, Bo figured it was best to leave him alone.

Bo was deep in thought as he tried to put the pieces of the puzzle together. Bo felt trapped but at the same time exhilarated. He was finally getting the truth, but he was deeply concerned by its implications.

When Bo returned to the office minutes later, Bart of Diamonds was gone. No note, no letter, nothing. Bo waited over half an hour for Bart's return but eventually gave up and phoned Ruby to inform her that he was finally calling it a day and leaving the office. Things would soon get even more mysterious.

By the time Bo arrived at home, Bart of Diamonds had already called Ruby and asked her to apologize to Bo for his premature exit. He asked Ruby to let Bo know that he would be in Europe for a month or so. His last words to Ruby were, "Don't worry. Everything is just fine and under control." *Famous last words*, thought Bo, sipping his cold Bud Light from a can and propping his legs up on the coffee table with Max and Bella under his feet.

Chapter
Twelve

or the next month or so, Bo and Ruby continued to lead their idyllic lives. Bo was busy with work and Ruby's Café continued to be the local hot spot. Bo began receiving monthly bank statements from the Bank of the Grand Cayman and watched as the interest compounded. The interest alone generated in excess of $2.5 million after deducting the costs of administration per year. Bo heard nothing further from Bart or from the Russians. Bo and Hank had finally fully recovered from their injuries and were back to training regularly. Bo thought it wise to keep Hank from investigating any further in order to protect him. Bo felt personally responsible for Hank's injuries and vowed to keep him away from any additional harm.

Just when all seemed quiet, Bo received the Hungarian death certificate for Joe Marx in the mail from Paul Schwartz. There was no letter, just a certified death certificate, and a cashier's check made payable to the estate of Joe Marx for $20,000. Several days later Bart called from Mexico.

"Hey, Bo, long time no speak," muttered Bart.

"How have you been?" asked Bo.

"Sorry, I have been out of pocket recently, but I will be coming back next week. The kids, Dana, and I are all fine and sunburned. I directed Paul Schwartz to send you Joe's death certificate in order to formally open his estate. Please prepare whatever you need for me to sign, ASAP. Okay, my friend?"

"Fine," said Bo. "I'm glad that all is well. What address and social security number should I use for Joe?"

"Just use the Old Port Cove address and I'll have Paul get you a key to satisfy your numerous questions, and to take an inventory."

"That would be great," replied Bo. "I'll get to work on preparing the Probate estate pleadings."

"See you soon. Bye."

As Bo listened to the dial tone, he knew that with each phone call and every minute he spent on this matter with Bart, he was falling further and further into the black abyss.

Bo, still troubled by the phone call, took out his Florida Rules of Professional Responsibility and began to carefully read them. Ethically, Bo was living on the edge. The Rules provide that an attorney shall not violate the attorney-client privilege unless the attorney believes there will be irreparable harm to another or to the client himself. The primary example illustrated a scenario that if a client informs his attorney that he intends to kill another or himself, then the attorney must ethically disclose the matter to the proper authorities. Since Joe never actually informed Bo about his stolen diamonds, Bo rightly believed he had no duty to disclose it. Further, since Bo was only Bart's estate planning attorney, he was not in violation for failing to inform authorities regarding the sale of the diamonds, so therefore ethically he was in the clear.

Now, believed Bo, Paul Schwartz has most certainly breached the Rules of Ethics. Bo vowed to make Paul as uncomfortable as possible when he dialed Schwartz's law office.

"Paul Schwartz, please. Bo Martin calling on behalf of Bart Sinclair," he told the receptionist.

"Yes, Mr. Martin, hold on one second."

Moments later, Paul picked up the phone. "Yes, Bo."

"Hi, Paul. I just spoke to Bart, and he said you have a key to the Old Port Cove condominium where Joe was living. I will need to get if from you." Paul at first denied having the key, but when pressured again by Bo, he miraculously located it in his file.

"Great," said Bo. "I have a court appearance in thirty minutes. I'll pick it up afterwards."

"Fine," said Paul. "I'll have it ready for you."

"Thanks. Goodbye."

Bo sensed that Paul did not want to provide him the key, which he thought peculiar.

Paul's office was located in the elegant, black thirty-story concrete structure dubbed "The Darth Vader Building," in downtown West Palm Beach.

It was situated along Flagler Drive and overlooked the Intracoastal Waterway with its magnificent view of the mansions of Palm Beach. Paul was available and even waiting when Bo arrived.

Paul stressed to Bo that if there was anything he could do to help, just let him know. Turning to Paul as he left, Bo stated, "Paul, have you read the Rules of Professional Responsibility lately where it discusses an attorney's duty to disclose a crime when it presently is or will be committed? You know you really should. Good-bye."

Bo left Paul with a slight smirk on his face as he walked out the door.

It was Thursday, and Bo was anxious to meet his friend, Hank after work for their weekly bridge run. Bo thought afterward they could search the Old Port Cove condominium together. After rinsing off in the Martins' pool with the red dogs, Hank and Bo drove off to inspect Joe Marx's condominium.

The condominium was located in an upscale development in North Palm Beach, about twenty minutes north of Palm Beach, but worlds apart financially. After checking their names with the security guard, they soon located the right building. The condo unit, number 303, was located on the third floor of the seven-story building. Bo figured it was worth about $250,000. The unit consisted of two bedrooms, two bathrooms, a small kitchen, and a tiny family room.

The furniture was old, yet comfortable, and the place was spotless. There was nothing expensive in the entire unit, and one thing Bo found unusual was that there was not a single photograph in sight.

Bo opened the refrigerator door and quickly shut it tight to contain the smell of sour milk and rotten vegetables. At first glance, Bo felt Joe had not planned a long trip.

Hank examined the bedroom, the closet, and the toiletries. Everything was in order, nothing seemed out of place, and it appeared that Joe had not planned to leave on any extended trip. Joe's wardrobe was simple yet complete. The bed was clean and extra towels hung from the shower towel racks.

Bo next proceeded into the guest bedroom. The drawers, closet, and guest bathroom were completely empty, and it didn't appear the room was ever used. Bo's eyes, however, spotted a small desk in the corner of the room and hoped to find some information. Unfortunately, the desk was also completely empty. No stamps, no envelopes, no paper, no pens, nothing. Bo thought it quite odd.

"Where is his mail?" exclaimed Bo.

"I don't see any financial records, letters, tax returns insurance matters, or any bills for that matter either," exclaimed Hank from the other room.

Hank, who was now in the kitchen, located the liquor cabinet. It appeared that Joe Marx certainly loved his vodka. "Hey, Bo, there's enough vodka in here to last a lifetime—Stoli, Grey Goose, Smirnoff—you name it, and he's got it in here."

"Check the freezer, Hank."

Hank did as Bo requested and found six more bottles in the freezer. Bo always wondered why alcohol didn't freeze, ever since his college days in the fraternity house. As Hank was shutting the door one bottle caught the gleam of his eye. It was short and square with a large pouring mouth. Hank paused and then removed the bottle from the back shelf in the freezer. There was something in the bottom of the bottle.

"Hey, Bo, you better come in here!"

Bo couldn't believe their good fortune. Within seconds, Bo and Hank had poured out the contents of the bottle into the sink, and in the bottle were two keys.

Bo examined the first key, easy enough. Clearly it belonged to a safe deposit box. The second key appeared to belong to a post office box. Fortunately for them, both of the keys were marked with the name of the respective institutions.

"Pay dirt," remarked Hank.

"Good work, my friend. I would never have even noticed the bottle."

"It was nothing," shrugged Hank. "Now let's go snooping!"

"Wait, unfortunately we don't officially have authority to utilize the keys. The bank and post office will need some sort of identification. Since neither of us look like Joe Marx, we can't very well just march in there and gain access."

"You just watch me tomorrow," replied Hank. The two men spent another hour rummaging through the condominium finding nothing of interest. Afterwards, the two men arranged to meet at noon the following day.

When the guys arrived at the bank the following day, Hank leaned over to Bo and proclaimed, "watch an expert at work." Bo stayed behind and watched his friend in action.

The young woman assistant at the Bank of North Palm Beach smiled and said hello and ushered Hank over to her desk at the entrance to the safe deposit boxes. She accepted the key in Hank's hand and promptly departed into the manager's office. Within thirty seconds, she and the branch manager, a heavyset woman, proceeded to question Hank regarding the key. The papers in their file specifically stated that Joe Marx was the only one allowed entry in the box. Without a court order, the bank would not grant Hank access, and he was sent away with no more questions asked.

Hank left the bank looking extremely dejected. Bo could have told him he was going to strike out, but because Hank was trying to help him, he kept his thoughts to himself.

"I'll have better luck at the post office," stated Hank, rather convincingly. Bo knew otherwise but continued to remain silent while Hank drove them to the local post office. Fortunately for Bo, he had handled the estate of the postal teller's father, and before he allowed Hank to speak, Bo stepped in front and exclaimed, "Hi Monica, how are you?"

"Oh, hi Bo. Nice to see you again. I hope all is well with you. I've been meaning to call your office and schedule an appointment. We need to come meet with you to revise mine and my husband's wills, but we've just been so busy! What brings you here?"

"Monica, this is my friend Hank. He's a private investigator. We have a post office key for a client of mine and we would like to get his mail."

"Hold on; let me check our files. It'll just be a second."

Bo winked at Hank, who was still smarting over his lack of success at the bank. Meanwhile, Bo felt confident he would gain immediate access.

"Sorry for the wait. According to our records, nobody except Joe Marx is allowed access to the box. Do you have a power of attorney, Bo? If not, I'm sorry, but I won't be able to help you today. His box is not the normal run of the mill kind that usually doesn't require postal consent to gain access. I'm sorry, but it's my job. I hope you understand Bo," said Monica.

"Sure, I understand. Take care, Monica, and just call Ms. Everett to set up an appointment."

"Okay. Bye."

As the two men exited the building, it was Hank grinning this time.

"Smooth, just smooth. We are now zero for two. What next?"

"Well, I've got an idea, but it will take some time. We'll have to come back in a few weeks."

"A few weeks? Are you serious?"

When Bo got back to the office, he proceeded to prepare all the necessary probate pleadings for Bart's signature in order to open the estate of Joe Marx. In two relatively short hours, Bo had prepared all the necessary court documents.

Bo stared at the legal pleadings and realized he was now standing on the edge of the cliff. He was placing his entire legal career on the line with Bart of Diamonds, a noted and confirmed liar and—don't forget—killer. Bo asked himself for the hundredth time, *Why am I getting further involved with a man I do not trust? I know he is a crook. I know he is dealing with the Russian Mafia, who would kill me at the drop of a hat. I have reason to believe that Bart has had something to do with the deaths of his previous wives and maybe even his parents. I know his attorney and accountant have shady financial dealings with him. Most importantly, I know that by handling this estate, I will be risking my law license, my career, my firm, and maybe even my life. So why do I find myself still working for him?*

Bo realized he simply had read too many Robert Ludlum and John Grisham novels. However, the simple fact of the matter was that Bo was curious. He knew curiosity killed the cat, and it could easily be his demise, but quite simply, he was growing a little bored of his elderly clients and their tax and estate plans, and he couldn't resist some crazy legal adventure. So Bo vowed to satisfy his curiosity and find out everything he could about Joe Marx. *I owe it to the man,* reasoned Bo.

The last legal document Bo had prepared for Bart's signature was a fiduciary power of attorney. This specially designed form would give Bo the authority to gain access to the safe deposit box and post office box without having to inform his client, Bart Sinclair. Bo knew that Bart would sign whatever he presented to him, and this form would hopefully enable Bo to find some answers. "So much for trust," Bo said to himself and laughed.

It took about another three weeks for Bo to receive the signed pleadings back from Bart. However before filing them with the court, Bart had oddly instructed Bo to email/fax the documents over to Paul Schwartz. Bo, following orders, sent all the forms except the Power of Attorney, which he exclusively maintained in his sole possession.

It was Ross Brown who first telephoned Bo. "Hi, Bo. Ross here. I note that you will be opening the estate of Joe Marx soon. I just wanted you to know that Bart's corporation will be taking back the car and condominium and will thereafter handle all the bills."

"That's great," replied Bo. "What do you plan to do with the furniture and clothing?"

"The furniture will remain as it is, but we could have Goodwill pick up the clothes."

"I have a key. Why don't I take the clothes to Goodwill myself? There didn't seem to be that much, and I'll get a charitable deduction, personally for Bart."

"Sounds good to me."

"I plan on opening up the estate tomorrow at the courthouse, and I'll swing by later to pick up the clothes before dropping off the key at Diamond and Sons."

Seconds later after Bo hung up with Ross, Paul Schwartz was on the telephone. "Bo, my friend, how are you? And thanks for emailing me the pleadings. It all looks good to me, but I would like from hereafter for you to copy me on everything you send to Bart and everything you file with the court. Okay?"

"Sure," said Bo. "No problem. Gotta run. Bye." Bo certainly did not want Paul looking over his shoulder, but he knew he had no other choice.

The following day on the way to the courthouse, Bo reflected once again on this unprecedented situation. Here I am going to open the probate estate of a man I'm not fully certain, is really dead, and I also don't know if I'm breaking the law with any of my actions. Probate is only for the dead!

The probate judge, who was extremely fond of Bo and his excellent reputation, admitted the Last Will and Testament to Probate and entered the Order appointing Bart Sinclair as Personal Representative of the estate without blinking an eye.

Bo realized there was no backing out now.

Bo was certainly filled with mixed emotions as he proceeded directly to the post office while telephoning Hank to meet him there. In what seemed like no time at all, the two men converged on the North Palm Beach Post Office. As usual it was filled to capacity with mostly retired senior citizens, shuffling along the line, using the counter as a crutch. They both thought to themselves that someday that would be them! Hopefully, not someday soon, though!

Bo and Hank waited for what seemed like an eternity, as they listened to customers complain from everything ranging from the increase in the price of stamps to their health problems to their ungrateful children. The two of them certainly did not look forward to growing old. Simultaneously, the two best friends looked at each other and vowed not to whine about everything when they do get old. They both envisioned themselves competing in running races well into their eighties. Granted, they realized their speed might be reduced to that of a brisk walk, but it would be better than remembering what once was and then complaining about everything else.

Unfortunately for them, Monica had the day off, and the two men were asked to kindly wait until the supervisor was available. They waited for quite a while until they were almost at their wit's end when the two were finally met by a supervisor, who was obviously very flustered.

"Can I see the legal papers?" demanded the woman.

"Sure, here," said Bo, as he handed the Letters of Administration and the fiduciary Power of Attorney to the woman.

After reviewing the papers thoroughly, the woman then requested the death certificate.

Bo spoke, "Ma'am, the original is with the court. The documents that you have in your hand authorize me to have access to the post office box. You don't need anything further, and you certainly do not need a death certificate."

"Young man, let me inform you that I am an officer of the US Government, and I must follow proper guidelines and procedures. I'm sure you understand that."

"Oh, I do," replied Bo, rather indignantly. I can assure you there is no other paper work that you need to allow me access. Please just let us retrieve the contents of the box, and we'll be on our way."

The woman, beginning to become a bit more flustered with the two of them staring at her, finally relented and opened the post office box of Joe Marx.

The two men were hoping for lots of mail, bank statements, and some sort of lead into the secret life of Joe Marx. What they found was a single white envelope.

Hank spoke first, "Only one envelope? What's up with that?"

Bo reached into the box and retrieved the envelope. It was unsealed and contained the following handwritten note:

To Whom It May Concern:

If you are reading this letter by now you will know that I am deceased. My story is not a happy one and I am an old and bitter man.

My wife and daughter were murdered by Victor Butin. I made it my plan, my sole purpose in the days I had left to destroy Victor for what he did to my family.

I have made millions of dollars selling diamonds and have given most of it away to charity, as material possessions mean nothing to me.

I have used and abused many individuals, my latest, being Bart Sinclair. If Bart is in trouble with the law, let this letter absolve him from any and all liability.

I am a criminal, I am guilty, and I pray to God to forgive my sins.

Joe Marx

Bo and Hank were both at a loss for words as they reread the handwritten letter.

"Well, Bo, now what?"

Bo just shook his head. "I don't know, Hank, I honestly don't know."

"Well, let's see what's in the bank. What can it hurt?" asked Hank.

The two men traveled in Bo's car to the Bank of North Palm Beach. Neither man said much, each eagerly awaiting the contents of the box.

Fortunately, the men did not have to wait long, as the assistant vice-president was very obliging and considerate.

"Mr. Martin, I bet you have to do this a lot, considering your profession?"

"Yes, unfortunately you are right. It never gets easier going through a deceased's personal belongings." The safe deposit box was very small. Bo was hoping it would be a bit larger. As Bo and Hank proceeded to empty the contents onto the table in their private room, they were both surprised once again.

Inside was one extremely large, beautiful—make that exquisite—diamond solitaire. It had to be fifteen to twenty carats. There was also about twenty thousand dollars in hundred-dollar bills and three passports with Joe Marx's picture, all under different names. There was also an old picture of a young Joe Marx with a pretty brunette woman and a young girl. The thought of Ruby holding a beautiful baby flashed through Bo's head. They certainly looked like a happy family. There was one other envelope.

Bo picked up the envelope, opened it up, and proceeded to read it out loud to Hank.

To Whom It May Concern:

If you were able to locate my safe deposit box key, you must know that I am now dead. I hope that my plan was a success and that Victor Butin is wondering how he lost fifty million dollars. If not, I am a failure and my life was a complete waste.

The diamond is real and worth in excess of three million dollars wholesale, six million dollars retail. The cash from the sale of the diamond should be distributed evenly to Bart's children pursuant to my Last Will and Testament. Please destroy my passports. The picture is the only reminder of my painful past.

Please do the right thing!

If this is being read by Victor Butin, MAY YOU ROT IN HELL!

Joe Marx

Bo was almost afraid to handle the diamond, and Hank wanted to have nothing further to do with the diamond or the money. Things were getting just too weird, as he felt like he was caught up in a gangster-type B-rated movie!

"Bo," asked Hank, "now do we call the authorities?"

Bo looked him straight in the eye and replied, "Not on your life!"

"That's exactly what I was afraid you were going to say. We are up shits creek without a paddle!"

"Come on now, Hank, we are much more informed than ever before. We now have a place to start. This whole thing has been one big puzzle, and now we have the first piece to start putting it all together."

Bo, the optimist, was upbeat. Hank, the rational one, was worried.

"Pandora's Box is open, and we are in for a wild ride," exclaimed Hank. "They do serve you three square meals a day in prisons, don't they?"

"Let's go," was all Bo had to say, as the men left the bank with the contents in Bo's beat-up brief case.

Chapter
Thirteen

---

*V*ictor Butin barked out orders to his petite yet beautiful oriental maid. He was in a foul mood, and even the unbelievable view of Central Park from his multimillion dollar penthouse, failed to improve his disposition. The maid continued on with her work, trying hard to stay out of the old man's way.

Victor was now in his mid-seventies and for his age still possessed a pretty inspiring physique due to all his years of weight lifting, and he still looked very impressive in his custom Armani suits. Victor never remarried after his brief first marriage ended in heartbreak. It was as if Victor's once warm and kind heart turned to ice the moment he saw his wife in the arms of another man. Victor became a different person that day. Even members of his own family became afraid of him, and needless to say, his former wife's lover met his unfortunate demise not too long after that fateful day.

In any event, Victor was in a particularly rotten mood. For a man with homes in Monaco, Switzerland, and New York, he definitely was not hurting for money. In fact, it became a game to him, the more he got, the more he wanted, and on and on. Victor was about to receive his final shipment of diamonds. His blackmail and extortion of his ex-wife and the DeBeers family was coming to an end, and this was going to be the last cache of diamonds. Fortunately, this stash was the best and largest of them all. The diamonds were absolutely magnificent. Victor expected to clear upwards of $50 million from their ultimate sale, exclusive of Joe Marx's cut.

For years Joe's company, A Trading Co., acted as the intermediary for the sale of the diamonds. Joe consigned the diamonds to various jewelers, and upon each sale, the proceeds were deposited into A Trading Co. From there, Joe would wire the money to Victor's designated accounts worldwide. Victor trusted Joe and believed that Joe would never cross him.

Yet despite many years of unfettered success, Victor always covered his bases. With that much money on the line, you can never trust anyone completely. Victor had always believed Joe was somewhat odd. What kind of man makes millions of dollars yet never acquires any material possessions? What kind of man never cheats and accurately accounts for every penny and every diamond ever sold? *Joe was remarkable, but why?* thought Victor.

When Victor had acquired his latest expensive collection of gems, he turned over all the stones to Joe. Victor made necessary precautions since this was his last deal, and he didn't want anything to go wrong. First, he paid off the vice-president of the Bank of England in the Isle of Man where A Trading Co. was located to inform him of any and all activity in Joe's corporate account. Second, Victor had Joe's personal phone and the phone to A. Trading Co. tapped. He then assigned his trusted assistant, Marty Zorkof, and his two faithful former weight lifters, Igor and Ivan to monitor all telephone calls from a leased warehouse in West Palm Beach and to also keep a closer eye on Joe. Victor had a transmitter placed on Joe's car so Igor and Ivan could follow his every move. Since Joe didn't do much, except drink, their job was rather easy, or so they thought.

Victor knew that most of the sales of gems over the past years had come from Diamond and Sons Inc., owned by Bart Sinclair in Palm Beach, Florida. On several occasions, Victor had actually visited the Worth Avenue store, and even purchased an item or two for a female admirer. Based on his information and belief, Victor was confident that the gems would be sold and that efforts were being made to sell the flawless diamonds.

Victor started to become alarmed when no money was being transferred to the Isle of Man account. Normally the sales occurred primarily during the winter season in Palm Beach, and the sales proceeds came at intermittent times. It had been just over three months since the stones were delivered. During that time, other lots of stones were sold and the proceeds received, but none of the latest batch of gems and not one penny of the expected fifty million dollars had been deposited.

Victor had even gone so far as to extend himself financially with his latest purchase of a London mansion in anticipation of the forthcoming fifty million dollars.

When the sale proceeds still had not materialized, Victor personally visited Paul Schwartz. Paul was extremely cooperative with Victor and his two big friends.

Paul had provided Victor with copies of Bart Sinclair's corporate income tax returns, financial statements, and all other information that Victor had requested. Paul was a grade-A rat and informant, and the disclosure of the financial information was certainly a breach of ethics and a direct violation of the attorney-client privilege. But Victor operated in a world full of informers and snitches, and Paul Schwartz was a good inside man, and if the price was right, it made him all the more willing.

Paul reported directly to Victor, and on numerous occasions kept him abreast of all of Bart's dealings.

Still several more weeks went by and nothing. Victor believed there was a problem and finally placed a call directly to Joe to get to the bottom of everything. However when there was no answer, Victor became infuriated and slammed the phone down. He immediately placed a call to Paul.

"Paul, this is Victor Butin calling."

"Oh, hi Victor; hold on a second, and let me close my door," replied Paul.

"How are you, Victor?" asked Paul.

"As soon as I find your Mr. Sinclair and Joe Marx, I will be terrific! Now tell me, how is our friend Mr. Sinclair?"

"Very well, I believe. He has been away for a few months now and if business was bad, I seriously doubt whether he could get away for such a long period of time."

"So as far as you know, everything is well at Diamond and Sons?"

"I believe so. I know for a fact that one extremely wealthy fellow has been purchasing a good deal of diamonds. Bart told me he has a winner if that means anything to you?"

"Yes, it certainly does," said Victor.

"Do you know where Joe Marx went?"

There was a brief moment of silence before Paul spoke, "I, I, I don't know. I am presently very busy with a trial, and I haven't seen or heard anything about him. Like I said, Bart has been out of the county for a while. I have spoken with him on a couple of occasions, but he has never mentioned Mr. Marx."

Victor sensed Paul's stammering and went right to the punch line. "Paul, is there something you are not telling me? You know my background. If I ever find out you are not being honest with me, I am sure you know the consequences!"

"Well, I don't know if this is of any great importance, but I do believe Joe may have found himself a woman."

"A woman! When? Where? Who? You have got to be kidding me. This must be some sort of a joke. Joe Marx is a loner and has been ever since his wife and kid died many years ago."

"Listen, Victor, it is probably only a rumor, but that is what I heard."

Victor screamed into the receiver, "You have not heard the last of me."

Literally seconds later, Victor was spewing profanities into the phone at Marty. If Victor was face-to-face with him, Marty would be a dead man by now or at least certainly impaired.

Marty responded hysterically to Victor. "Victor, Victor, Victor, listen. The last we heard from Joe was yesterday, and we are headed over to his apartment right now to check things out. I will call you as soon as we find out anything!"

"You're damn right you will," said Victor and with that, slammed the phone down and in the same motion grabbed a Waterford goblet and hurled it against the wall shattering it into a hundred pieces. "Nobody crosses Victor Butin. *Nobody!*"

Chapter
Fourteen

*M*ilton Rogers stood unabashedly clad only in his silk pajama bottoms while admiring the Atlantic Ocean from his multimillion dollar Palm Beach mansion. The naked woman lying in the ruffled bed a few feet away softly called his name. Mrs. Rogers was in her early thirties and still looked quite youthful, and she was eager to have Milton return to bed. However, Milton ignored her plea. Minutes later Milton, who was about to turn the age of sixty-five, walked back to the bed.

"Get up. You need to leave now."

"But, Milton, what happened to us being together all day? I made many sacrifices to get here."

"Just do as I say. My wife may return soon, and I don't think she would like to see her daughter-in-law in her bed. Do you?"

"You really can be an ass sometimes, Milton," remarked Mrs. Rogers, as she gathered her clothes and prepared to leave. "I don't know why anyone puts up with you."

"Yes you do. It's because I'm rich."

With that said, Milton proceeded to light his cigar and contemplate the rest of his day.

"Oh, please leave through the guest entrance, just in case someone on the grounds may see you."

"Whatever," said the young Mrs. Rogers, "Annie" to those close to her, and sashayed out of the room in quite a huff.

Alone at last, thought Milton, as he reached to pour himself a brandy to go along with his Cuban Monte Cristo cigar. It was not yet two in the afternoon, but Milton's day was done.

Milton Rogers grew up on the streets of Brooklyn, New York. His father died at a young age, and his mother never remarried. She focused all her energies on raising her son. She brought him up to love books and reading and to rise above their one-bedroom one-bath flat. She pushed young Milton hard and relentlessly to excel in school. Rather than play outside with the other children, Milton studied literature. He read books and studied English.

Milton and his mother's hard work paid off, as he excelled in school and was awarded a college scholarship to NYU. When he realized, early in his collegiate career that he would never be an award-winning author, Milton focused his energies on publishing. Although he could not write professionally, he recognized talent when he read it. In a relatively short time, his little publishing company that he started right out of school with what little money he scraped together began to grow.

Ever the optimist, Milton met his future wife, Brenda at a time when his company needed a serious infusion of capital. Brenda, the daughter of a bank president, convinced her father to loan Milton the much-needed funds. Milton realized he needed the money for his publishing company to grow, but was not pleased with the terms. "If you want the money, you must marry my daughter," uttered the bank president. It's as simple as that; no marriage, no money."

Milton liked Brenda enough, and she sure was something to look at as well as being very accomplished in the bedroom, but Milton wasn't sure about marriage, right now. However in the long run, the thought of an extremely wealthy father-in-law made up Milton's mind pretty quickly, and he soon made Brenda his wife. The loan enabled his publishing company to expand. Meanwhile in an effort to satisfy the increasingly more stringent demands of his father-in-law and to obtain further funding, Milton and Brenda produced four offspring. Grandpa was indeed proud, and the banking relationship proved beneficial to all.

Milton worked day and night while Brenda tended to the boys. Unfortunately, the boys did not inherit Milton's mental genes or his almost inhuman drive to succeed. Not one of them would ever become a successful businessman. As Milton's publishing empire grew, so did the extravagant tastes of Brenda and the boys. Nothing was too good for her or her boys. Sports cars of their choice at age sixteen, boats, guns, European vacations, and the latest and most expensive of everything else were provided for the boys.

Milton grew to resent the hell out of his children and their pampered lives. What he resented most of all was that he had such little control over their upbringing. It was not only because he was just too busy with work, but his wife wouldn't hear of it. She didn't want her precious boys listening to things such as "A little hard work wouldn't hurt you" or "You have to work hard and achieve your own success!" On numerous occasions, the boys were afforded jobs in Milton's publishing empire. None of the four ever amounted to a hill of beans, and all were basically spoiled brats. When the going got tough, they just quit and went running back to mom. They were lazy, dumb, and not worth a nickel. Milton would have liked to have thrown them out on their own, but unfortunately, he had his wife and father-in-law standing in the way of that.

The boys enjoyed their father's money and power and were soon able to engage their voracious appetites for booze, women, and drugs. DUIs were dismissed, drug deals vaporized, and barroom fights were just simple misunderstandings that could be resolved with their father's money.

Milton secretly despised each and every one of them. Maybe that was one reason he enjoyed young Annie so much. It was his way of getting back at his oldest son.

As the boys ended their wasted twenties for some inexplicable reason, Milton worried about their futures. All four lived solely off the money Milton and Brenda provided them. They all resided in million-dollar homes, craved only the finest and most expensive cars, jewelry, and clothes, and had never worked an honest day in their lives. Now with children of their own looming in the very near future, "Grandpa" Milton was faced with a major dilemma.

Milton and Brenda knew that upon their deaths, 35 percent of their estates would go to the IRS. Milton hated the IRS and believed the Rogers family had paid more than their rightful share in taxes. He also knew that his publishing empire would become valueless in a short time under the control of the boys. Further, Milton was tired of the stress of running the publishing empire singlehandedly and wanted to relax, unwind, and enjoy his life and hopefully, his grandchildren.

One night after cataloging Brenda's extensive jewelry collection, Milton came up with a brilliant plan. *If I could convert my stocks and bonds to tangible assets, I could transfer them to the boys without the IRS's knowledge, and avoid the 35% gift tax*, thought Milton. The boys could then sell the items at their leisure and enjoy the proceeds tax-free. It was a brilliant plan, or so he thought.

The very next day, Milton visited Diamond and Sons Inc., and began to collect and gather information. In addition, Milton and Brenda undertook gemology and appraisal courses online. They had also researched the internet and learned a great deal from it. Together the two had learned all about gems and had actually become semi-experts—Milton much more than Brenda. Milton devoured as much information as he could, and in less than two years, he had indeed become an expert in the diamond business. Brenda loved Milton's new interest, and he showered her with stunning and brilliant diamonds and jewels. Diamonds were definitely Brenda's "best friend"!

In the interim two years, the Rogers boys individually and collectively, had attempted and failed in at least six businesses. Food, construction, sales, marketing, retail, and yachting were among their failures. The boys just could not get over the "work" thing, as they always just wanted to be out playing and spending money. The boys were smart enough to realize, however that their father was getting close to the end of his generosity and decided they had to find some sort of legitimate business to prosper in. The boys were only knowledgeable about the recreational drugs they consumed and how they spent their father's money. "Drugs that's it, we will learn about the drug trade," laughed Lee, the oldest Rogers's son.

It was Lisa Rogers, the wife of Milton's youngest son, who made a statement that further guided Milton's master plan. Lisa had just dined the previous evening with Dana Sinclair at the Sinclair's mansion. She couldn't get over their wealth and was extremely envious. She said over drinks, "I've met Bart Sinclair, and he is an idiot. If he's not drunk or fishing, he's out womanizing. He is not much of a businessman and even keeps his business records on slips of paper. He has literally no accounting system, and rumor has it that he has been sued on several occasions for allegedly changing out the stones of customers. I've even heard that he can't tell a real diamond from a fake one. How he makes his money is beyond me, but Dana says the markup on jewelry is incredible. So with mom's (Brenda's) jewelry, which Milton bought for her over the years, he probably made over a one hundred percent profit. Why don't we get into the jewelry business?"

The Rogers boys all thought it was a stupid idea but not Milton. Lisa's suggestion was the nail in the coffin for Milton's ingenious plan, or so he thought.

Milton spent several more months meticulously working on his plan. The sale of his publishing empire would gross nearly $500 million. However, the long-term capital gains tax of 15 percent would take a $75 million whack out of his sales proceeds. Milton abhorred the thought of paying the IRS such a huge amount and had pursued all the legal avenues to reduce the $75 million income tax bill.

Milton also realized that upon the death of both he and Brenda, the remaining $425 million would then be subject to an inheritance tax of an additional 35 percent, resulting in an estate tax bill of nearly $150 million. Only $275 million would be available to his four sons. Undoubtedly, they would squander their inherited wealth in record time. Even though Milton really disliked his sons, he absolutely abhorred the IRS! To Milton it was a no-brainer. He was willing to do whatever it took to minimize taxes and maximize the benefit to his family.

Milton vowed not to let the IRS get the bulk of his lifetime achievement. He had made far too many sacrificesover the years to build his publishing company to see it all go to the government. Hell, he even had married Brenda and raised four children in order to grow the company.

The impending sale of his company would be paid in two installments. $250 million at the time of closing and the remainder on the one-year anniversary date of the sale. Milton was to receive 99 percent and he had only allocated a paltry 1 percent to his valued employees. Milton really cared little about his employees including his lifelong secretary and his chief officers, despite the fact that they had worked diligently for him for so many years.

Money, or rather the lack of it, was what drove Milton, and the fear of losing over 40 percent of his net worth to the IRS was something he simply could not handle. Milton had hired the brightest and most aggressive CPAs and tax attorneys to help him minimize the impending impact of taxes. However, not one of his tax advisors had provided him with the answers he wanted to hear. All the sophisticated estate and tax planning techniques required him to relinquish control of his assets to his boys, and that was something he would never do.

One week before the sale of his company, Milton Rogers's solution finally materialized. *Damn the consequences to innocent people*, he thought. Even though his sons were lazy good-for-nothings, he vowed to protect them. After all, it was his children and his good name. Milton's plan would save his money and his family, and in doing so, he would outsmart the IRS. To Milton, it was a win–win–win strategy.

In his two and a half years of study, Milton had become a certified CAI jeweler. He treated himself by flying to Utah for a few weeks' vacation. At first, Brenda was hurt by his desire to go alone, but she soon relented when she started thinking about what she could do while he was away: maybe her own little vacation, shopping trips and luncheons with the girls, spas treatments, and much, much more.

However, Milton did not arrive in Provo, Utah for a vacation. He was there to learn everything he could about synthetic gems. In the jewelry business, the Federal Trade Commission mandates that gems sold as "synthetic" must match the chemistry and structure of natural gems.

The traditional method of synthetic gems was to start with a seed gem, a natural stone the size of a salt grain, which is then used to set a pattern of future crystal growth. Crystal growers then spend weeks adding aluminum oxide to the seed gem and placing it under high pressure and temperature. In little over two months, a seed gem can grow from an inexpensive two grams to a pricey fifty grams in weight.

Milton had discovered that synthetic diamonds made from carbon had been around since 1954 when General Electric scientists first created them. These manufactured diamonds were only slightly less hard than real diamonds, but the silicon carbide gems actually sparkled with more brilliance.

After two weeks, Milton unfortunately came back from Utah empty-handed. He had hoped to buy the Provo, Utah, synthetic diamonds company. The owner, a ruffled former GE scientist, refused to part with ownership of his company, despite an impressive cash offer. Milton was incensed but undeterred. His time schedule was ticking away, the core of his plan was lacking, and he could feel it all slipping away.

Fortunately for Milton, the old man gave him the name of a young scientist, out of Gainesville, Florida, looking for seed capital and a silent partner to manufacture colorless artificial diamonds. Brad Penny was the name of the young thirty-year-old University of Florida scientist who, through overseas training and his own trial and error, had copied and improved on a method to re-create intense pressures and temperatures to better fuse carbon atoms together to create a synthetic diamond. Using this state-of-the-art technology, Brad employed lower pressures over longer times in his patented novel presses to create his colorless diamond.

The major synthetic manufacturers in the industry could only produce yellow diamonds. The heating process under their traditional methods released some nitrogen, which turned the diamonds yellow. So Brad's new process was quite revolutionary. Milton was bound and determined to convince Brad that together they could capture the market.

Chapter
Fifteen

The four-hour car trip it took to get to Gainesville was almost three hours longer than it actually took Milton to convince Brad to form a partnership. The duo wasted no time in getting their partnership started. Milton's desire to create colorless artificial diamonds was soon going to be a reality. Brad was able to jump start his program immediately. The results were historic.

In a little over an intensive six-month period backed by Milton's several million dollars of capital, Brad had successfully completed the production of flawless brilliant colorless synthetic diamonds. Milton was ecstatic! The first mass production of the colorless diamonds coincided with the sale of Milton Rogers's publication company, and the initial $250 million. Milton had successfully laid the ground work for his grand plan.

Milton summoned his four sons and their wives including Annie to the family oceanfront mansion in Palm Beach.

Naturally the boys were a little nervous; they knew their father did not approve of their lifestyles, and they always felt like they were treading on very thin ice inside Milton's mansion. They never doubted for one moment that their father could cut them off financially at any time. They all arrived timely and settled into small talk.

Lee, the oldest, was the first to speak, "Well, what do you think the old man has in store for us? My wife and I need at least two million dollars per year to get by. How about you?"

In rapid progression, Lance, Lawrence, and Luke all answered that they too needed around two million dollars per year to get by. Between club memberships, boating, clothes, vacations, houses, cars insurance, and never-ending socializing, even two million dollars, seemed like roughing it.

Lance responded next, "Now that Dad's company is being sold, do you think Dad will just give us a portion of the sales proceeds?"

"What, are you nuts?" answered Luke. "Besides Mom and Dad need some of that money for themselves. The most they can give to us is twenty-eight thousand dollars per individual, per year under the current estate and gift tax laws."

"My attorney tells me that for Mom and Dad to give me and my wife two million dollars per year, they have to pay the IRS an additional seven hundred thousand dollars in gift taxes. That means it takes almost eleven million dollars per year to provide us our eight million dollars after taxes. I'm sure that pisses Dad off!"

"Now with the company being sold and us no longer on the payroll where will the money come from?" questioned Lawrence.

"It looks like we all might have to start working" quipped Lee.

Luke responded, "As the youngest, I think we all need to stick together. We have to stand up to dear old Dad. Are we all in agreement then?" They all nodded their heads and raised their drinks in unison just as Milton strolled into the massive formal family room.

"Please sit down, and thanks for coming. You all look well," Milton remarked, as he gave Annie a sly little wink. Milton walked over to the bar and mixed himself a dirty martini, since everyone else was already sipping on one, but he knew it was more like their second or even third, as they all drank like fish!

When Milton was ready, he began his speech.

"You are all probably wondering why I called you here." All heads nodded.

"As you know, I sold my company and you are now officially unemployed. Your mother and I plan to enjoy our retirement, and we also do not plan on supporting you for the rest of your lives. After the goddamn IRS steals its share, we won't have much left for ourselves. Unfortunately, there is not enough to go around."

You could have heard a pin drop as the eight of them were sitting with their mouths on the floor and their heads spinning. The boys were speechless, but their wives were utterly horrified.

Milton knew they were all sweating bullets. *What worthless kids I have,* thought Milton. *They will definitely toe the line and follow me in my master plan. Anything to keep from actually having a real career and making their own money!*

Lance spoke first. "On behalf of all of us, we must say that we are at a huge loss. Naturally, we all had assumed that we would one day ultimately run the company. But now you have sold it from underneath us. Of course, we are happy for you and Mom. But what are we to do?"

Milton had expected such a self-centered response from his worthless children.

"Give me a fucking break," yelled Milton. "Have I not attempted to employ each and every one of you and your spouses in the family business? Have I not supported your pathetic attempts to run your own worthless ventures? Have I not given you each millions of dollars per year just so you can grow up to be a bunch of worthless losers? Have you any idea that each time I give you a dollar, I have to give the IRS thirty-five cents as well?

"Well, don't all answer at once! What's wrong? Has the cat got your tongue, or has all that private school education ruined your pathetic minds?"

Milton was pacing the room and flailing his arms as he spoke. His face had turned a crimson red. "What good are any of you? Tell me please."

Luke, the youngest was the next to speak. "Dad, we're sorry. We know that we have disappointed you, and we all feel terrible about it. However, we are your family, and we will do anything you tell us to do."

Next it was Lee's turn. "Dad, unfortunately we have come to rely on you and Mom for everything. We really can't make it without your generosity. We need over a hundred thousand dollars a month between all the bills and expenses. And of course, we want to have children to carry on the Rogers name."

Milton snapped back, "Why, so I can support them as well? Another generation of losers!" The room suddenly grew very silent. All four boys' heads were bowed, each sensing the absolute worst. *No money! What on earth are we going to do?* they all thought.

Just when the boys had lost hope, Milton slowly reeled them back.

"Don't look so glum, you sad and worthless bums. You are my boys—of course, I am going to help you. More importantly, I need your help."

The boys immediately perked up, but not as much so as their four young wives, who were all silently rejoicing. Everything was not lost—they would still have money. Thank God!

By now, Milton had all the boys' complete attention. "Lee, Lance, Lawrence, and Luke, what do you do best?"

The boys were silent. Not one could provide an answer. "Think for once in your miserable lives!" shouted Milton.

"Well," said Lawrence. "We all have excellent taste."

"Good, what else?" Again, nothing but silence. "I can see that your wives like the finer things in life—like designer clothes and fine jewelry."

"Yes of course they do," uttered all of the boys simultaneously.

"Is that so?" Those spoken words were exactly what Milton wanted to hear. He pulled a velvet bag out of his jacket pocket and said, "Well, take a look at these," throwing several colorless diamonds at each son. The boys scrambled to collect all the diamonds Milton had thrown in their direction. Their wives marveled at the brilliant stones. They all inspected them closely, examining their color, carat, and clarity.

"Are we going to sell these stones?" questioned Lance.

"Yeah," muttered Lee. "What do we know about diamonds? We were once interested in retail, and you know how bad that experience was. I don't know if we could get certified in the jewelry business. It would take a lot of work."

"Heaven forbid," exclaimed Milton. "God help you if you have to actually work for a living. W-O-R-K is not a four-letter word, people!"

Lawrence stood up and said, "Dad, whatever you want, we can do it. We will do anything you ask, and I promise, we will not fail you ever again." He sounded so sincere that Milton laughed inwardly.

"You're damn right you won't fail me. I will make sure of that!" demanded Milton.

"Take a closer look at the diamonds. Can you notice anything? Compare the stones to those on your wives' fingers, wrists, necks, and ears."

The boys did as instructed. Each took several long minutes to compare the diamonds, and so did their wives.

"Well, I'm waiting," exclaimed Milton, as he tapped his foot on the mahogany hardwood floor.

Luke spoke, "Dad, these diamonds are flawless. From what I can tell, they are some of the nicest stones I have ever seen. They must be worth a lot of money."

"Check closer," prodded Milton.

The boys once again examined the gems. It was Annie who then spoke up. "These are real, I know real from fake, and I know these are real stones."

Everyone nodded and agreed that the stones were real and that they must be worth a small fortune. They looked up to the standing Milton, and awaited his response.

"Well, well. You all agreed that your strongest attribute is that you could tell the real thing from the fake. The in versus the out. The hip versus the non-hip." Milton let these words sink in for a moment longer.

"Well, let me tell you something. You guys *pass*. Congratulations! Now give them back to me."

The wives hesitated to hand the stones back over to Milton. They all believed they were letting hundreds of thousands of dollars slip through their greedy little fingers.

When Milton had recovered all the diamonds, he placed them back into the velvet Crown Royal purple sack and continued speaking. All the while, he amused himself with his daughters-in-law fake smiles, knowing how badly they all wanted to keep the diamonds in their possession.

"Hold those thoughts for just a while until I return," said Milton as he exited the room. When he was gone, the kids spoke all at once.

"Can you believe those gems? They were absolutely beautiful? I would die for those diamonds! What's Dad up to? How much do you think they're worth? Gosh, my friend Dana would be impressed. Honey, could you get me a new diamond necklace?"

Milton was in a much better mood when he returned and walked in on the kids' animated discussion and waited for silence. "I don't want to alarm you or include you into my master plan right now, but I just want you to know several things.

"First, I expect your total, and I mean one hundred percent, cooperation in this family endeavor."

"Second, you will be asked to move temporarily out of Palm Beach. One of you will most likely reside temporarily in Los Angeles one in Dallas one in Miami, and the last one in Boston."

"Do I hear any objections so far?" asked Milton.

All the boys and their wives looked at each other, but all agreed to a temporary change of address. No one dared to speak out.

"Third, I will need each of you to work with the federal government, the FBI, the US attorneys, private investigators, and scores of attorneys. Do you have any problems with that?"

Though it sounded a little intense, the consensus was a resounding "No."

"Fourth, are you willing to lie under oath and do whatever is asked of you whenever it is required in order to protect the Rogers family?"

Once again, all nodded in agreement. Lying was actually no big deal to the Rogers children.

"Very well then. My plan will make each and every one of you extremely wealthy. I am not talking millions, but rather tens of millions. Can you live with that?"

All the children unanimously voiced their willingness. They were high-fiving and hugging each other. "Whatever you want, Dad, whatever you want."

Milton thought to himself and smiled, *My plan is foolproof.*

Chapter
Sixteen

*M*eanwhile back in Gainesville, Brad Penny was ecstatic. He had long believed that he could mass-produce a colorless artificial diamond that possessed spectacular brilliance. He basically had stolen the actual concept from a Belgium scientist he previously worked under, but he had substantially improved on it.

Everyone in the diamond industry was well aware of the fact that Antwerp, Belgium, was the diamond-polishing capital of the world. Therefore, Brad worked and studied his trade for several years in Belgium under one of the country's leading scientists. Before returning back to Gainesville, he had extracted from his years of apprenticeship the cutting-edge technology needed to produce colorless diamonds.

When a disguised Milton Rogers had appeared at his doorstop in Gainesville, it was as if all his prayers were answered. Milton provided the money for a state-of-the-art lab just outside the University of Florida in the nearby town of Alachua. He also provided the cash necessary to hire quality UF grad students, lured by the attractive thirty-dollar-an-hour wage. Students were lining up to work at his lab, appropriately named Clear Inc. Clear Inc., was in actuality an offshore quagmire of shell corporations, so intertwined that the true owner or any individual name was unobtainable.

Milton singlehandedly provided everything for Brad under the most secretive terms imaginable. Not one of the UF students had a clue who or what they were working on or for. However at thirty dollars an hour, they didn't complain.

Of course, Brad worried about the unbelievable privacy protections and restrictions from the guy with a terrible toupee. However, the future promise of extreme wealth helped to alleviate his fears. Although he would rather have been paid by check, he and all the employees at Clear Inc., accepted their cash payments. Brad was required to pay each student cash at the end of each workday. No student ever laid eyes on Milton or had any contact with anyone other than Brad. Brad was in lone possession of the cash, which Milton funded each week by Federal Express from a post office box under a foreign name and fake address.

Brad was also provided one cell phone. There were no other phones in the Alachua lab itself, and nobody was allowed to bring a cell phone to work. There was also no mailbox and surprisingly, no business cards or records. Brad was simply provided a Federal Express manila envelope full of cash, each week, out of which he paid the employees, electric, water, and himself. Naturally, Brad helped himself handsomely to all of the extra cash at the end of each week. *Who cares, we are all going to be rich*, thought Brad, as he pocketed the weekly excess.

The actual implementation of his novel presses utilizing lower pressures but over substantially longer times proved easier than Brad had ever imagined. It was a huge success. Once the first batch of colorless diamonds was complete, Brad was somewhat stunned by Milton's specific instructions. He naturally assumed they would begin manufacturing thousands of diamonds. But, much to his surprise, Milton limited the first production run to 150 specific carat and cut diamonds.

Brad thought to himself, *What on earth is this man thinking? Why aren't we manufacturing more diamonds, and why these specific shapes and sizes?* Nevertheless, Brad begrudgingly did as he was instructed and continued to pocket all the extra weekly cash.

With the manufacturing of the synthetic colorless diamonds running smoothly, Milton proceeded to implement his next step.

Milton had become a frequent visitor at Diamond and Sons Inc. in Palm Beach. Almost every other week he had wandered into Bart Sinclair's store examining and admiring the beautiful merchandise. He personally had witnessed Bart's lack of quality control, lack of bookkeeping records, and overall lack of business acumen.

Milton definitely liked what he saw.

He was even more elated when he researched the Palm Beach County court filings and uncovered several lawsuits against Bart Sinclair, all for allegedly switching stones. Although the suits were eventually settled out of court and permanently sealed, he had all the ammunition he needed and was ready to strike.

The day after the sale of Milton's company and his first cash installment, he approached Bart personally.

Bart was becoming increasingly annoyed by Milton's numerous visits, but as a natural salesman, he continued to be pleasant and courteous toward him, knowing his potential. When Milton approached Bart and asked him if he had a moment, Bart wasn't really expecting anything big.

"Bart, have you got a moment?"

"Sure."

"I just want to thank you for your generous hospitality and for answering all of my numerous questions."

"No problem, Milton. You and your family are nice people and great customers, so whatever I can do for you is my pleasure." Bart proceeded to work on his display presentation when Milton said the magic words. "I sold my company, so I have some extra cash sitting around. I would like to spend some of it on your prestigious diamond collection."

Bart had learned through the grapevine that Milton's company was worth several hundred million dollars, so naturally that statement got Bart's immediate attention. He promptly stopped what he was doing. "Well in that case, please come into my office. Phyllis, honey, hold all my calls. I'm going to be busy for a while." Bart's office was rather small and casual. There were many pictures of Bart and his family. There were awards and trophies and plaques on top of every file cabinet. Milton smiled to himself when he observed all the clutter.

The two men sat on the comfortable identical leather couches. Bart earnestly listened to Milton's every word.

"Bart, as you know, I am very interested in getting into the diamond and jewelry business as a collector. My wife adores jewelry, and now with the sale of my company, I would like to be a major consumer. I don't plan on selling any of the jewelry I intend to purchase as I just want to be a collector. I am impressed by your store and friendly staff, and I feel that your diamonds are impeccable. Your prices on diamonds also tend to be reasonable, and I think we can reach a mutual agreement."

Bart was elated and tried to hold back his emotions. His heart was racing, and all he saw was dollar signs.

"Well, Milton, what exactly do you have in mind?"

"I want to spend one hundred million dollars over the next two years, and I am solely interested in diamonds. I am mostly interested in the colorless diamonds.

It was music to Bart's ears. Bart made a significantly higher markup on the diamonds he procured through Joe Marx. This was indeed his mother lode!

"Okay. Do you want the diamonds loose or in settings?" asked Bart curiously.

"To tell you the truth, Bart, I am interested in the larger colorless loose diamonds. I want to tinker with creating my own settings if you don't mind."

"No, not at all. In fact that makes my job easier. Let me show you what I have on hand out of my personal inventory. It will just be a minute."

Milton waited while Bart went to his enormous safe to withdraw the merchandise. When Bart returned, Milton's smile lit up once he had an opportunity to examine some of the stones. Milton thought to himself, *My synthetic stones are even more brilliant than the ones placed before me, and these are excellent quality.*

Bart stood over Milton grinning from ear to ear.

"Now, what would you like?" asked Bart.

"Bart, I would like five of each cut and size beginning with one carat and proceeding up to twenty carats. I have a wife and four daughters-in-law, you know."

Bart's mind was working overtime. He believed that he could fulfill Milton's request, but it would take a while, and Joe Marx would really have to hustle in order to fill Milton's request. Bart also realized that even with Joe's 50 percent share, Bart's profit would be in excess of $50 million.

Milton's next question caused Bart some alarm. "And, Bart, I do not want to pay the six percent Florida sales tax of six million dollars. I'll write checks out to you personally, or to your wife or kids or any other entity, but not to Diamond and Sons Inc. Do you have problem with that?"

After a moment's hesitation, Bart answered somewhat leery, "No, Milton, not really." Bart wanted to ask him some probing questions, other than the obvious, but he didn't want to risk losing all that potential money! *I'm going to have to spend some time calculating the prices and it will definitely take me some additional weeks to procure the stones,* Bart thought.

"What time frame are we looking at?"

"It is October 3 today. I would like half of the stones before Christmas and the other half next year, prior to Valentine's Day. Can you handle that?" Milton asked raising his eyebrows.

"I don't think that will be much of a problem," said Bart. "How are we going to negotiate prices?"

"Look, Bart, as you know I am very wealthy. I want to be treated fairly by you. Of course, I don't expect to pay wholesale prices, but I don't want to be cheated either. I know you have to make a living, and I just want my money's worth. As a deposit and a token of my good faith, here is a check in the amount of ten million dollars. I'm counting on you, Bart. Please don't let me down."

"Oh, no, you can definitely count on me!" Deep down inside, Bart was praying to God that his supplier, Joe Marx, would be able to fulfill this once-in-a-lifetime request.

Bart should have sensed he was being manipulated, but the lure of money proved overwhelming, and Bart did not give it another thought.

With that said, Milton stood up, handed Bart the check made payable to Bart Sinclair with a firm handshake, left the office, and walked out of the store. Bart went back into his office, pinching himself with his unbelievable luck. He couldn't believe his good fortune. He felt on top of the world.

Minutes later after Milton had left the store, Bart placed a call to Joe. Joe, naturally, didn't answer, and Bart left a somewhat frantic message on his machine. "I'm on my way over. Don't leave the condo. I'll be there in less than half an hour. Don't worry, it's only good news."

It actually took Bart closer to forty-five minutes because he caught two separate drawbridges. Bart hated waiting at drawbridges while the idle rich aboard their yachts or sailboats slowly passed down the Intracoastal Waterway, making all the motorists idle, helplessly in their cars.

As Bart entered the condominium, he was elated to see Joe somewhat sober and coherent. After all it wasn't even 5 p.m. yet.

"I just listened to your message, Bart, so tell me, what is the good news?

"You won't believe it, but I have a client who wants to spend one hundred million dollars on loose diamonds!"

"He's got to be a fed—stay away from that trap," replied Joe instantly, as he continued to work on his *New York Times* crossword puzzle.

"No, honestly, he is a wealthy publisher who just sold his company and wants to begin assembling a diamond collection. Hell, he lives over in Palm Beach at the south end, and he has previously spent over one and a half million on jewelry from me over the past several years."

"I think you might be a bit too anxious there, Bart. Give me his full name and address, and I'll research him myself," responded Joe coldly.

"You do that," replied Bart. "You'll see. He is legit, I tell you. Legit."

"Okay, very well then. Now tell me exactly what does he want?"

"He wants five stones of each cut and size starting with one carat and increasing all the way up to twenty carats!"

"Jesus Christ, Bart, now I know you are screwing around with me!"

"Why on earth would I screw around with you and waste your time and more importantly, mine! He is a once-in-a-lifetime customer, and we must keep him happy!"

Bart did not inform Joe of Milton's desire to avoid the 6 percent Florida sales tax. *No use worrying the old man*, thought Bart.

After Bart had provided Joe with all the particulars, he left the condo to go home and celebrate with his young wife, Dana.

Joe remained sitting. He, like Bart, was ecstatic. Only, Joe knew how to conceal his emotions. Inside he was burning. *This is it*, thought Joe. *My time to finally avenge my family and get back at Victor has finally come!*

Joe made a few phone calls and conducted numerous Google searches on Milton Rogers and the entire Rogers family. He liked what he saw. By the end of the evening, Joe had made significant headway.

Milton Rogers was indeed a very wealthy publishing magnate. He had started with nothing and built his publishing empire the hard way. He was ruthless, cunning, and could not be trusted. In each and every business venture, it appeared that he had been involved in some sort of lawsuit. The civil lawsuits sometimes led to criminal lawsuits but received little publicity in the local newspapers. It was clear to Joe that the man was no stranger to litigation. However, more importantly, Milton was not a fed or part of the federal government. All of Joe's research confirmed that Milton Rogers had indeed sold his publishing empire and was sitting on more cash than one could imagine. From everything that Joe could decipher, Milton was actually telling Bart the truth.

Joe then proceeded to do something extremely rare. He put down his vodka and went for a walk. Although he had already gulped down three glasses of straight vodka, he was not even feeling the least bit tipsy. Joe needed to think clearly, and a walk and some fresh air was the best therapy. About an hour later, Joe was dripping in perspiration, but he had come up with his plan to once and for all destroy Victor Butin. He was mentally and physically energized. After showering, he placed his first call.

"Victor, this is Joe. How are you?"

"Fine, replied Victor. How are you, my friend?"

"I am great," replied Joe. "And I think I might make your day right now."

"I don't know about that, Joe. To tell you the truth, it is getting harder to do business these days, and my relationship with my supplier is sadly coming to an end."

"Well, Victor, I have one final mind-blowing deal for you. I figure that you can make fifty million dollars' profit in the next three months. Of course, I will take my twenty percent cut."

"Have you adequately researched everything?" answered Victor, trying to sound relaxed and conceal his rising excitement. "With such a huge deal, it is hard to believe that the buyer is not a federal agent."

"Yes, Victor, no need to worry. Everything has been checked out, and the individual is going to purchase the gems through a local Palm Beach jewelry store."

"Who?" demanded Victor. "Is it Diamond and Sons Inc.?"

"I'd rather not say at this time. Just trust me that it is all legit. Once again, Victor, I have researched the buying party in detail. He's clean with no government attachments and no drug money involved."

"Okay, I trust you, Joe. You know I always have. What is it that you need?"

"Jesus Christ, you're kidding me. Right?" This was all the response Victor could muster after Joe had finished giving him all the details of the deal. Victor had Joe go over everything again, just in case he missed something.

"No. The customer plans on spending one hundred million dollars. He just sold his company for over five hundred million dollars, and now he wants a magnificent gem collection. He has an oceanfront mansion in Palm Beach, and he has fought the IRS personally and corporately on numerous occasions. He is no stranger to litigation and likes to push the envelope."

"How much up-front money"?

"Ten million."

"That is good. That is very good."

"He wants the gems by Thanksgiving. Is that a problem, Victor?"

"What protection or collateral do I have?"

"You have me," replied Joe. "You don't need anything else, and just after the first of the year, you will have your money—all forty million of it."

Victor thought it over for several seconds before responding. "Are you sure everything is on the up and up? I have never given you so many stones without collateral."

Joe interrupted Victor and declared, "Victor, haven't I always been faithful to you? Haven't I always made sure you were paid? You just said that you have always trusted me. If you don't trust me now, then you have a serious problem. This is a chance of a lifetime. Victor, even you can retire on this amount of money."

Again, silence.

Victor spoke slowly, "Okay, I am in. My final shipment from South Africa is due in London, but I can move up the delivery date if I have to. I personally will see to it that the diamonds are hand-delivered to you. If you screw me over on this, I don't need to tell you the consequences now, do I?"

"No, you don't," mustered Joe. "Thank you."

Victor concluded the conversation by stating that Joe would be hearing from his men soon. After the phone conversation ended, Joe went to the freezer and poured himself yet another stiff glass of Grey Goose. He was still perspiring. I've done it! "I am finally going to get Victor Butin!" he said to himself.

Victor immediately began making plans. He called his personal attendant, Marty to inform him of the situation. Marty in turn, immediately summoned Igor and Ivan. These two were bodyguards, or rather thugs that assisted Victor and Marty in different matters. You really didn't want to make these two former weight lifters mad. They singlehandedly could take your head off with one blow if they wanted to. Within twenty-four hours, all three men were gathered in Victor's palatial penthouse.

Victor explained the details of the sale of the gems. He was relying on Marty and his sidekicks to transport the gems, deliver them to Joe, and then shadow Joe until the money was ultimately wire-transferred into Victor's accounts.

Victor trusted the men implicitly and knew that they would carry out his orders. The men all feared Victor and his powerful family's connections. Basically, they knew that Victor would go to any length to destroy his enemy and their families.

The following day all four men once again gathered at the penthouse. "So," Victor said, "Marty, Igor, and Ivan, you three, will transport all the gems to North Palm Beach, Florida, and will personally deliver them to Joe Marx. After delivery, you will remain in Florida and keep an eye on Joe until I advise you that the money has been wired to my account."

"We understand," replied Marty. "Is there anything else?"

"After I have received the wired funds, I want you to kill Joe Marx."

"Are you serious, Victor? Haven't you worked together for over thirty years?" inquired Marty.

"Yes, but he will no longer be needed, and he knows too much. Just do it, and I don't care how! The three of you will begin operations in an old warehouse in West Palm Beach. It will be all set up for you, handing the street address over on a small sheet of paper. You will also place a wiretap on Joe's phone as well as a tracer in his car. I want to know where he is and what he's doing at all times. Have you got that? Any questions?"

The three men nodded their heads in unison.

Marty asked as they were leaving, "Is there anyone else you want us to watch while we're down there?"

Victor looked at Marty for a second and then said, "Yes, now that you mention it, why don't you keep an eye on Bart Sinclair and his jewelry store, Diamond and Sons Inc. I am pretty certain that's the company where the stones will be sold and where the wire transfers will most likely originate from."

"Okay," said Marty. "You can count on us."

"I hope so. I certainly hope so for your sake," snickered Victor.

Meanwhile back in Palm Beach, Bart had already begun to count his money. He determined the individual cost of each diamond in the collection based on the current market prices. Bart next included a discount of 20 percent (since Milton was one of those one in a million, or rather one in 50 million, customers) and figured that the total cost would indeed be approximately $100 million. How convenient!

After receiving affirmation from his trusted friend, Joe Marx that the diamond request could and, more importantly, would be fulfilled, Bart phoned Milton.

"Milton, this is Bart. I just wanted you to know that I believe I have secured all the merchandise you have requested, and everything is on track.

"Very good, Bart! That is great news." *It is all coming together now*, thought Milton.

"When will the diamonds be ready for inspection?" Milton inquired.

"I'm hoping by Thanksgiving. Is that good with you?"

"Perfect, absolutely perfect," said Milton. "There is still no problem with the sales tax?"

"Oh, no, not at all, replied Bart. We will overcome that obstacle at a later date."

"Just let me know who to make the checks out to."

"Now, Milton, as much as I trust you from now on, we will require either a wire transfer or cashier's check if that is not too much to ask for."

"Oh, no, not at all," said Milton. "I expected as much." Milton was a little annoyed about the checks, but he didn't believe, deep down that Bart was truly that dumb to accept personal checks.

"Very well then," said Bart. "I will call you when the shipment comes in. Take care."

The next call Milton made was to Brad Penny's cell phone.

"Hey, Brad. I hope you and your team have been working on those stones I requested."

"You know, you really should give me your number in case there is a problem."

"Brad, the situation is going to stay just the way it is. I think you are being compensated enough that you shouldn't have anything to worry about, are you not?"

"Yes, I was just thinking about your end."

"Brad, I will take care of myself, and you just take care of manufacturing the diamonds, okay? Now once again, have you begun making the stones as we discussed? I will need five stones for each carat diamond, as previously stated."

"Yes, I am in the process of finishing up the emerald cuts, and the rest should be finished by Thanksgiving if all goes well."

"If!" shouted Milton. "I don't want to hear an 'if.' It sure as hell better be done!"

"Okay," stammered Brad. "All is well. You can count on me!"

When Milton hung up the phone, Brad felt extremely uncomfortable. He had originally agreed to make no notes and keep no records of his operations. Now, however, he had the nagging feeling that he was being set up. He didn't trust Milton, and so he began keeping a journal detailing each and every part of the diamond operation. He kept this journal in his safe deposit box. And in an abundance of caution, he put his childhood friend's name (Stacey Gwen) on the box as well and gave her a spare key. She knew what to do if anything ever happened to him.

Stacey Gwen was definitely worried about her friend Brad. She always was and always would be there for him. She couldn't understand all the secrecy concerns and privacy protections. So much so that she decided to do a little investigating on her own.

Stacy visited the Alachua County courthouse to examine the real estate deeds. She had no last name to go on and no first name. She finally came across the real estate legal description for the Alachua warehouse. She naturally assumed she would find a legal name and address. Unfortunately, the property was titled in the name of a Bahamian Corporation. There was no name of the president or any director at all. There was only a PO Box in Miami. She had hit a brick wall.

Stacy wasn't about to give up that easily. She was deeply concerned for Brad, and her curiosity was definitely piqued. Although she couldn't financially afford to fly over to the Bahamas, she did the next best thing. She employed her nephew, a sixteen-year-old computer whiz to do an exhaustive search of the Bahamian Corporation called "The Four L's, LTD." Her nephew spent days scanning the internet and even broke into the Bahamian Ministry of Deeds computer system to discover any information regarding the owners of the company. The best and only information that her nephew could provide Stacy was that the owner had a Miami post office box and that there were really four separate owners, all beginning with the same first and last initials. There was no other information available. Whoever had purchased the company had definitely covered their tracks well.

Stacy, quite understandably, was now concerned more than ever for Brad's personal safety and convinced him to carry a gun with him at all times. Brad did not object to the idea for he was also quite concerned at this point. He continued to keep his journal and in an abundance of caution, used loose-leaf paper each and every day rather than his normal log. If Milton happened to catch him with the log only the final day's entry would be lost, not everything else.

By November 15, the last manufactured diamonds were completed. Brad had been instructed to let the University of Florida students who had been working with him go. Milton had informed Brad that he was going to send his sons to Gainesville. Again, Brad's gut told him something was wrong. It was a Friday afternoon, and after dismissing all the employees for good, Brad had the warehouse all to himself. Putting his gut instincts aside, Brad was extremely happy. He had skimmed more than enough money to put a nice down payment on a beautiful southern-style home in Gainesville and had planned a visit with Stacy's father to ask for permission to marry his daughter. Brad's state-of-the-art manufacturing process of colorless diamonds would revolutionize the diamond industry, and he knew that in the near future, money would not be a problem. With that pleasant thought, a rare smile came to his face.

Unfortunately, his smile soon dissipated as he watched the man with the terrible toupee waltz through the door.

"Hi, Brad," said Milton. "I hope I'm not intruding. My wife and I were visiting friends in Jacksonville when we decided to drive on over here. I'm glad you're still here."

"Where's your wife?" asked Brad, straining his neck to see if she was in the warehouse.

"She's in the car. She's not feeling too well."

"That's too bad. Is there anything I can get her?" asked Brad rising from his seat in an effort to stand eye to eye with Milton.

Brad began walking toward the door when Milton moved to block his exit.

"Can I see the diamonds?" inquired Milton.

"Sure," said Brad. "They are all in the safe, exactly as you had ordered. All one hundred diamonds are accounted for. I placed five in each bag and identified the twenty bags by the appropriate corresponding carat."

Brad's hands were shaking as he fumbled with the combination. He hoped that Milton didn't see his trembling hands, as he was consumed by fear.

Milton carefully examined all the bags. Indeed, everything was accounted for, and they were exquisite!

As Brad watched Milton put the stones into a briefcase, he had this sense of dread pour over him. He attempted to make a dash for the exit door but was met there by one of Milton's men, who appeared from out of nowhere.

The man grabbed Brad by his shirt and threw him back into the warehouse, slamming the door behind him.

"Now, Brad where were you going in such a rush? Are you afraid of me? After all I've done for you, why don't you trust me?" laughed Milton.

"Ah, ah, I do trust you. I just wanted to make sure your wife was okay."

"Oh, I see. So you're not afraid."

"No, sir," gulped Brad. "You haven't given me any reason to be concerned!"

Milton moved over to Brad's desk and began to examine its contents. In the upper right-hand drawer, he found the loose-leaf piece of paper. Brad winced when he listened as Milton read its contents. Brad still had his gun tucked safely behind his back. He knew the guard was armed, as he could see a gun tucked into his belt, partially hidden by his jacket. He couldn't tell if Milton was armed or not. Brad realized that he would have to shoot the guard first if he had any chance of surviving.

Brad sensed that he had to act fast. Unfortunately, he paused for just a second too long. In his delay, the guard had drawn his gun and aimed it at Brad.

Milton spoke, "My, my, Brad, you have been a very naughty boy. Not only have you been skimming cash from me, but you have been making notes in direct violation to my orders. I thought you were a smart young man. Now, unfortunately, I suspect otherwise. Where are the rest of your notes?" asked Milton in his condescending voice.

"I don't know what you're talking about, Milton," somehow Brad managed to speak, his mouth was dry as dust.

"Now, Brad, we have already searched your apartment, and we found nothing. There must be some notes hidden somewhere. So where are they?"

"I told you, there are none."

The guard approached Brad with both hands on his semi-automatic weapon. Likewise, Milton inched closer to Brad until he was face-to-face with the young man.

"Don't make me say this again. Where are the rest of your notes?" demanded Milton.

"There are none." Just as Brad's last word was spoken, Milton lashed out and struck Brad square on the jaw with a wicked right hand. Brad immediately fell to the floor, bleeding out of his nose and mouth. The pain was intense.

"Let me ask you again," screamed Milton. "Where in the hell are the rest of your notes?"

Brad blurted out, "Go to hell."

At that moment Milton delivered a kick to Brad's mid-section. You could virtually hear the cracking of bones as blood spurted out of Brad's mouth.

"Where are the notes?" cried Milton. "If you know what's good for you, you will answer me now."

In one desperate and final act, Brad blurted out "fuck you," as he simultaneously reached for his gun. He tilted on the ground and came up firing. His bullet struck the guard squarely in the chest. The gunshot spooked Milton, who ducked and shielded himself from the gunshots. The wounded guard retaliated by firing his own weapon several times before collapsing. All three gunshots hit Brad directly.

Within seconds both men lay dead at Milton's feet. This was even better than planned, Milton thought. He then nonchalantly stepped over the lifeless bodies and walked outside to his rental car.

Milton returned with highly flammable cleaning chemicals and began dousing the warehouse and all its contents. Then with baseball batting gloves on, he began smashing the place with an aluminum baseball bat, trying to make it appear as if a robbery had taken place.

Milton was convinced that the authorities would conclude the crime scene was a robbery. If there was any further investigation, the robbery was probably due to the large amount of cash on hand used to pay the University of Florida students.

As he was walking out the metal door, he struck the match that soon ignited the entire warehouse. When he was safely away and seemingly unnoticed, he glanced back into his rearview mirror to see the warehouse in flames. Milton zigzagged his way back to the interstate and proceeded to return to Jacksonville to catch up with his accomplice and alibi, Brenda. Milton figured they wouldn't be late for dinner after all.

Chapter
Seventeen

s planned, Victor was able to acquire and successfully deliver the requested diamonds to Joe. Joe couldn't have been happier, and he promptly called Bart with the good news. Joe then drove his car with the diamonds to Bart Sinclair at Diamond and Sons Inc. Of course Joe was closely followed by Victor's watchmen just to make sure the diamonds reached their destination without any problems. Joe was armed with a small handgun as he crossed Worth Avenue with his briefcase in hand, watching out for any sort of suspicious activity. The briefcase containing the diamonds was the most expensive collection of gems he had ever seen or handled.

The sun was just visible over the taller buildings on Worth Avenue, but because it was still before 9:00 a.m., none of the stores were open. Bart, upon seeing Joe approaching the store, made sure that his own gun was securely in his belt and that the security guard was on his toes. Bart's gun was not for Joe of course, as he had done business with Joe many times, but because of the enormity of the delivery, he didn't want to be caught off guard by anyone or anything. Bart opened the door and escorted Joe immediately inside. Bart gave a quick look up and down the street and stepped back inside the store, quickly locking the door behind him. Bart made sure the delivery was done before regular store hours for obvious reasons. Bart proceeded to open the massive safe and placed all one hundred diamonds in the enormous steel container. Both Bart and Joe were sweating. The two old friends were mutually satisfied and delighted.

"This calls for a drink, don't you think, Joe?"

"Of course, it is the only way to start off a good day. Grey Goose on the rocks."

"Coming right up."

After the drinks were poured, the two men positioned themselves on the leather couches. Both for a moment, were at a loss for words.

Joe spoke first. "This is the last deal we will ever make together, my friend. However before it is finished, I will need a good attorney. Not your criminal attorney, Paul Schwartz, but an honest, good attorney."

"I know just the one. His name is Bo Martin, and he is as honest as there is."

"Great. Give me his number if you have it."

"Thanks," said Joe as Bart wrote Bo's name and number on a Post-it note.

Chapter
Eighteen

*J*ust days before Thanksgiving, Milton accompanied by Brenda visited Diamond and Sons Inc. Worth Avenue was somewhat calm, as most of the Palm Beachers were still residing up north in their primary residences. They were preparing for the Thanksgiving holiday before migrating south to their Palm Beach winter homes after the holiday. Within weeks, Worth Avenue would be swamped with tourists, snow birds, and Christmas shoppers.

Bart was in his office making arrangements for a winter marlin fishing tournament in Walker's Cay, Bahamas when the Rogers entered. Minutes later Bart was ushering them into his office. Bart was overanxious and began speaking rapidly.

"Well, I have the diamonds you requested. They are all flawless. I am sure you will be more than pleased."

"Could we see them now?" requested Brenda. "I'm just dying to see the collection."

"Yes, Bart, please do show us," countered Milton.

Bart excused himself and entered the vault. He returned moments later carrying five velvet pouches which contained the one hundred diamonds. He had previously separated the stones into five bags, each containing twenty lots of diamonds beginning at one carat and increasing to twenty carats.

Milton took his time inspecting them all very closely. He was very pleased with the stones.

"I must say, Bart that I am certainly impressed with your execution of my request. All the diamonds appear flawless, clear, and brilliant. I knew you were just the man to trust. Brenda was so pleased with her other stones, she insisted I do all my business with you. From the looks of it, I am glad I did! Well, let's get down to business, okay?" said Milton, not one to mince words.

"I know that you wanted a cashier's check, but wouldn't a wire transfer be easier for both of us? I can have my bank wire transfer the sum of forty million dollars to your bank account today. Just give me the wiring instructions, and I'll do it as we wait."

"Sure, Milton that sounds fine with me." Bart just wanted to close the deal. He had been waiting for this for too long, and he didn't see the harm in the wire transfer. In fact, it was easier than cashing a check. He couldn't believe this was actually happening.

Moments later Milton was on the phone with his private banker providing him the verbal authorization to transfer the requested funds.

"Well, Milton, which stones do you want? I can give you fifty now and then fifty later in January at the time of your next payment."

At this point, Brenda blurted out, "Honey, I would like them set in several different settings. You know, just like your sketches. I sure do hope you brought them with you. Did you, Milton?"

Giving Brenda a little wink, Milton pretended to be embarrassed as he took the sketches out of his briefcase. Of course this was all part of their brilliant scheme. Milton slowly presented Bart with his jewelry sketches of several designs for bracelets, necklaces, rings, earrings, and chokers.

"As you can see, my husband has spent a great deal of time on his drawings. I would like for you to create these pieces, using the stones."

"You what?" exploded Bart. "That was not part of the deal. I would have to hire a new employee at this time of the year, our busiest season, and have him work around the clock for you." Bart paused for a moment before continuing, "I'm sorry, but I don't think I can help you there, Mrs. Rogers."

Brenda played it to the hilt and sulked into the leather couch. "I only want to make Christmas special for my family."

If looks could kill, thought Bart to himself.

Milton addressed Bart calmly, "Now Bart, couldn't you satisfy my wife? I will pay whatever you ask. How about two hundred thousand dollars for the extra work? That should be more than enough to hire a master craftsman for two months' work?"

Bart was definitely not happy. He really didn't trust an employee to work with so many expensive diamonds, and his own craftsman was going to be swamped throughout the holidays. He figured he could hire someone new but had no idea where he would find someone on such short notice that was qualified for the job. Brenda's request would be a royal pain in the ass. Nevertheless, Bart reluctantly agreed and took a quick look at the sketches. The illustrations incorporated sixty diamonds, which was ten more than Milton had paid for.

While Bart was examining the drawings, Milton spoke up. "I know we dip into the second part of the sale, but on January 2, you will get the other fifty million dollars." Naturally, Milton was lying. "Here is a personal check for two hundred thousand dollars for your troubles." He handed the check over to Bart.

Bart took the check and then proceeded to speak. "I personally will make sure that all the diamonds are set in accordance with your illustrations. I just want you to realize that I am not taking any responsibility for these designs. Not to be rude, but I'm afraid that some of your designs are somewhat intricate and may be very hard to re-create exactly as you have drawn."

"Well, go forward with the designs, and if there is a problem with any of them, let me know, and we will work with the designer," answered Mrs. Rogers.

"That is very accommodating of you, Mrs. Rogers, thank you. I will do everything in my power to create your designs, as close to your drawings as possible. I will make sure they are ready by December 23. Now please realize my store will be extremely chaotic at that time, but I will do my best to personally meet with you. I do hope you understand."

"Oh, sure, absolutely," answered Milton, speaking for both of them.

"Have a nice Thanksgiving," they said as they left the store.

Nestled back in their Rolls Royce, Brenda turned to Milton and asked: "Was that easy or what."

"You were terrific, darling, absolutely perfect."

"Well, thank you, my knight in shining armor. You weren't so bad yourself."

Meanwhile, back at Diamond and Sons Inc., Bart received a telephone call from his bank informing him that the forty million dollars had indeed been transferred into his account. Bart thought of phoning Joe Marx at once, but decided against it. *Why not allow the interest to accumulate for me?* thought Bart. *I'll let Joe know when the full hundred million dollars is in my account.* Bart figured one month's interest would be enough to fund his entire fishing tournament to Walkers Cay. And that's only if he lost. Bart hated to lose.

Bart was extremely lucky to find a recently retired master jeweler who just happened to be looking for some extra cash during the holiday season. It took the master jeweler exactly twenty days to complete all the settings that the Rogers requested. Bart was so pleased that he was able to perform the work so quickly and at a cost of less than forty-five thousand dollars that he gave the man an additional five-thousand-dollar bonus.

On December 20, three days early, Milton and Brenda picked up their jewelry. Fortunately, the store wasn't too crowded, and Bart was able to give the Rogers his undivided attention.

Brenda acted so excited. "I just love the settings. Aren't they absolutely exquisite?" she gushed. Milton countered, "Why, honey, they are just what you wanted. The children will have a fantastic Christmas, and you will be the Belle of the Ball at every social occasion this upcoming season."

Bart thought that he'd throw up. The jewelry designs were hideous, and he wanted it known that in no way were the designs tied to him or Diamond and Sons Inc. But he couldn't be rude and had to restrain himself from speaking out.

Bart next asked, "Do you want any of the pieces gift wrapped?"

"Oh, no. I do all the Christmas wrapping," replied Brenda.

"Well at least let me escort you to your car."

"Before I forget, here are my final illustrations. Could you have the remaining stones set accordingly?" requested Milton.

Bart grabbed the illustrations and briefly glanced them over and once again struggled from actually blurting out to them just how wretched they truly were.

"When do you want them completed by?"

"How about January fifth?"

"I will wire the remainder of the money when we pick up the jewelry. Is that fine with you?"

"I'll say it is," said Bart and smiled.

Bart accompanied Milton and Brenda outside to their car, even though by now the store was very busy. Worth Avenue was swamped with traffic and shoppers.

As Bart walked back to the store, he thought, *There is something about a fool and his money.*

Likewise, Milton turned to Brenda and said, "Bart really is an idiot."

Chapter
Nineteen

C hristmas was always a wonderful time for Bo and Ruby. Ruby closed
the restaurant from December 20 through January 7 each year to give
her and her employees a breather before the onslaught of the snow
birds. Bo also tried to keep business as light as possible. Granted, there were
always the last minute end-of-year annual gifting techniques and the funding
of charitable remainder trusts and charitable foundations, but Bo for the most
part, kept his workload to a minimum.

As usual, the Martins' house was decorated impeccably with Christmas
bows, wreaths, figurines, and gardow everywhere. The prized Vizslas were
smart enough not to poke their noses in any Christmas decorations, especially
the tree. They did not want to face Ruby's wrath.

Ruby always prepared Christmas dinner, and every year it was better than
the last. Bye and Teresa Martin loved every minute of it, and the neighbors,
Mike and Sophia Milner, did their share in making the day wonderful.

When the doorbell rang interrupting dinner, Bo hesitated but proceeded
to answer it. They all wondered who it could be. To their surprise it was none
other than Bart Sinclair bearing gifts and good tidings.

"I know you're very busy now. I just wanted to wish you a very Merry
Christmas and let you know that Joe Marx, a dear friend of mine, will be
calling on you before the holidays are over to discuss his estate plan. Make sure
to accommodate his wishes."

"That's wonderful," said Bo. "Don't worry about me. I will take care of
him"

"I won't worry a bit and sorry to intrude. Take care."

"You too. Merry Christmas!"

When Bo reentered the dining room carrying a case of Opus One, the ladies were very pleased.

"Open up a bottle of the wine. Nineteen eighty-nine was an excellent year for Opus One," exclaimed Sophia.

"Who with good taste, brought you the wine?" asked Ruby.

"Bart and Dana Sinclair."

"Well they definitely have good taste. We will certainly have to reciprocate their generosity," said Ruby, joined by Sophia.

Chapter
Twenty

Two weeks later, Bart was on cloud nine. The final jewelry pieces were assembled and prepared according to the Rogers's illustrations by January 5. Bart had previously informed Joe Marx of the big day, and Joe was also feeling pretty antsy.

Joe couldn't shake the feeling that he was being watched. He had known and worked with Victor Butin for too long to ever truly feel comfortable, and he had thought he had seen Russian bodyguards on several occasions. Joe wasn't taking any chances, and in an abundance of caution, he secretly had purchased a small Nokia cell phone during one of his rare visits to the Gardens shopping mall.

Joe knew that in most likelihood, he was being watched and that his car and condo were undoubtedly bugged. With such a huge amount of money on the line, who wouldn't take those precautions! On one occasion when he returned from the grocery store, he noticed that several items in his condominium were slightly moved. He figured it could only be the work of Victor because only he and Bart had a key to the condo, and Bart almost never ventured from Palm Beach to North Palm Beach.

Most Palm Beachers actually feel like they are actually slumming it when they drive off their beloved island. The only times some well-heeled Palm Beachers leave their secured oasis is to fly out of the West Palm Beach airport or attend a ballet or opera at the Kravis Performing Arts Center in West Palm Beach. Everything else is self-contained on the island. Granted, the prices of everything are usually higher, but what does that matter to the wealthy?

Joe had been busy making phone calls to coordinate the transfer of his monetary share. Over the years, Joe had created several corporate accounts in foreign banks. He maintained balances in each foreign account sufficient to pay the extravagant annual fees and to provide him with financial security. The rest of his money, he gave to charity.

Joe originally created A Trading Co. Inc. in the Isle of Man, many years ago, and kept a balance of slightly over two million dollars in it. The Isle of Man company was owned solely by him, and the annual reports listed Joe M. as the sole director.

Joe then established AA Trading Co. Inc. in Panama, several years later and also maintained an account balance of slightly over one million dollars. Joe most recently created an account in Grand Cayman under the name A. Trading Company Inc. He deposited only five hundred thousand dollars into the account but made a personal visit with Harrison Frazar, the bank vice-president. He let it be known that millions of dollars would ultimately be wired under his sole command from his companies in the Isle of Man and Panama. In fact, Joe provided Harrison with his corporate information, revealing account information and wiring instructions. He wanted to make sure that Harrison would not be surprised with the amounts of money, and most importantly, would always maintain his secrecy. Lastly, he made certain that Harrison would work with Joe's ultimate successor.

Joe distrusted bankers and lawyers. However, he believed that if he met them face-to-face, it was less likely that he would be cheated. His philosophy was that it's easier to swindle someone you've never met than someone who you've spent time with.

Chapter
Twenty-One

As planned on January 5, Milton and Brenda Rogers arrived at Diamond and Sons Inc. and were instantly greeted by Bart Sinclair. Bart was so on edge and antsy that he barely could contain himself.

"Well, I hope you and your family all had a Merry Christmas and a Happy New Year," commented Bart.

"We certainly did, Bart, and on New Year's Eve, everyone remarked at how beautiful and exquisite Brenda's jewelry looked."

"You will probably have an excellent year. We saw everyone at the Breakers New Year's Eve black tie charity affair, and everyone remarked about the jewelry," exclaimed Brenda.

"Hell, Brenda was literally dripping in them, as well as our daughters-in-law. The girls are still admiring their diamonds. I don't think they have taken them off yet! And of course if the girls are happy, the boys are happy too," boasted Milton. "I didn't want to tell anyone that I had designed the settings for modesty's sake, but one of my daughters-in-law let it slip. Sorry about that, Bart. I wanted the store to take all the credit for the beautiful pieces."

"Oh that is quite all right, Milton. Let credit be taken where it is due." *Thank God,* Bart thought to himself *if anyone actually believed that Diamond and Sons designed and created those pieces, it would just be humiliating!* "I am just absolutely pleased that everything has worked out to your liking."

"Funny, we didn't see you or your lovely bride at the Breakers Bash. You know it is the biggest and most important social function of the year!" interjected Brenda.

"To tell you the truth, Milton, I was here working on the jewelry settings."

"I bet," Milton said with a smirk.

"Anyway, you missed a wonderful evening and a great chance to pick up some new potential customers."

"You know these new-money computer technology nerds are invading the island. There were so many new faces. I sort of miss seeing the old-money crowd," said Brenda.

"I know exactly what you mean, darling."

"What we need is a technology recession in order to get rid of some of these obnoxious people," laughed Brenda.

"So much for small talk. Can we see the pieces?" asked Milton.

"Certainly. Come into my office. I'll just be a moment to get the items out of the safe." When Bart returned, he handed the pieces to Brenda.

Brenda once again exclaimed, "How exquisite and absolutely stunning. Milton, you've really outdone yourself this time. They are even more beautiful than the last pieces. I absolutely love them!" Brenda then kissed a slightly embarrassed Milton on the cheek.

"Oh dear, I'm just glad you're happy." Milton then turned to Bart.

"Well, Bart, I must say we both are really pleased. You have gone out of your way to satisfy us, and I want you to know that anything you ever want or anything you ever need, I will be there for you. I mean that with all my heart."

"Well, thank you, Milton. That means a lot to me, coming from you."

"Let's now complete the sale," declared Milton.

"Absolutely! Please use my phone if you need it to make the necessary calls."

Milton made the call to his broker, and then they all waited patiently. While to Bart it seemed like hours, it was only several minutes later when Bart received confirmation that the sum of $50 million dollars ($50,000,000) was successfully wired into his account.

"Now, you sure about that little sales tax concern?" asked Milton.

"I have already taken care of that," replied Bart.

"Good because we don't want any trouble whatsoever."

"Don't worry, Milton, don't worry."

"Well, my dear, are you ready?" asked Milton with his left arm extended toward his wife.

"Yes, darling, and you know what? I am starved. How about we go to Amici's for lunch?"

"Anything you want," replied Milton.

Bart interrupted, "I think it would be better if you put the jewels into your safe at home before going anywhere. Although this is Palm Beach, you can never be too careful."

"You're right. What are we thinking? Thank you," responded Brenda.

Bart again escorted the Rogers out to their car while closely eyeing the street for any suspicious activity. The Rogers were safely in their Rolls before Bart felt more comfortable. As he watched them proceed down Worth Avenue, he found it hard not to smile from ear to ear.

Brenda turned to Milton in the car and exclaimed, "Don't you think you laid it on a little thick at the end?"

"No, I just wanted him to know how we felt. That's all."

"Well, we've got a lot of work to do. We need to have it all done by the end of January. February 12 will be here before you know it."

When Bart returned to his office, he picked up the phone and called Joe.

"Hi, Joe, it's Bart. If you didn't have a good New Year's, you will now."

Before, he could finish, Joe interrupted him. "Bart, I'm real busy right now. How about we have dinner tonight at your place?"

"Sure, Joe, sounds good to me. Is seven o'clock okay with you?"

"Great. See you then."

Bart thought it odd that Joe was so standoffish and rude but quickly dismissed it. He too was probably preoccupied with his good fortune, and was busy figuring out what he was going to do with it all.

"I'm fifty million dollars richer," said Bart to himself, pinching himself once again. His arm looked like it had been bitten by a hundred mosquitos with little red marks up and down from so much pinching. "After I dummy up the numbers, receipts, and invoices, I'll make it look like a twenty-million-dollar profit and pay taxes of about forty percent and owe roughly eight million dollars to Uncle Sam. Six percent, or one million two hundred thousand dollars, will go to the State of Florida for sales tax, and the rest is mine." *Finally*, thought Bart, *I am truly rich!*

Later that evening, Joe personally viewed in his rear mirror, the two Russians following him in their black Cadillac. *Not good*, thought Joe, *but so far no surprises.*

Bart was already slightly inebriated by the time Joe arrived.

"Come on in, Joe, and let me get you a drink. Tonight you really deserve one. We both do!" Joe helped himself to the Grey Goose, poured himself a drink, quickly threw it back and poured himself another one.

"So, Bart, tell me what is the good news. You are already two sheets to the wind, so let me guess, the sale went through."

"I'll say. The one hundred million dollars is in my company's trust account."

"Well, I'll drink to that," said Joe, as he helped himself to another straight-up vodka.

"You have never let me down, old friend, and I know that your father would have been mighty proud of you, Bart."

"My old man was never proud of me, but at least I have finally made it. I've really made it, haven't I?"

"Yes, you have, my friend. Indeed, you have."

"Bart tomorrow I'd like you to wire transfer the money to my corporate account in the Isle of Man. The company, as you well know, is called A Trading Co. Here are the wiring instructions." Joe handed Bart his card with all the necessary information.

"You need to wire transfer the entire fifty million first thing in the morning, so no more drinking for you. England is five hours ahead of us, and I'll notify them of the upcoming wire transfer."

"Don't let me down now."

"Oh, no, don't worry about me."

At that moment, Joe could smell the burning of what most likely was dinner. Both men heard Dana yell. Although she certainly was beautiful, her cooking skills were atrocious. When Dana came into the den where the two men were sitting, it was obvious that she was flustered and had been crying.

"I'm so sorry, guys, but I ruined the spaghetti sauce that I had spent several hours making."

"That's okay," said Bart as he awkwardly stood up and took her hand in his. "We'll just order out and have it delivered. Nothing can put a damper on today."

"I'll second that," joined Joe as he raised his glass.

"Order from wherever you like, honey. Whatever you want, will be fine with us, right Joe?"

"Oh sure, absolutely," said Joe, trying so hard to be encouraging but all the while thinking, *How can you mess up spaghetti sauce?*

After dinner, as Joe was leaving the Sinclair mansion, he again spotted the black Cadillac. They must be getting a little nervous, thought Joe.

Chapter
Twenty-Two

Joe had retained a private investigator to take a look into Bo Martin. His background, his family, his business, and his finances were all investigated. Joe was extremely pleased with the results. In fact, Joe had also conducted a little investigation of his own and had personally observed Bo when he was out coaching runners and again after he had won a local running race. In every situation, Bo was generous, caring, and open. People seemed to genuinely like him. It didn't take Joe long to figure out that Bo was extremely honest and trustworthy.

Joe had really never been able to trust again after the tragic loss of all his family by the hands of Victor Butin. He knew eventually that he would have to trust someone. After serious thought and consideration, he decided that Bo Martin was that person.

Joe felt hopeful that Bo could handle the task at hand. He hated the fact that he could never disclose to Bo all the particulars and realized that Bo would most likely serve his role as an unsuspecting and completely innocent victim. Nevertheless, Joe knew that time was running short. He decided to visit Diamond and Sons Inc. in the morning to confirm the wire transfer and persuade Bart to personally introduce him to Bo Martin.

When Joe arrived the next morning at the Worth Avenue store, Bart was fortunately in his office. Bart looked like crap and was evidently extremely hung over, but he had managed to correctly wire transfer the money to Joe's corporate account overseas. Bart was in the middle of making up fake invoices and sales slips when Joe walked in.

"You look like shit."

"Thanks, I feel like it. However, you should be pleased the money has already been wired. The confirmation is around here somewhere. He shuffled through his stack of papers before finding the faxed confirmation. "Here, here it is," said Bart, handing it to Joe.

"Thanks."

"No, thank you. Thanks for also being a good sport about dinner last night. My wife was really upset."

"Think nothing of it. Her beauty more than makes up for her lack of culinary skills," laughed Joe.

"Yeah, I certainly didn't marry her for her cooking," smiled Bart.

"Well, Bart, I've got a favor to ask of you."

"Sure, what's up?"

"Can you get me an appointment with your attorney?"

"Who, Paul Schwartz? Let me call him right now. You know I let it slip that I had a good year, and already he's hitting me up for more legal fees."

"No, not him. The other one, the younger one?"

Oh, Bo Martin."

"Yes that's him."

"What are you making out, a will?" asked Bart.

"Something like that," countered Joe.

"By the way, what are you going to do with your money? I know you have to pay off your supplier, but you also probably made out like a bandit," said Bart while making a mischievous grin.

"Well, Bart to tell you the truth, I want to leave my estate to you and your family."

"You what?" Bart blurted out, as he choked on his words.

"You've been good to me. You've never demanded anything of me. You've allowed me to live in your condo and drive your company car. With your spending habits, I know you can never have too much money. Plus, I've already given away most of my money to charity anyway."

"Well, Joe, I have to say that I am deeply honored. To tell you the truth, I am actually quite shocked. I really think you should think about it some more before making a final decision."

"No, Bart, my mind is made up, and that is that. What I have in mind is the creation of a trust for you and your family but administered by a neutral third party. Do you trust Bo Martin?"

"Hell, yes," replied Bart. "He is the successor trustee on my estate planning documents, I believe. I absolutely trust him with my family's well-being."

"Well that ices it for me. Let's go see him together."

Bart looked at his watch and then at his pile-high stack of papers before saying, "How about now? My head is pounding, even more so after what I just heard from you, and I really could use a walk."

"Sounds great."

It took the two men over ten minutes to walk over just three blocks to Bo's office. The weather in Palm Beach in January was unusually cool with a strong northerly breeze, and the two men fought against the wind their entire walk. They were clearly windblown when they greeted the receptionist.

"Hi there, I'm Bart Sinclair. I don't have an appointment, but I'm a neighbor as well as a client of Bo's, and I have a pressing matter I would like to speak with him about if he is available."

"Let me see what I can do. Just a minute, Mr. Sinclair."

In a few minutes the elderly Ms. Everett entered the waiting area. "Good morning, gentlemen. Mr. Martin is on a conference call right now. As soon as he's off the phone, he will meet with you. He will be a few minutes if you don't mind waiting."

"No, not at all; sounds great. Thank you."

The two men helped themselves to some much-needed strong coffee and muffins that were in the reception area, and within fifteen minutes, Bo bounded into the lobby.

"Good morning, Bart. So nice to see you. The wine was excellent! Hope you had a nice New Year's."

"Oh, yes we did. Thank you."

"Bo, this is my dear friend Joe Marx. He would like to meet with you."

"Nice to meet you, sir. Come this way into my office."

As the men sat down, Bo closely examined the elderly gentleman. Joe Marx was about five foot six inches tall and weighed about one hundred forty pounds. He was mostly bald with some gray short hairs cropping out on the sides of his head. He was deeply tanned and appeared in excellent shape and health except for his alcoholic-looking bulbous nose. He had to be at least seventy years of age and of European descent. He was dressed rather conservatively and looked basically like any other senior citizen in south Florida. He wore no jewelry, and Bo couldn't get much of a sense of the man.

His eyes were black and showed absolutely no emotion. Other than his eyes, nothing else about him was out of the ordinary.

When he spoke, the German accent came through loud and clear.

"Mr. Martin."

"Please call me Bo."

"Well, Bo, my name is Joe Marx. I have been in the import/export business all of my life. I have made lots of money and given away most of it to charity. All of my family members are deceased, and I have nobody to leave my estate to. I, therefore, want to create a trust for the benefit of Bart Sinclair and his family."

At those words Bo leaned forward on his chair. He stared Joe directly in the eye. "Mr. Marx before you do that, I have an ethical duty to make sure that you are not only of sound mind but also not being unduly influenced by Mr. Sinclair."

"Believe me," muttered Bart, "I have not put him up to this."

"Mr. Martin, Bo, I have thought long and hard about my decision. I have also privately investigated you personally. Trust me, this decision is being made fully and freely by me, and I am not influenced in any way by Mr. Sinclair." Bo debated whether to allow Bart to even remain in his office, but since Joe seemed extremely coherent and independent, he allowed Bart to remain in the office.

Bo proceeded to start taking notes, all the while thinking, *I've been investigated by this old man?*

"So do you want a revocable trust to take effect upon death? With a revocable trust, you are in complete control of your money, and you can make changes at any time you want. Revocable trusts are the most common estate planning documents."

"No, Mr. Martin, I want it created now, and I do not want any of the money."

"So you mean an irrevocable trust?"

"Yes, exactly."

"Well, most irrevocable trusts are used to own life insurance and take effect upon death. If I understand you correctly, you want a trust to take effect now? Do you understand that you can never change the trust, and that once it is created, you can have no incidence of control over the money or the trust itself?"

"Yes, exactly. I am fully aware of that. As I said before, I know what I am doing."

"Are you a US citizen?" asked Bo.

"No."

"So, I don't have to worry about the United States Gift Tax provisions. Will the money be administered here or overseas?"

"Overseas. The money will never be in the USA."

"Okay. And you want the beneficiaries of this trust to be Bart Sinclair, his wife, and his children?"

"Yes."

"Do you want them to receive all the income and some principal, or do you want the trustee to have some discretion?"

"I want the trustee to have total control over everything."

"Okay. So the irrevocable trust will be a full discretionary trust providing the trustee with complete discretion over both the income and the principal distributions?"

"Perfect."

"Now, who do you want the trustee to be?"

"You."

"Me?" answered a quite shocked Bo.

"Yes, you."

"But, I don't even know you?" shot back Bo.

"As I said, I have had you personally investigated, and I have given this much thought and consideration. I do not make decisions hastily. Believe me, I have done the research, and you will serve as the trustee if that's okay with you."

"Well then, Mr. Marx, I would be honored to serve as the trustee over the Joseph Marx irrevocable trust."

"Based upon what you have stated, who would you like to serve as a successor trustee in the event of my incapacity or death?"

"Let's leave it up to Bart or his children if you can't serve. Can you do that?"

"I can do anything you want, Mr. Marx. Because you will be creating an irrevocable document, I want to make certain that it is exactly what you desire."

"I understand completely."

"Now, you do know that you could designate a bank or a trust company to serve as the corporate fiduciary."

"I know, but I detest bankers and do not want an institution in charge of overseeing the trust. In fact, can you keep the trust private?"

"Generally, irrevocable trusts are private documents. Only the trustee and the beneficiaries are provided with information. A trustee can sue and can be sued. With the increase in attorneys, there always will be frivolous lawsuits. You can't totally insulate a trustee from litigation. Are you concerned about litigation, Mr. Marx?" asked Bo curiously.

"Oh, no. Definitely not."

"Please tell me, Mr. Martin, I mean Bo, what is the annual charge for your services?"

"Typically financial institutions charge a fee based upon the percentage of the value of assets. Their fee is usually one to two percent per year."

"That is fine with me. How about you, Bart?"

"I would have no problem with two percent," said Bart, who was trying to pay attention but still couldn't help but daydream about all the money he would soon have.

"Okay, two percent then. Now tell me, how much money are we talking about Mr. Marx?"

"I am talking millions."

"Oh, I see. Would you be willing to sign an affidavit stating that this money did not come from drug smuggling?" questioned Bo, trying to act unfazed by the word *millions*.

"Definitely. I assure you, drugs are not involved."

"Well that makes me feel much better." A broad smile appeared on Bo's face for the first time.

"Now I am going to need your personal information, such as your full legal name, address, social security number, phone, etc."

"I'd rather not," replied Joe.

Bo shot Joe a look of concern.

"Bo, I have personally hand selected you. You don't need that information. Use Bart's address on everything. I don't want any mail or rough drafts. In fact, I never want to receive anything at all from you. Just prepare the trust as we have discussed, and I'll sign it. From there the money will be placed in the trust, and you will faithfully administer it. Correct?"

"Yes in a manner of speaking."

"Bo, I trust you. Bart trusts you. If you administer it correctly, there will not be any problems. Once I've created the trust and then funded it, I will be completely out of everything. Understood?"

"Yes, sir," replied Bo, who still couldn't believe what he was hearing. Bo had dealt with many eccentric individuals in his career, but this man topped the cake.

"Well then, no need to take up any more of your time. Have a draft prepared ASAP. Here, here is five thousand dollars. That should be enough," said Joe sliding the cash across Bo's desk.

"No, take your money," countered Bo, trying to push if back to Joe.

"I insist." As Joe and Bart stood up, Joe reached out his hand to Bo and said, "It has been a pleasure meeting you. Take good care of yourself."

"Thank you. You too."

"Bye, Bart."

"I look forward to hearing from you," replied Bart winking at Bo.

As the two men left the office, Joe spoke first. "I really like that young man, and I believe he will do an excellent job."

"Oh, I have no doubts. And, Joe, thank you again for your generosity."

"No, thank you, Bart."

The walk back to the jewelry store was much easier with the wind at their backs. Once there, they turned to each other and shook hands. Joe turned away and started toward his car, he threw his arm back in a wave goodbye, and said, "See you later." Bart returned the gesture and walked back into his store.

As Joe drove to his condominium, his mind was racing. He really liked Mr. Bo Martin and just hoped he was tough enough to handle the inevitable future onslaught. *Heck if he can't muster the courage, then he can always resign,* thought Joe. Deep down, Joe was pleased with Bo and knew he had made the right choice.

The very next morning Joe contacted the bank in the Isle of Man and wire transferred the sum of $50 million to his company, AA Trading Co. in Panama. Two days later, Joe transferred the entire amount to the Bank of Grand Cayman account for A Trading Co. He made and received confirmations, via his own personal Nokia phone while he was out walking in his condominium development. He made sure never to discuss business or money matters over his condominium's telephone. Several days later, he met Bart at the jewelry store and signed the trust document and affidavit before Bart's notary. Joe made sure to fill in a date that was five years earlier.

The following day Joe had to do some fancy driving before he was able to lose the black caddy that was following him. Once that was accomplished, Joe embarked on a short day trip to the Grand Cayman Islands. Immediately upon his arrival, he met with Harrison Frazar, vice-president of The Bank of Grand Cayman. The meeting took place that afternoon.

"Harrison, you look well today. I hope I caught you at a good time. I don't have an appointment."

"Thank you, and an appointment is not necessary for you," replied Harrison.

"How have you been, Harrison?"

"Very good, and by the size of your account, I know that business must be fabulous."

"You could say that I had a good year."

"I'll say so and drink to that."

"Can I get you anything? Coffee? Tea?"

"Vodka would be nice."

"Very well, vodka coming right up," said Harrison. Joe knew that Harrison's assistants would be scurrying to find the expensive vodka. For as much as the bank is charging, he figured they better have the good stuff.

Moments later, the vodka had arrived.

"Ah, thank you," said Joe as he took the glass from the secretary. He shot it back in a matter of seconds. "Thank you again that hit the spot!"

"Very well then. What brings you to the Cayman Islands?"

"Well, I would like to change the ownership of the accounts."

"The ownership? I don't think that's possible. The account is in the name of A Trading Co., Joseph Marx, president. If you were to attempt to transfer the account to an individual name, it would be red flagged by the US government, especially considering the vast sums of money involved, and there could be penalties. I'm sure you don't want that now, do you?"

"Oh no," replied Joe. "What I am simply planning on doing is transferring the ownership of my stock in A Trading Co. to a trust. That's all."

"Hmm in that case, there will be several forms to fill out."

"I figured as much, and that is why I came here personally. Here is the name, address, phone number, fax, and email of the new trustee and his business card. Here is also a copy of the trust document. The trust will be the sole shareholder of A Trading Co. You will eventually meet with the new trustee. As you can see from the document and the information I have provided you, the trustee's name is Bo Martin, and he is an attorney in Palm Beach, Florida."

"I presume that Mr. Martin will personally pay a visit to the bank."

"Oh, yes and very shortly," replied Joe.

"Good. It will take some time for me to prepare the necessary forms."

Harrison Frazar then inquired, "You must be selling your company for a small fortune. Could we perhaps assist in the sale of the company or in the investment of the sales proceeds?"

"That won't be necessary, but thanks anyway," answered Joe.

Damn, thought Harrison. *I'm sure the bank could have generated tremendous fees to handle that large transaction.*

Meanwhile, Joe sat patiently. *If Harrison only knew how much the actual sale was for, he would have been sick. Absolutely, sick to his stomach,* Joe thought.

Exactly one hour later, Joe emerged from the Bank of Grand Cayman and headed straight to the nearest bar. Four shots later, Joe was feeling no pain and was pleased with what he had accomplished.

Even though Joe was in paradise, he didn't once venture out to the beach or ocean. He still had too much to do.

When Joe returned back to West Palm Beach, he instantly became aware of his most daunting task. Joe, determined to see his revenge fulfilled, began making his last arrangements.

Joe planned for Bart to approach Bo within two weeks to purchase A Trading Co. However before that time came, Joe personally contacted one of his former attorneys, Phillip Houseman to represent his ownership in A Trading Co. Joe wanted to make certain that his personal identity was kept a secret. Joe also knew that Bo Martin would become extremely suspicious if he sensed there was anything fishy going on regarding the purchase of A Trading Co.

Joe also realized that Bart Sinclair had a big mouth, especially when he was drinking. Rather than allow Bart to breach the security, he insisted that Bart inform his personal attorney, Paul Schwartz, and accountant, Ross Brown, regarding the trust. He wanted these men to be informed of not only the creation of the trust but also the purchase of A Trading Co. by the irrevocable trust.

Joe went to great lengths to explain that Bo Martin would be the sole trustee and would have complete control of the trust. Joe had personally witnessed Paul Schwartz's outright greed and was sickened by it. For all Joe was concerned, he believed that most lawyers thought of themselves first and their clients second. Bo Martin on the other hand, placed his clients first and his own personal needs second. He was indeed unique!

After paying Phillip Houseman handsomely for his future services in the matter, Joe watched from afar and witnessed the actual transfer of ownership in A Trading Co. to Bo Martin, trustee of the Joseph Marx irrevocable trust. Joe made certain that the Joseph Marx's name was deleted on all records at the Bank of Grand Cayman so that the only ownership record reflected the following: "Bo Martin, Trustee."

Harrison Frazier confirmed that everything was exactly as Joe desired.

Utilizing his own personal zeal in his quest to avenge his tragedy at the hands of Victor Butin, Joe secured his latest passport, driver's license, credit cards, and even American Express platinum card. Joseph Marx had painstakingly made arrangements to simply blend into the French countryside. Ten years earlier, he had purchased a small estate approximately one hundred kilometers outside of Paris. He had titled the property in the name of Jean Pierre (the most common name in France, aka John Smith in the USA). Joe's forged papers all reflected the name Jean Pierre.

In Budapest, Hungary, Joe had many years earlier, saved the life of a young gentleman. The young man was a grave robber who was caught red-handed one evening, digging up the remains of a recently buried widow, hoping to procure her wedding ring. Joe intervened on his behalf, had the charges dropped, and secured a job for the young man as an intern in a local mortuary. After years of hard work, the man had now acquired and managed his own funeral home. He owed his life to Joe and hoped one day he would be able to repay his kindness.

Joe placed the phone call to his friend. He made it from a public telephone booth, just around the corner from his condo and perhaps one of the last remaining pay phones in all of Florida. When his friend heard Joe's voice on the telephone, he knew immediately that the time had come.

"My dear friend, how are you?"

"Very well, and you?"

"Can't complain. How long has it been twenty . . . twenty-two years?"

"About that."

"I've followed you throughout the years, and I was very happy to learn that you now own your funeral home. People are always dying, so I trust that business is good."

"I have been truly blessed. If it wasn't for you, Joe, I probably would be dead myself! Life is good for me and my family."

"Wonderful."

"So, what do I owe this long-overdue call to?"

"I need a favor," replied Joe.

"Anything."

"You know Dr. Worazek?"

"Yes, quite well. He's the best doctor around here."

"Well, he and I go way back. He is going to handle my death."

"Your what?"

"My death. Yes, you heard me. After my death, my identity will be changed, and you will probably never hear from me again."

"Okay, I am not going to ask any more questions—it already seems way over my head! Just tell me what I can do to help you."

"I need you to prepare my death certificate."

"No problem, but you will also need a body in your place. Correct?"

"I thought that was also where you could help me out, owning your own funeral home and everything."

"Well, it is your lucky day. It just so happens that I have an unidentified male in the freezer. He has been there for months now, and there is no longer any inquiry into his unfortunate demise."

"That's great. Can you prepare it up within a couple days' notice, my friend?"

"I can and will do anything you ask."

"You may catch some heat on this, and some nasty Russians may try and beat down your door."

"That's okay. I am a big boy now, and there will be no missteps."

"Very well, then. There are some names and addresses of the people in the United States and London who I want you to mail by Federal Express, the certified death certificates." Joe gave him the names of Bart Sinclair, Paul Schwartz, Phillip Houseman, and Harrison Frazar. Before hanging up with his old friend, Joe sincerely thanked him for handling this matter.

"Joe, it's my honor and pleasure to finally be able to help you. I owe my life and all my happiness to you!"

"Well, thank you. I wish you all the best."

"Take care, Joe."

"You too."

Joe then walked back to his condo to make his travel arrangements. Using his home phone, Joe called several airlines to inquire about travel to Budapest. However, he made sure not to make any final reservations on his home phone or even his cell phone, just to be safe. He booked his first-class tickets to Budapest, Hungary at the same public phone he had used a day earlier.

The next to last step in Joe's plan would take place simultaneously with Bo and Ruby Martin's upcoming trip to the Grand Caymans to transfer ownership in A Trading Co. to Bo Martin, trustee and new president.

Joe also officially closed his accounts and wire transferred the money to separate French accounts in the name of Jean Pierre. Joe figured that over five million dollars was more than enough for an old man to live on. Plus, he still had several million in diamonds that he would carry with him.

Finally, Joe wrote the two notes hoping and praying that someday Bo Martin would find them and use the evidence to further proclaim Joe's unfortunate demise. The post office box and safety deposit box were the safest two places that he could come up with.

When the day finally came for Joe to leave for Europe, he left his house with nothing in tote. Joe had on a pair of khakis, a polo shirt, and his walking shoes. He headed out as if he was on one of his usual walks, knowing that he was still being watched. Joe started out on his usual route that took him behind one of the adjoining condos only to reappear moments later. However, this time, as soon as he got behind the building he jumped into a waiting Uber and headed toward the airport. As the plane left the West Palm Beach terminal, Joe settled back in his seat, ordered his vodka, and dreamed of his future life in France.

Chapter
Twenty-Three

eanwhile, back in West Palm Beach, the two Russians, Igor and Ivan, were bored out of their minds. They had listened in on Joe's telephone calls and had noted that he was making inquiries about a trip to Hungary. It was not clear when or even if he would be going, and since Marty was away on another matter in Key West, the two men decided not to inform Victor Butin until it became certain when Joe would be leaving.

When Marty returned from the Keys, he was outraged that the men had failed to notify him or Victor of Joe's plans of a trip, even if it was not certain.

"What the hell was your job? You stupid morons. Your instructions were very simple. You were to watch Joe's daily movements, listen in on all his conversations, and keep Victor informed the first moment you became aware of anything suspicious, like him planning a trip! What were you thinking? We are all dead men!"

"Did he discuss the sale of jewelry? How many suitcases did he bring? How long is he staying? Idiots!"

"Marty," exclaimed Ivan, "we both are pretty sure that Joe is still in North Palm Beach. He never actually booked a flight to Hungary; he was only making inquiries, and when we were watching him yesterday, he was just going about his normal walk.

"When is the last time you to actually laid eyes on Joe?"

"We saw him yesterday when he was going on one of his daily walks. I don't think there is anything to get concerned over yet," explained Ivan.

"Let me ask you two morons something, did you see with your own two eyes, Joe Marx return from his walk?"

"No, we did not see the point in waiting for him to return. Every day it is the same thing: he goes for a walk, and one hour later he returns; he is like clockwork."

"Oh My God, you two are so fucking stupid! Come on, we are taking a drive to Joe's condo, and you two better hope he is there!" screamed Marty. Marty knew that for his sake too, Joe better be in his condo. On the way to the condo, Marty received the dreaded phone call from Victor. Marty let Victor know immediately what he was doing. "We are on are way over there and will let you know as soon as we find anything out and, Victor, I am sure everything is fine," Marty tried to sound reassuring as he wiped the sweat from his brow with the back of his hand.

Once at the condo, much to their dismay and fear, they did not get any answers. Marty picked the lock in a matter of seconds and entered the condominium. Everything appeared normal. Marty did find a travel itinerary and even some brochures and newspaper clippings on Budapest in the garbage can. "So boys, according to this piece of paper, Joe Marx left for Hungary yesterday, just about three hours after he went for his walk! The only good thing is that according to the itinerary, he is due back in five days. They looked around a little bit more, and Marty was somewhat pleased when he noticed that most of Joe's clothes were in their drawers and on the hangers. From a cursory inspection, it definitely appeared that Joe was only on a short trip and would be back by the end of the week. Why Joe chose Budapest to visit was not something Marty was too concerned about.

Marty knew that he should not piss Victor off any more and immediately placed the call to him.

"Victor, this is Marty. How are you?"

"Well, I suppose that depends on what you have to tell me!"

"Well, I just wanted to inform you that it looks like Joe went on a little trip."

"I hope one of your men has followed him! You know he has fifty million dollars' worth of my diamonds!"

"Victor, you are alarming yourself for no reason; at this point, we know the diamonds are at Diamond and Sons. They are not in Joe's personal possession."

"Screw you, I know he does not actually have the diamonds, but he does have fifty million dollars of mine! Now tell me what you *do* know!"

"Well, Joe flew first class to Hungary for a week's vacation."

"He did what?"

"He's in Budapest, Hungary."

"What in the hell is he doing there? Why didn't one of you follow him?"

"Victor," said Marty hesitantly, "we have monitored all of his calls and have inspected his condominium. Trust me, he is planning in returning in five more days."

"You imbecile! Joe has never done anything like this before. He's planning something. If you lose him, Marty, you will have to answer to me!"

"Well, Victor before you jump the gun again, we do know that he never picked up any diamonds from Bart Sinclair, and we know that his checking account still has only about ten thousand dollars in it."

"Is that so?"

"Yes."

"Well in that case, I feel a tiny bit better, but I am going to contact my family over in Russia. They have contacts in Hungary, and maybe they will be able to pick him up. I won't rest until Joe is back there in Florida. It is not like him to simply take off."

"Granted, it is somewhat out of his character, but he has been holed up in the condominium for several months now. We have followed him virtually every day and we have monitored all his phone calls."

"Still, I will feel better when he is located."

"Me too, Victor, me too."

"I'll keep in touch."

Nearly twenty-four hours later, Victor's phone rang. The blood drained from Victor's face when he received word from his contacts in Hungary that Joseph Marx had died from a heart attack in his Budapest hotel room.

The facsimile of the newspaper report simply stated that Joseph Marx of North Palm Beach, Florida, died of a sudden heart attack shortly after arriving to his hotel. Dr. Julius Worazek confirmed the death. Officials were trying to contact family members but so far have not been able to locate any. Victor thought, *Family members . . . none.* "I want to see the body!" screamed Victor. Unfortunately for Victor when the member of his gangster family actually visited the Hungarian funeral home, it was learned that through a mix-up at the mortuary, the body of Joseph Marx had been inadvertently cremated. They received the remains and a bill, but there was nothing else except ashes. Joe's monogrammed watch, passport, traveler's checks, and driver's license were the only identifying pieces of information.

"That son of a bitch that son of a bitch!" was all that Victor could say over and over again. His informants confirmed a male body had indeed been cremated by the mortuary and that all the personal contents belonged to Joseph Marx. Finally, there was no questioning the integrity or honesty of Dr. Julius Worazek. The man's reputation was beyond reproach. Joseph Marx was indeed dead!

Chapter
Twenty-Four

Meanwhile, Joe was extremely pleased with everything. Nothing had gone wrong. By now the official death certificates had been FedExd to everyone, and undoubtedly, Victor's men would have confirmed his death. He smiled when he envisioned Victor going ballistic on his men.

Joe knew that once his death was confirmed, then all attention would be placed on Bart Sinclair. Even though Bart was a boozer and womanizer, he wasn't stupid. Bart would utilize the legal services of Paul Schwartz and all his snitches. Bart now had more than enough money to buy his way out of any trouble, Joe reasoned. After all if you can't pay off the police in Palm Beach, what good are they?

Joe recognized that Victor would come directly after Bart, but Joe also knew that it would be too little too late. Bart had done nothing illegal. He bought and sold expensive jewelry. Bart always knew in the back of his mind that Joe had been getting smuggled merchandise, but he never came out and asked about it. The less he knew, the better, and if his knowledge didn't go any further than Joe, then all the better for him. At this point with Joe Marx dead, Victor was dead or at least nonexistent. It was not like Victor was able to go to the authorities. The only thing Victor had at his disposal was Marty and his two goons.

When Bart would ultimately be interrogated by Marty, the records would confirm the payment of $50 million by Bart Sinclair for the one hundred diamonds. Their inquiry would end abruptly at the Isle of Man, due to its secrecy laws. Joe's death would leave Victor Butin with absolutely no recourse.

Bart purchased all the diamonds, and legally, there was nothing for Victor to proceed against.

Joe also knew that Bart would ultimately take the Will that he had signed before the notary public, which left every asset owned in Joe's individual name to Bart's children to Bo Martin to have it probated in Palm Beach County, Florida. Joe only hoped that Bo would find the two hidden notes, as well as give him a heads-up regarding Victor Butin. It would be the only message Bo would ever receive to watch his back. *Poor Bo*, reflected Joe.

As Joe peered out over the French countryside from his new residence, he was finally at peace. Nothing can go wrong, or so he thought. *Damn you to hell Victor Butin!* he thought.

Chapter
Twenty-Five

Unfortunately for Bart and Bo—and for Joe as well—Milton and Brenda Rogers had devious intentions of their own that would soon place everyone at great peril.

On February 12, Brenda Rogers raced into Diamond and Sons Inc. hysterical in tears. She was carrying one large and extremely ornate box containing all the jewelry pieces. Brenda bypassed the store employees and headed straight for Bart's office.

"I have to see Bart. It's an emergency."

"Well, he's out to lunch at Taboo. He should be back in less than an hour."

"I'll wait then," barked Brenda, still in tears.

Sure enough, less than an hour later, Bart entered the store. The place was packed. Valentine's Day was less than forty-eight hours away, and it was the height of the Palm Beach season. Brenda was the last person that Bart wanted to see.

"Mrs. Rogers, Brenda, so nice to see you," said Bart with his fakest of smiles.

"Bart, I have a huge problem."

"How can I help?"

"We all hate the jewelry designs. The girls think the designs are hideous and now refuse to wear them. I never liked the designs myself, but I did not want to upset my husband. Milton is quite devastated by all of this, as you can imagine."

"So, what can I do?"

"I want you to, quite simply, remove all the diamonds from the settings. Then I'll divide them up and distribute the diamonds to all the girls. They each can come to you on their own and have you recommend various settings."

"Well if that's what you want."

"That's what we all want. The only problem is that time is of the essence. I want to give the diamonds away tomorrow. Can you take them apart in less than twenty-four hours?"

"Well, the jeweler I used to create the pieces is no longer with me, and I really don't have anyone that can take them apart. Plus, I honestly don't trust anyone with the gems."

"Can you do it?"

"Me?"

"Yes, you? How long could it take?"

Bart was truly at a loss for words. He personally hadn't worked on jewelry pieces in over fifteen years. Sure, he could take the diamonds out himself, but it would take him all night to finish the work.

"What do you say?" chided Brenda, refusing to take no for an answer.

"Okay, but it won't be cheap."

"Oh what does that matter, Bart, just do it. I'll be back tomorrow. And thanks, you are the best." Brenda flashed him a cutesy smile and blew him a kiss as she left the office.

Bart took the large box into the back room and immediately started the careful deconstruction of the jewelry. He had had two martinis for lunch, and his mind was elsewhere as he disassembled the pieces without really closely examining any of the diamonds.

Meanwhile, back in the Rolls, Milton was waiting impatiently for Brenda, as she stepped into the car. "Well, how did it go?" he asked anxiously.

"The store was quite busy, but it couldn't have gone any smoother. In fact, I think that he was going to take the diamonds out himself. Can you believe that? He couldn't tell a fake from a real diamond if his life depended on it." They both laughed out loud.

It had taken Milton and Brenda almost a full month to replace all the real diamonds with the manufactured diamonds from Brad Penny's lab. Although Brenda was curious as to what happened to Brad, she was much too afraid of Milton to ever ask him directly. Milton had a violent temper and a sadistic mind. She knew that Milton also had numerous mistresses and lied to her about everything, but she, nevertheless, was still in love with the man. Brenda

figured she had spent far too many years with him by now, and there was
no point of going through a messy and an unquestionably expensive divorce
proceeding. She had money and power, and with Milton's cunning mind,
she was going to ensure that her children would be financially set for their
respective lives. *My children are my life*, thought Brenda, as she and her husband
leisurely drove to their home on South Ocean Drive.

When they arrived home, they quickly headed to their secret room.
Milton and Brenda had created their own gem lab. Milton had been extremely
careful to purchase the most innovative gemology equipment with cash, using
a middleman. It was there in that lab where Milton had methodically removed
each and every diamond and replaced the real gems with the fake diamonds.

The cost had been enormous. Almost three million dollars had been spent to
create the synthetic diamonds. Two men had been killed, and an entire warehouse
had been destroyed, and with it, all the-state-of-the-art manufacturing equipment.

Milton and Brenda stood there in the lab staring at all of the shimmering,
beautiful diamonds. They were speechless. Milton then picked up the
telephone and called his State Farm insurance representative.

"Bill, this is Milton Rogers. How are you today?"

"Fine, how are you, Mr. Rogers? Happy belated New Year's."

"And to you too."

"Bill, I'm calling to inform you that my wife and I have gotten into the
jewelry collection business."

"Oh, so I take it you are not retired."

"Heavens no. I am just venturing into different areas. My latest area of
interest is in diamonds. I am just fascinated by them, so much so that I just
recently spent over one hundred million dollars on diamonds from Bart
Sinclair of Diamond and Sons Inc."

"You're kidding me. Right?" asked the agent sounding quite shocked.

"No joke. The sales are complete, and tomorrow my wife and I are
picking up the diamonds. I thought it might be good to have them appraised
and then insured."

"Well, yes. You definitely need them insured, and to do that you will also
have to have them appraised, and from the amount you're telling me you have,
this isn't going to come cheap!"

Milton practically choked on his words, "What the hell do I care how
much it costs. Just get it done and soon!"

"Very well then. I will make some phone calls and try to get someone
over there this week."

"That's fine, Bill. Let me know when."

"Sure thing. I'll get right on it."

Milton next placed a call to Jim McDonald. Jim McDonald was a former US assistant attorney. He was a short Napoleonic man, extremely egotistical, and highly confrontational. When Jim was unable to rise through the ranks of the United States Attorneys' office, due in large part to his un-redeeming personal qualities, he quit and went into private practice. He received no offers from any of the larger, well-respected law firms and settled with a medium-sized law firm in West Palm Beach, known for its viciousness and unethical antics.

Jim had represented Milton on numerous occasions. In each situation, Jim had used his connections with the US Attorneys' office to threaten possible criminal sanctions, outside of the civil proceedings. Jim acted like a bulldog in court and would think nothing of lying or cheating to help his client.

In all actuality, he was just like Milton. The two men were quite fond of each other, and their relationship blossomed. Over the last ten years, Jim had been successful in saving Milton several millions of dollars. Jim literally attacked his opponents with both legal and illegal approaches, and he really did not care if innocent people got hurt in the process.

Jim's two most important accomplices were an assistant US attorney, Steve Fleishman, and the local newspaper columnist, Mae McReynolds.

Steve Fleishman was your typical nerd. He was a C student in law school and naturally was unable to find a job in the private industry, upon graduation. He had never held any position of authority, and therefore, he loved the power that came with being an assistant US attorney. What he lacked in salary from the government, he more than made up for with the cash that Jim McDonald paid him on the side.

The arrangement worked out wonderful for Milton as well. Milton would sue a party in the civil circuit court. Most of the lawsuits involved contractual obligations or employee entitlements regarding his publishing empire. Jim would file the civil lawsuit and demand an absurd amount of money in damages for Milton and his company.

At the beginning of the discovery process, Jim would contact Steve at the US Attorneys' office. Steve would immediately institute a federal investigation into the defendant. Just the mere involvement of the US Attorneys' office would virtually scare the defendant into settling the civil matter in a manner benefitting only Milton. The threat of actual incarceration was too intimidating to all of the parties that Milton sued.

Then to make matters even worse, Mae McReynolds of the *Palm Beach County News*, would write front page inflammatory articles on the defendants. Her stories typically included unflattering photos of the defendant and were written unbelievably one-sided in favor of Milton Rogers and his companies. She also would always include the fact that the US Attorneys' office was in the midst of an ongoing criminal investigation of the defendant.

The negative publicity alone often helped Jim in settling Milton's civil matters. Never was there any unflattering article written about Milton or his company. For all the public knew, Milton and his companies were the good guys, and Milton was well known in the community for his charitable contributions.

Eventually when the lawsuit was settled, Jim or Milton would then pay off both Steve and Mae, and since Jim made enormous fees, they were compensated handsomely for their involvement. It was a tremendous opportunity for all three individuals.

"Jim, this is Milton. How have you been?"

"Quite well, thank you."

"I know that you've probably heard by now that I sold my company.

"Yes, I had heard, and it didn't make me very happy, as I am sure you could have guessed. You were one of my best clients. I sure hope that you get into something else very soon because I could use another lawsuit, as things are getting a little tight around here."

"Well, Jim, I think that you may be in luck. I've got a really big lawsuit in the making."

"You do? What, may I ask, is the litigation?"

"It involves my new business endeavor. I think I've been screwed over."

Jim could barely contain his emotion. "Well, come to my office immediately. I would love to represent you again."

"I know you would, and you will. I still have to take care of a few things before I am ready to meet with you."

"Absolutely. Call me as soon as you are ready; I am here whenever you need me," said Jim, sounding a bit needy.

"Talk to you soon, Jim."

"Bye, Milton."

Chapter
Twenty-Six

When Brenda arrived at Diamond and Sons Inc. on February 13 around 1:30 p.m., the store was bustling with people. Many white-haired gentlemen were making last-minute purchases while their chauffeurs waited patiently by the doors of the building. All the store employees were hustling back and forth. There was a phrase that the employees joked they never heard on the day before Valentine's Day: "Let me think about this purchase and come back later."

Brenda wasted little time in locating Bart, who was engaged in some serious negotiations with a very distinguished middle-aged man over an exquisite necklace. Brenda butted right in.

"Hey, Bart, are we ready to go?"

"Excuse me," Bart said to the gentleman, "Brenda, I am just about finishing up here. Just give me a few minutes, okay?"

"Well, just a few minutes, Milton is in the car, and you know how much he hates to wait."

Bart thought for a second, apologized to the gentleman, and then scurried into his locked office. Moments later he returned with the ornate jewelry box and handed it to Brenda.

"Here you go, Brenda. Just as you requested, I did everything myself."

"Thank you. Thank you. Just send the bill to Milton. You are such a dear."

"Have a nice Valentine's Day."

"You too."

Bart quickly went back to the gentleman, apologizing for the interruption.

Back in the Rolls, Milton and Brenda anxiously examined the box. They laughed all the way home.

"Can you believe he couldn't tell the gems were fake? I can't believe you pulled it off, Milton. I am so proud of you!"

"You have to admit, the synthetic gems are amazing. Without a trained eye, not many would be able to tell they were fake."

"Oh, Milton, you would have known, no doubt."

"Maybe, but probably not."

Over the next two days, Milton and Brenda disassembled their secret room and turned the lab back into a guest bedroom. There was literally no trace of any gem paraphernalia, books, catalogues, or pieces of equipment. Taking no chances at all, Milton had rented a large pickup truck and had taken everything to the Broward County dump where he made certain it could never be located again.

The following day, hours before a planned family dinner, the tangible personal property appraiser, hired by Milton's insurance company, arrived at the Rogers's mansion. The huge formal dining room was set in anticipation of the family dinner, and they even hired extra staff for the occasion. Milton wanted witnesses. For that reason alone, the Rogers had cleared a table adjacent to the kitchen and formal dining room for the purpose of the appraisal.

The appraiser wasted little time in getting down to business. For the next two hours, he examined each and every diamond. All four Rogers boys and their wives had arrived at the mansion and intruded on the inspection, just as Milton had planned.

Toward the end of the examination, the appraiser started fidgeting, and beads of sweat began to form on his forehead. He started furiously writing notations in his notebook and frequently glanced back and forth from the diamonds to his notes. Finally, the appraiser spoke.

"If I may be so bold as to ask, where did you purchase these diamonds?"

Milton answered, "They were purchased from Diamond and Sons inc. Are you familiar with Bart Sinclair?"

"Oh, yes I am. He has an excellent reputation on the island. When, may I ask, did you purchase the gems?"

"Well, they were originally purchased in December and again in January for tax purposes. I had the stones set in designs that I had created myself. Unfortunately, my wife and the girls hated my designs. So several days ago, my wife, Brenda took the pieces back to the store and had them dismantled back into the loose stones you see before you."

"Very good, and how much, may I ask, did you pay for the stones?"

"Well with sales taxes and everything, we paid approximately one hundred million dollars."

"Can I see the sales invoices?" asked the appraiser.

"We don't have any."

"You don't have any?"

"No. Bart Sinclair runs his store very informally. He just has never got around to preparing an invoice for us yet."

"So I see."

"Why? What's wrong?" asked Milton.

"I'm afraid you don't want to know, and before I jump to any conclusions, I recommend that you get a second opinion."

"Why, what on earth for?" demanded Milton.

"Mom, Dad, what is wrong with the diamonds?" inquired Lance, butting into their conversation.

It appeared that every one of the Roger's clan then spoke at once. The appraiser was bombarded with questions.

"Hold on one second. Don't all speak at once, and let me try to explain. I have personally never seen better diamonds. They are of the highest quality."

All at once the children breathed a huge sigh of relief. However, Milton stood rigid staring at the appraiser, hoping to hear those famous words.

The appraiser next words were: "But they are fake."

Everybody except for Bart and Brenda literally fell to the floor. Lee was the first to shout, "What do you mean they're fake?"

"You've got to be kidding," chimed Lance.

"That son of a bitch," hollered Luke, joined by wife, Lisa, who stated coldly, "I just knew that the Sinclairs had too much money. What a bunch of crooks!"

Lawrence tried to answer calmly, "Are you telling us that the gems that you have before you—and that my parents paid one hundred million dollars for—are worthless?"

The appraiser thought before responding, "I wouldn't declare the synthetic diamonds to be worthless, but they are not real and are certainly not worth the price you paid for them."

Milton next spoke, "I have been a businessman all of my life. I have worked hard to accumulate my wealth, and I think I am an excellent judge of character. I trusted Bart Sinclair. I researched into his background, and I never believed in a million years that he would cheat me or that I, Milton Rogers, could ever be hoodwinked."

"Well, as I said, it is my recommendation that you get a second opinion, but I believe the diamonds are exquisite fakes and probably worth no more than five million dollars. State Farm Insurance Company will not insure them for more than that amount, I can guarantee you that much."

"You don't know, or can't imagine, how truly devastated I am at this moment. My family and I probably need some time alone. Will you prepare a written report and provide Bill, our agent at State Farm, the name of another jewelry appraiser?"

"Why, certainly. I hate to be the bearer of bad news, but I hope that you can get this resolved immediately. This could ruin Diamond and Sons Inc. I wish you all the best."

"Thank you, and thanks for coming," said Milton as he ushered the appraiser to the door.

When Milton returned, the family was silent. The girls were devastated and the Rogers sons were infuriated.

Milton quickly defused the situation when he said, "Let's eat. After dinner on the patio we will discuss financial matters."

All agreed, even though they had clearly lost their appetites.

Chapter
Twenty-Seven

The food was excellent: tender fresh Mahi Mahi fillets, covered with a tropical mango salsa, succulent red potatoes, fresh asparagus, and frozen coconut sherbet for dessert. Not one family member mentioned the gems. All were instead immersed in gossip, discussing who was getting divorced, who was pregnant, who was seen with another's husband or wife, and who recently had the latest in cosmetic surgery. The Rogers family was consumed by their own personal self-importance on the island. They made sure to obey the unwritten laws of Palm Beach—they were members of the "in" clubs (Sailfish Club, Bath & Tennis Club, and the Everglades Club) attended church at the famous and beautiful Bethesda-By-The-Sea, shopped only on Worth Avenue, and made sure to partake in all the high society functions.

The Palm Beach Shiny Sheet was the biweekly Palm Beach newspaper that photographed Palm Beachers in all their glory. The Rogers family always felt slighted when they were not included in the pictures of the gala events.

The Rogers sons all photographed well. Further, since not one was currently employed, they had lots of time to work on their perpetual tans. Unfortunately, all four battled the bulge and took after their mother. Even though Brenda was by no means obese—she actually looked quite distinguished and healthy in her physique—she had to work endlessly to maintain looking the way she did. On the other hand, the boys were lazy even when it came down to their health. They did not put as much time and effort into staying in shape, as did their mother, and they were all starting to sport that Michelin tire look. Their wives actually took after their mother-in-law in the sense that they had their endless workout regimes. And even though none of them were quite yet thirty, they did everything they could to stay ahead of their biological clock. They included regular trips to their plastic surgeons for Botox, chemical peels, and whatever the newest breakthrough was in age-defying treatments. Of course they all had had their boobs done, and two of them were thinking about the Brazilian butt lift. The girls were very jealous of each other and had to keep trying to outdo each other. They were also all vying to become the first pregnant daughter-in-law to produce the first male grandchild.

Milton sat observing his boys and their wives. *How pathetic*, he thought. Here, I have given them everything, and not one has an original thought or ambition. Even their wives, except for the lovely Annie, will ever amount to anything. Unfortunately, Milton and Brenda had a family of all takers rather than givers. *Well at least they will be wealthy*, thought Milton. *Maybe, just maybe, my grandchildren will become successful. On second thought, I highly doubt it.*

Chapter
Twenty-Eight

ictor Butin was staring out at the historic landmarks of London from his penthouse suite. Although age had definitely slowed him down physically, his mind was as sharp as ever. He was consumed by his feelings of hatred for the late Joseph Marx.

"How could he do this to me? God damn him to hell," he ranted.

Victor had been in constant communication with his family contacts in Budapest. From everything that they could tell, Joseph Marx did indeed die of a massive heart attack. The episode occurred within an hour of his checking into the hotel. His bag one small carry-on, was not even unpacked yet, and he had just made dinner reservations for one at seven o'clock that evening. There really was nothing suspicious about the incident.

Dr. Julius Worazek just happened to be dining in the hotel restaurant when he heard all kinds of commotion in the lobby. He overheard that one of the guests had just called down saying he thought a man was having a heart attack.

"What room is he in?" screamed Dr. Worazek, "I am a doctor!" Dr. Worazek worked on reviving the man for several minutes, but it was a lost cause. The doctor contacted the local mortuary instead of going to the hospital. What was the point in the hospital? The guy was long since dead.

Numerous witnesses saw the gurney with the dead body encased in a black body bag. However, nobody, not even any of the hotel staff, recalled seeing the dead man's face.

Victor thought that extremely odd.

Joe Marx was confirmed dead at the scene by Dr. Worazek, and the body went directly to the local mortuary. There were several cremations scheduled for that same evening, and the proprietor inadvertently cremated Joseph Marx's body, along with the others.

Several witnesses confirmed an irate Dr. Worazek publicly scolding the proprietor for his shoddiness and negligence. "How on earth can you cremate someone before the next of kin has yet to be notified and actually confirm his identification!" he was overheard screaming.

All of Joseph Marx's personal belongings were found at the mortuary, along with the remains. From everything the contacts could discover, Joseph Marx was a complete stranger, and there was no connection found between him and either Dr. Worazek or the mortician. No payoffs were uncovered or any other bribes detected.

Further, no rental cars were either leased out or turned in, and no automobiles were purchased by any American or anyone fitting Joe's description.

Victor was not yet convinced. For some reason, he had this nagging suspicion that Joe was alive. Ever since Victor had worked with Joe, he had thought him extremely odd. As he acquired wealth and power, Joe seemed to give his money away, never really desiring or wanting anything of real value. He had no vices other than vodka and had no outside interests. And most importantly after all these years of working together, Joe had never double-crossed Victor and had been nothing but honest and straightforward, even after what happened all those years ago! Victor was never really sure if Joe knew that he was the one behind all his tragedy, but he guessed he probably did. He could never truly understand why Joe had never sought vengeance against him. Victor just assumed that Joe knew it would be useless to try and go up against such a powerful family and decided it best just to join sides with them. Yes, Victor should have been convinced.

Well, maybe the man is really dead, thought Victor. Too bad he couldn't spend the ten million from Victor's eventual $50 million windfall. Victor was now more than ever determined to locate the money, and he knew just where to look!

Victor grabbed his cell phone and called Marty.

"Marty, have you been to Diamond and Sons today?"

"Yes I have. Business couldn't be better from what I could tell. The store was packed, and everyone looked like they were spending lots of money."

"That's very good."

"Any word on Joe Marx?" asked Marty.

"Well, it is official. It seems Joe died of a massive heart attack. He had several thousands of dollars on him, but nothing else."

"Then the diamonds must still be here at Diamond and Sons unless they have already been purchased.

"Marty, I will be arriving in Palm Beach next week. I will be staying at the Breakers. Continue keeping an eye on Sinclair!"

Meanwhile, unbeknownst to Marty, Bart Sinclair, his wife, Dana, and children were out enjoying themselves in Walkers Cay, Bahamas. Bart had worked extremely hard through most of February. Business was going great, and the $50 million from the sale of jewelry to the Rogers had made Bart feel invincible.

Bart had already doctored up his own personal files (what little they were) and had notified his accountant, Ross Brown of his big sale. In an abundance of caution, Bart had paid the IRS and the State of Florida's Department of Revenue all the necessary income tax and sales taxes, respectively, based upon his doctored statements.

Bart had then funded the children's trusts, which Bo had suggested that he and Dana create for each of the children. He also prefunded an irrevocable life insurance trust to help pay the estate taxes, upon his ultimate demise.

Bart had been thinking incessantly about death ever since Joe's unfortunate heart attack. Joe had really saved Bart's life. The gems that he had supplied him allowed Bart to compete against some of the more established jewelry stores and acquire significant wealth in the difficult marketplace of retail jewelry. Bart could never have done it without Joe's help, and because of that, he never questioned Joe where the gems had come from. Bart didn't even want to venture a guess.

Over 80 percent of his diamonds were purchased through Joe. With Joe's death, Bart would have to find another supplier, and he knew he would never find another Joe Marx. This situation was going to put a serious burden on Diamond and Son's earnings. Thank goodness for that once-in-a-lifetime sale with the Rogers, and now coupled with Joe's trust, Bart would survive and maintain his lifestyle. Well, he might also have been thinking that an early retirement would be pretty nice also!

Bart was extremely pleased that Joe had created a trust for his and his family's benefit, and he trusted Bo Martin, the trustee, completely. He knew that he and his family were in good hands.

Still, Bart wondered exactly how much money was in the trust, how much income would the principal generate, and when, exactly, would he begin receiving the monthly distributions?

By now Bo most likely would be getting ready to probate the Last Will and Testament of Joe Marx. In a couple of months, Bart knew that his children would inherit whatever Joe had in his individual name. Bart realized it couldn't be much. The condo and car were already owned by him, and the contents weren't worth all that much. Still, something was better than nothing.

Bart had also paid Paul Schwartz his annual $120,000 retainer for his legal protection. Bart had relied on Paul for everything, but he still hated paying Paul $10,000 per month simply to be available whenever needed. *Everyone has to make a buck but not that much*, thought Bart.

Whatever concerns Bart did have were soon wiped away when a giant blue marlin hit the ballyhoo and started tail jumping along the surface of the deep blue Atlantic Ocean.

The entire Sinclair family was thrilled to watch their father fight the beautiful fish. Bart sat in the mahogany fighting chair, slowly reeling in the gigantic animal while his children and even Dana stood mesmerized by the entire ordeal.

Four hours later, an exhausted but elated Bart and family watched as the enormous fish was photographed and released and slowly swam away into the depths of the ocean. *It doesn't get any better than this*, thought Bart. Little did he know what was in store for him when they returned to Palm Beach!

Chapter
Twenty-Nine

It didn't take long for a second appraiser to inspect and review each and every one of the diamonds. The second appraiser was just as methodical and meticulous as the first. Again, the questions he raised were virtually the same.

"Where did you purchase the stones?"

"When did you purchase the stones?"

"Have they ever been out of your possession?"

"How well did you know Bart Sinclair?"

"Have you contacted an attorney?"

Milton and Brenda answered all of his questions with deep concern. It was all an act, but the appraiser didn't know that. After more than three hours, the appraiser left the Rogers's oceanfront mansion, reiterating once again that the gems were all fakes. Truly extraordinary fakes, but fakes nonetheless, and definitely not worth $100 million.

Milton was extremely relieved, and with a smugness that was part of his persona, placed a call to his attorney, Jim McDonald. Jim was away on vacation and wouldn't be back for another week. "No, he didn't take his cell phone with him, and no, he didn't plan on checking his messages," was all his secretary had to say.

Nonetheless, later that evening Jim returned Milton's call.

"Milton, how the hell are you?"

"I've been better to tell you the truth."

"Well, as you've probably heard, I am on vacation at the moment. I won't be back for at least another week. But what can I do to assist you?"

"Oh, nothing that can't wait until you return. By the way where are you?"

"I'm in Vancouver, taking in the sights and spending money that I don't have."

"Oh, is that so?"

"Yes, unfortunately, it is."

"Well when you return, I have a monster case for you. So go ahead and spend your money. I will make you a very rich man."

"Oh, Milton that is music to my ears!"

"Well, enjoy your vacation, and call me when you get back into town."

"Thanks, Milton. Take care."

Within the next three days, the second appraiser provided Milton with his final appraisal of the gems. State Farm Insurance Company was also provided with copies. The average of the two appraisals listed the true value of the diamonds at $5.5 million. Certainly far less than the one hundred million dollars that Milton had paid. Bill from State Farm, phoned Milton as soon as the reports hit his desk.

"My God, Milton, what the hell is going on?"

"I was screwed over, pure and simple," replied Milton, sounding glum.

"But, Milton, you are one of the most meticulous businessmen I have ever met. How could this happen to you?"

"I really don't know what to say. My wife and I are devastated."

"Did Bart Sinclair really pull a switcheroo on you?"

"That is what it looks like at the moment."

"My God. And to think that he has such an excellent reputation on the island. I sure hope that you plan on getting to the bottom of this right away. You understand that State Farm cannot possibly insure the gems for one hundred million?"

"Oh, I understand completely. At this point it doesn't even make any sense to insure them at all."

"Precisely," said Bill, crying to himself because the insurance premium alone on a hundred-million-dollar policy, would have paid for his new Mercedes.

"I'll tell you what. When my attorney gets back from vacation, I'll have him call you. His name is Jim McDonald."

Bill had heard of Mr. McDonald and was somewhat shocked when Milton told him that he was his attorney. Bill knew that Jim McDonald was a real prick. Not the kind of guy that a successful multimillionaire would want to be associated with.

Oh, well, thought Bill. *To each his own.*

"I look forward to speaking with him. I wish you luck, Milton."

"Thanks. Take care."

"Bye now."

Chapter
Thirty

ust days before Victor's scheduled visit to Palm Beach, he suffered what doctors called a mild stroke. Marty flew to London to help attend to Victor's personal affairs.

Marty was shocked to find Victor somewhat in a state of financial distress. Most of Victor's money was tied up in non-liquid assets, such as his several homes, automobiles, joint ventures, and limited partnerships. Victor had always spent money like water, and his taste for the finer things in life had always led to one sort of liquidity crisis or another.

Victor had been counting on the $50 million ($40 million if he were to pay Joe Marx his $10 million) to secure his final years of life.

Unfortunately, the untimely demise of Joseph Marx and Victor's inability to confront Bart Sinclair face-to-face caused Victor much concern and anxiety.

Igor and Ivan had continued to report daily from West Palm Beach, and they had not seen Bart or his family members for over two weeks. They informed Marty that Bart was on his yacht fishing off the Gulf of Mexico.

The infamous Paul Schwartz, Esq., had also confirmed that Bart and his family were indeed fishing in the Bahamas. Victor was beside himself because he still had no proof that any of the gems had been sold or even if the gems were still in Palm Beach. Each day that passed caused Victor more stress, which further attributed to his personal health issues.

Finally after three weeks of rehabilitation, Victor was ready to travel to Palm Beach and confront Bart Sinclair face-to-face.

Victor was totally in the dark about the tumultuous events that had transpired in Palm Beach during his convalescence. Undoubtedly, he would be sick when he heard the news.

Chapter
Thirty-One

*U*pon Jim's return from his vacation, he personally visited with Milton and Brenda Rogers at their gorgeous oceanfront home.

Milton had kept meticulous records of all his visits, telephone calls, and daily records of his transactions with Bart Sinclair. If Jim didn't know better, he would have sworn Milton was up to something with all his itemized documentation. *It was almost too perfect*, he thought.

In any event, Jim listened incredulously to the transaction of events between the Rogers and Diamond and Sons Inc. He did not interrupt Milton once during his nearly one-hour dissertation.

When Milton finished, Jim sat dumbfounded. So much so that Brenda asked, "Are you okay, Jim?"

"Oh, a . . . a . . . I'm just shocked that's all. I know of Bart Sinclair's reputation in the jewelry business, and I just can't believe he would do something like this, especially on a deal so huge where he knows you would undoubtedly get the jewelry insured. I know he drinks a lot and likes to womanize, but to do something like this, and then to top it off to try and dupe someone like you, it is just ridiculous. Milton, are you sure you are not leaving anything out at all?"

"No, Jim. That's it in its entirety."

"And, why did you decide to get into the diamond-collecting business in the first place?"

"Well, I was in the process of selling my business, and I knew I would have too much spare time on my hands. I know most people travel when they retire, but face it, there isn't anywhere we haven't been two or three times already, and plus, as we all know, Brenda's favorite hobby is wearing jewelry! So we decided to pick an interest that we both could be involved in, and investing in diamonds and starting our own collection seemed the best way to accomplish that."

Just at that moment, Brenda piped in, "It is so nice to actually be a part of my husbands' life. Even though we have been married close to thirty-five years, I feel as I hardly know him! You know he traveled so much or was always busy with some big project or other and I was busy raising the boys."

"I can understand that," said Jim. "Let me have a look at the invoices."

"There are none."

"What?" asked Jim incredulously.

"We, I mean Bart, never got around to filling them out. All that I have are the two wire transfers."

"You mean to say that you have no invoices to substantiate the sale of one hundred million dollars?"

"That's correct. Is that bad?"

"For Christ's sake, Milton, why didn't you call me in the first place? When you ran your publishing empire, you conferred with your attorneys on everything before you ever acted. What exactly were you thinking?"

"Lay off! Can't you see that I am embarrassed and humiliated enough as it is?" countered Milton, trying to suppress his veiled anger.

After a few moments of silence, Jim spoke again.

"We need to meet with Bart Sinclair and his attorney. I do not want to file a lawsuit without trying to resolve this first."

"You're the attorney, Jim. Whatever you say."

"Fine then. Let me go over all your information again, and then I'll arrange a meeting. In the meantime, don't tell anyone, not even your boys about this matter. Hopefully, it will just be a big misunderstanding."

"Too late," chimed Brenda. "We already told the boys and their wives."

"Shit," muttered Jim. "Listen, talk to the boys and their wives and tell them mum's the word for now. Wait until you hear from me again before talking to anybody else."

"We will. Thanks again, Jim."

"No, thank you, Milton. If what you say is true, this will be the biggest jewelry lawsuit ever in the United States."

As Jim left the mansion, all he could think about was his attorney's fee. *I will handle this case on a percentage fee basis. Twenty-five percent plus costs*, thought Jim. *Not too shabby!*

Chapter
Thirty-Two

T he moment Bart and his family returned from their fishing
expedition, Paul Schwartz called him.

"Hi, Paul, how are you?" answered Bart.

"I'm fine, Bart. I hate to be the bearer of bad news, but I received a
courtesy phone call from that shark of an attorney, Jim McDonald, and he
wants to meet with you early next week. He says that he represents Milton
and Brenda Rogers."

"That's fine with me. The Rogers are my biggest customers."

"Oh, really?"

"Yes, they help me afford you and your ten-thousand-dollar monthly fee."

"Is that so? Well not to alarm you, but I don't have a good feeling about
this."

"Don't worry. I haven't the foggiest idea what it's about. But, trust me, I
have done nothing wrong."

"Okay. We'll set up a meeting for next Tuesday at eleven a.m."

"See you then. Better yet, call me on Monday to remind me again."

Bart got off the phone and yelled to Dana, "I'm going to walk over and
see Bo Martin, honey. I shouldn't be gone long."

Bo was outside trimming some dead palm fronds with the red dogs when
Bart lumbered over.

"Hi, Bo. You got a minute?"

"Sure, Bart. Hold on, let me open the gate."

Seconds later the prized Vizslas were licking Bart and treating him like royalty. Bo thought, *He can't be all that bad—the dogs like him at least.*

Bart didn't mince words, "How is the estate coming along?"

"Well, I have complied with all the Florida laws and have published the notice of administration. It will run for ninety consecutive days, and creditors can file claims against Joe's estate during that time period."

"Has anyone filed any claim yet?"

No," answered Bo.

"I also found some cash in a safe deposit box, as well as a letter.

"Great," said Bart.

Bo did not reveal to Bart, the existence of the huge diamond or the Russian thugs. He did attempt to elicit more information, though.

"Do you know of a Victor Butin?"

"I heard Joe speak of him sometimes."

"In what way?" inquired Bo.

"Well, I'm not really sure, but I think he may have been Joe's diamond supplier. I never asked him who his supplier was, and he never relinquished that information."

"Is that so?"

"Yes."

"Anything else?" asked Bo.

"Not really. You see I purchased about eighty percent of my diamonds through Joseph Marx and his company, A Trading Co. Joe supplied me with the diamonds on a consignment basis, and when they eventually sold, I paid his company, A Trading Co., the price we agreed upon."

"So, you never actually met Joe's supplier then?"

"No, but on a few occasions I heard him mention the name Victor Butin about jewelry shipments."

"Can you remember something more? Anything else about the man?"

"Well, I believe I may have seen him once or twice. I believe he is Russian. If I remember correctly, he came into the store with Joe one time, years ago, and bought some jewelry if I recall. I did not personally assist him in his purchase, and I know he paid cash, so I never really got his name, but I believe I remember Joe calling him Victor."

"Do you think the gems could have been stolen?"

"I can't say. I doubt it though."

"Don't give me that crap. Did Joe charge you the going rate on the jewelry, or was it deeply discounted?" demanded Bo.

"That's none of your business now, is it?"

"Well, it just might be. You see I am the trustee of his trust, and I want to make sure that you and Joe and whoever this Victor fellow is, are on the up and up."

"Trust me, the gems were all real, and they were of superior quality. Sure, Joe sold them to me at a big discount, but then again, I could move the merchandise. Hell, he dealt with my father for years before me!" whined Bart, revealing more information to Bo than he originally intended.

"Okay, let's just leave it there for now."

"So, Bo, tell me, how is the trust doing?"

"Well, it's all invested very conservatively in treasury bills, treasury notes, municipal bonds, and blue chip mutual funds of both large cap and small cap stocks."

To Bart it all sounded great. He wasn't the most financially astute investor. "When can I get some money?"

"When do you want it?" retorted Bo.

"Well, not at this moment, since I'm sort of flush, but in the near future, I will need it to supplement my income. You know with Joe's death, my main supplier is gone. It will be much more difficult to turn a profit now."

"I understand," said Bo. "I will also provide you with a semiannual report. When the first one is finished, I will mail it to you."

"Thanks, Bo. Well that's all I wanted. By the way, we don't have any more travel plans for a few months. Maybe we could have dinner soon."

"We'd love that," said Bo trying to sound somewhat convincing.

"Well, gotta run."

"Take care."

"You too."

As Bo watched Bart walk back to his mansion, Bo felt the sense of dread again. Why didn't I mention the diamond? What am I going to do with it? I have a duty to disclose it, report it, and then pay estate taxes on it. Fortunately, the estate tax return isn't due until nine months after death. A lot can happen in that time.

Chapter
Thirty-Three

The meeting between Jim McDonald and Bart Sinclair, accompanied by Paul Schwartz, Esq. took place in Bart's disheveled office promptly at 11:00 a.m.

"Thank you for meeting with me," stated McDonald.

"Our pleasure," responded Paul.

"Rather than exchange a bunch of pleasantries and beat around the bush, let me tell you that I'm afraid you have a big problem. I wanted to meet with you face-to-face in the hope of settling this matter before litigation."

"What is this about?" chimed Bart.

"As you know I am here representing Milton and Brenda Rogers. They have provided me with detailed records including telephone calls, store visits, wire transfers, and other backup information. From what I have uncovered—and believe me I have already spent numerous hours reviewing materials in this matter—the Rogers bought one hundred million dollars' worth of diamonds from your store. The diamonds were delivered to them just prior to Christmas, December 23 to be exact, and again in January. Fifty million was transferred to your account in November and another fifty million in January."

"In addition, the Rogers provided you with illustrations and paid you an additional two hundred thousand dollars to set the stones according to their designs."

"In February, the Rogers were disappointed with all the settings. Brenda delivered the stones directly to you, and the following day, she picked them up from you, which would have been February 13."

"Have I left anything out?" Jim asked.

"No, you are correct so far," said Bart with a serious look of concern on his face.

"Several weeks ago, my clients had their gems appraised by two separate appraisers. They had contacted their insurance representative to purchase tangible personal property insurance, and their agent recommended an appraisal.

Bart, who was beginning to sweat a little bit, and Paul sat still as they listened to Jim.

"Here are the two appraisals." Jim handed copies of them to both Bart and Paul, who reviewed them briefly.

When Bart had finished scanning both appraisal reports he shouted, "What the hell is this bullshit?" Are you implying that I sold them fake stones? Because if you are, you can take your ugly ass out of here right now, you scumbag!"

"Now, just hold on, Bart," calmed Paul.

"Jim, are you suggesting that Bart sold your clients fake diamonds?"

"That's exactly what I'm saying, and I'm not suggesting anything. Your client, Paul, sold fake gems to my clients, and if you don't pay the one hundred million dollars back within the next fifteen days on behalf of my client, I will sue you for civil theft and demand treble damages. That's three hundred million dollars if you care to multiply," said Jim, smiling and looking directly at Bart, who was now bright red with anger.

"Get out of my office," hollered Bart. "Take your papers and yourself, and get the hell out of here. Now!"

"Okay, so be it. I guess I'll see you in court. I was really hoping we could resolve this amicably."

Bart was so livid he could spit. He kept muttering to himself, "This is wrong, this is wrong, this is wrong."

It took Paul twenty minutes to even get Bart to sit down and focus.

"Tell me, Bart, what's going on?" asked Paul.

"I swear to you on my children's lives that I never sold the Rogers any fake diamonds!"

"Are you sure?"

"Yes, completely. I analyzed each and every diamond when I received them from Joseph Marx. They were impeccable and flawless. All one hundred of them."

"I used the best jewelry maker to set the stones, and I know for a fact that the stones were genuine when the pieces were delivered to Brenda and Milton. Hell, I myself, dismantled the pieces when they wanted the stones separated."

"Did you examine them closely at that time?"

"To be honest with you, it was right around Valentine's Day, and I just popped all the stones out. I really can't say that I remember too much at all. I was just so damn busy. The store was packed."

"Do you think that they could have switched the stones?"

"They had to. Who else could have done it?"

"Are you sure?"

"Positive. What gets me is that the fakes, according to the appraisals, were perfect. I don't think there even exists, clear synthetic diamonds that are actually brighter than the real thing. I know that nitrogen causes the diamonds to turn yellow. But the appraiser says the diamonds were superior to anything that he had ever seen if they are indeed fakes."

"Wait, let me get this straight," asked Paul. "Are you telling me that you know of no person or company capable of manufacturing fake gems of this kind of quality? Is that what you are telling me?"

"Yes, I am. What am I going to do?" By now Bart's redness had vanished, and he was turning white with fear.

"Well, you certainly didn't make a good impression on McDonald. Tell me, how much money do you have?" asked Paul

"Well, those stones cost me fifty million dollars."

"Well that's great! All we have to do is contact your supplier, and we can prove the legitimacy of the stones."

"Unfortunately, Paul, my supplier is dead."

"Not Joseph Marx?" gasped Paul.

"Yes. Oh. No!"

"Is there anyone else who can confirm the genuineness of the stones?"

Bart thought long and hard before answering, "Maybe, maybe Victor Butin."

Paul shuttered to himself. *No way is the Russian mobster ever going to testify on your behalf!* thought Paul.

"I also paid the IRS and the State of Florida over six million dollars. I've spent over four million dollars on a new boat, and my wife and I bought life insurance, and I funded all the kids' trusts, so I probably have close to thirty-five million dollars remaining."

"What about the trust?"

"Joe's trust?"

"Yes!"

"I have to ask Bo Martin. I can't say for sure. Well don't bring that trust up just yet."

"Oh, don't worry, I won't," responded Paul, trying to calculate the sum of money in Joe's trust. "Bart, this could get very costly, and it could get even uglier. There will be criminal charges filed as well."

"I know that, Paul. Oh Jesus, what the hell am I going to do? All along it seemed that something just wasn't right, but I kept on going ahead because I let all that money blur my thinking! Shit!"

"We're going to have to discuss my fees. I'd rather get it out of the way now if you don't mind. I'll need a million-dollar retainer right away. Let's hope that this doesn't hit the papers. Negative press will obviously be devastating to your business. Let me go back to the office and prepare up our retainer and fee agreement."

With that said, Paul left the office leaving Bart all by himself.

Bart thought to himself, *This isn't happening to me. How could this happen?*

Chapter
Thirty-Four

It took Jim McDonald a little over two weeks to prepare the voluminous civil complaint. The complaint named Bart Sinclair individually, Bart and Dana Sinclair, jointly as husband and wife, and Diamond and Sons Inc. as the defendants. The plaintiffs, Milton and Brenda Rogers, were suing the defendants for numerous counts including racketeering, conspiracy, RICO violations, fraud, deceit, unjust enrichment, and civil theft and sought in excess of three hundred million dollars including attorney's fees and costs.

When Jim was finished with the Complaint and all its accompanying attachments, he phoned Milton and Brenda to come and review his masterpiece.

Milton was thrilled when he finally concluded reading the entire lawsuit. Brenda gave up within minutes of trying making sense out of all the legalese.

"I've got to hand it to you, Jim. This Complaint is great. I understand now why it took several weeks to draw it up!"

"Well, Milton to tell you the truth I haven't even looked at another case in the last two weeks. It was extremely exhausting, but also I haven't worked on anything so exciting in my whole career! I've researched every case like this on the internet, and this lawsuit is the largest jewelry fraud case in the world. This case is going to be monumental, and it is going to take up a lot of time, plus a lot of extra work from my associates."

"I understand that, Jim. Whatever it takes to get this done, Brenda and I have the utmost faith in you and your abilities."

"Now let's talk money here," said Jim clasping his hands in front of him on his desk.

Milton knew what was coming and braced for it.

"I can either charge you an hourly rate, my usual rate being five hundred fifty dollars per hour, associates at two fifty per hour, paralegals at one twenty-five per hour, or we can handle this case on a contingency basis or a combination of the two. What would you prefer?"

"Well, Jim on a contingency arrangement, you get paid when we get paid. Correct?"

"Yes that's correct."

"And how much of a percentage would you take?"

"Well, my standard is one-third. However in light of our previous working relationships and our friendship, I would do it for twenty-five percent."

"That seems kind of steep," piped Brenda.

"Or, we can just handle it on an hourly basis. To give you some idea of how much time is involved, I would venture to guess that at this point in time, I have personally spent in excess of two hundred hours. So that's over one hundred thousand dollars already, not including anyone else's time."

"I see," nodded Milton and Brenda, each independently of the other.

"I have both types of fee contracts available. It really makes no difference to me," said Jim, who was bluffing, of course. Jim had no intention of handling the case on an hourly basis and counting every minute of his day that he spent working on the matter.

Milton knew that Jim desperately wanted to handle the case on a contingency basis as well. So he kept Jim hanging just long enough to worry the attorney. After about a minute's worth of silence, Milton spoke, "It's a tough call, but I think you should handle it on a contingency basis."

Jim was extremely relieved. "Well that's fine with me." He informed his secretary to print up the standard contingency contract, and after making minor revisions, he provided the Rogers with the contract.

"Here is our standard contract. You both need to sign where indicated."

"Good," said Milton, as he and Brenda reviewed the five-page document before signing where instructed.

Milton was eager to sign the Complaint and get the ball rolling. His next appointment was with the accountant, and he didn't want to be late.

As Milton and Brenda started to rise from their chairs, Jim asked if they could stay a little bit longer, since he had a few more questions to ask them.

"Okay," responded the Rogers. Milton sensed what was coming next.

"How do you feel about publicity? I know you may feel humiliated and somewhat dumbfounded about all this."

"Well we are a little embarrassed of course, but do whatever it takes to get this case won!"

"I understand fully. Now, how about the involvement of the FBI and the US Attorneys' office?"

"Sure, I guess," responded Milton thinking this was exactly what he had hoped for.

"If you say so," said Brenda trying hard not to smile too much. Inwardly she was so excited. Her husband had played Jim perfectly.

"Speaking frankly with you, what Bart Sinclair did to you is criminal, and he should be put away for a long, long time."

"We feel the same. There is no way Bart did not know his diamonds were fake!"

"Good that's settled then. I will personally handle the publicity and the criminal aspect as well."

"Fine," uttered Milton.

"Be prepared for some minor unflattering publicity though."

"Oh, we will," chimed Brenda, as she and Milton moved toward the door.

"We will keep in touch, as this slowly moves through the judicial system," Milton said jokingly.

"Say what you will, it's the best system in the world," replied Jim.

"We know. Thanks, Jim."

"No, thank you."

When the Rogers had left, Jim was euphoric. *This case is going to elevate my reputation and seal my financial security. Thank you Milton Rogers!* he thought.

With a copy of the lawsuit and appraisals in hand, Milton and Brenda met with their accountant less than an hour later.

Will French was the senior partner of his Big Eight accounting firm. He had personally handled the Rogers's tax returns for the past fifteen years. Since April had already passed, the Rogers return was on extension and due August 15. Another extension could be granted for hardship until October 15.

Will was already upset with Milton for not having paid more in estimated taxes on April 15, especially in light of the sale of his publishing empire. *The penalties and interest could be in the millions,* thought Will. Milton, no doubt, would be pissed. Will did not want to incur the wrath of Milton. He had witnessed firsthand Milton's rage regarding previous business transactions gone bad, and he did not want to ever experience that again.

Will nonetheless was pleased to see both Milton and Brenda. Normally, Milton came alone.

"Please sit down. What can I get you? Anything?"

"No, we're fine, Will. You look tired."

"To tell you the truth, I still haven't recovered from April 15, tax day."

"Oh that is right, you *must* be exhausted!

"What have you got there," asked Will.

"Oh, this, well this is why we're here."

"Really? Now you do have my full attention."

"This is a Complaint against Bart Sinclair."

"The diamond jeweler in Palm Beach?" asked Will.

"The same. You see, we purchased a large, a very large, amount of diamonds from him."

"Really? How much?"

"One hundred million dollars' worth."

"You what? Is this some kind of joke? I can't see you spending that kind of money on diamonds." Will was laughing as he spoke.

Brenda interrupted him, "To tell you the truth, it really was my idea. I knew that Milton needed to find a hobby, and I love jewelry. I thought it would be something we could do together."

Will knew that Milton had a wandering eye, and he sensed that it was also a way for Brenda to keep an eye on her man.

"Yes, so I see. But why not start small and work your way up?"

"You know me, Will, I only want the biggest and best, and the same goes for Milton!" said Brenda smiling.

"Understood," replied Will.

"But how does the Complaint tie into your huge income tax liability for last year?"

"You see, the stones we bought were fake."

"Fake?" exclaimed Will. "You've got to be kidding me. All of them?"

"We are dead serious. It shows we were taken for over ninety-five million dollars. All we have left are fakes, worth five million or so."

"My God! What a shame. I'm so sorry for you," said Will sincerely.

"Well, thanks. Now we need to report the forty-five million as a loss for last year and fifty million as a loss for this current year."

"Are you sure it's a complete loss?"

"Unfortunately, yes. And Sinclair is going to fight us for years in court," chimed Brenda.

"I know how litigation can be. We've been involved in a malpractice action for over two years now, and the outrageous attorney's fees now exceed the actual alleged loss."

"So, you can see, we need to take the loss on our income tax return immediately."

"I understand completely. This loss means that you will most likely incur no penalties or interest, and furthermore it will save you thirty-six percent in taxes. I know it's a far cry from one hundred percent, but at least you can find some solace in the fact that it's not a total loss."

"Thanks, Will. But, unfortunately, it doesn't put food on our plate."

"Now Milton, we both know there is not any concern there. Can I keep a copy of this Complaint and appraisal? I would love to take the time to read it thoroughly."

"Sure, I got this copy especially for you."

"Thanks."

"In the next few weeks, we should have your income tax return completed after recalculating your investment loss of forty-five million dollars. If I should encounter any difficulties, I'll just call you. Are you planning on going away in the near future?"

"We will be summering on Martha's Vineyard, as usual, but you know how to reach us there."

"Understood. Well, I wish there was something I could do to help with your loss. Thank goodness you sold the company, or it would have taken years to wipe off that ninety-five-million-dollar loss!"

"I guess we should be happy with that," said Brenda, as she and Milton stood to leave.

"You can say that again."

When Milton and Brenda were back in their Rolls, Milton spoke first, "It is all coming together, my dear. Only one more loose end."

Milton thought to himself by *reporting the loss of forty-five million dollars in the past year we will save almost nineteen million dollars in income taxes. The loss of fifty million dollars this calendar year will save another twenty million dollars in taxes for a total income tax savings of thirty-nine million dollars! Not too shabby!*

Plus, he mentally added that in addition to the income tax savings, they would save an additional $35 million in federal estate taxes ultimately upon his death. *I would bet that Will French would just die if he knew the real truth. Am I a genius or what? And I've never even read the Internal Revenue Code*, he thought.

Back in the office, Will reflected on his day. Milton sure didn't act like a man who had lost ninety-five million dollars. Something didn't seem right. *He intentionally failed to pay his estimated income tax in January, knowing full well that he had suffered an enormous loss. But the appraisals were not completed until May. Curious, very curious! If I didn't know better, I would say that Milton was definitely up to something*, he thought.

Chapter
Thirty-Five

When Paul Schwartz arrived back at his office, sweating profusely from the scorching heat of South Florida, the last person he wanted to see was sitting in his office.

"My dear friend Paul, so nice to see you again," said Victor Butin, as he rose slowly from Paul's personal chair.

"Nice to see you too, Victor," said Paul rather sheepishly.

As soon as Paul had shaken Victor's hand, the door closed behind him, and the two Russian sidekicks stood barring the door.

"I see you've brought reinforcements. Are you afraid of me, Victor?"

"Not in the least. But I am an old man, and I like a sense of security. I'm sure you understand."

"Certainly. So what can I do for you?" asked Paul, as he sat stiffly in his client's chair while staring intensely at Victor, who looked quite comfortable behind the large desk.

"I'm here to check into my investment."

"What investment?"

"My arrangement with Joseph Marx."

"Joe's dead, so I guess you're out of luck." Paul attempted to rise but was forcefully thrown back into his chair by Igor.

"Not so fast, Mr. Attorney. I want to know exactly where my money is."

"Well, Victor, you may be in a bit of a jam—make that a huge *jam.*
You see, your man, Joseph Marx, consigned a large lot of diamonds to Bart Sinclair."

"Tell me something I don't know."

"Okay. Do you also know that Bart Sinclair has been paid and most of the money spent?"

"He what?" shouted Victor. His cheeks immediately rushed to crimson.

"Oh, it's true, all right. I just came from a meeting with the buyer's attorney."

"Do you mean buyer or buyers?"

"Buyer. A husband and wife bought all the stones."

"That's incredible! I can't believe it."

"Well, it was true."

"What do you mean, it was?" asked Victor, curious about Paul's use of the past tense.

"Victor, the buyers now allege the diamonds are all fakes."

"Nonsense. I know for a fact they were all flawless. How dare you insult me that way!"

"That's exactly what Bart Sinclair said as well. Unfortunately, two separate appraisers have appraised the gems and have concluded they are all fakes—beautiful fakes, yet fakes nonetheless. Here, take a look," said Paul as he handed his only appraisal copies to Victor. Victor's hands were shaking as he reviewed the appraisals. After a few minutes of silence, he asked, "So where's my money?"

"I believe you'll have to figure that out on your own. The papers that I saw showed that Bart wire transferred A Trading Co. LLC, Joe's own company, fifty million dollars."

"You're kidding me? So what you're telling me is that Bart paid Joe the money already. I thought the deal would conclude around Easter."

"You were misinformed."

"And now Joe's dead."

"Looks that way."

"So where's the money now?"

"Hell if I know, Victor, but I figure it is still in the A Trading Co. account." Paul knew very well that the bulk of the money was in Joe's irrevocable trust, but he was not about to tell Victor that! At least not yet!

"Did Joe leave a will?"

"Yes, I believe he did."

"Damn. Who did he leave his assets to?"

"I believe he left them to Bart's children."

"His kids? He doesn't even know them, does he?"

"I don't know about that, but I am pretty sure they are who he left everything to," said Paul, nodding his head and becoming more comfortable by the minute.

"Well then, who is in charge of the estate?"

"A local Palm Beach attorney by the name of Bo Martin."

"Never heard of him," Victor lied.

"He's a nice guy, honest, and well liked."

"I am sure he is. Well, I guess we need to pay him a visit next."

"I think that you should. That's a wise idea."

"You're not lying to me about the money, are you, Paul? You do know what happens to people who lie to me."

"I swear on my wife's life; I am telling you the truth. But, Victor if what the buyer is claiming is true, then there is going to be a lot of negative publicity. If the FBI gets involved and can trace the gems to you, you could be implicated." Paul was telling the truth, and he could see the look of concern flashing across Victor's face.

"I know for a fact the gems were real! I know now that they were sold. I have been informed by you that the money was wired to A Trading Co. in January, and the amount wired was fifty million dollars! Correct? What more do I need to know?"

"Well, would you testify on Bart's behalf, as to the authenticity of the diamonds?"

"Hell no! All I want is my money. Got that?"

"So, you're not going to help Bart?"

"And what, risk facing the FBI, a lying no-good federal prosecutor, a federal judge, and the possibility of prison? I am a businessman. All I want is my money. That's it. Now, please leave. I have to make a few phone calls."

"But Victor, this is *my* office!" whined Paul.

"Out!" shouted Victor. Slowly Paul did as he was asked. It was an easy decision with the two Russians staring down at him. They snickered, as Paul walked past them out the door of his own office.

Victor immediately phoned Marty at the West Palm Beach warehouse.

Fifteen minutes later, Victor received confirmation that $50 million had indeed been wire transferred to A Trading Co. from Bart Sinclair's Diamond and Sons Inc. in January. For some reason this wire transfer had never been disclosed to either Victor or Marty.

A somewhat relieved Victor sat behind the large desk. He was smiling as he joked with the two large Russians. He waited again for a second call from Marty.

Unfortunately, the second call jolted his world.

"You what?" shouted Victor.

"I can't tell you where the money went," said Marty.

"How come?"

"It appears that the money went to some company in Panama."

"How soon will you be able to determine where it went?"

"Victor, I will have to visit both the Isle of Man and Panama. It will also cost a substantial amount of cash to access the privileged information."

"Whatever it takes, just do it. And find John Spears, the vice-president of the Bank of England in the Isle of Man. I paid him too much money to keep me advised on anything to do with that account!"

"Okay."

Paul watched from his lobby as Victor and his two friends exited his office.

"Oh, Victor, can I have my office back now?"

Victor shot him a look that could kill, as he spoke, "Sure, but I will be keeping an eye on you. My friends here will also."

Chapter
Thirty-Six

When Bart returned to his Palm Beach home, all he wanted was a stiff drink. He was still reeling from the shock of earlier today when he and Paul Schwartz had met with Jim McDonald.

"How could the gems be fake? I had checked them all myself. Am I losing my mind? Can they really create clear fake unblemished diamonds? Did Joseph Marx double-cross me? But why?" he said to himself. Nothing made sense to him anymore.

Fortunately for Bart, Dana was out with the kids. He was all alone. Thank goodness! As he poured himself yet another drink, a black STS Cadillac appeared in the driveway. "Now who could that be?" Bart asked himself?

When he answered the door, he saw an elderly but immaculately dressed gentleman.

"Hello Bart, my name is Victor."

"Victor, yes I believe we have met briefly once or twice before." No sooner had Bart extended his hand to Victor when the two Russians grabbed him and threw him back into the marble tiled foyer.

"Why don't you make yourselves at home," said Bart, trying to calm his nerves and straighten out his shirt.

"I believe we will. Is there a room where we could talk?"

"Absolutely. I'll lead the way."

Victor observed all the beautiful pieces of art and furniture and was immediately impressed with Bart's interior decorating style.

"You have excellent taste, Mr. Sinclair."

"Well, thank you. And how can I help you."

"I want my money. It's as simple as that."

"What money are you talking about? I don't owe you a penny."

"My friend, can I call you my friend?"

Bart shot Victor a questionable look, "Sure, why not."

"I don't believe that you have my money. But Joseph Marx certainly does."

"Now listen here, Victor, I have known Joe Marx for a good many years. He never cheated me once in all that time. I recently paid him fifty million dollars for his lot of diamonds. Now you can come to my office on Monday and see for yourself the account where I wire transferred his money. I have no knowledge where that money is now."

"That's too bad, isn't it?" replied Victor.

"For you maybe, but not for me. I have my own serious problems." The stiff drinks had begun to reduce Bart's inhibitions, and he soon took offense.

"Victor, would you like a drink?"

"Sure. Vodka, Tito's if you have it."

"No problem. How 'bout your two pals over there?"

"They'll have vodka as well."

Once Bart had poured and delivered their drinks, he sat in the study's leather sofa.

"Let me tell you about the gems."

"Sure, I'd like to know the full story," declared Victor.

"As you may not know, I bought over eighty percent of my gems through Joseph Marx. Joe mentioned your name a few times, so I guessed that you were his supplier. In all actuality, I never really cared who the hell his supplier was."

"All I knew was that he sold me gems that I desired at a cost that was significantly reduced. He also provided me the gems on consignment. I always paid Joe punctually after the sale of any gem, and I either wrote a check payable to A Trading Co. Inc. or I wire transferred the money to A Trading Co. Inc. Joe never asked for any paper work, and everything we did was basically on a handshake.

"I trusted Joe implicitly. He was like a father to me. Hell, he even lived in my North Palm Beach condo and drove my company Lincoln. He never told me much about his personal life, except that he was once married. He never spoke about any family members, and I never really broached the subject. He was also good to all my kids and my current wife and even my ex-wives, for that matter.

"I know he had to be wealthy because hell, he made me and my father very wealthy. Through your stones, I presume, I am able to keep a fairly low overhead, even for Palm Beach. I sell top-quality jewelry at very reasonable prices. Tiffany, Hamilton and Bailey, Banks and Biddle all hate me because I sell superior merchandise for less. It's as simple as that!"

"Tell me something I don't know."

"Okay. Are you ready? One of my wealthy clients recently sold his publishing empire. His name is Milton Rogers, and his insane wife is Brenda. They were regulars in my store. Always looking, always asking questions— always too nosy for their own damn good. Come to think of it, it was like they were casing my store, me, and all my employees for months.

"Finally, out of the blue, he informs me he wants to spend one hundred million dollars on pure cut diamonds, starting at one carat and increasing up to twenty carats. I called Joe immediately, and then I guess he called you."

"Go on," replied Victor.

"Well, the gems that Joe provided me were flawless. I mean absolutely perfect. The Rogers were thrilled. In November, I got paid fifty million, and in January, I received the additional fifty million. After delivery of all the diamonds to the Rogers and the last payment, I then paid Joe his fifty million dollars.

"I personally had the stones set according to illustrations provided to me by Milton Rogers. The designs were hideous, and right before Valentine's Day, a crying and distraught Brenda Rogers asked me to disassemble the pieces and give her the loose individual diamonds. She said her children would independently come to me to have them reset."

"Did the kids ever come back?"

"No, not yet."

"Okay, then what?"

"After Valentine's Day, I took my family on a long fishing vacation. We had a great time. When I returned, I learned that Joe had died of a heart attack in Budapest."

"Did he tell you he was going on a vacation?"

"No, but then again, he didn't really tell me anything."

"Then what?"

"He had made a will and left it in my safe, and I gave it to Bo Martin, and he is now probating the will."

"How much money is in his estate?"

"Funny you should ask. I, myself, thought there would be millions. So far, Bo has found very little."

"What about A Trading Co?"

"Well, Bo informed me there was no longer an account in the Isle of Man. Furthermore, there was also no account over there in Joe's own name." Bart vowed there was no way he was going to spill the beans about the trust, so he left it at that.

"Who are the beneficiaries of the will?"

"My kids. Can you believe that?"

"Miracles never cease," said Victor sarcastically.

"And that is all I know concerning Joe."

"You don't say."

By now Bart had finished his drink, and he got up and poured everyone another round. He needed another shot to help his confidence. Feeling somewhat inebriated, he asked, "Victor, I need your help."

"Me? How?"

"Well, I am probably going to be sued by Milton and Brenda Rogers."

"Why?"

"They say the gems I sold them—your gems—were fakes. I have gemology degrees and licenses and also a masterful eye. I know for a fact the diamonds were real."

"So what's the problem?"

"I have read the appraisers' reports. According to the reports, the fakes are worth five million dollars. These fakes are truly unbelievable. I know of no company or entity that manufactures clear, super clear perfect synthetic diamonds."

Victor thought about what Bart had just said before responding. "So what you're telling me is that you didn't sell them fakes because you don't even know where to purchase that high quality of fake diamonds?" asked Victor incredulously.

"Exactly," Bart replied, realizing that for an elderly man, Victor was sharp as a tack.

"Why can't you just show them what you paid by the invoices?"

"Because Joe is dead, and we have no paper work. I can't prove otherwise. I can only demonstrate that I couldn't provide them fakes because these fakes are too perfect."

"That is a bullshit argument, my comrade. Listen to yourself. You are trying to prove a negative with another negative. Your case is an uphill battle, even for a greedy American like yourself."

"That is why I need your help."

"I'm sorry but I can't help you."

"Why not?" asked Bart incredulously.

"Because my family has many enemies and many secrets. I can never divulge where I acquired the stones."

"Why not?" asked Bart, now trembling with fear.

"Because it would put me in a great deal of danger. I am not a young man. All I want and need at this stage in my life is my money. With it, I will live out my life in peace and security."

"So you won't sign an affidavit?"

"Hell no! Listen, Bart, you seem to be a nice guy. I believe you trusted Joe, and I understand that he made you a wealthy man. But unfortunately, I can't help you. I'm sorry."

Victor and his two goons stood to leave.

"You don't need to escort us out. We know the way. Good luck, my friend."

When they were gone, Bart stood and looked out over the Intracoastal Waterway at his yacht and powerboats. He noticed his hands were shaking. "Please God, let this lawsuit go away," he prayed. Moments later Bart was relieved when he saw his lovely wife, Dana. He hugged her and the kids as soon as they came through the garage door.

Chapter
Thirty-Seven

Jim McDonald was enjoying his pecan-encrusted yellowtail snapper while engrossed in a discussion with Steve Fleishman, the assistant US attorney, and Mae McReynoldsof the *Palm Beach Times*. They were at the highly fashionable Charley's Crab Restaurant in Palm Beach. Opus One was on the table, and the expensive wine was flowing freely. All three individuals were having a wonderful time, and better yet, it was all free, courtesy of Milton Rogers, of course.

After they had devoured their succulent entrees, but before the desserts and coffee had arrived, Jim handed Joe and Mae copies of the six-inch-thick Complaint, along with the attachments and appraisals. In addition, he handed Joe a detailed list of the names and addresses of all of Bart Sinclair's employees. Joe also received a list of Bart's main jewelry competitors. It was worth noting that all the competitors were extremely jealous of Bart's success.

Jim then handed Mae copies of all previous lawsuits filed against Bart Sinclair and his company, Diamond and Sons Inc., as well as stories that Milton had compiled regarding the deaths of Bart's parents and his first two wives.

Finally, and most importantly, each received a plain manila envelope containing thousands of dollars. Twenty thousand dollars each to be exact. Steve attempted to thumb through the stack of hundreds while Mae calmly slipped her envelope into her purse.

"For Christ's sake, Steve, there is twenty thousand dollars in there. Trust me."

"Oh, I do."

"Then why are you counting the money?"

"It's just so much money and it is all mine. You know the government doesn't pay us squat, and with my house, cars, and the kids' school payments, this money will really come in handy."

"Well get yourself under control there, Steve, and just remember there's lots more where that came from."

Jim had their full attention now, and he proceeded to fill them in on the entire story, focusing on the main points of the lawsuit before concluding what their own future respective parts would be in this matter.

By the time the desserts were picked over and the Opus One was all but finished, Steve and Mae knew their upcoming roles.

Mae was going to write and publish on the front page of the *Palm Beach Times* (preferably the headline) about the largest jewelry fraud case in the world. She was also going to include all the previous lawsuits Bart Sinclair had been involved in and other negative information extremely detrimental to Bart. In addition, the article would also detail all of Milton and Brenda Rogers's wonderful attributes and their philanthropic endeavors.

Based on the soon-to-be-published newspaper article by Mae, Steve would then institute an immediate federal investigation of Bart Sinclair. Also, an IRS audit would be started as well.

At the end of their dinner, all three toasted Milton Rogers, and that they all would definitely keep in touch. They all knew that Bart Sinclair's life, as he knew it, was going to drastically change—for the worse.

Chapter
Thirty-Eight

Milton was attending to the final stage of his master plan. He had just flown overseas and was now sitting in the plush office of his dear friend, Jean Valhomme overlooking the entire City of Antwerp, Belgium.

Milton and Jean went back many years. Jean's wife, Elle, was once an aspiring young writer, who at her husband's urging, came to Milton to be published. Milton was just beginning to build his publishing empire, and he took a chance with the beautiful young woman. Elle Valhomme's first book was an enormous success, and Jean was ecstatic. Over the next two decades, Elle went on to write many more novels. Unfortunately, none ever attained the commercial success of her initial book. But Milton continued to publish and promote her books, nonetheless.

Jean truly appreciated and admired Milton's devotion to Elle. Jean in the interim, had begun his own empire, focusing on the illegal drug trade. He started off manufacturing LSD in small abandoned warehouses. As his business grew and the money mushroomed, he became more and more sophisticated in not only the manufacturing of illicit drugs, but also in the actual distribution of the narcotics. He also started legitimate businesses as well, using his ill-gotten spoils in an effort to diversify and keep the government officials off his back.

At one pointb about ten years ago, Jean needed to launder his vast sums of cash. He approached Milton, and together the two men mutually benefitted. It was relatively easy for Milton to launder the cash among his extensive publishing empire, and in return, provide Jean clean and laundered sub-companies with large bank accounts.

Over the recent years, the two men's lives drifted apart. Jean had mostly become legitimate, and he had learned and adopted all the most sophisticated money-laundering techniques. Milton had less and less use for Jean's cash deposits, and Elle had pretty much quit writing altogether. Nevertheless, the two men had remained loyal friends.

When Milton had called Jean, out of the blue to inform him that he was flying into Antwerp, Jean suspected something was up.

Now, as Jean sat behind his mammoth desk, he listened to Milton talk pleasantries. Jean knew that Milton was not one to mince words and soon would get to the true purpose of his visit.

"Well, enough about the past and my family. You are probably wondering why I'm here."

"The thought did cross my mind," replied Jean, smiling.

"I know that you are still involved in numerous business enterprises, most of them legal now, of course."

"Absolutely."

"What I have in mind is something, let's say on the dark side."

"Exactly what do you have in mind, Milton?"

"Look, Jean, I read the papers, and I study trends."

"Go on."

"I am here to discuss the drug, Ecstasy."

"Ecstasy? With you retired and sitting on a publishing fortune, why would you be interested in Ecstasy?"

"Look, Jean, I'm not wired, and I'm not a confidential informant. Yes, we both know that I am a very wealthy man, but let's just say I am getting a little bored, and besides, you know how much money Brenda and the boys spend. Shit at the rate they go through it, I will be a pauper in no time! I need your help, and I believe you can assist me and my family and in return make a very nice profit for yourself."

"Ecstasy—also known as MDMA (methylenedioxymetha amphetamine)—is a stimulant with hallucinogenic properties, which can cause anxiety, dehydration insomnia, and brain damage. It is mostly manufactured here in Belgium. In America it has become the most popular social drug. One pill can last four to five hours. It creates a euphoria that produces a sense of love and a feeling of love for others. It is an extremely emotional drug, which greatly heightens your senses and makes one sensitive to the touch," spouted Milton from memory.

"In America its use is prevalent among the teenagers and young adults in their twenties, and it can be found at just about any dance party. I believe the kids call them raves.

"Prices per tablet can run anywhere from twenty-five to forty dollars. The pills come in many colors and shapes and are sometimes referred to as 'Lucky Charms,' like the breakfast cereal with its multicolored marshmallow treats."

When Milton had finished his lengthy dialogue, Jean spoke next.

"That's pretty good. Thanks for the education. Now I know what Ecstasy is! But if you don't mind, I really should get back to business," said Jean, rising from his seat.

"Dammit, Jean, I am serious here. I have a huge deal for you."

"Okay, okay, Milton, I'm listening."

"My boys have created an offshore corporation in the Bahamas called 'The 4 L's.' In the corporation are perfect, uncut, brilliant diamonds with a street value of over one hundred fifty million dollars."

"You're kidding me, right?" laughed Jean.

"No, no, Jean, I am not kidding!"

"Are they stones or pieces of expensive jewelry?"

"They are stones and extremely easy to fence. No more problems with having to launder your excess cash."

"Go on." It was clear that Jean was interested, and he leaned forward to listen to Milton's every word.

"Plus, the stones are not hot. They were bought and paid for by me and my wife. There will be no trail to them and no federal heat regarding their ultimate sale."

"I'm listening, please continue."

"I would like to trade you the diamonds for the pills. And to make the deal sweeter for you, I will reduce the value of the gems to exactly what I paid for them one hundred twenty-five million dollars. That's a profit of twenty-five million for you, right off the bat."

"Milton that's a lot of pills."

"I realize that, but I feel that you could handle it."

"Thanks for the confidence, but as you know, I have been out of that business for quite a while."

"Like I said," replied Milton, "I feel you are up to the task!"

"Okay, so just say I am in. How where you thinking about them being delivered?"

"Well, Jean, you are a little bit more experienced in the shipping of this kind of merchandise, so I will let you decide the safest path to take, but I would like the ultimate delivery of the pills to be Palm Beach."

"Once the pills are delivered to you, then what happens from there?"

"Oh that's for me and my boys to handle."

"Milton, just because the shipment is delivered safely, doesn't mean all is good! Are all the kids clean?"

"Yes, no major arrests, and they and their wives are very involved in the Palm Beach community and the church."

"Well that is a good start, but are they street-smart? The last thing we all want is a deal gone bad because of their stupidity."

"I get your drift. But don't you see that the diamonds make this super clean? No money to launder. No invoices or bills of lading. Just a simple delivery to Palm Beach!"

"A single delivery of over fifty million pills?" Jean extorted. "My ass this is simple. It will be the largest shipment ever."

"Fine, then increase your bulk rate per pill by fifty cents."

Jean's eyes lit up. "Why, you are so right Milton, my going rate is two dollars per pill, but because of the high risk involved with you and your neophyte sons, the cost per pill will be two fifty to you, my friend."

"That's fine with me," replied Milton, not willing to haggle over any price.

"Not so fast," countered Jean. "The value of your stones will be counted as only one hundred million dollars. Plus, I want my jewelry expert to inspect your gems beforehand."

"You drive a hard bargain," protested Milton. "However, I believe that I can live with that."

"Where or when can I see the gems?"

"I had them federal expressed to your office. They should be here after lunch," replied Milton.

"What! You are a crazy son a bitch, Milton. You had over one hundred million dollars' worth of diamonds Fed Expressed! What did they say when you told them how much you wanted to insure the package for?" cautioned Jean.

"Come on," said Milton. "All this talk had made me hungry; let's go grab a nice bite to eat."

The two men left the office with Jean still shaking his head over the Fed Ex package. When the two men had returned from lunch, sure enough the Fed Ex parcel was already waiting for them. It was packaged as a bag of marbles, but inside among the marbles were the diamonds.

"You are really something, Milton," smiled Jean.

"Let's meet with your jeweler, now."

After a few phone calls, the two men were soon traveling in Jean's Mercedes toward the jewelry district. Jean was packing heat just in case there was a problem, and Milton appeared as calm as ever but was starting to drag, a little bit by the long flight and new time zone.

The outside of the store was nondescript and plain. Once inside, Milton was not about to let the stones out of his sight, so he sat in the back room with the older, bespectacled jeweler and watched as he began his inspection. Jean placed several calls on his cell phone while pacing out in the front room. His gun was safely tucked into his back belt loop. His mind was reeling. Could he manufacture that many pills? Yes. Could he deliver them to Florida? Yes. Could he sell the gems? Hopefully. He would soon know.

About an hour later, the jeweler had completed his appraisal of the gems. He began by commenting that the gems were all real and that they were all of superior quality.

Both Milton and Jean now sat in silence. Based on the jeweler's own personal evaluation, the stones were worth in excess of one hundred twenty million dollars' retail value.

Jean interrupted the jeweler when he asked, "How much could I sell them for wholesale?"

The jeweler replied, "You would need to sell these stones in many parcels. No jewelry store could purchase them all. You could use an intermediary that I know of, and he would most likely pay no more than one hundred million dollars. Plus if they are stolen, the price could go down substantially."

"The gems are not stolen," piped Milton. "They are mine. Bought and paid for."

"I see. Well in that case, I believe that you, Jean, could get one hundred million dollars for the entire collection from a single intermediary. You may get more if you shopped them around, but I wouldn't take that route if I were you."

Jean felt pretty confident, and of course, Milton was beaming. Later, as the two men drove back to Jean's office, they negotiated their deal.

The gems would remain in Antwerp, Belgium in a designated place. Only Milton would have the combination to its safe. Upon the successful delivery of the Ecstasy pills to Palm Beach, Milton would provide Jean the combination.

Jean naturally wanted to keep the stones in his possession, but he trusted Milton enough to go along with the deal, although he certainly was not thrilled with their arrangement.

Jean figured out in his head that his cost for manufacturing each pill, including shipping and overhead, was about one dollar. In essence, he was betting fifty million dollars that Milton was an honest man.

As Milton sat back in his plush first-class seat on his return flight to the States, he was extremely content. Not only was he able to unload the gems, but he also was in a position to quadruple his money. He had already made arrangements with several distributors to buy the Ecstasy tablets for upwards of ten dollars per pill.

If everything went according to plan, each son would soon be worth over $100 million tax free. Milton would never have to worry about their lazy asses again.

Milton and Jean figured it would take six to eight weeks for the delivery, more than enough time to finalize all the arrangements and to deal with his knucklehead sons. After his meeting with Jean, and before catching his return flight back, Milton visited several young maidens in an Antwerp brothel. He shut his eyes, and a large smile emerged. *Life is good*, thought Milton. Life was very good!

Chapter
Thirty-Nine

The main headline of the *Palm Beach Times* read: "Palm Beach jeweler sells fake gems." There was no use of the word "alleged" anywhere in the article. Every paragraph ripped Bart Sinclair apart and led the reader to believe that Bart was nothing but a lying, cheating, womanizing fraud. The article was simply devastating. Worse still, the photographs of Bart, his store, and his family were atrocious. The pictures even made him look guilty. The final paragraphs of the article also contained glowing words of praise for Milton and Brenda Rogers. *I couldn't have written a better article myself,* Milton thought as he put down the paper and called his attorney, Jim McDonald.

"Jim here."

"Hi, Milton. What you think?"

"I love it. I absolutely love it."

"There's more to come. I've been on the phone already with Steve Fleishman, and the FBI have assembled a team of four investigators. Steve also talked with the US district attorney, and he now has the green light to go after Bart. Better yet by the end of the week, the IRS will also come knocking."

"I owe it all to you, Jim."

"Well, the fees are going to be huge. I am thinking about hiring two private investigators. They are former FBI agents, and I want to immediately start tracing Bart's assets. Once we get a judgment, we will need to attach the assets before the government steps in."

"Anything you say, Jim. Oh, and can you tell Mae that she is the best?"

"I'll pass it on."

"Good. Well, Jim, keep me informed."

"Always."

When he hung up, Milton fretted about his upcoming dinner with the kids. He hated the idea of having their spouses in the know but realized it was best if everyone was on the same page. *One disgruntled wife could spoil all the cards*, thought Milton.

When Bart Sinclair read the headlines, he felt the ground fall from beneath his feet. Virtually, the entire front page and all of page six vehemently attacked him. It was devastating and worse than any *National Enquirer* article. He would sue. Damn Mae McReynolds, damn Milton and Brenda Rogers, and everybody else! "I'll see you all in court!" he shouted throwing the paper against the wall.

Bart's wife, Dana, sobbed after reading the article for a second time.

"My God, Bart. It makes you worse than Jack the Ripper and Bernie Madoff, combined. You and I both know you've made mistakes in the past, but this is vicious. What will our friends think? What about your business? Our poor kids! Our lives are ruined!" said Dana, crying hysterically.

"Now, now Dana, everything is going to be okay. I promise you," said Bart trying to control his young wife and sound convincing. It was a hard sell.

Dana with tears streaming down her red-flushed face asked, "Bart, did you sell them fake diamonds?"

"On our kids' lives, I swear to you I only sold the Rogers real diamonds."

"Don't you lie to me! Not now and not about this," said Dana sternly, slowly trying to compose herself.

"I'm not lying. I swear, honey."

"Well, the kids are not going to school Monday, and I'm not venturing out in public either. It's your problem, now you handle it!"

Bart was on the phone moments later to his attorney, Paul Schwartz. Bart's head was spinning, he had a serious headache, and it wasn't even 7:30 a.m. yet.

"Paul, what the hell is going on?"

"Bart, we are going to sue the *Palm Beach Times*. We are going to sue Jim McDonald and also that piece of shit writer, Mae McReynolds."

"Paul, how can they print this trash? What happened to being innocent until proven guilty? She makes it seem that I am a criminal."

"You are not a criminal, and we will win this case."

"Now what do I do?" whined Bart.

"You just hold your head high and act like you did nothing wrong. You got that? Act as if nothing ever happened."

"Easy for you to say. One million people didn't just read about you and your supposed criminal acts!"

"Hang in there, my friend. Just take it day by day," said Paul in closing. "Keep in touch."

"I most certainly will."

Meanwhile, Bo Martin couldn't stop shaking. He had read the article three times. He had known about Bart's past history because Hank had personally investigated him. What he couldn't understand is why he got him involved.

When Ruby saw Bo sitting at the kitchen table in his board shorts looking sheepishly white, she asked, "Is something wrong, honey?"

"You could say that," answered Bo. "Here, read this," he said, as he handed the newspaper to Ruby.

When Ruby had finished, she looked up at Bo.

"My God! Is this true? He is such a scumbag. And to think that I thought he was an honest and successful businessman. Thank goodness you had nothing to do with him. Right, dear?"

Bo didn't answer. He didn't even look at her. He couldn't.

"Honey, tell me you didn't have anything to do with Bart Sinclair. Please, tell me no."

Bo again said nothing and just shook his head.

"Oh my God! Does this have anything to do with our trip to Grand Cayman?"

By this time, Bo couldn't even look up. He was still staring at the ground.

"It does. Oh my God. You're going to go to jail, aren't you? Tell me, dammit," Ruby screamed hysterically.

Bo stood up and attempted to give Ruby a hug.

"I'm not going to jail. I have done nothing wrong. At least I think I've done nothing wrong."

"You think! I believe you had better be more convincing than that, Mr. Hotshot Attorney!"

"Look Ruby. This is just a civil lawsuit between two super wealthy men."

"Yes, but now the FBI and the IRS and the Justice Department are looking into it. That's a heck of a lot of people. Where there's smoke, there's fire. That's what my dad used to spout."

"I know what the article says, but you can't believe everything you read," said Bo rather unconvincingly.

"Well, it's pretty clear to me that he sold these people one hundred million dollars' worth of fake diamonds!"

"There are two sides to every story. Trust me." With that said, Bo took the two red dogs and headed off to the beach.

Bo couldn't wait to go for a run and think clearly for himself. He was really scared, but what did he really know?

First off, Joseph Marx was his client. Joe had created a trust for the benefit of Bart and his family. Joe then funded the trust with shares of stock in a company called A Trading Co. The trust owned 100 percent of the outstanding shares of the company, and the company bank account contained over $50 million. Bo was the sole trustee, and his fiduciary duty was to Bart and his family.

Second, do I have a duty to find out the source of the money? thought Bo.

Must I even ask? Bo figured the answer to both of these questions was a resounding no!

Third, was the money in the account a result of the jewelry fraud I had just read about?

Fourth and final, is Bart Sinclair a crook? Once gain Bo was clueless. The one troubling feature that kept concerning Bo was that ignorance of the law is not a defense.

When Bo had finished his run and he and the dogs had rinsed off in the pool, Bo figured he must speak to Bart Sinclair personally.

Chapter

Forty

Victor Butin was enraged when he finished reading the article from his penthouse balcony at the Breakers overlooking the Atlantic Ocean.

"That son of a bitch Marx! How could he be involved with that two-bit fake punk Bart Sinclair?" ranted Victor.

Based solely on the article, Bart was already tried and convicted. Victor realized that Bart's business was now destined to fail. Also once the federal government became involved, then Bart would face racketeering, conspiracy, mail fraud, and money laundering charges. It was only a matter of time before the federal net would completely ensnare Bart Sinclair.

What Victor didn't want happening was any mention of Joseph Marx and his $50 million. If the government or even Milton Rogers became aware of the diamond payment transfer, then the US government would undoubtedly attempt to freeze the account wherever it was located.

Victor realized his only chance was to beat the Feds to the money. The funds had to be somewhere in Panama.

Victor called his underling, Marty.

"Marty, have you found anything out yet."

"Well after paying off several people, I've determined that the money from A Trading Co. Inc. in the Isle of Man, was transferred to the Panamanian National Bank and to a company called AA Trading Co. Inc. From what I have gathered, the president and sole shareholder of that account was Joseph Marx. The address used was Joe's North Palm Beach, Florida, condominium."

"Excellent news. Excellent work." It was rare for Victor to give compliments.

"Well, not so fast," quipped Marty.

"What do you mean?"

"The Panamanian account was cleaned out over two months ago by Joe."

"It what? God damn him. So where the hell is the money now?"

"I honestly have no idea, Victor. I have approached three of the Panamanian banks' officers, and not one of them could be bought off. Without an insider's help, I'm afraid I can't do anything further."

"Don't you worry. I'm sending Igor and Ivan down to Panama to join you. As you are well aware, I will use whatever means it takes to uncover that information."

"Sure, Victor. Well, do I dare ask how things are there in Florida?"

"Terrible," replied Victor. "The press reported today that Bart Sinclair sold fake diamonds totaling one hundred million dollars to some Palm Beacher, who is now suing Bart."

Marty was quick to speak. "That doesn't make sense, Victor. I know the gems we delivered to Joe were real. I also know that the same gems were sold to the Rogers. That means only two things: either Bart switched the real gems with fakes or the Rogers switched the stones themselves and are lying about the genuineness of the stones."

Victor paused for a moment. "You may have something there, Marty. All morning I thought it was Bart Sinclair, and now maybe you're right. It could be the Rogers who are the crooks. Isn't that interesting?"

"Well, what's important now is that we trace where the money went. We have to locate it before the US government attempts to freeze the funds."

"Act quickly, my friend."

"Will do, Victor."

"Let me know the instant you find anything out."

Chapter
Forty-One

All morning long, Bo's mind was preoccupied with the newspaper article and Bart Sinclair. Ruby was livid, and Bo was extremely worried. Fortunately, Hank had called, and the two of them made plans to meet for lunch.

At the small Italian hotspot called Amici's, they were escorted to a table toward the back of the already cramped restaurant.

"Thanks for coming Hank."

"My pleasure. So, what do you think?" Hank wasn't one to mince words. "Do you believe the money in the trust represents the proceeds from the Rogers sale?"

"Without a doubt," replied Bo.

"That's what I thought. So if the answer is yes, do you have to go to the authorities?"

"I don't have a clue," responded Bo, honestly.

"Well, since you don't know for sure, why don't you do nothing? Hang tight and see how this pans out."

"Easy for you to say," replied Bo.

"That's why you get paid the big bucks and can afford to take your poor friend out to lunch."

"Very funny."

"Well, I have the diamond from the estate with me," said Bo.

"You do?"

"Yes. Let's go see if it is real."

"That's a great idea."

The two men didn't even finish their pasta dishes when Bo paid the tab leaving a generous tip, and off they went to visit another jeweler friend in Palm Beach.

After waiting nearly thirty minutes for the jeweler to become available, the large heavy-set man sat down and closely examined the diamond. He handed it back to Bo before speaking.

"What do you want to know?" he asked as he took off his black-horned rimmed magnifying glasses to rub his eyes.

"Is it real?" asked Bo.

"Of course it is real. It is also extremely rare and exquisite."

"How much is it worth?" questioned Hank.

"Well if you were to sell it retail, the stone is worth in excess of four million dollars. If I were to buy it, I wouldn't offer you over two million dollars."

What a relief, thought Bo. Hank could see from the look on Bo's face that he was extremely pleased.

"Tell me what I owe you," asked Bo taking out his wallet.

"Nothing, Bo. Just next time you get some estate jewelry to sell, please think of me first. Although I do suppose my business will be picking up after the Sinclair scandal. Can you believe it?"

"I'm sure it will be," mumbled Bo, sheepishly, "but I absolutely will keep you in mind, and thank you so much for your time."

"My pleasure."

When the two men had left the store, Bo felt much more at ease.

"Now what do you think?" asked Bo.

"Well, based on the jeweler's cursory appraisal, I feel that the diamonds were real and that Joe sold Bart the real goods. Therefore, the money in the trust represents proceeds from the legit sale of the diamonds, the real diamonds, and I don't see any fraud or any crime."

"That's great."

"So, what do you think Bart did? Do you believe he sold Milton Rogers fake gems and pocketed the money?"

"As I told Ruby this morning, I have no idea at all. It's really just another fight in civil court between two really rich men!"

Chapter
Forty-Two

If only it were that simple. Steve Fleishman had already met with Milton and Brenda Rogers and had taken their videotaped statements at the federal building. A jewelry appraiser hired by the US Attorneys' office was inspecting the fake gems, and four FBI agents were assigned to the case. This was an incredible amount of manpower assembled for what appeared to be a mostly civil matter.

The IRS had already called Ross Brown, and an income tax audit investigation was being initiated for the preceding three tax years against Bart Sinclair individually and Diamond and Sons Inc. Ross was dumbfounded. He had never seen such incredibly swift action by the IRS. He realized that someone with a lot of power was pulling their strings.

To make matters even worse, the State of Florida Department of Revenue had requested additional sales tax information and had decided to request an additional two years of sale invoices. Ross Brown would be quite occupied with Bart Sinclair's income tax and sales tax problems for the next sixty days. He figured he'd hit Bart up for at least a $250,000 advance. He certainly didn't want Bart to claim poverty and an inability to pay. Ross himself was beginning to have doubts about his own client.

In less than two weeks' time the federal grand jury, based solely on Milton and Brenda Rogers testimony and their supporting documentation, found reasonable cause to indict Bart Sinclair on racketeering, conspiracy, mail fraud, wire fraud, money laundering, and obstruction of justice charges. All told, Bart Sinclair was facing over one hundred sixty years in prison.

The sign at Diamond and Sons read "Closed for Inventory Purposes," but Bo knew better. Bo hadn't slept well at all since the first article had appeared. The second article announcing the indictment had also made headlines and had run the same atrocious pictures. Bo didn't blame Bart for closing the store. Hell, the man was facing life in prison. He should be home with his family.

As Bo was peering inside the blackened store window, as he walked to lunch along Worth Avenue, Bart Sinclair, who happened to be sitting inside by a mirror, saw Bo's reflection and came rushing to the door.

"Don't go, Bo. Please come in. I'm ah, ah, doing the inventory."

"I'm really sorry about everything, Bart. If there's anything I can do, please just ask. Ruby and I have wanted to call or come over, but we thought we would give you time with your family to figure things out."

"I understand completely. It's been a real trying couple of weeks."

"If it helps any, Ruby and I are behind you all the way. If you need anything, let me know."

"Since you offered Bo, tell me how is the trust?"

"The market, although it has been very volatile, has stayed about even. All the trust money is invested and waiting for me to make an income distribution to you and your family."

"That's good," said Bart and nodded. "I haven't told anyone about the trust, and I just wanted to make sure it was in good hands."

"Well, rest assured, this is one thing that you don't have to worry about."

"Thank you, Bo. I'll call if and when I need it."

"Okay, and Bart, good luck, and hang in there."

"Thanks, I really do appreciate it, but I think I am going to need a lot more than luck!"

As Bo was leaving, he stopped and debated before asking another question. He couldn't hold it in anymore and needed to know the truth.

"Bart, let me come right out and ask, did you sell the Rogers fake jewelry?"

"I swear to you on my children's lives that those diamonds were real. I did not sell them anything fake. Trust me, Bo."

Bo, looking Bart straight in the eye, said "One more question then."

"Did you purchase all your diamonds from Joseph Marx?"

"Yes. Yes, I did."

"Where did he get them from?"

"A Russian by the name of Victor Butin, I believe."

"I see. And you swear to me that everything was legitimate?"

"Bo, Joe sold me the diamonds for much less than I could get them anywhere else. They were most definitely real. Never in my life have I sold a fake stone. I'm making too much money. Why on earth would I get greedy all of a sudden?" I have to tell you that I never questioned where Joe's supplier, Victor Butin, got the diamonds from, and I never really cared."

Bo felt that Bart was actually telling him the truth.

"Well, just between us, there was a large diamond in Joseph Marx's safe deposit box."

"Yeah, I know."

"You what? You already knew that?"

"Joe told me. It was a way to test you, Bo. Joe put it there and said if you ever told me about it, you were an honest man and that I could trust you with anything. You just passed the test. But then again, I've always trusted you."

"As an officer of the court, I have a duty to declare it as part of the estate. The sad part is that thirty-five percent of its value will go to the IRS in estate taxes, which are due very soon."

"Oh, I see," said Bart looking fairly troubled.

"But, Bart if you tell me that the diamond was yours, and that Joe was just holding it for you as a test to me, then it wouldn't be part of Joe's estate. Do you understand?" Bo was hoping that Bart was able to follow Bo's logic.

Bart nodded and then slowly answered, "The diamond is mine. It is not Joe's. It was all a test."

"Honestly?"

"Honestly!" Bo was deeply relieved. Despite all of Bart's troubles he was still able to think rationally.

"Great. I'll be back in ten minutes."

Bo literally ran down the street to his office and stood before the small concealed safe. He spun the correct combination, opened the box, grabbed the diamond, and hurried back to Diamond and Sons Inc., completing the trip in less than ten minutes.

"Boy that was quick," muttered Bart.

"Here you go. One beautiful diamond," said Bo handing the impressive stone over to him.

"Thanks," said Bart eagerly accepting he diamond.

"For what it's worth, I had the diamond appraised."

"You did?"

"Yes. This one is real and worth about four million dollars, retail."

"I know," replied Bart. "And thank you again for your honesty."

"I'll keep in touch. Remember, Ruby and I are here for you." Bo did check both ways on Worth Avenue to see if anyone was watching him as he left the vacant store.

Chapter
Forty-Three

Both *60 Minutes* and *20/20* had run feature stories on the world's largest jewelry scam. Of course, Bart could not speak to the media, and his attorney, Paul Schwartz, looking rather plump and ghostly white, seized upon the opportunity to promote himself while attempting to help Bart. Unfortunately on both occasions, he failed miserably, making Bart look even more guilty to the American public.

To make matters worse, Milton and Brenda Rogers made the most of their interviews, and they could not have done better. They dressed appropriately and said all the right things. They were the ideal martyrs, and perfectly played the part of the poor sympathetic victims.

At the end of each show, the overriding consensus was that Bart Sinclair was definitely guilty, and Milton and Brenda were as innocent as newborn babies. Both the criminal and the civil proceedings were slowly winding their way through the court system, and Bart's attorney fees were mind-boggling.

Paul Schwartz had already burned through the first million dollars and he had asked for and received another million. Paul's former partner, Don Dannon, the son of an extremely wealthy Midwest family, was handling the civil litigation onslaught.

Virtually every day, Jim McDonald had scheduled a deposition or was requesting additional documentation from Bart Sinclair. Don had his hands full and was doing his very best to keep up.

Don was a relatively short man about five feet two inches tall with a receding mop of blonde hair. He was a fishing fanatic and had an adorable wife and three lovely kids. Don was a board-certified civil litigator and had been practicing litigation for over twenty years.

However, never before had he faced such a vindictive and menacing opponent as Jim McDonald. Early in the beginning of the litigation, Don figured out that Jim McDonald was leaking information to the FBI and was assisting the federal government on a daily basis.

Don also soon realized that Jim McDonald was simultaneously trying the case in the media. He knew that Jim had a sympathetic voice in the *Times* reporter Mae McReynolds with her now weekly front page headline condemning Bart Sinclair for one thing or another. Mae definitely knew how to keep a case in the headlines. Her feature stories were pointed and extremely damaging to Bart.

Don had now spent numerous hours with Bart Sinclair, his personal and criminal attorney, Paul Schwartz, and his accountant, Ross Brown. While Bart had clearly manipulated his company books—something that Don dreaded would eventually be revealed—he actually believed in Bart's innocence. He just had a gut feeling that Milton Rogers was lying, and his intuition had never let him down. Unfortunately for Bart's sake, Don had yet to find any real evidence to put a dent in the Rogers's lawsuit.

However, everything wasn't coming up roses for the Rogers either. It had been over four months since Jean Valhomme had promised to deliver the Ecstasy tablets. Each day caused Milton more concern.

The four Rogers children, Lee, Lance, Lawrence, and Luke, were growing restless. They had each temporarily moved to L.A., Boston, Miami, and Las Vegas, respectively, and attempted to make the connections that Milton had commandeered. Each son had negotiated with characters whose names were "Slinky," "Fats," "Spice," and "Cool Breeze." Individuals they would never have wanted to meet, much less do business with.

The Rogers's kids were extremely naive in addition to their laziness, and Milton was constantly worried that something would go wrong. In fact, he counted on it. He highly doubted that The 4 L's Inc. could turn $100 million into over four $400 million. But it was certainly worth a try.

Milton also knew that Jim McDonald was only representing him for the money, and he was wary of that greedy man. Milton couldn't care less whether he recovered a dime from Bart Sinclair. Since Jim arranged to take the case on a contingency basis, Milton was no longer fronting the attorney fees and paid little attention to the civil lawsuit. He was out over $2 million in legal fees but didn't mind the initial outlay. It was simply a cost of doing business.

Milton was most tired of dealing with Steve Fleishman from the US Attorneys' office and assisting all the FBI agents. Milton was convinced that the government only hired morons. Each time he dealt with them, he came away feeling more and more confident that his master plan would work, and his children would be financially secure for their lifetimes. But it was so hard trying to reeducate the Feds, time after time.

Milton realized that the only way the FBI ever made progress on a case was when someone snitched. Milton was certain that nobody in his family was going to snitch or be snitched on. He would make damn sure of that!

Chapter
Forty-Four

During the final stage of the estate administration, Bo had again inquired about the fake diamonds. Bart seemed very anxious to discuss the fabulous fake gems as well since neither Paul Schwartz nor Don Dannon had really focused on the synthetic diamonds. Everyone had just accepted the fact that the gems were fakes.

Two independent appraisers as well as the government's own appraiser had all inspected, analyzed, and then valued the manufactured stones. It was uncontested that the value was approximately $5 million.

Bo remembered his discussion clearly.

"So, Bart" asked Bo, "where did you allegedly purchase these fake gems? I'm sure they're going through all your invoices to determine when and where you bought the synthetics."

"That's just it, Bo. It's what I've been trying to explain to my attorneys. I have no idea, make that no clue whatsoever where you could even purchase such realistic fakes. You see, Bo, there is no company that I am aware of that has the technology to manufacture a clear synthetic diamond."

"Wait, let me get this straight," interrupted Bo. "If I understand, what you're saying is that you couldn't have sold the Rogers the fake diamonds because there is no entity that you're aware of, who has the technology available to manufacture them? But someone did."

"That's it," said Bart shaking his head up and down.

"Well, then where did the Rogers acquire the fake diamonds?"

"That's the hundred-million-dollar question, my friend. It's what makes me stay up at night and troubles me the most. I have no idea."

"So let me get this right, said Bo. Again, it is your legal defense that you couldn't have sold the Rogers fake diamonds of that brilliance because you don't even know where you could have actually purchased them? There has got to be a company or two."

"That's it; doesn't sound exactly open and shut, does it?"

"Well, what do your lawyers say?"

"Other than they need more money, they are not focusing on the fake diamonds aspect at all."

"Why not?"

"Just because there is too much being thrown at them from the government and that prick, Jim McDonald. My attorneys are always on the defensive. I need someone to take the offense for a change."

"Definitely. It sure would seem that way to me."

"Will you be my offense, Bo?"

"Bart, I'm not a litigator at all. I wouldn't even know where to begin."

"Listen, I trust you implicitly. These other guys are only in it for the money. Be my investigator. Try to find out everything you can about the synthetic diamonds. Travel to Russia or Belgium and wherever else there is a big diamond import-export business, and examine the labs over there."

"But, Bart, I've never done this sort of thing. I am an estate lawyer only."

"Listen, Bo, I'm facing life in prison and bankruptcy. I need your help. Use the money from the Trust. Pay yourself handsomely. I don't care what it costs. Help me. Please help me."

Bo could see the look of fear, frustration, and desperation in Bart's eyes.

"Okay. I'll see what I can do."

"Hurry. The trial in the criminal matter is in less than six months."

"I'll do my best."

"Thank you so much, Bo. I knew I could count on you! Thank you!"

Chapter
Forty-Five

Spring had just ended and it was now summertime, and most of the snow birds had migrated back up north. This was the time of year that Bo and Ruby relished. They mostly had the island to themselves and could now get dinner reservations at almost any Palm Beach restaurant. Even the most popular West Palm Beach dining establishments, had little or no waiting lines. In spite of this lull, they themselves also went north for a good part of the summer.

It was the first week of June, and Bo and Ruby had just arrived in Nantucket for their annual vacation. Ruby loved this time of year because it meant that she got to go out and buy new summer outfits. She also thoroughly enjoyed the time that she had with Bo, all to herself. She didn't have to compete with Bo's clients for his undivided attention. Plus, Nantucket was absolutely beautiful in the summer.

The Martin family had a large home and a smaller cottage on their compound near Cisco beach just off Hummock Pond Road about five miles from Main Street. Bo and Ruby and the red dogs summered in the small cottage. It was two bedrooms with two baths and had just enough space for them and the dogs.

Bo and Ruby rented a jeep for the entire summer. The red dogs loved riding in the open-aired jeep with the wind flapping their long thin red ears.

Nantucket allows dogs everywhere, so Bella and Max naturally felt right at home in the laid-back but extremely affluent community.

Since the early 1990s, Nantucket had prospered immensely. The price of homes on the island had quintupled in value, and Bo and Ruby, unfortunately, realized that their idyllic oasis was changing.

Where you once saw only old trucks, jeeps, and station wagons, you now saw Lexus, Mercedes, Range Rovers, and BMW SUVs. The new rich were snapping up all the older homes, tearing them down and constructing large mansions with huge hedges and privacy gates.

Nantucket had definitely changed. The new money had transformed the island into a mini New York. Business and money became the primary focus, and everyone was hustling, even while on vacation.

Bo and Ruby wondered to themselves how the locals could afford such outrageous costs. Affordable housing was just about nonexistent, and the cute and energetic college summer interns were replaced with Caribbeans, willing to sleep eight or ten per room and work long hours for low wages.

Bo and Ruby decided to go for a drive as soon as they got to their cottage to check everything out. Ruby was yelling at Bo, so he could hear her over the topless jeep, "I hope it's not too crowded this summer."

"Well, I don't know about that, honey; this is the new place to be and be seen. Mom and Dad say it is already pretty congested all the time in town."

"I know. I just wish it was like when we first visited your folks."

"Yeah, it was pretty peaceful, wasn't it?" said Bo and smiled, reflecting on years past.

"Maybe with the stock market depressed, the young multimillionaires won't be able to afford Nantucket!"

"Wishful thinking, sweetheart. Wishful thinking."

"So, Bo, you are staying the entire month of June with me, aren't you?"

"Well, I've got some business to take care of."

"Oh, Bo. Damn you. What now?"

"I've got to go over to Belgium for a short trip. I am taking Hank with me."

"Belgium?"

"I know you wouldn't have wanted to go there in the summer and be away from here, so I'm taking Hank along with me. Plus, he will be able to help me out with a few things."

"It's about Bart Sinclair, isn't it?"

Bo couldn't lie. "Of course. Who else has been taking up all my time lately? We're trying to locate the source of the synthetic gems. I've told you all about it."

"I know, but why now?"

"His criminal trial is in less than five months, and thus far, he is looking pretty guilty."

"You really think he's innocent?"

"Yes, I do. Plus, I'm getting paid top dollar to investigate so that you can play all summer."

"I'd rather just be with you. I'll get bored all by myself with only your folks."

"I figured you would, and that's why Sophia will be flying up the week after next to stay with you. It was supposed to be a surprise, but I don't want you to be too disappointed."

"Really? Oh that is great! I can't believe she didn't even give me a hint. Oh she's going to get it from me when I see her! Well, I guess it's okay then; go on your little trip to Belgium. Sophia and I will manage, somehow."

Great, thought Bo

"When are you leaving?"

"I will be here in Nantucket for about a week and a half. I am going to meet up with Hank in New York and go from there.

"How long will you be gone?"

"Probably about a week or so, maybe a little bit longer. I should be back here with you before the end of June."

"We'll still have fun, I promise you."

Bo knew that Ruby would be angry with him so that's why he had asked Sophia to join her in Nantucket. The two women couldn't stand to be apart for even a week, and Bo knew that Ruby wouldn't stay mad at him for long once she knew she would be having company.

Chapter
Forty-Six

The flight to Belgium was long and uneventful. Hank and Bo had been actively investigating the source of the synthetic gems. Even with extensive internet research, they had put in hundreds of hours and had come up with absolutely nothing. Hank and Bo were running out of ideas and time, and Bo knew that Bart was becoming distraught. Nevertheless, they continued on.

Hank had come across the name of a Russian scientist who advocated using lower pressures over a longer period in an effort to avoid the release of nitrogen, and prevent the synthetic diamonds from turning yellow. The gentleman was willing to meet with Bo and Hank, but only for an hour.

Bo and Hank were exhausted when they arrived at their small hotel and they immediately crashed, skipping dinner altogether. The next morning after a nice long run, the two men were eager to meet with the scientist.

Sergei Isimov was about sixty-eight but looked considerably older. He stood hump-backed from years of straining over a laboratory table. Fortunately, he spoke English pretty well and greeted the two men warmly.

Bo had illegally swiped one of the fake gems from the government's exhibitof all the stones purchased by the Rogers. In its place, he had inserted a yellowish one-carat diamond. He knew it was only a matter of time before Steve Fleishman would find the deviance, and all hell would break loose. Only Hank knew that Bo had "borrowed" the stone, and he would never tell a soul.

The Russian scientist listened intently to Bo and Hank as they explained the purpose of their visit. The man said nothing. After completing his spiel, Bo handed Sergei the synthetic diamond. The Russian's eyes lit up, and he spent the next fifteen minutes carefully analyzing the gem. Bo and Hank stood in silence.

Finally, the Russian spoke. "It's beautiful, isn't it? I knew it could be done, and to think that maybe it was my technology that made this creation possible. I'm thrilled."

"Well, do you know who could have manufactured this particular diamond?" asked Bo.

"Yes, I believe so."

"You do?" both Hank and Bo couldn't believe their ears. It was as if all their hard work was worth their efforts.

"Sure. He is a young American who worked with me for a year or so. He is brilliant—a real genius—and he most likely is the manufacturer. He is the only person I know to have ever come close to something like this," he said, holding up the fake diamond. "I am sure it is him!"

"Great. What's his name?" asked Hank.

"His name is Brad Penny, and he is a graduate of the University of Florida."

"Have you heard from him recently?" inquired Bo.

"No. He left rather abruptly, a few years ago, just when we were so close to producing the first perfect synthetic diamond." It was clear that Sergei was reminiscing when he spoke fondly of Brad. "Damn, we were so close, and once he left, I was never able to figure out the missing component. But apparently, Brad did!"

Bo watched Sergei's complexion turn a few shades of red before speaking again. "Do you know of anyone else or any other company in the world that could manufacture a colorless synthetic diamond?"

"No, not of this quality. But I am sorry, gentlemen, but your time is up," Sergei said rather curtly.

"But we have several more questions for you," pleaded Bo.

"No, gentlemen, I must be going. Your time is up. You see, I just realized that something I had been working towards my whole life has been stolen from me by an impetuous American, and now you want to take up more of my precious time. Good day, gentlemen," said Sergei and bristled away, closing the door behind him.

Bo and Hank were elated to finally have a name and a possible break in the case. When they returned to the hotel and saw the antiquated communication systems with limited internet connection, they knew that they had to get back to Palm Beach immediately.

Bo thought of his beautiful wife, Ruby, and knew that she wasn't going to be happy. Bo had promised to fly directly to Nantucket, but since he had only been gone a few days, he still had some time. Bo further rationalized it by thinking that since she was with her best friend, Sophia, she wouldn't miss him too much.

Since Bo and Hank weren't into sightseeing and didn't know much about Belgium's history, nor wanted to, they caught the earliest flight home.

Chapter
Forty-Seven

Meanwhile, back in his New York City penthouse, Victor finally received the call he was anxiously awaiting.

"Victor, this is Marty."

"Jesus Christ, Marty where the hell have you been? I thought I would hear from you days ago!"

"I'm just fine, Victor; thanks for asking. Oh, and by the way, thanks for sending Ivan and Igor down here; they have been a big help in certain situations if you know what I mean."

"What news do you have for me?" asked Victor, getting right down to business.

"Well, Victor with the assistance of Igor and Ivan, we were able to convince the bank vice-president to disclose the information we wanted. And just in case you were wondering, the man's not dead. He may never have the use of his index fingers, but he finally cooperated completely."

"So where is the money?"

"The funds from AA Trading Co. were wired transferred by Joseph Marx to A Trading Co. located in the Grand Cayman and deposited in the Cayman National Bank."

"So that's where the money is located?" exulted Victor.

"Not only located, but there exists over fifty million dollars in the account."

The sense of dread that was looming over Victor for the past several weeks just seemed to drift away like a cloud, and he suddenly felt like a million bucks, or rather, fifty million bucks!

"The name of the man in charge of large accounts at the Cayman bank is Harrison Frazar. And guess what? He will divulge any information we want, provided he is well compensated."

"Well of course, he shall be taken care of! How much does he want?"

"One hundred thousand dollars, and he will tell us whatever we want."

"That doesn't sound like very much money to rat out your clients. Are you sure he can be trusted?"

"Absolutely, Victor. Mr. Frazar didn't hesitate for a second to agree to give us the information, as long as he gets his money."

"All right, Marty. Tell me where to wire the money, and make sure nothing happens to the banker until you get the information. Is that understood?"

"Understood, Victor, but I must tell you, Igor and Ivan are getting pretty restless; there are no gyms down here, and they have a lot of pent-up energy, if you know what I mean!"

"You just keep them under control until you get what you want."

Moments later, Victor stepped out onto the terrace and took a moment to appreciate the incredible view. *Soon, very soon, I will have my money*, thought Victor.

Chapter
Forty-Eight

In two days, Marty had all the information he needed. Mr. Frazar was eager to talk after the money had been wired to his personal account. Harrison Frazar confirmed that A Trading Co. Inc. was opened by Joseph Marx. He also confirmed that there existed over fifty million dollars in the corporate account.

The next information he provided took Marty by surprise. The corporation was owned by a Trust. The trustee and individual in control of the account, however, was not Joseph Marx. The name of the new trustee was none other than Bo Martin, Esq. from Palm Beach, Florida.

That son of a bitch, thought Marty. *To think that we had interrogated him, and he never disclosed the existence of the trust or his fiduciary role. But where were the trust documents? Definitely not in the office of Martin and Martin.* Heck, he had personally checked the office himself.

Marty disclosed all the information to Victor, who pondered over how to proceed. Victor called the law office of Martin and Martin, P.A., and spoke with Ms. Everett personally.

"I need to speak with Bo Martin immediately."

"I'm sorry, but he's not here. He's currently on vacation in Nantucket. He won't be back until after the fourth of July, but I can tell you that he checks in every day. Can I take your name and number, and I'll pass your message on to him?"

"That's okay. I don't want to ruin his vacation. I'll call back when he returns."

"Well, I'm sure Bo and his wife will appreciate your not wanting to disturb their much-needed vacation. Have a nice day."

Seconds later, Victor was back on the phone with Marty.

"Book tickets to Nantucket, Massachusetts. He's vacationing for the entire month of June with his wife."

"Will you be joining us?" asked Marty, hoping that the old man would decline the offer.

"As a matter fact, yes. I've heard that Nantucket is beautiful. Plus with Igor and Ivan, I don't think it will be too hard to convince Mr. Bo Martin to wire transfer the money to my personal bank account."

"If he knows what's good for him, he most certainly will, boss. See you in Nantucket."

Chapter
Forty-Nine

Despite their jet lag, Bo and Hank proceeded directly to Hank's office as soon as once they arrived in balmy West Palm Beach.

Hank went to work immediately, and within minutes, had the insurance company's mainframe computer working on locating the whereabouts of a Brad Penny. After about three minutes, the information appeared on the terminal screen.

That is odd, thought Hank. "It appears that his last known address was Gainesville, Florida. But there is no recent activity. It's like he disappeared," stated Hank.

Bo was pacing quietly back and forth when Hank informed Bo about the lack of any present information, and Bo was extremely disappointed.

"Check the Office of Vital Statistics for death certificates. He may be dead," said Bo.

Moments later the computer confirmed Bo's worst fear. Brad Penny was in fact dead. It took literally seconds before the *Gainesville Sun* Newspaper article describing Brad's death appeared on the computer screen.

Both Hank and Bo read the article with earnest. "How very strange," said Bo. Hank agreed.

"His death is just too clean. No surviving spouse or family members. Gunshot to the chest and a subsequent fire at the warehouse."

"I wonder what was in the warehouse," asked Bo. Then he added, "Most likely, manufacturing equipment for synthetic diamonds."

"You know if I didn't know any better, I'd say his death was arranged," said Hank.

"Well, I would say a gunshot wound to the chest is not ordinary. I have seen thousands of death certificates over the years, and I rarely see a self-inflicted gunshot wound to the chest. You know what this means, don't you?" questioned Bo.

"Road trip!" exclaimed Hank. However before we leave, let's get a quick run-in, a long hot shower, and a good night's sleep. My body's own time clock is out of order."

"Agreed," said Bo.

The following day, Bo and Hank were on the Florida Turnpike, headed to Gainesville, Florida, mostly known as the home of the University of Florida Gators. It was about a four-and-a-half-hour drive, and Hank had brought along his wireless laptop.

Hank scanned all the newspaper articles regarding the death of Brad Penny and the warehouse fire while Bo drove. The local authorities had virtually closed the case, and determined that Brad was killed in a botched robbery attempt. An African American, Anfernee Robinson, was also found shot in the fiery remains. Anfernee had a long rap sheet and was mostly a street thug.

The police had concluded that Anfernee had attempted to rob Brad when the shooting ensued. During the scuffle, a piece of machinery accidentally caught fire. Both men were presumed to have died from their respective gunshot wounds before their remains were charred in the fire, which destroyed the entire warehouse and all its contents.

Police believed that Brad was running an illegal drug-manufacturing business. He paid his employees cash, in direct violation of the state and federal employee tax withholding laws. None of the college or part-time employees, questioned by local authorities knew the exact nature of the business, but they speculated it may have had something to do with drugs and jewelry.

Police had searched Brad's apartment with a fine-toothed comb and found over thirty thousand dollars in cash, which they concluded was from his illegal manufacturing operations. They found nothing else concerning what he exactly manufactured. No papers, no worksheets, and no records. The actual owner of the warehouse was protected by so many layers of partnerships and limited liability companies (LLCs) that it was virtually impossible to uncover, but the insurance coverage would, most likely, cover the warehouse loss.

After scouring over all the written information for most of the trip, Hank turned to Bo and said, "Something just isn't right; everything is too coincidental."

"I know exactly what you mean. I just hope this doesn't lead us back to Bart Sinclair. You know that death has a way of following that man around."

When Bo and Hank arrived in Gainesville, the first thing on the agenda was a visit to the famed Burrito Brothers to get the best burritos in the south. After completely stuffing themselves, they went directly to the local police department.

Hank used his insurance investigator credentials to convince the desk clerk to allow them to speak with the lieutenant in charge of homicide, Mr. Ray Brown. Fortunately, Brown was in and willing to talk. Bo and Hank cautiously entered the small drab office.

"Gentlemen to what do I owe this pleasure?"

"Good afternoon, I'm Bo Martin, and this is my partner, Hank." Hank handed Brown his card. "We're in Gainesville to follow up on the death of a young man named Brad Penny."

"Oh, well. What can I do for you? Please sit down."

Hank began, "We have reason to believe that Mr. Brad Penny was manufacturing synthetic diamonds, and quite possibly, the man who hired him for the job also had him murdered."

"Now, I've heard everything," exclaimed Brown, placing his large hands behind his head. "What do you take us for up here in Alachua? Buffoons! Where on earth did you come up with this absurd idea?"

Bo chimed in, "We just came back from Belgium where we met with a Russian scientist who was working on a procedure to manufacture colorless synthetic diamonds. Brad Penny worked for him a few years ago, and he confirmed that Brad had taken his technology with him when he unexpectedly left his research team. Time is of the essence. So would you mind if we look at your files and visit the warehouse?"

Brown quickly realized that Bo and Hank meant business. Brown's gut also told him that Brad Penny's death was a little too suspicious, and he agreed to give the men a break.

What have I got to lose? he thought to himself? "Tell you guys what, I'll personally accompany you."

"Great," said Bo and Hank simultaneously.

It took the trio about thirty minutes to arrive at the warehouse site. During the entire car ride, Brown described the police findings. Anfernee Robinson was a local thug. He ran some dope, pilfered some merchandise, and mainly victimized the innocent and unknowing college co-eds. However, he was not known to be violent. Never before had he been arrested for any violent act.

The police had a witness who said Anfernee got into a Lincoln Continental, driven by an elderly distinguished white male on the day of Brad's death. Unfortunately, the witness was also high on crack cocaine and totally unreliable. She later died of an opium overdose.

Most of Brad Penny's neighbors recalled him as being very quiet and unassuming. They say he worked long hours and that he was a real loner. One neighbor remembered seeing him with a younger woman, dressed very casually in army fatigue pants and wearing a baseball cap. Unfortunately, the investigation found no such person who fit that rather bland description in a college town. Also, no family members stepped forward to acknowledge Brad. So his remains were cremated, and his cash remains in the police lock-out room.

"That's about it," concluded Brown.

"What about the owner of the warehouse?" asked Hank.

"We have been unable to locate the owner but believe the company confirmed it had fire insurance. It appears the company rented the warehouse to Brad on a handshake deal, and Brad paid a year's rent by cashier's check in advance."

"Here's the road. Take a right," interrupted Brown.

The blackened and charred remains of the warehouse stood intact. The owner had not even bulldozed the place. The three men got out of their car and walked about through the remains. Immediately, Bo and Hank recognized some of the same machinery that they had briefly observed in Belgium at the Russian's facility.

Brown chimed in, "This is mostly manufacturing equipment. My experts believe it most likely was used to manufacture jewelry. However, I have my doubts."

"Lieutenant, this equipment looks brand-new. Did any of your guys contact the manufacturer to see when it was purchased and by whom?"

"No. Why should they?"

"Just checking," said Hank as he wrote down the serial numbers of several large pieces of equipment.

After about ten minutes, Brown stopped and asked the men what they were thinking. "Please guys, I could use your help," he pleaded.

Bo figured it couldn't hurt and began to explain to Brown their theory that Brad was murdered by the man who hired him to manufacture synthetic gems. He manipulated a local thug to make it look like a robbery-murder and to throw off the authorities on the real reason for the murder.

Brown was dumbfounded. "What was this guy involved in that would prompt someone to murder him?"

Bo and Hank answered in unison, "How about one hundred million reasons!"

"I see," responded Brown after hearing more answers on the drive back to the Gainesville police station.

Bo and Hank dropped off Brown, who had taken the equipment serial numbers and was going to immediately have someone get on tracing it. Then Bo and Hank drove to Brad's apartment.

The apartment manager had already sold the bulk of Brad's personal belongings and furniture to help cover the rent, but the men were not surprised to learn that the unit was subleased. The manager was extremely unhelpful, but he did remember a young female companion. He heard her name once but couldn't remember it.

For most of the remainder of the day, Bo and Hank knocked on doors and learned nothing new. They were tired and still fighting off their jet lag.

In one last-ditch effort, Bo and Hank visited the Gainesville newspaper headquarters and bought a half-page ad. The electronic accompanying ad was free. They didn't have any alternatives. Their ad read:

"Anyone knowing information about Brad Penny, call 561-863-8000. Reward money $$"

Hank had used his own cell phone as the number to call. The two men hoped for a miracle.

Later that same evening, the men jogged around the University of Florida, mostly admiring the beautiful coeds and the historic buildings. Bo told Hank all about the old Bell Tower. "Rumor has it that if a virgin graduates, the bell will ring. Never in the school's history had the bell rung."

"Funny, very funny," replied Hank.

After dinner, the men called their wives. Bo thought it odd that he was unable to contact Ruby. She must be having fun with Sophia, thought Bo.

Chapter

Fifty

O n the contrary, Ruby was not having fun at all. She and Sophia were
tied up and gagged. They were presently on the floor of an isolated
horse farm, well off the beaten path toward Madaket. The old
farmhouse was rather hurriedly rented out by Victor, who had paid cash for
the entire month's rental.

The women were terrified by the huge Russian men who held them
captive. The Russians had faked car trouble on Hummock Pond Road, and
when the girls stopped to ask if they needed help, the huge men grabbed them
and threw the women into the back of the van. Marty then had them take the
girls' jeep and follow the van back to the farmhouse in Madaket, which was
only a ten-minute drive away.

Naturally, the girls were terrified. Ruby sensed that their kidnapping was
somehow related to Bart Sinclair. Sophia was petrified, and she kept looking to
Ruby for a source of comfort. Ruby tried valiantly to hide her fear.

The girls had been tied up for what seemed like hours before the door to
the barn opened and an elderly well-dressed man appeared, followed by the
two giants and another man.

"Take off those gags," shouted Victor. "Also the ropes. Where are your
manners?"

Ruby and Sophia were relieved to finally regain feeling back in their
hands and feet and to breathe through their mouths.

Ruby stared at Victor before yelling, "Who the hell are you guys!"

"Now, now, please no need to get hostile. We are civilized. I mean you no harm."

"Tell that to the two guys behind you," snapped Sophia.

"Come, come. Calm down now. Nobody will get hurt if you simply cooperate."

"Then why the hell were we kidnapped?" snapped Ruby, "Are you some sick practical joker!"

"Kidnapped? Oh that's a little extreme, don't you think? Look, you're comfortable in a nice barn. Here. Have something to eat."

"We're not hungry," blared Ruby. "We want to go home now if it's all right with you."

"I'm sorry, but I'm waiting for your husband to come rescue you."

"My husband? Who, Bo?" questioned Ruby.

"Yes. He is your husband, isn't he?"

"He's in Belgium, you idiot."

"No, he's not."

"He most certainly is," shouted Sophia trying hard to hide her fear. "Why do you think I'm with Ruby? I'm Bo's stand-in until he gets back."

"But, his secretary told me he was in Nantucket," responded Victor with a concerned look on his face.

"Bo changed his mind at the last minute, and Sophia came in his place. I honestly have no idea when he will return to Nantucket. I haven't even spoken to him in two days." Ruby was telling the truth.

"Damn," said Victor, pounding his fist against one of the wooden stall doors.

"Now what?" asked Marty.

"Let me think, would you?" quipped Victor.

"Listen, let us go, and we won't say a word to anyone. Okay?"

"We can't do that because you know what we look like."

"So what? I also believe that those two big goons were the same guys who beat up my husband and his friend, Hank."

"You are indeed too smart for your own good," retorted Victor. "You are not going anywhere. Have you got that?"

"Look, I don't really know who you are, but this is a pretty small island, and even though you think we're out in the country, they can find you pretty fast."

"But I need your husband. Call him," demanded Victor, thrusting his cell phone into Ruby's hand.

"How? In Belgium. Oh sure thing," joked Ruby.

"Damn it. Why is nothing easy? Guys, look after the girls while Marty and I have a talk."

As they left, Ruby and Sophia took turns making faces at the huge Russians. They were still frightened, but slowly they were gaining collective strength.

Marty spoke first. "She's got a point, Victor. This is a small island, and you know the Martins will put an APB out on them pretty soon after they fail to report back. If they catch us, we're in big trouble."

"Granted, but if we let them go, they will run to the authorities."

"I know; that's why we need to leave now. Let's leave the island immediately and purchase tickets for Igor and Ivan. They'll leave the girls, and it will take the women at least an hour and a half to get back to their Nantucket house. By then, we'll all be gone."

"It's risky, Marty."

"Yes, it is, but what choice do we have now? We can't keep the girls from talking. And, we don't want to hurt them, do we?"

"Lord no. Not yet."

"Then let's leave. Cut our losses now before it's too late."

"I guess you're right. We'll make them suffer later."

With their minds made up, Marty and Victor left for the airport to purchase four tickets. They boarded the first plane out. It went to Boston on Cape Air, and they left two tickets for Igor and Ivan for the next plane out. Marty then called the Russian goons and told them to hide the jeep's keys and rush to the airport where they would find the tickets to Boston, waiting for them. Time was of the essence.

When the goons had left, Ruby and Sophia untied themselves and sprinted out the barn door. "I know where we are," exclaimed Ruby. "If we run for about half a mile, I know a house where we can use the phone."

"Let's go," said Sophia.

Sure enough, the girls found the house and were met at the door by a waspy thirty-year-old, closely guarded by her trusty yellow lab.

"We need your phone quick," explained Ruby.

"Right over there. What's the problem?" asked the startled woman.

Ruby had dialed the police and was soon on the line describing the four men and asking that all planes out of Nantucket be stopped at once.

It took a little convincing before the police responded and could arrive at the airport. Fortunately, they arrived just when the Russian goons were attempting to board their plane. Surrounded by four officers, the Russian goons gave up without a fight, and after two hours, Ruby and Sophia were still with several police officers at the local police station.

The Russians weren't saying a thing. Most unfortunately, Victor and Marty had managed to evade the authorities at Boston's Logan Airport. Two minutes earlier and they too, would have been nabbed.

Chapter
Fifty-One

Bo and Hank woke up the next morning, bright and early, and ran, reviewed the newspaper ad, and made their daily plans. It was going to be a long one. Bo checked his cell phone, as he was becoming concerned about Ruby.

His phone rang.

"Hello."

"Oh, thank God you're okay. Oh, honey, I love you so much."

"I love you too; what's up?"

"We were kidnapped yesterday."

"You what?" exclaimed Bo.

"Yes, kidnapped. Four Russians. The older gentleman and his sidekick got away, but the police caught the two huge Russians."

"Were they enormous and ugly?"

"Yes, giants."

"Both Hank and I have met them, I believe. Are they talking to the police?"

"Who knows? But, Bo, they thought you were here in Nantucket. They kidnapped us to get to you."

"I am so sorry. Are you all right?"

"Oh, we're fine. It ruined our entire day yesterday, but we'll make up for it today by going shopping."

"Be my guest. It's on me."

"It's always on you, my dear. But, now you owe me a vacation, just the two of us."

"Done."

"Hey by the way, we are getting a great signal from Belgium."

"Honey, I'm not in Belgium. Hank and I are in Gainesville, Florida."

"At the U of F?"

"Yes. We think we located the manufacturer of the fake diamonds."

"That's excellent."

"The only problem is that he's dead."

"Oh, no."

"It seems we take one step forward and two steps back."

"How long will you be in Gainesville?"

"Probably a couple of days with any luck."

"Okay. When you're done there, get your butt up to Nantucket! That's an order."

"Aye, aye, Captain. See you soon. I love you."

Hank had overheard the entire discussion.

"Those two Russian goons must be really pissed.

"You betcha. Now let's see if Lt. Brown can help keep those goons in Nantucket while we try and figure out who hired Brad."

"If it's Bart Sinclair, he's a dead man," said Hank.

"But if it's Milton Rogers, then what?" asked Bo.

"Then we really have a mess on our hands."

"I know what you mean," said Hank, begrudgingly.

Lt. Brown was successful in keeping the giant Russians detained. The Russians were on their way via ferry to Boston, Massachusetts to be arraigned on kidnapping charges. They would be held in the county jail, pending their initial appearance. It was highly unlikely that they would be allowed to post a bond, since they were significant flight risks.

The Russians were maintaining their silence and ignored any lines of communication.

At the first opportunity he got, Lt. Brown asked Bo and Hank why the Russians were involved in the manufacturing of synthetic gems. Needless to say, both men said it was a long story, and they didn't think it would be of any interest to him. Lt. Brown knew there was much more to the story, but he dropped the subject.

Lt. Brown was also happy to report that his men had been successful in locating the primary equipment manufacturer. The equipment was entirely brand-new and was purchased by none other than Brad Penny.

Bo and Hank were clearly disappointed with the news. They had hoped the equipment was purchased by either Bart Sinclair or Milton Rogers or some corporation controlled by either man.

"Sorry about the news," said Lt. Brown into his phone.

"Give me the number and the name of the manufacturer again," asked Bo.

Moments later, Bo was on the phone with the manufacturer. Bo was interested in how the machinery was purchased. After holding on the line for what seemed to be an eternity, Bo received an answer. "Thank you so much," said Bo as he hung up the phone.

"So?" asked Hank. "What did you find out?"

"Just as I expected. The money for the purchase of the equipment was paid by cashier's checks, but the initial minimum deposit was wired by a Bahamian corporation called the Four L's."

"Somebody messed up!" exclaimed Hank.

"And we're going to find out who," vowed a determined Bo.

Hank and Bo were headed for lunch when Hank's phone rang.

"Hello," answered Hank.

"Yes, hello. I'm calling about the ad in today's *Gainesville Sun.*"

"Well, thank you for calling. Were you a friend of Brad?"

"What's this all about?" asked the young female caller hesitantly.

"Ma'am, we are just investigating Brad's death. In all honesty, we believe there is more behind the story and feel that someone else may have been behind his death."

"You swear?"

"Scout's honor."

"Well, there is a lot more to the story, and I should know because I'm his, or I was, his friend."

"B-I-N-G-O," mouthed Hank to Bo.

"Tell me where we can meet? My partner and I are staying at the Holiday Inn at the corner of University and 34th Street."

"Well, I don't get off work until six o'clock. How about we meet at Leonardo's Pizza Palace, right across from your hotel?"

"That would be great. Oh by the way, we are two old runners, six foot four and the other six foot. I'm the good-looking one, though. My name is Hank."

"Well, I'm about five foot four, and I'll probably be wearing baggy jeans and a baseball cap. My name is Stacey."

"See you tonight, Stacey. Bye."

Bo and Hank checked back with Lt. Brown later in the afternoon to see if his people had any more information. "Nothing," replied Lt. Brown.

When Lt. Brown asked if they had received any phone calls regarding the ad, Bo replied, "No, not yet."

Bo and Hank were extremely anxious and nervous about their six o'clock meeting. Hank had received three other phone calls regarding the newspaper ad, but not one was legitimate.

Bo and Hank arrived at the pizzeria fifteen minutes beforehand and chose a seat that allowed them to see the customers entering the restaurant.

Sure enough, shortly after six o'clock, a young woman dressed in baggy jeans and sporting a Jacksonville Jaguars' football cap sauntered into the restaurant. She immediately saw Bo and Hank waving their hands, and she hesitantly walked toward them.

"Sorry if I'm a little late."

"No problem. We haven't even ordered yet and hope that you will join us for a bite to eat."

"I'm Bo, and this is Hank."

"Nice to meet you two," she said, shaking their hands. I'm Stacey, and the garlic rolls here are out of this world."

The waitress soon took their order, and after the pleasantries, Bo got down to business.

"We are sorry about the death of your friend, Brad. We recently were over in Belgium and met with an individual who formerly hired Brad."

"Oh, I know all about him. He called Brad a lot of bad names, and accused him of stealing his invention. He was Russian right?"

"Right."

"So you know about Brad's work?" questioned Hank.

"Why, of course! Brad was a real genius. He was a loner, and it took me for what seemed like forever to gain his trust. Eventually I did, and we became good friends. Not boyfriend-girlfriend, actually, more like soul mates. I think Brad was gay. So I kept our relationship on a casual level. I did love him, though." Tears started to roll down her freckled cheeks.

"It's okay," said Bo, offering a napkin to absorb her tears.

"I'm sorry, but I'm still trying to deal with his death. I'm about all he had. He had no family and really, no friends to speak of."

"So tell us about the diamonds," asked Bo, trying to steer the subject back in the right direction.

"When Brad returned from Belgium, he immediately went to work in the evenings at the University's metal laboratory. He convinced the professor to let him use some of their sophisticated equipment. After about a year, Brad himself, had created a piece of machinery that he said eliminated nitrogen or the stuff that turns diamonds yellow. He was so excited, you know. We even went out and celebrated. I remember it like it was yesterday.

"Look here," said Stacy. Both men eyed her necklace with the three-carat diamond dangling from it. "This was his first creation. He gave it to me and said that some day, he was going to be rich."

"Did Brad talk about money a lot?"

"Oh, sure. Seeing how he didn't have much and scrimped by week to week. Fortunately, living in Gainesville, Florida, is not too expensive. And I helped him out, occasionally. My folks are sort of wealthy."

"Oh, I see," said Hank, eyeing her intensely.

"A few months later, Brad received a phone call, and then had a meeting with a mysterious stranger."

"Who was it?"

"I don't know, and Brad didn't ever know his real name. The man was going to pay Brad over a million dollars if Brad was successful in making single solitaire diamonds, ranging from one carat to twenty carats."

"You don't say," chirped Bo, noting that those specific carats were identical to the sizes purchased by the Rogers and sold by Sinclair.

"The man had Brad lease a warehouse in Alachua and then had Brad order all the necessary equipment, which Brad would need in addition to his machine. The machines cost about a million dollars. The man also gave Brad cash to pay for the help he needed. I, of course, solicited students from the University. Brad paid cash to all the kids, and they worked real hard." Stacey now had the men's total attention.

"It was odd, but Brad made sure that none of the students ever knew exactly what he was working on. Brad kept telling me that he was sworn to secrecy. He didn't tell anyone anything. Trust me."

"How did Brad end up with so much cash in his apartment?" interjected Hank.

"Well after Brad was almost through, he realized that he could skim off some of the employees' cash and that the mysterious man would never know it. Brad wanted to buy a truck, real badly. He also talked about what he was going to do with the one million dollars."

"Towards the end, Brad was real secretive, even with me. It was like he knew something wasn't right. I just got the sense that he didn't trust the man at all."

"Did you tell any of this to the authorities?" asked Bo.

"No. They usually are a bunch of assholes. So I said nothing."

"How come you called about the ad then?" queried Hank.

"My conscience told me that I needed to clear the air. It wasn't about the reward if that's what you're thinking."

By this time, the delicious garlic rolls were served, and the thick Chicago-style pizza pies were too enticing to ignore. All three devoured the food and ate in relative silence. When the plates were cleared, Bo spoke again.

"Do you think Brad was killed by a local thug, or do you think there is more to the story?"

Stacey remained quiet before answering, "At first I thought it was just a botched robbery. However, the more I analyzed it, the more I believe that Brad had suspected the worst. Heck, I didn't even know he had a gun until one night I saw it sticking out of his jeans. I said, 'Are you crazy?' He just stated that the gun was for his protection and that his new technique would revolutionize the diamond industry."

"I see," said Hank, patting his full bloated stomach.

"You never met the mysterious man or heard his voice or saw him at a distance?"

"No, I never did. Brad didn't really say too much, except that he was in his sixties, tan, obsessed with privacy, and was extremely wealthy."

"You know what's weird? Two days before his death, Brad said that the diamonds were finished. His cell phone that the man gave him, rang, and Brad told me that the man would be in Tallahassee, but would see Brad soon. But Brad looked scared when he hung up the phone."

"Do you know where the phone is?" asked Hank.

"No. I presume it was destroyed in the fire."

Bo and Hank nodded in concurrence and made a mental note of it to see if Lt. Brown had found a cell phone in the fire debris.

"Is there anything else that you can think of to help us locate the mystery man?" asked Hank.

Stacey then grabbed her knapsack and pulled out pages of Brad's handwritten notes. She handed them to Bo.

"He gave those to me and said to protect them with my life."

Bo and Hank quickly glanced through the numerous written pages. The notes, arranged chronologically, explained his entire manufacturing process. It was the actual blueprint on how to produce clear synthetic diamonds.

More importantly, though, it contained all his telephone and personal meetings with the mystery man. There was even a brief description of the man. Age sixty-plus, tan, and the father of several children.

Bo and Hank were thrilled with the notes. The notes themselves could be admitted into evidence in a court of law. Unfortunately, Stacey's statements would be inadmissible as hearsay.

It was readily apparent to both men that Brad's notes excluded Bart Sinclair as a suspect. They would now focus their energies entirely on Milton Rogers.

To Bo, however, it also reinforced his own belief that the proceeds in the Joseph Marx Trust were all legitimate and that he had nothing to worry about. Even Hank could sense Bo's renewed self-confidence.

Stacey gladly gave the men her address, phone number, social security number, and even her parents' address and phone number. She promised to help in any way possible. After they said goodbye and thanked Stacey, Bo and Hank felt closer to putting the pieces together. Little did they know that big trouble was brewing in West Palm Beach, Florida.

aul Schwartz sat uncomfortably in his spacious penthouse office facing Assistant US Attorney Steve Fleishman and his underling, Nick Long. Paul was not enjoying their intense discussion at all.

"Now Paul, we are under incredible pressure to bring Bart Sinclair to justice. Between *60 Minutes*, *20/20*, and the unrelenting telephone calls from Milton Rogers, his family, his wealthy friends, and even several influential Senators and Congressmen, everyone demands to see Sinclair serve serious jail time for his outrageous fraud."

"It's not a fraud. My client insists he's innocent. I have no authority to cop a plea deal."

"Listen," said Steve, "your client is going to be found guilty. In the federal system, you are not innocent until proven guilty. You are guilty, and the best you can do is cut your losses and accept a plea."

Paul was well aware of the federal criminal justice system and all its flaws. The US Attorneys' Office maintained a 90 percent success rate. The laws, the judges, and to some extent, the juries are inherently biased in favor of the prosecution. Because of this inherent unjustness, most federal criminal cases settle with the defendant entering a guilty plea.

Naturally, a plea deal cuts the sentencing severity of a federal trial conviction by more than 60 percent. So a majority of defendants, caught up in the federal system, simply accept plea arrangements in order to reduce their maximum sentencing guidelines significantly.

The defendants who decide to fight the charges and take their cases to court have slightly better than a 10 percent chance of success. Of course, criminal defense attorneys primarily make their money and develop their own reputations in court trials, and so they often neglect to inform their clients of the cards stacked up against them and the tremendous odds of failure at trial.

Bart Sinclair had steadfastly held firm in declaring his innocence. "I will not accept any plea whatsoever," were Paul's client's last words.

Steve Fleishman and his associate knew full well that Bart Sinclair would not settle, and the men were eagerly preparing for trial. However, Steve held some cards up his sleeve.

"You know your former client, Bubba Franks, who copped a plea two or three years ago for cocaine smuggling."

"Yeah, I remember Bubba. What about him?" queried Paul.

"Well, it seems he says he paid you with cash and cocaine. We've checked your income tax returns, and despite your most recent divorce, we see no reporting of any cash."

"So what's up with that?" asked Nick Long, finally able to join in the conversation.

"Why, you son of a bitch," said Paul. "You know full well that Bubba would say anything to get some years taken off his sentence."

"Well, Paul, my bosses want me to take it to the grand jury. We have income tax invasion, money laundering, conspiracy, and I'm sure I could add a few more charges."

"You wouldn't," grimaced Paul.

"Oh, yes, I would, and trust me, I will." The room was silent while Paul prepared to answer. Droplets of sweat were now forming on his bald forehead.

"Okay," said Paul. "What do you want?"

"We're looking for more convictions. Give us something we don't know."

Paul was now sweating profusely, and beads of sweat were running down all three of his fat chins.

Steve realized he had Paul, and he sensed that Paul would throw him a bone.

"Do you promise to keep me out of it completely if I do cooperate?"

"That depends on how good the information is that we get from you. And who we get. Of course, we love professionals, like yourself," said Steve grinning through his white-bleached teeth.

"Well, you didn't hear it from me."

"Okay!"

"In this Sinclair matter, have you found anything out on A Trading Co.?"

"Only that it is a corporation based in the Isle of Man, and that Joseph Marx was the president and sole shareholder. We also discovered that it was a legitimate jewelry distributor. We further acknowledge that Sinclair wire transferred fifty million dollars to said company. We also know that Joseph Marx apparently died of a heart attack and that the money was then wired to another of his companies in Panama before disappearing." Nick smiled to Steve and Paul after he finished speaking.

"That's it. That's all you have?" countered Paul.

"If Joseph Marx were still alive, we would have already indicted him too. We believe there is more to his and Bart Sinclair's relationship, but we don't have much to go on."

Now, Paul leaned back in his chair. The moment was on him. He could be a stand-up man and remain silent and face the music or be a true rat in every sense of the word. The Feds had not connected the dots. They were still clueless.

Paul debated whether to tell Steve, yet he knew that what information he had to divulge in order to save his own personal hide, despite the fact that it would drastically impair his own true client, Bart Sinclair.

"What I have to say is huge."

"So."

"So, I want total immunity from the Bubba Franks matter and any other matter I have ever been involved in."

"How do I know you are not bluffing?"

"What I have to say will probably enable you to convict my client and another attorney."

"Another attorney?" said Nick, who was just waiting for his chance to get a shot at a white-collar professional. Most prosecutors abhorred private successful attorneys because usually prosecutors were the "C" students in law school and were not offered any summer internships or exclusive jobs. Unfortunately, the "C" students were forced into working for meager amounts for local, state, or federal governments. They deeply resented all private attorneys—especially successful ones.

"Now, what do you have to say?" asked Paul.

Steve and Nick had a private dialogue before responding. "All right. We will give you full immunity for any of your past deeds."

"I want it in writing. Now." The two Federal prosecutors nodded their heads in complete agreement.

Paul then dictated a complete release and immunity agreement into his digital voice recorder and handed it to his secretary for her immediate attention.

While the men waited anxiously for the document, Don Dannon poked his head into Paul's office.

"Oh, I'm sorry. I didn't know you were in conference," said a surprised Don.

"That's okay. What can I do for you?"

"Nothing important," said Don, even though he thought it odd that Paul would be meeting in his office with federal prosecutors so close to trial.

Don glanced at the document that Paul's secretary was typing and immediately was aghast. How on earth could Paul sell out his client and friend, Bart Sinclair? Don was actually nauseous as he walked silently toward his own office and quietly shut the door.

After a few minor changes, the men signed the legal document. Paul put the original into his personal safe and provided Steve with two copies.

"Okay. Now what have you got for me?" Steve anxiously asked.

Paul began slowly. "Joseph Marx created an irrevocable trust. He named Palm Beach attorney Bo Martin as Trustee. The trust is for the benefit of Bart Sinclair and his family members. Bo has sole discretion over the trust income and principal."

"So what?" impatiently replied Steve.

"Well that Trust holds fifty million dollars from the sale of the alleged fraudulent diamonds."

"You're kidding me. Oh my God! You're right, Paul, you have just sold out your client," laughed Steve.

Paul realized his mistake immediately after he had ratted on his own client and the unsuspecting Bo Martin, which handed the US attorney his case on a silver platter. Naturally, it would be argued that Bart Sinclair sold fake diamonds, and the fifty million he allegedly paid for the real diamonds had in fact, come indirectly back to him. Furthermore, the federal government now could freeze the funds and use the money to repay Milton Rogers. Nobody would believe that Joseph Marx would give away fifty million dollars. Nobody! In addition, the government could prosecute Bo Martin for money laundering, wire fraud, and bank fraud.

Paul realized that if anyone ever found out what he had done, he would face disbarment and be subject to serious liability. But in Paul's own mind, it sure beat sitting in a prison cell.

With this newfound information, Steve Fleishman and Nick Long soon left Paul's office with ear-to-ear smiles.

Not too long after they had left, Paul sat alone in his plush office overlooking idyllic Palm Beach. He was shocked and surprised when Victor Butin and his sidekick, Marty, suddenly barged into his office.

Victor immediately drew his revolver and cocked the hammer. "You son of a bitch."

"What are you talking about? Please put that gun down, Victor!" said Paul hysterically.

"You knew."

"Knew what?"

"You knew that Bo Martin was in control of my money."

"I knew nothing of the sort. All I knew is that Joe had created a trust for Bart Sinclair's family and named Bo Martin Trustee." Slowly Paul was regaining his composure. He had to think quickly and carefully.

"Well, you should have informed me, and should have let me know immediately."

"How much is in the trust?" queried Victor.

"Fifty million."

"Seriously."

"Dead serious." Victor had now put the gun away and taken a seat.

"We need to discuss our future plans."

Paul listened to Victor and Marty explain how they had traced the money from the Isle of Man to Panama, and finally to the Grand Cayman Bank. A Trading Co. Inc. contained over $50 million, and the sole shareholder was the Joseph Marx Trust, Bo Martin, Trustee.

The men also discussed the botched kidnapping of Ruby Martin and their perilously close escape from authorities.

"That was so stupid," injected Paul. Paul felt a jolt of testosterone rush when he realized that the two big Russian goons were in prison and couldn't do him any personal harm.

"Stupid, yes, but we need to find Bo Martin and have him wire transfer the money."

Paul clasped his clammy hands together on his large mahogany desk, and calmly informed Victor that the US government most likely would freeze the corporate funds. When he finished explaining governmental seizures, Victor was extremely pissed, to say the least. He also realized that his only chance was to locate Bo Martin, and have him wire transfer the Cayman account funds to his own personal account before the authorities located him.

"Where the hell is Bo Martin? We heard he was in Europe looking for the manufacturer of synthetic gems."

"I don't have the foggiest idea where he is," answered Paul.

"Tell me something, Paul. Is there any chance of Bart winning at trial?" asked Victor.

"Honestly, it doesn't look good. But Bart's a fighter."

Deep down, Paul knew that Bart had virtually no chance of winning. It was a lost cause.

Chapter
Fifty-Three

Bo and Hank were about to leave Lt. Brown's office at the Gainesville police department and head back to Palm Beach when Hank received a call on his cell phone. Earlier Lt. Brown had informed the men that no cellular telephone was located in the charred debris. "In fact," said Lt. Brown, "no telephone even existed at the warehouse. What type of business is run without a telephone or computer?" he inquired.

Bo and Hank knew the answer to that, but they sure weren't going to offer any more assistance to him.

"Hello," answered Hank once the men were outside police headquarters.

"Well, Ms. Everett, so nice to hear your voice. Yes, Bo's here with me. Sure you can talk to him." Hank handed Bo his iPhone.

"Hello," said Bo. "Oh my God! No, thanks for calling Hank. Yes, it's okay. And, yes you did the right thing. Everything is going to be okay. Please don't worry. I'm fine. See you soon."

Hank knew whatever it was, the news was not good. Bo's coloring had instantly changed ghostly white, and a look of fear had come over his face.

"Are you okay, Bo?"

"Not really. Ms. Everett said the FBI and the assistant United States attorneys were just at the office. It seems that they have a grand jury indictment against me for money laundering, obstruction of justice, and racketeering!"

"Holy shit. What is it all about?"

"Hell if I know for sure. Ms. Everett told them I was in Nantucket on vacation. Looks like they're going to fly up there. I better warn Ruby. Can I use your phone again? My battery is dead, and I don't want there to be a trace so the Feds can't track my whereabouts, via my phone."

Moments later Bo reached Ruby on her cell. "Honey, this is Bo."

"Oh, hi dear. Are you on your way up?"

"No, and I'm afraid that I have got some pretty bad news."

"You're okay, aren't you?"

"Yes, I'm fine. I don't want to tell you where I am, but you're more than likely going to get a visit very shortly."

"By who? Tell me what's wrong."

"The FBI and some US attorneys."

"Oh my God! No, Bo. Tell me no!"

"I'm sorry but I can't. I, myself, don't know what's going on. Hank and I just uncovered some excellent information, but I think the government believes the money in the Joseph Marx Trust is fraudulent. I've got to prove otherwise."

"Where are you, honey? Are you safe?"

"I can't tell you, and I also can't say where we're going, but you can call Hank's cell phone and keep in touch—but only on his phone."

"Should I tell your folks?"

"No need to worry them, just yet."

"I trust you won't be coming up to Nantucket then?" said Ruby in a way that expressed pure fear.

"No. I'm going to be traveling light for a few days or so."

"Oh, honey. I'm so scared. Will everything be all right?"

"I certainly hope so. I love you, Ruby."

"I love you too, Bo!"

When Hank and Bo were back in the car, they immediately tried to unravel everything. Bo and Hank almost instantly concluded that someone had sold Bo out. But who?

Several hours later, they both overwhelmingly decided the snitch was none other than Paul Schwartz. Only Paul Schwartz, Ross Brown, Bart Sinclair, Joseph Marx, and Harrison Frazar, knew about the Trust. Since Joseph Marx was dead, and Bart Sinclair was fighting for his life, neither of them could be the culprit. Ross Brown was just an accountant. He was also a small potato, and really didn't know much about the trust or even where it was located. Harrison Frazar was in the Cayman Islands, far removed from Palm Beach.

No, both men decided that it had to be Paul Schwartz. My God by selling out Bo, he had sold out his very own client and trusted friend, Bart Sinclair!

Bo had figured it all out by the time the men had reached Orlando. The government was going after Bart Sinclair with everything they had. If it was ever found out that Bart Sinclair and his family were the beneficiaries of a trust created by the same man who had sold Bart fifty million in diamonds, then the government would easily convict Sinclair. The trust, Joseph Marx, Bo Martin, and the Grand Cayman account would be considered a ruse, conjured up by Bart Sinclair to bogusly demonstrate that he had purchased real diamonds when in fact he had clearly sold fake gems to Milton Rogers. Case closed. The Feds would pound the fraud into the juries' heads over and over again.

Bo shuddered at the thought of Paul Schwartz, sitting snugly in his penthouse office, knowing that he had sold his own client and Bo Martin down the river.

Hank stared intently at Bo before speaking. "I'm in this thing all the way with you my friend."

"Thanks, Hank, but you have a wife and child to think about."

"No, Bo. I'm in this to the bitter end. So, the way I figure it, we've got to ditch your car. We need to purchase another car in my name only. We also need to get some cash, clothes, and pay a visit to Harrison Frazar in Grand Cayman."

Bo realized everything that Hank had said was true. As long as nobody directly contacted him, he was not, knowingly, a fugitive.

Fortunately, both men had over $10,000 of cash between them, and with that money, they could charter a flight to the Cayman Islands and also purchase a cheap car. A real cheap car! The rest of the two-hour drive was spent in relative silence. They left Bo's car near the West Palm Beach Municipal Airport and bought a fifteen-hundred-dollar Dodge Dart from a small independent dealer in less than two hours.

The men then drove to Chalk's International. Hank chartered a plane to the Cayman Islands. Hank did all the talking, and Bo's name never even appeared on the registry. *It certainly paid to slip the clerk an extra five hundred dollars*, thought Hank.

The plane landed in Grand Cayman at one o'clock in the afternoon, enabling the men plenty of time to obtain a room and freshen up. It was the first time they had showered in two days. Then it was off to the bank.

Both men were quickly ushered into Harrison Frazar's office by his secretary before even Harrison realized they were there. Harrison nearly had a heart attack when he saw Bo, face-to-face.

Bo figured he needed to sweat the man out, since they weren't totally convinced he wasn't the snitch.

"Well, Mr. Martin, you nearly scared me to death," stammered Harrison.

"Cut the theatrics. I know what you did."

"Look, look, I, I . . . I was forced into it."

Bo looked at Hank, and Hank telepathically knew he needed to threaten the already petrified banker.

"I'm Bo's enforcer," said Hank. "Now fess up, or you're going to feel some of my wrath."

"All right, please don't hurt me."

"Go on," uttered Bo in his most serious voice. "We are waiting."

"You see," said Harrison, "I've got big gambling debts. I was approached by this Russian, Marty something, and two huge weight lifters. Biggest guys I've ever seen."

"Go on," repeated Hank, nodding along with Harrison's description of the Russian goons.

"They said they would kill me if I didn't give them information on A Trading Co."

"Yes."

"My life was at stake. So I told them everything."

"Such as?"

"Such as the fact that you're the Trustee of the Joseph Marx Trust, and as the sole shareholder, you have complete control of the Trust."

"Did they see the Trust?"

"No, no. It's right here in the file."

"Give it to me," demanded Bo.

"I can't."

"Give it to me now," shouted Bo. Begrudgingly, Harrison handed the trust over to Bo. Bo gave it to Hank.

"How much did you get paid?"

"Nothing."

"Don't lie. You're dead if you lie."

"Okay. I got one hundred thousand dollars from a wire transfer."

"Who sent the money?"

"I don't know."

"Bullshit," said Hank as he stood and approached Harrison.

"Okay, okay. It was a Russian LLC licensed to do business in the United States. I did my research and it turns out that Victor Butin is the treasurer."

"So I see," said Bo.

The men sat in complete silence for what seemed like several minutes. Harrison couldn't take the stress any longer and blurted out. "I'm so sorry. Please don't get me fired! I have a wife and two kids who depend on me."

"You should have thought of that before you breached your duty," said a stone-faced Hank.

"Look if there is anything I can do, I will. Anything."

"Now that you mention it," began Bo, "we will need five hundred thousand dollars cash in twenties, tens, and fives before the end of the day."

"No problem. Anything else?"

"Yes, the entire account needs to be transferred to a new account."

"A new account? I can't authorize that!"

"Yes, you can, and you will if you want to protect your wife and kids."

"You wouldn't."

"Just try me," said Bo. "You've compromised everything with your actions."

"Okay. What do you want?"

"I want a new account called 'The Trust.' No trustee, no address, no other information. Also, it must be finalized and confirmed before the end of the day. Only Bo Martin and Hank Miles can give the commands regarding The Trust."

"What you're requesting is against bank policy!"

"Do it or else face the music."

"Okay, I'll do it, but under extreme protest. If this ever comes to light, you will suffer the consequences, not me."

"Fine."

About two and a half hours later, Bo and Hank walked out of the bank, each carrying two hundred fifty thousand dollars in cash. Bo also had the confirmation that the trust proceeds were safe and secure from the government and from Victor Butin.

Hank spoke to Bo in jest, "It's bad enough that the US government wants your ass, but the Russian mob as well?"

"Thanks for your uplifting support, good man," said Bo with the first smile that Hank had seen in the past two days.

Chapter
Fifty-Four

O ver dinner, the two best friends plotted their next moves.
The following morning, after a barefoot run on the sandy white beach and a long swim, the two men chartered another plane back to West Palm Beach, Florida. Again, Hank paid off the ticket master, and Bo's name was omitted from the pilot's log.

Their trip was a success, and miraculously the Dodge Dart started right up. The air conditioning even worked, much to the delight of both men.

It was still early in the afternoon when the men walked into the Crazy Horse Saloon in North Palm Beach, Florida. The hardcore regular alcoholics were already at their designated seats, and it didn't take the men long to locate their man, Sean Heese. Sean was an immense man now, but in his glory years, he was a star running back for Palm Beach High School.

Sean was surprised to see the two men.

"Well, I'll be. How the hell are you two?"

Hank said, "We're just fine. And you?"

"Could be better."

Bo interrupted. "You want to make some money? Good money."

"Certainly. You know I've been down in the dumps lately with my wife leaving me and taking the kids."

"There will be no drinking on the job. Can you handle that?" asked Hank.

"Sure. What do you need?" Sean was now sitting erect and giving the men his complete attention.

Bo knew that Sean was once a top-notch private investigator before the booze led him down the wrong path. In fact, Bo's dad had used Sean on numerous cases, and always said that Sean was the very best.

Bo looked Sean squarely in the eyes. "We need you to bug a house and keep an eye on a Palm Beach family."

"How much will you pay me for this illegal bugging?"

"What do you want?" queried Bo.

"I want ten thousand dollars and all my expenses paid."

"It's a deal. Here is five thousand dollars now, and you will get the rest upon completion," said Bo, handing over the cash.

"I can live with that. Who are the people?" asked Sean as he stuffed the money underneath his large pot-bellied stomach.

"Their names are Milton and Brenda Rogers, and they live in Palm Beach. Hank and I can monitor the wiretap from your own house, Sean."

"Is there some reason why you are keeping a low profile?"

"Let's just say that discretion and extreme caution are warranted."

"We also need you to break in and install everything this evening. We've confirmed that the Rogers have a dinner reservation at the Sailfish Club at seven o'clock tonight. We think the best way to enter the house is from the ocean."

The men spent the rest of the afternoon plotting and helping Sean prepare the eavesdropping equipment from Sean's own living room.

"Feel free to stay at my house."

"Thank you. We will."

"Don't worry. We'll add it to your fee," smiled Bo.

Later that evening, their mission was a complete success. Sean was able to dismantle the burglar alarm, strategically place all the wiretaps and monitoring bugs, and reset the alarm without any problems.

When the men were safely back at Sean's home, they tested out the equipment before Milton and Brenda Rogers returned home from their society dinner.

Milton was in a foul mood.

"I can't believe they can't even locate Bo Martin. The FBI is incompetent. Goddamn Steve Fleishman and Nick Long. Those US attorneys are also idiots. Mae McReynolds can't wait to run a story on Bo Martin's indictment and his role as trustee over the fifty million dollars, but not until he is officially served."

"You know, honey, I don't like it that you now have an innocent attorney involved."

"Screw him."

"Everyone I know holds Bo and his lovely wife, Ruby in the highest regard. This is just going to devastate them. Milton, he could go to prison!"

"So what!"

"He's innocent."

"Look, honey, nobody is innocent. You got that. N-o-b-o-d-y!"

"Well, he's innocent of this matter."

"Don't you want your spoiled rotten kids taken care of for life?"

"Of course I do. I just didn't want anyone to get hurt in the process."

"Trust me, honey. Our plan will work out. If only that son of a bitch, Jean Valhomme, calls and lets me know when the shipment will come in. It should be here shortly."

"When we confirm the delivery, I'll have you fly over to Antwerp, access the box, and hand over the real diamonds to Jean."

"Why me?" asked Brenda.

"Because I'll be here with the boys, trying to distribute the Ecstasy tablets. The boys can't handle it themselves. Plus, I lined up all the distributors myself under the code name Diamond. Pretty catchy, huh?"

"Whatever, Milton. I just want the boys protected. Where will the money go?" asked Brenda.

"For the last time, woman, we created the Four L's Ltd in the Bahamas. When the pills sell, the money will be deposited over in the Bahamas bank. The boys and I will take our yacht over there with all the cash. The bank president will get one million dollars, and the rest will be deposited into the account. No questions asked. Later, the account will be divided four ways, and each boy will then be in complete control of his own account."

"Well, the boys have been waiting for months now, trying to "fit in" those major cities, Milton. Do you have any idea when the pills will be arriving in the Port of Palm Beach?"

"Soon, dear, very soon," said Milton, although his mind was miles away.

"My God," said the three men simultaneously as they turned off the recording equipment.

"Did you get all of that?" asked Hank.

"Sure did."

Sean looked at Bo. "This is some heavy shit, man. You have been set up. I always thought that Bart Sinclair was getting a bad rap, but I could never have expected this."

Hank also was shocked. "My God, what an excellent scam. Bo, we really need to act on this quickly."

Bo nodded and said, "I only hope we hear from this guy, Jean Valhomme, soon, before I'm arrested."

"We will. Trust me," said Sean. "I'm the best. By the way, my fee also just tripled."

Chapter
Fifty-Five

B o and Hank spent the next day monitoring the conversations inside the Rogers's mansion, as well as the numerous telephone calls. Together, they still couldn't figure out who Jean Valhomme was and his connection to the Rogers clan. Both men were also becoming somewhat uptight and extremely concerned. Sean was the only calm one.

"Give it time, give it time," said Sean.

Bo turned to Hank and said, "What if we can't prove the Rogers's scheme? We don't have the jewels. We don't have Joe Marx. We don't have this Jean fellow, and I'm staring down an indictment for money laundering, civil theft, racketeering, wire fraud, and probably the kitchen sink."

"Cool it, Bo. Calm down. You're one hundred percent better off now than we were before. Something will break. Trust me. You're too nice a guy to end up in prison. And besides, who else would I have to train with?" laughed Hank.

"Thanks, Hank. Thanks for everything," smiled Bo.

Less than an hour later, they received their lucky break when Lee and Lance walked into the Rogers's palatial home unannounced.

"Dad! Mom! Is anyone home?" shouted Lee.

"Maybe they're at the Beach Club playing tennis or sunning."

"No, their cars are out front. I know they're home. Dad's been anxiously awaiting a call from Jean."

"What's with this Jean fellow anyway? Wasn't he supposed to deliver the Ecstasy pills over two months ago?"

"Yes, but it will be an incredibly large shipment and security is much more stringent than ever before."

"Oh, don't worry about the Port of Palm Beach and its security officers. Dad has already paid off the top brass. When the shipment of pills does come in, there won't be any problems from the authorities."

"I sure do hope so. The last thing I'd want is to go to jail."

"Well, let's try the club and leave a note letting them know we're in Palm Beach and all the drug connections are set."

"You idiot. Don't write drug connections. Dad will kill you. You know how he is about secrecy."

"Oh, yeah. Sorry."

Bo and Hank sat numb in silence and disbelief. Bo's mind was reeling, as was Hank's. It was Bo who first spoke.

"Let me get this straight. Jean Valhomme is a drug smuggler. He is going to deliver Ecstasy tablets by boat into the Port of Palm Beach. Unfortunately, he hasn't called."

"So far, so good," replied Hank. "I'm with you."

"Let's go one step further."

"Okay."

"How are they going to pay for the drugs?"

"Not cash. The government has new requirements which pertain to cash deposits. Financial banks now must report any deposit in excess of ten thousand dollars. Wire transfers are traceable, and nobody is issuing cashier's checks for millions of dollars."

"You're right."

"So, don't you see?" questioned Bo.

"Not really," responded Hank.

"They're planning on paying for the drugs with the real diamonds. The diamonds are a lot more liquid and don't involve large deposits of actual cash. It makes it much easier to launder, than cash proceeds."

"Bo, assuming you're right, then if we can somehow thwart the exchange, we can recover the real stones and send Milton Rogers, his wife, and his idiot sons off to jail."

"Let's just pray that this fellow Jean calls."

Bo and Hank kept listening for anything, but all was quiet at the Rogers's mansion. The next morning there was activity, and Bo and Hank were on it.

Sean spoke excitedly, "See I told you not to worry."

Early that morning, the infamous Jean called Milton. Sean shouted to Bo and Hank. "Listen in. Hurry."

"Milton, this is Jean."

"Where the hell have you been? What took you so damn long?"

"Now, Milton, would I let you down?"

"I sure hope not."

"Well, don't worry about me or my wife or my son. We are all doing fine," said Jean tongue-in-cheek.

"That's just great. Now on to business," replied Milton, coldly.

"Well, Milton, everything is set. The merchandise is in route to the Port of Palm Beach."

"That's excellent. Just excellent!"

"Now, Milton. I'm out a lot of money. I want at least half the gems now."

"That's not part of the deal."

"Then I want your wife, Brenda to be in Antwerp and ready to deliver your entire merchandise."

"No way."

"It's my way or nothing. Got that, my friend?" There was silence before Milton spoke again.

"I hear you. I also understand you. Okay. If my wife and daughter-in-law fly to Antwerp and stay at the Ritz Carlton, they will be prepared to deliver you all the stones, but only after I acknowledge receipt of your delivery."

"Not on the phone Milton. You of all people should know not to say anything on the phone. Got it?" said Jean coldly.

"I've got it," muttered Milton. "I'll put the girls on a plane first thing tomorrow. When can we expect delivery?"

"I don't trust the telephone. There are always too many ears."

"Why don't you just fax me the necessary information then?"

"No paper trail ever," responded Jean.

"Okay. Then just give me the basics and I'll take care of the rest."

"Not until I see your wife and daughter-in-law."

"Are you serious, Jean?"

"Dead serious."

"If you so much as lay a hand or harm them in any way, I'll personally kill you. Have you got that?"

"Milton, I'll be waiting for them to come to my office, and only then, will I disclose the time and place. Until then, I bid you adieu."

"Yeah, yeah. See you soon."

Milton's next phone call was to his travel agent. He booked two first-class tickets to Antwerp. The earliest plane left at eight a.m. the next day. He purchased and confirmed the two tickets.

"Honey," yelled Milton.

"Yes, dear."

"Pack your bags. You and Annie are flying to Antwerp tomorrow to meet with Jean Valhomme."

"What about you?"

"I have to stay here with the boys and handle the delivery of the pills. You're going to have to hand deliver the gems to Jean once I confirm the receipt of all the Ecstasy tablets."

"We will need a code word or phrase," said Brenda really getting into the cloak-and-dagger aspect of their operation.

"Okay, honey. What do you have in mind?"

"Why not say 'diamonds are forever'? And Milton, your response or mine will be 'Sean Connery.'"

"How lame," said Milton, disgusted.

"But it works."

"Okay."

"How long will Annie and I have to stay in Antwerp?"

"I don't really know for sure. A week to ten days."

"Well, I'll call Annie now, and will you take us to the airport tomorrow?"

"Sure thing."

Meanwhile back at Sean's house, all three men stared at one another in disbelief. Without any spoken words, Sean got up and walked to the closet where he pulled out a suitcase.

"I don't expect either one of you to fly to Antwerp now, do you?"

Both Hank and Bo shrugged their shoulders.

"Plus, I intend on stealing some diamonds gentlemen!"

All three men smiled in unison.

"Do you really think the gems will be over there?" asked Hank.

"I do," said Bo.

"I do too," interjected Sean. "And I know that Brenda will be the one delivering them to Jean. Now that we know his last name, I can also do some surveillance work on him when the girls are sleeping or shopping. Plus, you will let me know ASAP whenever you hear a phone call from Jean to Milton, or vice versa."

"Now, Sean, you don't have to do this," said Bo.

"I understand, and yes, I do. Without those real gems, you are still in serious trouble, Bo. And I will now quadruple my fee for this trip. I am looking at getting my life back together, and with your fees, I will be back on my feet once again."

"No problem," said Bo and Hank in unison.

"Now go book me a first-class ticket," demanded Sean. Bo also handed Sean $20,000 in cash from the cash he had withdrawn from the trust.

"Thanks, Bo."

"No, thank you. And good luck!"

Bo was pleased that they were able to record the latest two conversations. Although the tapes could not be used in a court of law against Milton and his family, since they were illegal, they would be beneficial to Bo in his own criminal defense. Bo knew it was also inevitable that he would be indicted, and the news would be devastating to his legal career.

Bo was well aware that most Palm Beachers were extremely fickle. They like being considered part of the in-crowd. Presently Bo was part of the in-crowd. He knew that as soon as the indictment came out, his practice would precipitously deteriorate. His acquaintances would avoid him like the plague and it would take years to rebuild and regain the respect of the Palm Beach community. Most likely, his legal career would be over, and everything he knew, would be lost.

Bo couldn't even comprehend actually going to jail, but it was definitely weighing heavily on his mind. The last thing he would ever want was to be separated from Ruby and the red dogs.

Hank sensed his best friend's fear and tried hard to reassure him that everything would be fine. "Bo, we will get to the bottom of this. Sean will procure the gems, and we, my friend, will put a stop to the drugs."

"Do you think it's time to contact the Feds?" queried Hank.

"Not until we get more information. We have to catch them in the act."

"Well, what do we do now?" asked Hank.

"We go to the Port of Palm Beach and start surveillance on the docks."

"Let's get out of here. Put on your hat and glasses and try to look as inconspicuous as possible."

Chapter
Fifty-Six

The Port of Palm Beach is situated about one mile due west of the treacherous Palm Beach Inlet. On the south side of the inlet lies Palm Beach, and on the north side is Palm Beach Shores. It is an enclave of moderately priced homes in stark contrast to the multimillion dollar homes on Palm Beach. Once one has successfully navigated through the inlet, a rather large land mass called Peanut Island requires boaters to either turn left, and travel south to Palm Beach, or north toward the Intracoastal Waterway, which winds itself all the way up to New York.

In the 1960s, President John F. Kennedy commissioned a bunker to be constructed on Peanut Island in the event of war with Cuba. Now, the island housed a restaurant and large campsites for overnight stays.

Directly behind Peanut Island lies the Port of Palm Beach. The somewhat shallow depth of the inlet (thirty-five feet to be exact) precludes oversized yachts, oil tankers, or large cruise ships from using the Palm Beach Inlet. However, the bulk of the port's traffic includes freighters containing sugar, orange juice, and molasses. The biggest companies include Tropicana, US Sugar, and Crystals Inc.

Bo and Hank were able to slip by the grossly overweight security guard, who seemed more fixated on the television screen than in monitoring the entrance gate. Once inside, the two men dressed in jeans and t-shirts, quickly blended in among the numerous workers.

The Port was a hotbed of activity, and everyone seemed preoccupied with their own jobs. Nobody paid much attention to the two men.

The men worked their way toward the actual loading docks. There were three main docks. Only two were currently in use because the third appeared as if it were still under construction. Periodically, both Hank and Bo asked questions to workers, who were more than happy to answer them. Once a ship was safely docked, a huge crane promptly began unloading the numerous containers that the ships carried.

From what Bo could tell, Tropicana Orange Juice solely used the south dockage area, and all the others, primarily the sugar companies, used only the north dock.

The men also learned that the port accepted ships from seven o'clock in the morning until four o'clock in the afternoon. Only US ships utilized the south dock, and all foreign ships were required to use the north dock and properly clear US customs before any containers could be unloaded.

By the end of the day, Bo and Hank were satisfied that they had a sufficient knowledge and understanding of the port. They realized one more additional day would definitely be needed to plan their surprise on Milton and his boys.

Later that evening, Bo and Hank went to the Salvation Army and purchased work boots, hard hats, and t-shirts with pockets. Now, they would really blend in with all the other workers.

After a quick take-out dinner at Wendy's, the men returned to Sean's home and listened to all the Rogers family conversations and telephone calls until the wee hours of the morning. Unfortunately, no call from Jean came through.

At seven o'clock the following morning, the men once again snuck into the port and focused on the north dock. They even befriended the dock master, who told them all about the port and its inner workings. By the end of the day, Bo and Hank believed they were ready for anything.

Tired and mentally spent, the two men returned back to Sean's house and once again sat down to listen to the tapes. The good news was that Sean had called and was able to locate Jean's home and office and had followed the women to their hotel and a locker rental place where Sean presumed the gems were being kept. Sean sensed that the shipment would be any day now.

At six-thirty the following day in the morning, Bo and Hank intently listened to Jean's rather urgent call to Milton.

"My friend Milton."

"Nice to hear from you, Jean."

"Your wife hasn't changed a bit, and I really liked your daughter-in-law. Too bad she's taken. Right?"

Milton bit his tongue, but he was clearly annoyed. "I'm glad you've had the opportunity to meet with them. They are ready and willing to provide you with the goods but only upon my say so."

"Well, get ready, Milton. Tomorrow at three o'clock the Panamanian ship *Lourdes* will dock at the Port of Palm Beach. There are four containers. Number eleven, seventeen, nineteen, and thirty-three. You will need one large flatbed truck to transport the non-marked white containers. The man you must speak with is Ralph. He will load the containers onto your truck. Be sure to rent a big one.

"I want you to examine the contents of only one container. Don't check all four because it will draw too much attention. Ralph will call me once you have examined the container. I expect your wife to deliver the box to me within thirty minutes of Ralph's call. It will be later in the evening over here, and I will only require that she drop off the box at my house. My wife and I will be out for the evening, but my butler, Claude, who I trust with my life, will be here to accept the delivery."

"One more thing, and let me make it very clear to you. I will have your wife and beautiful daughter-in-law slowly tortured to death if you double-cross me. Understood?"

"Completely."

"Well, good luck, Milton."

"You too, Jean."

"Bingo," said Hank and Bo after the conclusion of the phone call.

Bo and Hank hoped that Milton would summon his boys to the mansion and they would confer in the den since the clarity from the bug in that room was by far the best.

By lunchtime the entire male Rogers clan had indeed assembled and were all sitting in the den area.

"Which one of you can drive an eighteen wheeler?" asked Milton.

No one said a word.

"You mean to tell me that nobody knows how to drive a truck? You worthless pieces of shit!"

"Sorry, Dad," joined the boys in unison.

"Okay. Does anyone know someone who can drive a semi?"

Again, not one boy answered.

Finally, Lee said, "Let's just hire someone to pick up the load and drive it to Dad's warehouse."

Milton thought about it for a second before speaking. "That's good, Lee. The four containers are destined to four separate regions. Your distributors can easily pick up each container from my warehouse in West Palm Beach. Are they ready?"

"They will be as soon as we call them."

"Well, it will probably take us a day to inventory the goods, so let's have the distributors pick up the containers in two days from tomorrow."

"Each of you call your contacts now. But not from this phone or your cell phones, idiots! Call from a public phone, please." Each boy nodded his head.

"Now, who do you recommend we call to pick up and take the containers to the warehouse?"

"How about Father and Sons Inc. They have a large semi and a flat bed," said Lance.

"Fine then. Make the arrangements. We all will be at the warehouse tomorrow night."

"I will call your mother," said Milton, "and everyone make your calls, and for Christ's sake, tell no one!"

Bo and Hank sat perplexed. "What do we do now?" questioned Hank, knowing full well that Bo had no idea either.

While Bo sat perplexed, the two men listened into the phone conversation between Milton and Brenda.

"Hello, dear."

"Yes, honey. Speak a little louder. Annie has the hair dryer on."

"We heard from Jean."

"Oh, great. Annie and I met with him, and he also told us where to deliver the package at his house. We know how to get there from the hotel, and a taxi can take us there."

"Listen up, Brenda. You must do exactly as I say. Got that?"

"Yes, dear, I understand."

"There can be no slip-ups. You will have less than thirty minutes to pick up the merchandise and deliver them to Jean from the moment I call you."

"I understand completely. I'm going to take a Ritz Carlton bag with me, and the taxi will take us directly to the box and from there to Jean's house. I really don't want to have anything with me tonight or in this hotel room."

"Smart thinking, Brenda. The boat will be docking around three p.m. We will inspect one of the containers, and then I will call you. It will be late tomorrow night or early morning when you need a taxi to make the drop-off."

"Now don't worry, Milton. Annie and I will handle our end. After all, we're doing this for my boys. I love you, Milton."

"I love you too, honey."

"Be extremely careful."

"You too."

When their conversation had ended, Bo quickly called Sean. The connection was somewhat muffled.

"Hello, Sean? Yes. This is Bo. How are you?"

"Just fine. Any news?"

"We just heard."

"Okay. Shoot."

"The pills are coming in tomorrow aboard a ship called *Lourdes* at three o'clock in the afternoon. We just overheard Milton's discussion with Brenda, and Brenda and Annie will take a taxi to the box rental place where they will pick up the gems, place them in a Ritz Carlton bag, and then deliver them to Jean's front door."

"Perfect," replied Sean. "That's all that I needed to know."

"Now, Sean, Jean also said if there was any problem, he would have the girls killed and Milton strangled to death with his own bare hands. So be extremely careful. What exactly are you going to do?"

"That's for me to know and you to find out. What about the pills?" inquired Sean.

"We're not sure yet."

"Well, good luck to you too. Stay in touch, and don't worry. I feel kinda good about this."

When Sean hung up, unfortunately neither Bo nor Hank felt good about anything. In fact, both men were actually petrified. Fortunately, out of the blue, Bo got an idea.

Bo picked up the telephone. "Now who are you calling?" asked Hank.

"You'll see."

"Hello. Mike, this is Bo Martin.

"Well, how the hell are you? Long time no talk. Thanks again for everything you did for us."

"Think nothing of it."

"Well, I'll owe you forever after all your support of me and my family when I was away in prison. Your letters and money kept me going and positive during my stay at Coleman Medium (a federal prison institution in Coleman, Florida). Now what can I do to help you?"

"You're still driving a semi, aren't you?"

"Absolutely. I'm making an honest decent living for a change, and I'm completely drug free."

"That's great because I need your help, big-time. Are you familiar with the Port of Palm Beach?"

"Sure. I pick up containers there ever so often. I have a TWIC card (Transportation Worker Identification Credential) that allows me access to all the maritime ports in Florida."

"And are you still best friends with the son of Father and Sons Inc.?"

"Yes. I was just with him yesterday, as a matter of fact. How'd you know?"

"I remember you telling me once."

"Okay. What can I do for you?" asked Mike, curiously.

"Can you by chance handle a pickup for him tomorrow, around three o'clock on the north dock from a ship called *Lourdes*?"

"How do you know a shipment is coming in and Father and Sons is picking up some containers?" inquired Mike, somewhat hesitantly.

"You don't want to know. Trust me."

"Let me call him now. Can I call you back?"

"How bout I call you back in a half hour?"

"Fine. Talk to you shortly."

The next thirty minutes seemed like an eternity for the two men. Hank was still amazed at Bo's connections and his wide array of friends and acquaintances.

Bo dialed Mike's number with trepidation.

"Hello, Bo." He answered.

"Yes."

"It's all set. I'm to pick up four containers, and this man Milton Rogers will inspect one container, and then I have to take them to a warehouse in West Palm Beach. I'm technically not working for Father and Sons Inc., so if there is something you want me to do, they will not be liable."

"Can we meet sometime today?"

"Sure, my best friend Hank and I, will be over in about half an hour."

"That's great. See you soon."

"Bye."

Bo was immediately back on the phone, this time calling another friend.

"Hi, Fred. This is Bo Martin."

"Hi, Bo. How are you? How you been?"

"Pretty good. And yourself?"

"Can't complain."

"I've got a favor to ask of you."

"Shoot. Anything."

"Do you still own a warehouse in West Palm Beach?"

"Sure do."

"Is there anything in it at the present time?"

"Well one of my tenants just moved out, so I definitely have some space."

"Great. I'd like to rent it from you for a while. Charge me whatever you want."

"Bo for you, there is no charge."

"What's the address again?"

Bo jotted down the address and made arrangements for it to be left open.

Bo made one final call whereupon he leased for thirty days, three large white containers to be picked up the following morning. As Bo and Hank traveled over to Mike's house, the two men were both hoping and praying that everything would work according to plan.

As Bo had expected, the meeting with Mike went great. Mike had no problem agreeing to let Hank ride with him to pick up the three new containers and to then utilize his services at the Port of Palm Beach.

Mike didn't ask what was inside the containers, and Bo did not reveal it to him. Mike also helped to make arrangements to have a crane ready at the rented warehouse, which was less than a mile from the Rogers's family warehouse.

It was Hank who suggested that Mike change the plates on the truck and use a fake name when entering the port security. Mike sensed that something was illegal but had no problem assisting Bo, even though he was putting his life of freedom at risk.

Later that evening, neither Bo nor Hank could sleep a wink. So at around two o'clock the men went for a much-needed run through Lake Park, Florida. They both wore hats and kept to the unlit parts of the neighborhoods. Together they discussed the final details.

Each man knew the substantial pitfalls they faced. What if customs searched the containers? What if Jean was conning Milton? What if the DEA was following the shipment? What if the FBI catches Bo? What if Victor shows up? What if Sean can't stop Brenda? What if Jean kills Brenda and Annie?

The answers to all these questions and concerns would be finalized within the next twenty-four hours, and their lives would forever be changed.

Meanwhile, breakfast at the Rogers's mansion was tense. Milton checked and double-checked all the final details and arrangements. The weather was expected to be beautiful with little chance of afternoon thunderstorms. He had called Brenda and Annie again, and everything was in order at their end.

The boys had also done their parts. Each distributor had previously coughed up $20 million representing 20 percent of the agreed-upon price per container in advance. Another 20 percent in cash would be paid upon inspection of the Ecstasy tablets, and the final 60 percent would be paid upon the sale of the pills or within sixty days of receipt, whichever occurred earlier.

The distributors were all extremely cagy characters, and if there was any trouble at all, the Rogers boys would definitely have their hands full.

Milton arranged it so that he, Lee, and Lance, his two oldest sons, would be at the Port of Palm Beach. Lawrence and Luke would remain at the warehouse and would notify the four distributors immediately upon delivery of the containers to the warehouse. Milton wanted to remain in total control of all aspects of the operation.

Chapter
Fifty-Seven

At the federal building, Steve Fleishman and Nick Long were fuming mad. "Where the hell is Bo Martin? He hasn't reported to work, nor has he even called in to check his messages. His cell phone is turned off. His wife and parents are up in Nantucket and the wiretap on the Martin phones has discovered nothing," yelled Steve. "We have to find him."

"Where could he be?" asked Nick.

Neither gentleman knew the answer. Steve was also feeling the heat from Jim McDonald and Mae McReynolds. Jim was pressing Steve to catch Bo so that he could include him as a defendant in the civil suit against Bart Sinclair. Mae had already written the scathing article, which she was eagerly awaiting to have published on the main page of the *Palm Beach News*. And of course, Steve was savoring to indict Bo on money laundering and RICO violations.

Plus, the federal criminal trial against Bart Sinclair was just weeks away. The government hoped to have already charged Bo Martin, as they planned to use him as a witness against Bart in the criminal trial. Through their notorious strong-arm tactics, the government hoped to convince Bo to roll over on Bart in return for a reduction of sentence. Basically, Bo was becoming the prosecutors' central figure in the case against Sinclair. Without Bo's help, the case rested on Milton Rogers's word versus Bart Sinclair's. Milton would be an excellent witness—an elderly rich man manipulated and defrauded by an unscrupulous jewelry dealer married to his third wife. Nonetheless, Bo needed to be apprehended immediately.

Bo and Hank met with Mike and his lovely wife. It was Mike's wife who painstakingly altered all three men's appearances. When she was finished, the men looked totally different. In fact, there was no way to identify any of them. Her work was that good!

After a delicious breakfast, the three men boarded the semi and drove to pick up the three white containers that Bo had leased with cash. Once they were loaded, the men dropped off Bo with the containers at the rented warehouse, and together they finalized their plan.

By two o'clock Mike and Hank said goodbye to Bo. Bo wished he could join them but knew he was better off coordinating matters from the warehouse. All three men were nervous but ready to experience anything.

Chapter
Fifty-Eight

he *Lourdes* arrived at the mouth of the Palm Beach Inlet precisely on time. The pilot boat captain navigated the foreign ship to the north dock, and the boat was secured and tied up by three-thirty o'clock in the afternoon.

Milton and his two eldest sons had been at the dock since two-thirty. Milton closely watched the dock for the appearance of any DEA agents, the police, or any other federal officials. Thankfully, none were around. The money he had spent on protection appeared well worth it.

Milton was also relieved to see the semi truck and two men who seemed ready to work.

It took more than three hours for the *Lourdes* to clear customs, and when the Port Authority agents departed from the launch, Milton and his boys grinned from ear to ear.

Milton proceeded next to introduce himself to Mike and Hank.

"Howdy, gentlemen."

"Hello. Hello."

"I see you are ready to load up your truck."

"Yes, sir. I have plenty of room to load your four containers. I know it's getting dark out. Do you plan on inspecting the containers first?"

"No. Just one."

"Okay. Just let us know when you're ready, and I'll instruct the crane operator to load all four onto the back of my rig."

"I will. By the way do you know where my warehouse is located?"

"Absolutely. I have the instructions somewhere around here," replied Mike looking down at nothing on the seat.

"Thank you."

"No, thank you."

When Milton passed, Mike turned to Hank and said, "What an asshole! I hope you stick it to him."

"We will, oh we will."

Hank and Bo had presumed that the Ecstasy pills would be encased in waterproof containers. They guessed right, especially since Bo had spent the day loading the three containers with boxes of empty waterproof containers.

Milton and his boys closely examined the contents of container number eleven. The pills were encased in two-by-four cream-colored boxes stacked from the floor to the ceiling of the container. They opened at least a dozen of the boxes, and each one was overflowing with pills.

Lee spoke after examining the last of the boxes. "Well, Dad, it looks like everything is here. Each of my boxes was filled with tablets."

Lance responded, "All of mine contained tablets."

Milton then spoke. "All of the boxes I inspected were also filled with pills. It appears that Jean came through."

Milton opened his cell phone and dialed.

"Hello?"

"Milton, do you know what time it is?"

"Sorry, dear. I just inspected the containers, and everything is fine."

"That's wonderful! We have been dressed and have been ready to go for hours now. I'm sure a taxi will be downstairs waiting for us."

"Well, be careful. You have thirty minutes."

"Talk to you soon, honey."

When the two women emerged from the Ritz lobby, Sean appeared in his taxi uniform and opened the back door of his "borrowed" taxi for the women.

"Where to?"

Brenda handed him the address to the storage rental and to Jean's home. "There's an extra fifty if you get us to the home in less than thirty minutes," said Brenda.

At the storage rental office, Brenda and Annie entered and emerged minutes later with a box, which Brenda then dropped into the Ritz Carlton bag. The box wasn't too large and sank to the bottom of the large plastic bag.

When Sean opened the door for them, he courteously grabbed the bag from Brenda and said, "Let me put this into the trunk for extra safety."

"Why do you think we need extra safety?" questioned Annie sternly.

"Because why else would you rent a cab at three o'clock in the morning and offer me more than fifty dollars to get you to some mansion?"

"You've got a point there, Mister. But no funny stuff."

"Don't worry, I want the fifty dollars."

What the women didn't know was that Sean had previously placed at least a dozen boxes of varying weights and sizes in the trunk with a couple of Ritz Carlton plastic bags, which Bo had informed him to do. Thankfully, he had chosen a box nearly identical to the one Brenda had placed inside the Ritz Carlton bag.

Sean conveniently switched his box and Ritz bag with Brenda's.

Sean drove carefully to the magnificent mansion of Jean Valhomme and opened the trunk to provide Brenda with the Ritz Carlton bag. Brenda didn't notice any discernible difference with the Ritz bag and waddled to the front door, rang the doorbell, and waited to hand deliver the bag and its contents to Jean's butler, just as she had been instructed. After the exchange, she promptly returned to the taxicab.

Once again Sean drove carefully back to the luxurious hotel and cheerfully accepted the generous $50 tip from Brenda.

After turning down the street and away from the hotel, Sean returned the taxi to where he had conveniently borrowed it and walked quickly with his box to his leased auto.

Sean then drove straight to the airport and within four hours was on a plane bound for Miami, Florida with the gems safely tucked inside his checked suitcase. Tempted as he was to drink like a fish, Sean instead opted for seltzer water and a lime.

Chapter
Fifty-Nine

ack in Florida, Mike and Hank had cleared the corridor of the port's elaborate entrance and proceeded west toward the West Palm Beach warehouse. Hank kept watching the rearview mirror and was pleased to note that neither Milton nor his boys decided to follow the semi.

Mike put the pedal to the metal and ran several "pink" lights before safely pulling into the rental warehouse where Bo was waiting impatiently with the crane. Bo had spent a summer operating large heavy machinery and within less than ten minutes was able to replace three of the four white containers with the newly purchased containers. Bo then spray painted the corresponding numbers on the new containers, making them appear identical to the original ones, and bid the men good luck.

When Mike and Hank reached the Rogers's warehouse, Milton and all four of his boys were already there.

"What took you guys so long?" shouted Milton.

"What are you talking about?" responded Hank. "We came straight here but got caught by a train. We didn't know you were timing us, mister."

"Just shut up and help with the unloading of the containers, would you?"

"Sure thing."

The crane that the Rogers boys had borrowed was old and barely operable. Hank worried that Milton would receive a call from either Jean or his wife, Brenda, and kept worrying that any minute he and Mike would be nabbed.

Fortunately, no call came through, and one hour later, the containers were unloaded and they were on their way to retrieve Bo.

So far, so good, thought Hank, as he and Mike drove cautiously down Australian Avenue to meet Bo at the warehouse.

When the men had returned back to Mike's home and had painfully removed their disguises, they finally had a chance to relax.

Bo and Hank couldn't thank Mike enough. Before they left in their Dodge Dart, Bo handed Mike fifty thousand dollars in cash and told he and his wife to immediately take a long trip. Mike was speechless and his wife was in tears.

"Thank you," said Mike.

"No, thank you," replied Bo. "Now get packing and get moving. Also, change the plates."

"Sure thing. Thank you both."

Hank hugged Mike, proceeded to the car, and joined Bo.

Chapter
Sixty

Now Bo and Hank faced a major dilemma. They were praying that Sean was successful in procuring the original real diamonds. Unfortunately, they wouldn't know anything until they returned to the Lake Park home and listened to the recorded messages. The return drive to Sean's residence was eerily quiet, as both men were consumed in deep thought.

There were only two messages. The first was a telemarketer, and fortunately, the second was Sean.

"Hey guys, it's me. Everything was successful. See you soon."

For a second, both men simply stared at each other.

"Do you think he would steal the gems and never return back here?" asked Hank.

"I really don't know. My Dad always told me, 'Money—it makes the blind see, the deaf hear and the mute speak.' But honestly, I don't think he would double-cross us. I really don't."

"I hope for your sake, Bo that he doesn't."

"Me too."

Bo figured that Milton and his sons would not examine the remaining containers until the following day. He reasoned that they would, most likely, celebrate the occasion and probably toss a few back.

Bo knew what he was going to do, but he wanted to know exactly what Milton knew before acting. Hank was left in the dark, wondering.

The men turned on the surveillance tape and began listening intently to the Rogers's conversations. Brenda had called saying that everything went well and that they would be returning home shortly. Fortunately, there was no phone call from Jean.

A phone call that did raise the hair on Bo's back was from Jim McDonald, Milton's civil attorney.

"Hi Milton, it's Jim. I just wanted to let you know that there is going to be an article by Mae on Bo Martin regarding the indictment and his abrupt absence. It's a wonderful article. I know you'll enjoy it. Also, Bart Sinclair's trial is in several weeks, but the Feds may have to postpone it until they can locate that Martin fellow."

The next message was from the second oldest Rogers's son, Lance. "Hey, Dad, we're at R. J. Bradley's Saloon, celebrating. Why don't you drive over here and have a drink with us?"

R. J. Bradley's was the famous West Palm Beach bar frequented by the Kennedys, Vanderbilts, Duponts, and other young aristocrats. It was not uncommon to see very inebriated women dancing on top of the bar in the early hours of a Saturday or Sunday morning. It was a fun local hangout, which served and catered to the rich.

Bo knew that Milton would not celebrate until the goods were sold and the kids' bank accounts fattened.

When Lance called again with the music and conversation noise from Bradley's blaring in the background, making it almost impossible to hear clearly, Milton shouted back to him, "I'll see you at eight o'clock tomorrow morning at the warehouse. Go home and get some sleep," he barked.

Bo knew what he had to do. Quickly Bo and Hank, wearing hats helping to partially disguise their identities, walked to the nearest pay phone.

Bo placed the call to the Palm Beach County Drug Enforcement Agency (DEA) and after what seemed like an eternity, was able to finally speak to an actual human being and not some machine.

"How can I help you?"

"I'd like to report a drug deal."

"Is it currently in process? Please give me your name and number and the vicinity of the drug deal."

"You don't understand; this is a significant drug deal."

"Okay, please give me your name and number."

"You don't understand," said Bo a second time.

"We can't help you until we have some basic information."

"Listen, lady, I don't need any help. I'm trying to help you and stop hundreds of thousands of Ecstasy pills from being released on the street."

"Did you say Ecstasy?"

"Yes, ma'am."

"Who are you?"

"Let's just say I'm a concerned citizen."

"You know this call is being monitored, don't you?"

"Listen up," said Bo. "There are four large containers housed currently in a warehouse at 1100 Australian Avenue in West Palm Beach. The warehouse is owned by Milton Rogers. One of the containers is filled with thousands of ecstasy tablets. Tomorrow morning at seven o'clock, they will be transported to trucks and moved. You must act quickly and catch the culprits in the act. Don't dillydally," were Bo's final words before hanging up abruptly.

Bo then turned to Hank and said, "We've done everything we can do. Now we just wait and see."

Chapter
Sixty-One

Less than two hours later, Paul Schwartz was awakened by a phone call.
"Hello, Paul?"
"Yes."

Just wanted to let you know that the DEA is going to pull a caper tomorrow morning at a warehouse owed by Milton Rogers. Supposedly there are lots of pills there."

"Really. Why in the world would Milton Rogers be involved with drugs?"

"That's all I know."

"Thanks, thanks a lot."

Paul couldn't fall back asleep. He had just finished another grueling week of preparation for Bart Sinclair's federal criminal trial. He was also tired of the malicious articles condemning Bart Sinclair. Already Bart had lost over twenty pounds with his incessant worrying. Bart was scared to death about serving prison time, and he was beginning to crack under the pressure.

Paul also didn't want Bart to know that in the federal criminal justice system in Palm Beach, the local United States Attorneys' office maintained a 90 percent conviction rate.

Clearly, Paul had his hands full. The facts were certainly against Bart. Bart had previously been accused of switching stones, Milton Rogers was an upstanding citizen and made a remarkable witness, Bart made few invoices, Joseph Marx was dead, and Bart was extremely rich. However, a drug conviction would certainly hurt his credibility substantially.

Paul also realized that as soon as it was disclosed that Joseph Marx had created a trust for Bart and his family with all the money from the diamond sales, then Bart would most likely be convicted.

What a shame, thought Paul. He wondered if Milton Rogers's arrest of drug charges would in any way help Bart. For one thing, it would drastically reduce Milton's credibility. Secondly, it could cast serious doubt in the minds of the jury, and a reminder that there are two sides to every story. Finally, and hopefully, it could go a long way into helping delay the federal trial of Bart.

Paul knew he was not a top-notch trial attorney. His specialty was in negotiation and plea bargaining before trial. He loved the publicity of a highly publicized trial but realized his limitations in the courtroom. However with the money Bart had paid him, he knew he had to prepare and proceed to trial.

Back in Palm Beach, Bart Sinclair fretted to his wife.

"Why haven't I heard from Bo Martin? What on earth is taking him so long? Why hasn't he called to at least give me a heads-up? Do you think he absconded with the trust funds?"

"Listen up, Bart. You know that Bo will do everything in his power to help you," scolded Dana. "Have some faith for Christ's sake. What have you got to lose?"

"I know, I know. But, we're only a few weeks away, and I'm looking at a lifetime behind bars."

"Now, you listen up, my dear. And you listen good. We need you. I need you. Your children need you. You have to stay strong and focused. You never sold Rogers any fake diamonds—right? You never exchanged the real stones for fakes—right? You never purchased any fake gems—right? You have no idea even how someone could manufacture synthetic clear diamonds—right? So please, Bart for my sake and the children's, remain positive, okay?"

"Yes, dear, I'll try!"

Chapter
Sixty-Two

Steve Fleishman had received word from his DEA informant that a warehouse owned by Milton Rogers was going to be raided at seven o'clock the next morning. He called Jim immediately to warn Milton about the upcoming raid.

Bo and Hank sat dumbfounded as they listened to the tape of Jim McDonald's phone call to Milton.

"Milton, this is Jim."

"For Christ's sake, do you know what time it is?" yelled Milton.

"Time for you to get your ass out of bed and down to your warehouse."

"What the hell are you talking about?"

"I just received word from the US Attorney Steve Fleishman that a warrant was just issued to raid a warehouse located at 1100 Australian Avenue at seven o'clock tomorrow morning. Rumor has it that you are the owner."

"Oh shit," was all Milton had to say before slamming down the phone.

Within thirty minutes all the boys had been rounded up (all of them hung-over) and a semi truck had been obtained to haul all four containers away.

Each boy had also contacted their distributors and asked for a delay due to a change in plans. The distributors were all infuriated because they each had paid twenty million dollars, so far for nothing.

Milton called in his markers and was able to relocate the containers by six o'clock in the morning to another warehouse in nearby Lake Park.

Milton was already incensed when he returned home, just in time to catch the wrath of Jean.

"You stupid old man!" exclaimed Jean on the telephone.

"What?"

"You double-crossed me."

"I did no such thing," professed Milton.

"Then why am I standing in my house and looking at a bag of marbles?"

"You what?" shouted Milton.

"Yes that's right. I am holding marbles. Not diamonds, but worthless marbles."

"Well that's impossible. Brenda delivered them directly to your servant."

"Not so, my former friend. You were smart to have them leave Antwerp so quickly after the exchange. But get this straight. You have twenty-four hours to return my diamonds, or I swear that everyone in your family will meet a horrendous death."

This can't be happening, thought Milton. *How could this happen? Why now?*

Milton was trying to narrow down the list of possibilities of who could have set him up when he heard Jean click off.

All Milton could come up with was that somehow Bart Sinclair was behind all this mess. He was so mentally and physically exhausted that he soon fell asleep in the den.

Meanwhile, Bo and Hank were ecstatic. They now had virtually destroyed Milton's master plan.

Bo also knew that the US Attorney was corrupt, and so was Jim McDonald. Bo believed this information would certainly help Bart Sinclair, as well as himself.

Unfortunately for Bo, the Sunday morning's newspaper headlines read, "Missing Palm Beach Attorney Faces Indictment."

It was one of the nastiest, most one-sided, scathing pieces of journalism he had ever read. In fact, Bo's hands trembled, as he read and reread the article. Even Hank was speechless. Words could not soothe or convey the hurt and devastation that Bo felt and tried to blow off.

Bo called Ms. Everett at home to explain.

"Bo, is that really you?"

"Yes, ma'am. Sorry I've been out of touch."

"I understand. I've been running interference for you for ten days now to be exact."

"I know, and I appreciate it."

"Your work is piled up three feet high, and I doubt you'll ever be able to return all your calls. Your emails are all unread. There must be over five thousand."

"I'm sorry I didn't call and check in earlier."

"You haven't done anything Bo. It's not okay. You know I love you like a son, and it just pains me to read such nonsense in the paper. And could they have picked a worse picture? Thank goodness your father and mother and Ruby are up north."

"I think that's the least of my worries."

"Look, you're in trouble, big trouble, so it's better to face it head on. You know when I go to the office on Monday it is going to be hectic, extremely hectic. What should I say, Bo?"

"Tell them to remain supportive of me and that everything will work out in due time."

"Okay, I will try. I will not tell a lie."

"I know and I don't want you to. Thank you for everything."

"You know I'd do anything you for, Bo. Anything."

Hank next came up to Bo and gave him a respectful pat on the shoulder.

"You know I love you and I'm behind you all the way. Unfortunately, I've got to go home and prepare for work tomorrow. You've got my cell phone. Call me throughout the day. My wife and daughter are really starting to miss me."

"I know. Go. Go home. And Hank, I owe you everything. Ask, and it's yours."

Bo suddenly felt all alone. He was confused and clearly frightened.

Chapter
Sixty-Three

When the doorbell rang, it was Dana who answered the Sinclair's front door.

"Why, Bo, we certainly didn't expect to see you today!"

"I bet you didn't. Is Bart here?"

"Oh yes, please come in quickly."

"Oh Bart, Bo's here."

Bart came through the kitchen clutching the local newspaper, which contained the scandalous article.

"Well, Bo, you certainly are a sight for sore eyes. How the hell are you?"

"I've been better."

"No shit, said Bart."

"Haven't we all," exclaimed Dana as she left to leave the two men alone.

"You know, I thought for a while there that you had stolen all the money and ran away. My wife, Dana, never doubted you for a second, but I had my concerns."

"I understand. I've spent some of the trust money, but what I have to say will definitely help you at your trial."

"Go on."

"I found out where Milton bought the synthetic diamonds."

"Where?"

"From a man named Brad Penny in Gainesville, Florida."

"Never heard of him."

"I doubt that you would. He's dead now. Killed in a suspect industrial fire where everything was destroyed."

"By who?"

"I would assume Milton Rogers. Unfortunately, I can't prove it, though."

"Can you at least produce some evidence of the fake diamonds creation?"

"Fortunately he had a female friend. Her name is Stacey, and she will testify as to the existence of the lab. She also wears around her neck the first synthetic diamond he ever created, and she gave me all his personal notes."

"That's terrific. I'm elated."

"Wait, there's more. But it's not good."

Let me sit down," was all Bart could say.

"Joe Marx never paid Victor Butin for the diamonds you sold to Milton and Brenda Rogers. In fact, the Trust consists of the entire fifty million dollars, so Victor Butin never was paid a penny!"

"Oh, I see. What should we do?"

"Well from what I've discovered, Victor Butin killed all of Joe Marx's family, and Joe planned after all these years to get him back one last time."

"I understand."

"I, as Trustee, don't want to give him a penny, but he knows that I am in possession of the trust and that I control all the money. Victor tried to kidnap my wife. His two huge henchmen are currently in the hands of the authorities. Yet, he's still after me."

"I see."

"It appears the real diamonds were switched by Milton and Brenda before they had you dismantle the pieces. In your haste, you didn't notice that they were fake. How you missed that, I don't know. The real diamonds were then used by Milton to purchase drugs. Milton's problem is that the diamonds were misappropriated, and the drugs were confiscated."

"You mean to tell me I was set up by Rogers, who then attempted to quadruple his money through selling drugs?"

"Exactly."

"Whoa that's tough to digest. Want a drink?"

"No, it's still morning."

"But it gets worse Bart. Much worse. Your own attorney gave me up as well as the identity of the Joseph Marx Trust. He informed Victor Butin of everything, as well as the US Attorney."

"Are you serious?"

"Plus, Milton's attorney, Jim McDonald is in cahoots with the US Attorney, Steve Fleishman, and the writer from the *Palm Beach News*. They are all on Milton's payroll."

"Where do I turn? Who do I turn to, Bo?"

"Unfortunately, I don't have those answers. I've got my own problems to face once I step foot in my office tomorrow morning."

"Tell me what to do. What would you do?"

"Contact a new attorney immediately. Ask for a stay in your trial, and basically pray. Here's Stacey's phone number. Get her a safe place to stay. She's your key."

"Okay, and Bo, thank you."

"Wish me luck."

"I wish us both luck, my Trustee."

Chapter
Sixty-Four

Milton was beside himself. Brenda and Annie had arrived safely but were already fast asleep after succumbing to the jet lag.

Milton had been successful in relocating the four containers to another location so that when the DEA conducted their raid, they found an empty building and no trace of anything. An extremely close call.

Milton knew Jean would be calling and demanding his money. He also knew the distributors would be demanding their money back as well. All the distributors were unsavory characters, and he did not want to upset any of them for fear of what they might do.

His cell phone rang, and Milton answered immediately, "Yes."

"Dad, we've got some bad news."

"What now?"

"Three out of four containers are empty."

"Empty?"

"Yes, they are nothing but empty boxes. No pills. Nothing."

"You're kidding me."

"We wish we were."

"What do we do now?"

"The distributors will be here in less than two hours."

"Oh shit. It's like someone has been bugging us and watching our every move. The two guys from Father and Sons must have switched the containers. That's why they were late in arriving at the warehouse."

"Stay where you are and I'll be there soon."

When Milton hung up, he went snooping around his house looking at the telephones. He stopped to unscrew the mouthpiece to the first phone. What he saw shocked but didn't surprise him. The cleverly installed bug was readily apparent to the naked eye. *Who could have done this*, thought Milton. *Who?*

By the time he had arrived at the new warehouse and met with his four sons, who by now were sober and scared, Milton had narrowed down the culprits to three people: Bart Sinclair, Bo Martin, or Jim McDonald. He didn't believe Sinclair was sophisticated enough, and he really couldn't fathom his own attorney stabbing him in the back, although it was not unfeasible.

He knew in his heart that Bo Martin was most likely the brains behind his current string of unexpected failures.

First things first though. After analyzing the situation, Milton figured each distributor would get 25 percent of the product from the remaining container. He then had his boys divide the pills into four equal parts. Since each distributor had already paid 20 percent, he figured he would have to call it even and suffer the 5 percent loss. The last thing he wanted was to have these murderous drug smugglers after his family.

All four sets of drug smugglers arrived on time and begrudgingly accepted only 25 percent of their direct allotment. Although they were all clearly disappointed, the free additional 5 percent helped to soothe their anger somewhat. When they were gone, Milton called to his boys. "Where is the eighty million dollars in cash?"

Lee informed his father of the money's whereabouts and what they had planned to spend it on. At least each son had twenty million.

"I'm going to need all of it."

"What? All of it," they replied in unison.

"Yes, don't you see? Someone stole the real diamonds and now we have to pay Jean for the pills."

"But Dad, who could have done this to us and why?"

"Let's say I have my hunches. Bring the money to the house right away. Who knows when Jean will be dropping in. Also, don't say anything inside the house. The house is bugged"

When Milton returned back to the Palm Beach mansion, he found Brenda and Annie tied and gagged and turned around to find Jean accompanied by four of his compatriots. They had flown directly over on his private jet.

"You didn't think you'd get away with it now, did you, Milton?"

Milton attempted to inform Jean that he was likely being audio recorded, but before he could say more, he was fiercely struck on the right side of his face by one of the large men.

"No sudden moves. You got that?" screamed Jean.

Fifteen minutes later in walked Lee and the boys, carrying eight duffel bags containing the entire $80 million in cash. Each bag weighed more than one hundred pounds.

All the boys stopped dead in their tracks when they saw the women tied and gagged, along with the four large men with Jean.

"Dad, what's going on?" asked Lance, staring closely at the blood on his father's face.

"Now that's a good question," yelled Jean. "I negotiate in good faith, and deliver the product to you as planned, and in return, I get marbles. Yes, marbles. Not the diamonds we bargained for. So now I'm out one hundred million dollars. I want my diamonds, and I want them now."

Milton slowly spoke next. "The money is in the duffel bags. There is one hundred million in cash." Milton lied, as usual. "The same as your diamonds. Somebody stole them from Brenda, and I'm working on who. But to satisfy our end of the bargain, take the cash equivalency, and leave us alone."

"Tell you what I'll do. I'll release all of you upon receipt and confirmation of the money."

Milton knew Jean would take the money and run. In fact, Jean didn't even make an attempt to actually count the money. He knew that Milton wouldn't dare cheat him again. Or so he thought.

Jean was still concerned about how he was going to return home with all the duffel bags of cash. When he examined the one bag closely, he saw ten million dollars written in small lettering. Quickly multiplying by eight, he stopped and turned to Milton.

"Now Milton if you have shortchanged me even by one hundred dollars, you will indeed be sorry you ever met me."

"You have my word," said Milton stone-faced.

Moments later Jean and his companions exited the Rogers's mansion with all the cash.

Quickly the boys ran to their mother and untied her. She embraced each and every one of them.

"Oh, thank God you saved me. I was so terribly frightened."

"It's over now," said the eldest son, Lance.

"What went wrong, Milton?" barked Brenda.

Milton stared directly at Brenda. "Tell me again what exactly happened with the gems."

Brenda talked slowly. "Well, Milton after we got your call, we caught a cab at the hotel."

"What did the cab driver say? What'd he look like? Was he an American by chance?"

"Come to think of it, he was an American."

"And didn't that raise your suspicion any, my dear?" ranted Milton.

"Not at the time, darling."

"Go on."

"We stopped at the box rental, and I went in and retrieved the gems."

"Did you put them in a bag?"

"Yes, yes I did. They were put into a Ritz Carlton bag."

"And you kept that bag in your lap?"

"Well, not exactly. I was really worried about them, and so the cabdriver sensed it and put the bag in the trunk of the cab."

"You're kidding me, right," said Milton, now virtually red in the face and screaming.

"He then drove to Jean's house, and the cabdriver opened the trunk and handed me the bag. I then walked up the stairs, rang the bell, and gave them to the servant who answered the door, as instructed."

"What happened next?"

"Nothing, really. Annie and I just travelled back to the hotel. It was late. Real late."

"Did the cabdriver ever get out of the cab?" asked Luke, the youngest son.

"No. He drove us back to the hotel. Said goodbye and drove off."

Milton was thinking hard. His face was still crimson red. "He must have switched the bag in the trunk of the car."

"Well, honey, he was real quick if he did."

"Oh, he did, all right. Jean wouldn't have flown overnight with his four henchmen unless he was cheated. I don't think for one minute he wanted to travel over here and accept cash payment. It's going to be very difficult for him to launder that amount of cash."

All eyes now fell on Milton.

"We've been had," he shouted angrily.

"What?" joined the chorus of voices. Milton walked out on the terrace instructing his family to join him.

"Our phones and house have been tapped, and our progress has been closely monitored. First, the gems were switched, and then the containers were switched. Someone has been ahead of us every step of the way. They have been monitoring all of our conversations."

"Do you think it's the FBI?" asked Lawrence.

"Not on your life," retorted Milton. "They couldn't find their heads if they weren't attached. The FBI only works because of snitches, and no one here in this room is a snitch. Right?"

A chorus responded, "Right."

"CIA?"

"Get serious."

"What about Bart Sinclair?"

"Now, you're getting closer."

"I really don't think that he could have masterminded this ploy. Whoever is behind this is good!"

"Then who could it be?" asked Lee, the oldest.

It was Brenda who answered. "My God, it has to be Bo Martin. He's the only innocent man. I knew we never should have crossed him, Milton."

"Oh shut up, woman. I think you would have recognized Bo if he were your cabdriver.

"True. But he's bright, smart, and cunning."

"Listen. Nobody, I mean *nobody* messes with the Rogers family and gets away with it," ranted Milton, causing the blood to continue to roll down the side of his face.

Lance spoke next. "What about our money?"

"Is that all you ever think of, you spoiled rotten retard?" sniped Milton. "Don't you realize that we are out one hundred million dollars?"

"What about our futures?"

"What about them?" shouted Milton. "Get a job. Work. You know the four-letter word you've never spoken or experienced."

"Very funny, Milton. Don't worry, boys. You father will think of something. He always does," calmed Brenda.

Milton left the group talking among themselves on the balcony and walked down to the beach. The lapping of the waves was therapeutic. Milton couldn't remember the last time he was burned in a deal. He vowed, then and there to get Bo Martin and fix him for good.

Chapter
Sixty-Five

B o had, what seemed to him, the world on his shoulders. As he walked into his office building on Monday morning around 10:00 a.m., all heads turned. He felt twenty sets of eyes pounce on him at once. Everyone was glad to see him. The associates, the paralegals, and the secretaries were all relieved. Their jobs seemed safe at least for the moment.

The mound of mail on Bo's desk was staggering. Ms. Everett had sorted all the mail into four separate piles. Urgent, important, necessary, and miscellaneous.

Bo spent all morning working his way through the urgent pile. Five full-dictated tapes later, he emerged from his office. It was then that he saw the pink phone messages. Literally one thousand in all. He was dumbfounded. However, Ms. Everett said, "Now, Bo, you've completed the urgent mail, get working on the important mail, and tomorrow you can start to make a dent in the phone calls. I'm telling everyone you're still away on vacation and have been for three weeks. I also stress to everyone that it was a planned vacation." *Three weeks*, thought Bo. *It seemed like years.*

"I don't know what I'd do without you."

"Neither do I. Now get back to work. I ordered you a turkey sandwich for lunch."

By 7:00 p.m., Bo had cleared away the last of his important mail. Ms. Everett and the word processors would be busy for at least the rest of the week, typing his numerous dictations. Feeling totally exhausted, but happy nonetheless, Bo called his wife.

"Sweetheart. How are you?"

"Oh dear God, I've missed you. Are you okay?"

"I'm just fine. I worked at the office all day and caught up on the important stuff. Tomorrow I have to return the phone messages."

"Have you heard anything more?"

"No, just that there was a terrible article in the *Palm Beach Post Times* on Sunday. Front page, and a bad picture to boot."

"I know."

"How?"

"Ms. Everett emailed us a copy first thing this morning. Do you want me to come home?"

"No, stay up there and enjoy yourself. No sense coming back here. I'm up to my eyeballs with work anyway, and I don't think I'd make too good of a companion."

"Tell me, how's Mom and Dad?"

"Well, your dad was outraged by the article, and your mom is trying to be strong and supportive and calming, as always."

"I sort of figured as much."

"Honestly, honey, your dad thinks your career is over. He has half a mind to come home and retake his lead role in the law practice. He said the Florida Bar will be contacting you next if they haven't already."

"To tell you the truth, I'd welcome him with open arms. If they had told me what being a lawyer actually was about, I promise you, I'd have quit in a heartbeat."

"Well, honey, try and hang in there. We'll probably be coming home in a few more weeks. The weather here in Nantucket is absolutely beautiful this summer, and the dogs love it here."

"I'm glad you're having a good time."

"I'd have a better time if you were here."

"Me too, honey. Me too."

As tired as Bo was, he was too frightened to go home. So after a short run, a hose shower, and a Taco Bell dinner, Bo was back at his office later that evening.

Bo pulled out his video camera and several tapes, and with an abundance of caution, began telling his story. When he was finished, Bo had made three separate tapes: one for the federal government one for the civil trial, and a personal one for his wife, Ruby. Each tape got better and more concise. Bo was clearly fearful for his life, and he wanted to get everything he knew on the record. Bo had made serious enemies. He realized that Victor could be lurking somewhere, and once Milton Rogers figured out he'd been had, Bo suspected the worst.

Bo also was worried about Sean Heese. Sean hadn't called since he returned from overseas, and Bo was frightened that Sean could have fallen off the wagon and lost the stones. Worse still, even double-crossed him.

Although it was well after midnight before he had finished everything on a lark, Bo phoned Sean. He answered on the first ring.

"Sean, I've been worried about you. How come you didn't call?"

"Honestly, Bo I thought of pawning the stones and retiring somewhere in the Caribbean. But you've helped me out too much. I've got them all, right here with me. Come over and pick them up. I don't want them around me. They are too much of a temptation for me."

"Sure thing. See you in twenty." To say Bo was excited was an understatement.

As Bo drove toward Lake Park, he had the feeling he was being closely followed. Bo intentionally ran a few red lights, conducted several one-hundred-eight-degree turns, and finally convinced himself he was no longer being watched. Still, Bo ended up parking his car at the local buffet and walked the remaining four blocks to Sean's residence.

It was a good thing because Victor and his henchmen had indeed gotten lost in the myriad of Bo's driving actions.

Sean was waiting for Bo when he arrived at the back door in complete darkness.

"I thought I was being followed, so I parked at the local buffet, and walked over here."

"Good idea. I really don't want anyone to know I was ever involved with you. Not that I don't like you, but I don't want to die just yet. I like living too much."

"Point well taken."

"Here's the diamonds."

"Aren't they just gorgeous?" said Bo counting each and every one of them.

"That they are. Any idea how much they're worth?"

"One hundred million dollars."

"Oh my God. I should have charged you more."

"Speaking of money. Here's your cash. You'll notice I doubled the quadrupled amount once you get it all counted."

"Oh, Bo. Thank you, thank you, thank you."

"You take good care of yourself."

"You too."

It was now 3:00 a.m., and Bo was feeling the effects of lack of sleep and lack of caffeine. Bo had given up sodas after finding out that the phosphoric acid had started to affect his hip, and most importantly, hurt his running.

Bo headed directly for Bart Sinclair's mansion. Bo called on his mobile and knew that he had woken up Bart and Dana.

"Do you have any idea what time it is?"

"Yes and no."

"Oh, it's you, Bo."

"Open the gates and come out with a gun. I'll see you in five minutes."

When Bo arrived the gate was open and Bo drove directly to the front door. Bart and Dana were in their matching monogrammed silk pajamas. Both looked worried.

"Hi, and sorry," said Bo.

"You're always welcome here," muttered Dana, although her handgun was still dangling in her right hand.

"What you got in the bag?" asked Bart.

"Step inside, and let me show you."

Once safely situated in Bart's den, Bo unwrapped the diamonds.

Bart examined them all very closely for the next ten minutes before saying a word. "Well, I'll be! These are the real stones."

"Are you sure?"

"Absolutely in fact, several of the large ones have the exact carat inscribed on them. Look here," said Bart, motioning Bo to look through the high-powered eyeglass.

"Can you prove it in a court of law?" inquired Bo.

"Yes, yes, I believe I can. Any expert could as well."

"Well, then, put these in the safest and most secret place you have."

Bart took the diamonds with him and disappeared from the room.

It was Dana who spoke next. "You know we tried to hire a new lawyer, but with the trial in less than two weeks, and the judge and prosecutor against any further delays, we were denied a postponement. No attorney has been willing to take it on. Not one!"

Dana's eyes were welling up with tears, and Bo knew that despite all of Bart 's faults, he had a woman who loved him dearly.

"To tell you the truth, I sensed that would happen. You have to remain strong."

"I'll try."

"I'll try what?" interjected Bart, as he returned to the den.

"None of your damn business," stated Dana. I'm going to make some tea. Anyone want some?"

Both men answered "yes."

"I guess she told you that we're stuck with Paul Schwartz. I tried to get it delayed and hire a new attorney, but the judge wouldn't allow it."

"That's okay. Did you talk with Stacey?"

"She'll be here tomorrow."

"That's wonderful!"

"Yeah. Considering the trial starts in less than two weeks."

"Let's call Paul."

"At three-fifteen a.m.?"

"Yes."

"Here goes nothing," said Bart, as he called Paul's home phone. After several rings, a groggy male answered.

"Do you have any idea what time it is?"

"Wake up," exclaimed Bart.

"I am up now, no thanks to you."

"Well, I'm here with Bo Martin, and I have some great news."

"What is it?"

"I am in possession of the original gems."

"You're what?" Bo could just envision Paul trying to inch his massive frame into a sitting upright position.

"I have the stones. All of them."

"Are you sure?"

"Positive."

"Don't tell me Bo Martin's involved."

"Let's just say I couldn't have done this without him."

Bo grabbed the phone.

"It's me, Bo. The stones are all safe and in a special place. When the time comes at trial, they will be available for you."

"I need those stones now."

"And what, risk them being lost or misappropriated? I don't think so!"

"Look here, you're in big trouble. I read the newspaper you know, and if I want the stones, I'm going to get them."

"Paul, I know about you and Victor."

"Who?"

"Don't pull Mr. Innocent on me. I know all about you and Victor Butin. I also know you're a low damn scumbag."

"I don't have to take any verbal abuse from you, Bo. You are going to be disbarred and go to jail."

"Maybe so. But if you so much as speak to Victor again, I'll notify the Florida Bar, and your license will be revoked."

"Is that a threat?"

"No, it's a statement. Do your job, and get Bart out of this mess. You hear me?"

"Yes, I do. Loud and clear."

"Well, goodnight."

"Goodnight." Bo's head was really throbbing now.

"Bart when the time comes, you're going to have to produce the real stones. You can never say how you got them. Understand?"

"Not even before the judge?"

"No. You'll have to take the Fifth Amendment on that."

"Okay. Whatever you say Bo."

"Well, get some sleep. The trial will be here soon enough."

"What about your tea?" asked Dana.

"Sorry. I'll have to pass. Thanks anyway."

"Goodnight, or should I say good morning?"

"Either way. See you both soon."

Bo was relieved to have gotten rid of the diamonds, as he drove the block to his house. He was soon to realize why.

Chapter

Sixty-Six

When Bo unlocked the front door to his house, he felt somewhat awkward entering his own home. It had been several weeks since he was last inside the house. With Ruby and the dogs in Nantucket, the house lacked the wonderful aroma of her exquisite cooking and the youthful energy of the red dogs.

Bo couldn't wait to climb into bed and sleep. It was now almost 4:00 a.m., and he knew Ms. Everett would be worried if he wasn't in the office by 8:00 a.m.

As soon as Bo hit the bed, two armed men appeared at the foot of his bed. In the darkness, Bo soon realized it was Victor and his henchman, Marty.

"Mr. Martin, so nice to see you again. You've been one busy young man."

"Is that so," said Bo as he struggled to an upright position in the bed. He was shirtless but had boxer shorts on.

"Your driving skills are excellent, I must say."

"Well, thank you," Bo replied.

"You know what I want, so let's cut to the chase and make it easy on you. You're a good-looking man, and I'd hate to have to rearrange your face. I want my fifty million, and I want it now!"

"I don't have it."

"No, but you know where it is, and you can certainly access it."

"Mr. Butin, why don't you just speak directly with your good friend, Harrison Frazar? I'm sure he's always willing to help if the money is right."

"Brilliant idea, Mr. Martin. The only problem is that he had a little accident. You see, he committed suicide."

"Is that so?" Bo was caught off guard by the information. The stakes had definitely escalated. He tried to hide his surprise from Victor.

"Trust me, we had nothing to do with his suicide. In fact, I'm very disheartened by his weak action. His final words were spoken with such anger and hostility."

"Oh, I bet. And did you enjoy killing Harrison?"

"I find no thrill in killing at all. I just want my money, and I want it now."

Out of the corner of his eye, Bo glanced at Marty's right fist and moved just in time to avoid a direct head shot. The force was not enough to knock him over, but the bodyguard was extremely quick for a short man, and soon Bo was tagged with several head and body blows that had him off the bed and sprawled out on the floor.

"We don't want to hurt you, Mr. Martin."

"Oh, well you have a strange way of showing it. But the answer is still no," said Bo with blood streaming down his chin.

Victor called off his associate and personally helped Bo to his feet.

Bo sensed that at least a couple of ribs were likely fractured. "If you kill me, you will never ever get your money."

"You think I don't know that."

"Look, I know what you're capable of, and I figure you killed Harrison Frazar after you found out that only I can access the new account."

"Touché."

"Well, I've got a solution to your problem."

"Oh, you do?"

"Yes."

"Go ahead. And this better be good. I don't need to remind you that your life is on the line now, do I?" said Victor as he arranged himself into the chaise lounge.

"That won't be necessary. You know anything about the drug Ecstasy?"

"Sure, who doesn't?"

"What if I told you I had at my disposal up to three hundred million dollars' street value in the tablets?"

"I'd say you're a liar, out of your mind, and have a very short life expectancy."

"How about an exchange?"

"Go on. I'm still listening"

"The tablets for my life in lieu of the money."

"You mean to tell me that you have access to the pills. How?"

Bo went through the entire sordid story concerning Milton Rogers and Bart Sinclair. By now his story was virtually down pat. He didn't leave anything out. When he finished, even Victor seemed awestruck.

"That story is so far-fetched that for some unknown reason, I actually believe you. I really do! Take us to the warehouse now."

"I'm tired, and I need some sleep."

"You'll do as I say. Grab him, and put him into the car," demanded Victor.

Bo winced in pain as he was thrown into the back seat of the black Cadillac STS. Bo was almost too tired and too injured to even keep his eyes open, but he managed to give the directions to the warehouse. Bo had hidden the warehouse key by the air conditioner and once at the facility, Bo unlocked the door to reveal the three large shipping containers.

Victor and his bodyguard took over an hour inspecting the containers.

Bo sat and dozed on and off during their entire inspection.

"Well, I'll be damned if you aren't quite right."

"I don't lie, Victor."

"And neither do I. We had a deal. Give me the keys, and I'll have them out of here by lunchtime."

Bo was in no mood to offer much resistance. The pain and lack of sleep had dulled all his senses.

As Victor was placing numerous calls, Bo caught a short nap. When he awakened, he found himself in the back seat of the Caddy and almost in Palm Beach.

By now the time was eight o'clock, and the weather was already unreasonably hot and humid.

As the car parked in his driveway, Bo used up all his strength to simply open the door and step gingerly outside.

Victor yelled from inside the car. "It's been a pleasure doing business with you. If you so much as place a call to the DEA or federal authorities, you're a dead man. And so is your wife and parents. I will personally take care of your wife."

"Oh Victor if you so much as call me ever again or talk to a family member of mine, you're the one who will be a dead man. I promise you that."

"You know something, young man. I like you. I really do. You have spunk. Don't worry, I'll never see you again. You have the Butin family word."

Bo hated like heck to give the pills to Victor, but he didn't really have much choice. Odds were that Victor would reship the drugs overseas, and so few if any, American lives would be harmed by the Ecstasy tablets.

And with the pills gone, Bo didn't fear about getting caught in possession of the drugs or involving Hank or Mike for the Port of Palm Beach heist.

Chapter
Sixty-Seven

Bo didn't make it in to the office until nearly eleven in the morning. Waiting in his lobby were Steve Fleishman and Nick Long, the two assistant United States attorneys.

"Gentlemen, nice seeing you this morning."

"We've come to serve you with this Indictment. As a matter of professional courtesy, we've hand delivered it and given you some time to turn yourself in and be processed. The Grand Jury found probable cause."

"When hasn't the Grand Jury found probable cause?" asked Bo. Let me tell you both a little something. You're barking up the wrong tree with me. Stop listening to Milton Rogers and his attorney, Jim McDonald, and focus on the truth," said Bo rather calmly.

Neither federal attorney said a word, as the two men turned and abruptly left the office.

Bo spent the rest of the day on the telephone. Fortunately, he found himself able to converse on the telephone at the same time he worked on a large federal estate 706 tax return that was due in less than one week.

Bo made inroads into returning his pink phone messages and was pleased to have taken the time to complete the entire estate tax return. At 5:30 p.m., Ms. Everett poked her head in the door to inform Bo that several reporters were outside the front door, and that he should use the back entranceway to leave.

It seemed that the assistant US attorneys had leaked service of the Indictment to the press. Money laundering and conspiracy were two terms that the public and most attorneys couldn't define, other than to know that it was not good.

On a hunch, Bo made a detour on his way home, just to make sure that the warehouse was empty. Sure enough, not a trace of a container was found. *Thank God*, thought Bo to himself. Bo next placed a call to his good friend Hank. By the shortness of his breath, Hank could tell Bo was injured.

"Bo, are you hurt?"

"Well, let's say I won't be running five-minute miles any time soon."

"Again?"

"But it's the last time, trust me," explained Bo with a hint of a smile on his face.

"Well that's at least one piece of good news. Speaking of news, did you know you were on TV?"

"I figured as much. Was it bad?"

"Let's just say that your reputation has now been soiled in the television media as well as in print."

For the next fifteen minutes Bo informed Hank of everything that had transpired, and even Hank seemed somewhat relieved.

"I sure hope you know what you're doing."

"Me too."

Chapter
Sixty-Eight

Later that evening Bo found time to speak with Ruby and his parents.

"Honey, are you okay?"

"To tell you the truth, Ruby, I have been better."

"You sound a little out of breath."

"I had a short run-in with Victor."

"Not again?"

"Yes, unfortunately."

"Anything broken?"

"Just my pride, and maybe a few cracked ribs."

"Honey, I'm coming home."

"I'd like that, I really would."

"Dear, your father would like a word with you." Bo waited for him to pick up the phone.

"Son, I have to say your mother and I are really worried about you."

"I know."

"A Grand Jury Indictment for mail fraud, conspiracy, and money laundering is extremely serious. You're looking at ten to twenty years if found guilty. Do you realize that, son?"

Honestly, Bo never thought about the actual prison time, but now he was seeing the light, so to speak.

"And, son if I may further pour salt into your wounds, the Feds have a very high percent conviction rate."

That's even better, thought Bo to himself.

"Now, call Lee Smith tonight. Here's his phone number. We'll be home in a few more weeks. Not that I want to face our friends and neighbors, mind you, but we still love you, and we're behind you all the way."

"Thanks for the support. I love you too dad."

Bo was very distraught. The last thing he ever wanted to do was to let his parents down. Bo had struggled so hard and so long to earn his father's respect, and now, he felt like a complete and total failure.

Later that night, Bo finally was able to sleep soundly and awaken refreshed.

Chapter

Sixty-Nine

THE TRIAL
Steve Fleishman and Nick Long wore their classic dark-navy business suits with white shirts and almost matching red silk ties. Paul Schwartz appeared in his Armani suit and Gucci loafers. The suit attempted to hide his rather protruding gut. Nothing could hide his three chins, however. Bart Sinclair looked rather peaked as he was dressed casually in khaki pants, blue shirt, yellow tie, and navy blazer. His wife, Dana, sat directly behind them in the first row.

Reporters were everywhere. Even the biggest magazines, such as *People*, *GQ, Town and Country*, and *Newsweek* had their representatives in the audience. Of course, Mae McReynolds was ready and waiting in the third row. Jim McDonald sat in the row just in front of her.

Fortunately for Bart, the presiding federal court judge was the highly esteemed Walter West. Walter was about sixty years old, and being a Mid-westerner, was known for his compassion and ultraconservatism. He had a reputation for being fair. He was tall, about six foot three, and had a mass of solid white hair.

At virtually the last moment, Paul Schwartz had added several more names to his witness list, which the government strongly objected to. The witnesses included a diamond expert from world renowned Sotheby's and of course, Stacey.

Fleishman and Long had no idea why Stacey was added at the last minute and vehemently objected to her inclusion. Paul apologized for the lateness but didn't give Fleishman any indication of why she was added as a witnesses or what she had to offer.

In an abundance of caution, Judge West had allowed both new witnesses. The judge also placed a gag order on the attorneys. He also prohibited the use of TV cameras in his courtroom, much to the dismay of all the local news stations. Bart Sinclair's trial had attracted almost as much attention as the William Kennedy Smith rape trial which was the most publicized trial ever in Palm Beach County, Florida. Only this time, the action ensued in the federal courthouse.

After cutting through much of the technical legal mumbo jumbo, which consumed almost the entire day, the judge called in the potential jurors.

In Palm Beach County, you have an extremely wide diversity of wealth. You have the extremely rich individuals of Palm Beach and farther west, the impoverished migrants of Belle Glade. This produced a wide variety of jurors from which to choose. The prosecutors attempted to seat the jury with individuals with higher education. While the defense was looking for jurors harboring a latent resentment for the government or that had relatives incarcerated.

Out of a possible list of over one hundred fifty prospects the jury would consist of twelve jurors plus two alternates.

The trial was expected to last several weeks, and both sides figured it would take a week to actually select and seat a jury.

Of course, Bo was on the witness list of the prosecutors, and Paul was worried sick about the Trust.

Bo was precluded from watching any of the trial because he was going to be a witness, which was just fine by Bo.

Bo spent the day trying to put out fires, finish a couple of sophisticated estate plans, finalize the two federal estate tax returns that were due shortly, and keep up on his phone calls.

Not that there were many calls. The newspaper article and subsequent news reports on his Indictment put a huge dent into his practice. Although he was still a member in good standing with the Florida Bar, most clients had dropped Bo as their attorney. It was only a matter of time before the Florida Bar would revoke or suspend his license.

Bo mostly dreaded his 5:00 p.m. appointment with Lee Smith, criminal attorney extraordinaire. Bo should have felt fortunate to actually get an appointment with the esteemed lawyer, but nevertheless, he was not keen on having to retain an attorney in the first place.

Deep down, Bo pretty much despised attorneys. Bo often watched how his contemporaries placed themselves first and their clients second. Bo always winced at reading the billable hours allegedly spent on a litigated case. He believed that hourly billing made liars out of all lawyers—even the honest ones.

Lee's office was located on the top floor of Phillips Point, the Pepto-Bismol–colored office building overlooking Palm Beach. The "valet only" parking was a dead giveaway that Lee's fee was going to be outrageous.

Ms. Everett had made sure that Bo left the office in plenty of time to make his 5:00 p.m. appointment. "Good luck," were her parting words.

Lee's impressive office consisted of a marble foyer with dark wood paneling, oriental rugs, and matching lamps. The decorating just screamed out "Money." Bo was forced to wait a good half hour before Lee poked his head into the visiting room. He hated waiting and understood the importance of punctuality.

"Mr. Martin," said Lee as he extended his delicate and finely coiffed hand, "I know your father quite well and look forward to working with you and resolving this most unfortunate matter. Did you bring your Indictment?"

"Sure, here it is," said Bo handing over the document consisting of almost 100 pages. He then followed Lee into his massive office.

Lee took several minutes to scan the full Indictment. Other than a few *hmm's* and several *uh's*, he said nothing.

When he was finished, he took off his glasses and spoke directly to Bo.

"Young man, I can't stress enough how serious these allegations are. You are looking at serving between ten and twenty years in federal prison. If convicted, you'll come out of jail an old man."

Bo just simply nodded his head. What a nightmare, he thought.

"There are two avenues we can take. The first is to fight the government with every penny and ounce of energy you have. The second is to attempt to negotiate a plea agreement, which would drastically reduce the amount of your time but would bar you from ever being an attorney. You would also forever be an ex-con."

"To make matters worse, Steve Fleishman is a ruthless federal prosecutor. He doesn't play by the rules, and he knows all the judges and is well respected by all of them."

"But I'm innocent," declared Bo.

"That doesn't make one bit of difference in the federal court system. The prosecutors don't really care if you're innocent. The federal system is designed to favor them, and prosecutors really hate lawyers, especially successful ones like you. In the federal court system, you are guilty until proven otherwise. Their ninety percent conviction rate is clear evidence of that fact."

Bo certainly didn't like what he was hearing.

"We'll initially take the position that you are innocent and file a not-guilty plea. Later, we will attempt a plea bargain. From there the decision is entirely up to you."

"So, I see," said Bo, trying to comprehend his unfortunate situation.

"Now the tough part. My up-front fee is one hundred twenty-five thousand dollars ($125,000). If we go to trial, I will want an additional two hundred fifty thousand dollars ($250,000), paid in advance. If you fail to pay, I will bail. And not to toot my own horn, I am one of the best. I will look after your best interest."

Bo was already seething over this ordeal, and now to learn that he had to cough up $125,000 made him sick to his stomach.

"I'm going to have to sell some stocks to come up with the money."

"That's okay. I'll file for an extension of our responsive pleading to the Indictment. I'll need the money within the week. Deal?" said Lee, extending his hand.

"Yes, it's a deal," said Bo, squeamishly.

"I understand through the grapevine that you will also be called as a witness in Bart Sinclair's trial."

"Yes. I'm afraid so."

"Well, just answer only the questions asked. Don't give any more information, and if you think any answer would harm your own personal case, take the Fifth."

"The Fifth?"

"Yes, simply state that you can't answer the question on grounds you might incriminate yourself."

"I understand."

"Well, good. Sorry to make this meeting so hasty, but I've got to go."

"Don't you even want to hear my side of the story?" asked Bo.

"In due time. In due time. When I get the money, we'll discuss your case in further detail."

When Bo left the office, he was incensed. Never in his entire life had he felt so helpless. Bo was only starting to understand the federal process. The more he learned, the more he feared. He now realized why there existed so many lawyer jokes. At least with Lee, Bo knew where he stood. Lee came first, and Bo came second. Right then and there, Bo decided that he would never ever put money ahead of his clients. Not that he ever did, but now he would never be a hypocrite, regardless of whether his firm failed or not.

Fortunately for Bo, his feelings and emotions perked right up when to his surprise, he saw his lovely wife, Ruby, standing at the front door of their house.

"Oh, how I've missed you," cried Bo.

"Dear, I've missed you so much."

Bo wanted to pick her up and squeeze her, but the fractured ribs precluded him from acting.

Ruby, sensing his hurt ribs, gently held him tight and whispered into his ear, "I'm here, and together we're going to get through this ordeal. I love you more than anything."

"I love you too," said Bo with tears in his eyes.

Chapter
Seventy

L ittle did they know, but at the Palm Beach Grille, a dinner meeting was taking place. Milton and Brenda Rogers were joined by Jim McDonald and Mae McReynolds. Milton was in control of the show.

"I asked you to dinner tonight because I need your help."

"Sure, what can we do?"

"We've got to take down Bo Martin."

"Take down, what exactly do you mean by that Milton? asked Jim. He's been indicted, we're suing him civilly, and he's a witness for the prosecution in Sinclair's criminal trial."

"Well, Jim, I've just learned from my sources that he's the trustee over that trust."

"Which trust?" asked Mae.

"The trust for Sinclair and his family."

"I've heard that rumor as well."

"Yes, but have you heard that it consists of all the moneys allegedly paid for the fake jewels he sold us?"

"You're kidding," responded Jim.

"I kid you not."

"Let me get this straight," said Mae. "You mean to tell me that Bart Sinclair paid money to his own trust, and the proceeds came from the sale of the fake gems to you?"

"Absolutely," joined Brenda.

"What a story!"

"Can you print it tonight?"

"Not tonight, but I can have it ready by Sunday's edition."

"That'd be great," said Milton as he took a large gulp of his Grey Goose and cranberry juice.

Over the next three hours of their five-course meal, the parties discussed Joe Marx, Bart Sinclair, the sale of the gems, and the existence of this infamous trust.

Chapter
Seventy-One

It took a full week for a jury to finally be seated in the Sinclair trial. The jury consisted of seven men and five women. Half had college degrees and only one had any extensive dealings with the legal system. Steve Fleishman and Nick Long were ecstatic. Paul Schwartz was not particularly pleased, but his lack of trial experience was already beginning to show.

The trial would begin on Monday, and the jury would remain sequestered throughout the entire trial.

Judge Walter West was pleased that a jury had been selected but was always concerned about the media and its possible effect on the jury. Try as he may, the jurors would undoubtedly see or hear something about this newsworthy case and perhaps use the information during deliberations.

Meanwhile, Bo and Ruby were just enjoying their time together. The red dogs remained in Nantucket with Bo's parents, and so Bo and Ruby had only each other to entertain, and they certainly made the best of it—Bo's hurt ribs and all.

Unfortunately, Sunday's paper put an abrupt end to Bo's temporary bliss. The article by Mae McReynolds was virtually a death knoll. The article painted Bo as a co-conspirator with Bart Sinclair regarding the sale of the gems. It discussed in hypothetical detail the trust and its terms and conditions. The article blatantly called for Bo to file a financial statement and account for everything to the public. This was something that Bo clearly was not required by law to do, but the article made it appear that Bo was embezzling funds and attempting to shirk his fiduciary responsibilities, and demanded a response.

The article made Bo sick to his stomach. It also made the cases against Bart Sinclair and Bo much stronger.

Milton Rogers was ecstatic as he read his Sunday paper. Mae had included every morsel of information that he had painstakingly spoon-fed her. She had hit Bo below the belt and, most likely, had ruined his legal career, not to mention his life. Only Brenda appeared worried, "Now, dear," she asked, "you don't think Bo has any other information he could use against us, do you? He is dangerous and has cost my children millions of dollars."

"Sweets, he's a dead man. We just sapped the life out of him. He no longer has any credibility, and he will not cause us any more harm," boasted Milton.

"I sure hope you're right."

Paul Schwartz read the paper with disgust. *Great, just great. Now Bart Sinclair is really in trouble!* thought Paul.

Bart and Dana sat together in their breakfast nook overlooking the Atlantic Ocean, sipping their coffee slowly and reading the headlined article.

"That's it, I'm toast," uttered Bart in disgust.

"Now, now, dear, it's not like this was unexpected," said Dana calmly.

"Tell me now? How in the world did Mae what's-her-name acquire all this information, and why now on the eve of my trial, did it have to come out?" screamed Bart.

"Honey, I don't really know. But you have to remain strong. Bo's not going to let you down. No way, no how."

"I sure do hope you're right!"

"When have I ever been wrong?"

Chapter

Seventy-Two

An early morning run did nothing to help lift Bo's spirits. In fact, every car that passed Bo along scenic North Ocean Drive seemed to stare down at him. He was certain that every passenger was talking about him and the Sunday front page article and picture.

Ruby did her best to help raise Bo's spirits, but in the end, let him be and went about her own matters. Ruby, herself, was frightened. She really didn't know much about the law and abhorred Bo's line of work (death and taxes). Try as she may, she couldn't imagine Bo in prison and away from her and the red dogs. Alone, she shut her eyes and prayed, "Please God, help me, help my husband. He's a good, fair man. Please."

Of course Bo hardly slept at all Sunday night and made certain to be the first one in the office Monday morning. Bo even closed his office door, something he only did when he had clients with him.

By the time Ms. Everett had arrived, three prominent families in Palm Beach had requested their files and original documents, as they were seeking counsel elsewhere.

"Bo, can we talk?"

"Sure, Ms. Everett, come on in and shut the door."

Alone, Ms. Everett spoke first. "I've watched you grow from a young, shy, and green-behind-the-ears man into an honest, hardworking, and fair individual. I don't know what you've done, but you can't hide in your office and shut out the world. Some people have already passed judgment on you and others will be watching you closely to see how you handle this ordeal before making their decision. Either way, you have to remain strong. You have to hold your head high, and you must always appear confident."

"I understand," said Bo.

"No, no you don't. First, you're going to keep your door open. Second, you're going to call these three families and speak to the men, not their gossipy wives. Third, you're going to appear on the local news tonight and defend yourself."

"I am?"

"Nobody, and especially not some local writer with an axe to grind, is going to bring down this firm. Have you got that, mister?"

"I do," exclaimed Bo.

"Well, good because the news cameraman will be here in thirty minutes. And don't worry the makeup woman will also be here. I don't want those dark circles to show up on TV."

Sure enough, almost a half hour later, a young reporter, a makeup girl, and the cameraman from the local NBC affiliate appeared at the office.

Bo was soon primped and ready. Bo answered the four predetermined questions posed to him. With each answer, Bo's confidence and outward demeanor improved. By the time he was finished, Ms. Everett was thrilled.

Meanwhile, the Sinclair case in the West Palm Beach federal building was moving along. Steve Fleishman spent most of the morning laying out the undisputed facts. The central point of the prosecution's case was that Bart Sinclair sold one hundred million dollars of fake gems to Milton and Brenda Rogers. Sinclair then engaged in tax fraud and money laundering by allegedly paying fifty million dollars to a trust created by a decedent, Joe Marx. The trust solely benefitted the Sinclair family, netting him a paper profit of $50 million.

Steve concluded strongly, "The facts, ladies and gentlemen, are surprisingly simple and clear. Bart Sinclair knowingly and willingly cheated and defrauded Brenda and Milton Rogers—who are wealthy, elderly, and uneducated in the jewelry business—out of one hundred million dollars. We have the fake jewelry in our possession, and each one of you will have the opportunity to examine the worthless gems. Bart Sinclair has no defense. At the end of this trial, you too will come to the conclusion that Bart Sinclair is guilty of all charges. Thank you."

Paul Schwartz rose and addressed the jury. Unfortunately, both his demeanor and presentation were clearly lacking as compared to the polished Steve Fleishman. In fact, Paul Schwartz was downright pathetic. He was surprisingly unprepared for the biggest trial of his career, and he was headed for destruction.

At the close of his opening argument, Bart lowered his head dejectedly. Dana sat stone-faced but was seething inside.

The local news ran the Bo Martin interview at both the 6:00 p.m. and 11:00 p.m. evening news. Ruby thought her husband was excellent and even Bo felt a little bit of pride.

Unexpectedly at 11:30 p.m., the Martins' doorbell rang. Normally the red dogs would have gone berserk barking and anxiously awaiting the visitor, but with the dogs away, Bo and Ruby were caught a little off guard.

Bo answered the door and was shocked to see both Bart and Dana standing before him.

"Please, come right in," said a surprised Bo.

"Thanks."

Ruby was already in the kitchen. "Coffee, tea, soda, or beer?" she inquired. Coffee was the unanimous choice, and Ruby began to brew a fresh pot.

"So what brings you over here, neighbor?" inquired Bo.

It was Dana who spoke. "We want you to be our trial lawyer."

"I am your lawyer."

"No, you don't understand. We want you to represent Bart in the courthouse."

Bo was taken aback.

"I'm speechless. I'm no trial attorney. I know nothing about criminal law, and I've never even cross-examined a witness in my life."

"So?" said Bart.

"So, you're involved in a criminal trial where you're looking at life in prison. You've got to be joking!"

Dana replied, "We're dead serious. You know much more about this case than anyone. You're smart, you're energetic, and you're the only person we trust. If we lose, we lose. The judge has already denied us the opportunity for new counsel."

"What does Paul Schwartz think of me working second chair with him?"

"Paul thinks it's great. The stress is killing him. Today, he was terrible. He's already drafted a motion for tomorrow to allow your appearance in the case."

"Guys, I'm flattered, even honored, but no way."

"Coffee's ready," said Ruby as she entered the room.

"What do you think, Ruby?" asked Dana.

"I think you've made a wise choice. My husband would be great."

"The prosecution would never let it happen. For Pete's sake, I'm a witness!" cried Bo.

"Paul's already spoken with them. They've agreed," said Bart.

"You guys are all nuts. All of you," yelled Bo.

Oddly, nobody flinched.

"You're serious?"

"Dead serious," muttered Bart.

Over coffee everyone including a begrudging Bo, agreed that it did make some sense.

As the Sinclair's were leaving, it was Ruby who pulled Bo aside.

"Honey, I'm here for you. Together we are going to help Bart and in turn, help you. I'll be your paralegal. Anything you need I can get off the internet.

"Sweetheart, I'm more afraid than ever before in my lifetime."

"I know together we'll get through this."

Chapter
Seventy-Three

The following morning, Judge Walter West's courtroom was buzzing. The ever-present media had a field day with the dynamic opening performance of Steve Fleishman versus the downright pathetic presentation of Paul Schwartz. Mae's headline article in the *Palm Beach Times* literally assured a conviction.

After last night's newscast featuring Bo Martin, the media were squawking among themselves over Bo's presence this morning in the courtroom. When Bo sat down beside Bart and adjacent to Paul Schwartz, several gasps were heard.

After Judge West entered the packed courtroom and everyone had settled in their seats, he summoned both sides to his podium.

"I have read this emergency motion, and I must say that after thirty years on the bench, I've never seen anything quite like it. Now, all of you please step back."

"Mr. Martin."

"Yes, your Honor."

"Do you really agree to serve as co-counsel for Mr. Bart Sinclair?"

"I do, your Honor."

"And do you understand the huge risk your client is about to undertake by having a tax attorney represent him in a complicated criminal trial where a virtual life sentence could be imposed if found guilty?"

"I do, your Honor."

"And have you attempted to dissuade your client from engaging an unqualified attorney to act on his behalf?"

At this question, Bart Sinclair stood up and addressed the court.

"Your Honor, I have requested to retain the legal services of Bo Martin. Mr. Martin, I know, is my estate and trust attorney. He has little if any, knowledge of the criminal system and virtually no courtroom experience. However, Mr. Martin is the most honest and hardworking attorney I know. My life is at stake, and I want him by my side."

"Very well. And do the Assistant United States attorneys have any objection to Mr. Martin's appearance as legal co-counsel?"

"Your Honor, although Mr. Martin has been listed as a prosecution witness, the government finds no other reason to object to his representation."

"Very well then. Gentlemen please take your seats. The motion to allow Bo Martin as co-counsel for Bart Sinclair is hereby granted. Further by the powers vested in me, I grant Mr. Martin the limited federal power to appear as legal counsel for Bart Sinclair, waiving any and all legal requirements for federal appearances."

Both Steve Fleishman and Nick Long sat down with huge grins on their faces. They equally despised successful civil attorneys and couldn't wait to see Bo fall flat on his face.

Even Jim McDonald, Milton Rogers's civil attorney, couldn't keep the smile off his face. This is going to be easier than we ever imagined. Just like killing two birds with one stone! He was virtually counting his fat fee.

Judge West further helped Mr. Sinclair by allowing the trial to be postponed for a couple of days to permit Bo Martin to catch up to speed.

No sooner had Bo left the courtroom than he grabbed Paul Schwartz and accompanied him to his Mercedes.

"Paul, pull all your staff off what they're doing and put them to work on this case. Order three new computer terminals and my people will be over to your office after lunch. Your conference room will be our official headquarters. Have three more telephone lines installed and pull Don Dannon off his civil cases. We're going to need all the best legal minds for this trial."

Before Paul could even respond, Bo was gone. Paul was dumbfounded but greatly relieved. If anyone could pull a rabbit out of the hat, Bo Martin had the best chance.

In the car on the way to his office, Bo called Ruby, and she accompanied by the neighbors, Sophia and her husband Burt, were more than willing and ready to help with the computer research.

Bo figured they had from Tuesday until Monday to uncover everything possible about Milton Rogers, Jean Valhomme, and Jim McDonald, Milton's civil attorney and confidant.

By the time the posse arrived at Paul's penthouse office, everything and everyone was in place. Even Bart Sinclair and his wife, Dana, were in attendance. Bo had previously informed Ms. Everett, and she was going to basically run his dwindling practice as best she could. Bo knew it was in expert hands.

Bo, appearing flustered but in complete control took instantaneous command of the mahogany boardroom.

"Thank you all for coming so fast. Keep track of your time because Mr. Sinclair is going to have one big whopping bill when all is said and done."

Everyone nervously laughed and seemed to settle down during Bo's speech. It was agreed upon that Ruby, Sophia, and Burt would handle the research. For extremely sensitive and hard-to-find data, Hank had agreed to loan his company's best computer expert and his company's huge mainframe computer to help.

Bo, Paul, and Don would handle the legal maneuverings and strategies, and all of Paul and Don's secretaries would act as floaters, helping wherever needed. Even Bart and Dana were called to service to perform several manual tasks.

It was unanimously agreed that the prosecution would start off their case with a bang and call Milton Rogers to the stand. After Milton, the men figured Brenda Rogers would be called and then be followed by one or more sons in an attempt to humanize the case and portray the entire Rogers family as innocent victims.

Don figured that the jewelry expert would follow next. After that, the men didn't know who would be called because the witness list contained almost thirty names.

If they were unsuccessful in personally attacking Milton and Brenda Rogers and besmirching the credibility of the jewelry expert, the case would be lost. It was as simple as that.

By Wednesday, the computers were humming along. Bo wanted as much information on Milton Rogers as he could get. He needed to know everything about the man: where he was born where he was educated, how many businesses had he run, how many lawsuits had he been involved in, tickets, accidents, close acquaintances, accountants, lawyers, lovers, and personal fetishes. Everything including the kitchen sink.

Hank's computer expert proved to be a tremendous help because he was able to pull up some highly classified personal information, such as individual income tax returns, corporate tax returns, gift tax returns, brokerage accounts, and other impossible information. All illegal of course.

The entire crew labored through fourteen-hour workdays, and by Sunday everyone was exhausted. They all felt tired but relieved at the same time. Everyone was also pleased to have assisted Bart. Dana had even grown on everyone in spite of her nouveau riche attitude and lifestyle. Ruby and Sophia suggested approaching Dana when the trial was all over and inviting her into the Palm Beach Junior League—an honor that Dana would virtually die for.

Sunday evening at the Martin residence found Bo and Ruby completely bushed.

"I'm exhausted," said Bo. "And what's worse is that the trial has barely begun."

"I know, dear, but you're completely prepared."

"Am I?" questioned Bo.

"Now don't go doubting yourself or your capabilities. I've watched you closely these past few days, and you totally command attention and respect. The jury is going to love you, and you're going to be great."

"I wish I felt the same, I really do."

Chapter
Seventy-Four

*V*irtually, the entire crew was at the overflowing courtroom Monday morning. Surprisingly, Mae McReynolds had not written another scathing article in the *Palm Beach Times* that Sunday.

Steve Fleishman and Nick Long were dressed in their very best dark suits, and together they made an impressive team. Paul Schwartz was attired in his usual Armani double-breasted suit that tried to hide his stomach, which amazingly appeared smaller. The stress was definitely affecting his appetite.

Bo wore his finest blue suit. With his broad shoulders and thin waist, he looked dashing—or so Ruby had said!

When all had settled down, Judge Walter West took command of the courtroom. He peered down from his large wooden stand and inquired, "Is everyone ready?"

"Yes, your Honor," said Steve.

"Yes, your Honor," replied Bo.

"Very well, then. Would the prosecution please call its first witness?"

Steve stood and confidently called Milton Rogers to the stand. Bo and Paul were relieved. *At least we guessed right*, thought Bo.

Milton Rogers slowly walked down the center aisle of the massive courtroom and took his seat in the witness box.

After reading him the required oath, Milton settled down. He was dressed casually in a white linen suit, and his dark tan blended well with his light mango-colored shirt and rep tie. Very Palm Beach chic.

For the first two hours, Steve Fleishman coached him through the most basic and generic questions. The main facts highlighted the date of the purchases, the discovery of the fake gems by the insurance specialists, the pain and humiliation suffered by the entire Rogers family, and all the emotional duress caused by Bart Sinclair.

Milton came across as a wealthy, self-made millionaire, who was unjustly wronged by Bart Sinclair.

Milton made several self-serving statements, which Bo immediately memorized and jotted down on his legal pad, just waiting for the proper time and place to question on cross-examination. Those points of interest included the fact that Milton stated he was testifying for the first time; that Milton was an unsophisticated investor of jewelry; that he had amassed his fortune honestly and fairly; that it was Bart Sinclair who convinced him to buy the diamonds because they were a great investment and hedge against inflation; that he had suffered physical and emotional problems resulting from the fraud; and that he was taking medication presently for depression.

By 4:30 p.m., the direct examination of Milton Rogers was completed. Steve Fleishman was elated. Jim McDonald was beaming. Judge Walter West called the court to a close, allowing Bo Martin the ability to cross-examine Milton first thing in the morning.

Milton Rogers had handled himself exceedingly well. The jury couldn't help but believe him and everything he said. In fact, Bo watched closely as the jurors indirectly frowned on Bart Sinclair as they left the courtroom. Bo certainly had his work cut out for him.

On his way back to Paul Schwartz's office, Ms. Everett rang Bo.

"So sorry to disturb you, but there's a Lt. Brown on the phone from Gainesville that wants a word with you."

"Did he leave his name and number?" asked Bo.

"Here it is. I hope it helps."

"Me too. Everything else is going as well as can be expected."

"You had several more clients request their files. They all are honest and sincere about it, but they all said they would return once your ordeal is over and sincerely wished you good luck."

"Yeah, right," uttered Bo sarcastically.

"Well, anyway, you've also had several people call and lend their support and backing. Don't worry Bo, it's all going to work out."

"I hope so."

"Good luck."

"You too."

The lieutenant of the Alachua police department was more than pleased to take Bo's return phone call.

"Mr. Martin."

"Yes, sir."

"Thanks for returning my call."

"It's been a while. Never thought I'd actually hear from you again."

"Just lucky, I guess," said Lt. Brown.

"To what do I owe this pleasure?" inquired Bo.

"Just wanted you to know that we haven't forgotten about the warehouse fire."

"Really?"

"Have you got a fax number so I can send you a composite of the elderly gentleman? We gathered the information from an eye witness who personally observed this elderly man."

"Sure." After a few seconds, Bo located the fax number at Paul's office and read it off to him.

"I really think you might actually like to know that in Alachua County, we do pretty decent police work."

"You never cease to impress me!" countered Bo.

"Well, good luck with all your problems down there."

"Thank you. Talk to you soon, I hope."

"Bye."

Ten minutes later Bo couldn't believe his eyes. The artist's rendering of the perpetrator's composite bore an uncanny resemblance to none other than Milton Rogers. He sat mesmerized by the faxed drawing.

This is good, thought Bo. *This is very good.*

Chapter
Seventy-Five

The following morning came much too soon for Bo Martin. On this important day Bo dressed in his navy and plaid Brooks Brothers suit. With a starched white shirt and red amoeba tie, Bo looked dashing. Ruby believed it would be extremely difficult for the women jurors to take their eyes off her husband.

All the other parties were impeccably dressed as well and wore confident expressions on their faces.

The morning's *Palm Beach Times* article by Mae McReynolds drastically over-embellished Milton's testimony and made it seem certain that Bart Sinclair's conviction was imminent once again.

One could also observe Milton Rogers self-inflated ego as well. Milton had a bounce to his step and today wore another ice-cream-cone suit. *Hopefully I can get him to melt*, thought Bo.

For the first thirty minutes, Bo asked Milton several easy questions. Milton slowly lost his strict self-defense mechanism and soon was into the flow of communication. Instead of responding with simple yes-or-no answers as instructed by Steve Fleishman, Milton was gushing information. Bo could sense that Milton felt over-confident and was merely trying to butter him up and fuel that massive ego.

Out of nowhere, Bo slowly began to lay the trap.

"Mr. Rogers, you stated yesterday that your testimony was the first time you've appeared in a courtroom. Is that true?"

"Why, yes," answered Milton loudly.

"Hmm," said Bo. "Then as defendant's exhibit number one, let me introduce these twelve separate court transcripts."

"Objection, your Honor," declared Steve Fleishman.

"Overruled," bellowed Judge West. "These exhibits are allowable."

"Can you explain these *twelve* separate transcripts of your testimony before various circuit courts?"

"Well, you see, um, well I must have forgotten."

"Oh I see," said Bo, walking toward the jury and fanning the thick exhibits.

"Your last court appearance was less than two years ago. You remember that one?"

"Well now I think I do."

"Mr. Rogers, let me remind you that you are still under oath and are required to tell the whole truth. Before I proceed, I want to make you fully aware of that."

"I certainly am aware of that, Mr. Martin," uttered Milton, appearing somewhat ill at ease.

"Do you know what any of these *twelve* separate court proceedings involved?"

"Not really. I can't recall exactly."

"How about your own truth and honesty for starters?"

"I am an honest businessman," shouted Milton.

"Oh, you are? Then why were you or your company named as a defendant in all *twelve* proceedings?"

"They were just business lawsuits," retorted Milton.

"Just business?"

"Yes," retorted Milton.

"Well, how about civil theft, fraud, blackmail, deceptive business practices, and slander and libel for starters?"

"Most of those were settled out of court, Mr. Martin."

"But, wait a minute, Mr. Rogers, you've already told this court that you are an honest businessman and that you've never testified before. Now, we know that's untrue. Were you lying then or are you lying now?"

"Objection," yelled Steve Fleishman, who had jumped out of his seat.

"Denied," bellowed Judge West. "Let me remind you, Mr. Rogers that you are under oath. Just answer the questions posed to you and we'll get this over and done with."

Jim McDonald wasn't happy with the direction the cross-examination was going.

"Well now that we know you are a liar and a cheat, let me resume my questioning," stated Bo over the tremendous "Objection" uttered by Steve Fleishman, who was now red in the face.

"Mr. Martin, please no self-serving statements," warned Judge West.

"Sorry, your Honor," replied Bo.

"I'll bet," exclaimed Steve in disgust as he took his seat.

"Mr. Rogers, you stated yesterday that you and your wife had no knowledge whatsoever of gems or gemology. Is that a correct statement?"

"Yes," said Milton, now sounding irritated.

"Good. Let me now introduce as defendant's exhibit number two Mr. Rogers registration in gemology classes at Florida Atlantic University. And as exhibit number three, let me introduce his grades for the record."

The jurors gasped, and Milton's face turned a crimson shade of red as he despised the direction this cross-examination was taking.

"You will note that his scores were all perfect hundreds but that in both courses, he failed to take the final exam thus earning him two incompletes."

"As defendant's exhibit number four, I present an affidavit from both of his professors who, let me paraphrase that Mr. Rogers was an excellent, knowledgeable student who absorbed the material and was a delight in class with his most insightful questions."

After the jury had taken it all in, Bo continued to press Milton.

"These classes were taken less than one year before you purchased the diamonds from Mr. Sinclair."

"So?" argued Milton.

"So, I find it extremely troubling that you forgot that you took two separate gemology courses."

"I'm a busy man," leered Milton.

"Busy studying about gems," responded Bo instantly.

By now Steve Fleishman was livid. "Objection, your Honor."

"Sustained," replied the judge. "Mr. Martin, please tone down your remarks."

Bo feigned an apology.

"Now tell me, Mr. Rogers, is there anything else pertaining to your knowledge of gems that you are not telling us?"

Milton looked worried and you virtually could see his mind thinking how to respond.

"No."

"What's that?"

"I said *no,*" Milton yelled back.

"Great," said Bo as he walked back to the defense table and grabbed two more exhibits.

"I'd like to introduce these two documents as defendant's exhibit number five."

You could have heard a pin drop as Bo walked over to the prosecutors and handed them the exhibits for their perusal. Steve Fleishman was pissed.

"Any objection, Steve Fleishman," asked Judge West.

"No, your Honor."

"Great," said Bo as he handed the exhibits to the judge's clerk.

"Mr. Rogers, do you recall attending two separate seminars on gemology?"

"Uh. Maybe."

"Maybe? Is that your answer? Please speak up for the jury to hear."

"I don't really recall."

"Well, Mr. Rogers, let me inform you again that the first three-day seminar you attended was eight months before you purchased gems from my client, and the second seminar was a mere four months."

"Now I seem to recall."

"Good. Do you also remember what the topic was of the second seminar that you attended?"

"Uh, no," said Milton rather squeamishly.

"Well, let me inform the jury here that the second three-day topic was on synthetic gems. That's right, synthetic gems," said Bo slowly. He stood silent, listening to numerous gasps from the jury.

"Isn't that odd, Mr. Rogers. Less than four months after your synthetic gem seminar, you allegedly buy one hundred million dollars of fake stones from my client."

"Objection. Badgering the witness," yelled Steve Fleishman.

"Overruled," said Judge West.

"Then could we at least have a recess?" pleaded Steve Fleishman.

Judge West, sensing that it was a good time for a break, called a lunch recess for two hours.

In the downstairs courthouse cafeteria, Paul Schwartz was beaming as he devoured his roast beef sandwich. "You were very good, Bo. I just wanted you to know that."

"Thanks, Paul. It means a lot, coming from you. We still have a long way to go, however."

"I know, I know."

After the lunch recess, it was clear that Milton had regained his composure. As he sat in the witness box, he glared at Bo. God, how he hated the young man!

Once again, Bo started Milton off with several easy questions. Milton's answers were now short and curt. It was obvious to all concerned that the federal prosecutors had spoken to Milton and attempted to coach him again.

Moments later Bo went in for the kill again.

"Mr. Rogers, you stated that Mr. Sinclair persuaded you to invest in the gems under the ruse that they were a wonderful investment?"

"That's correct."

"But from your previous knowledge based on your gemology classes and seminars, you had to have learned that diamonds were not a lucrative investment. You already knew that before you approached Mr. Sinclair about purchasing diamonds?"

"I can't recall."

"Well then, did you or did you not approach Mr. Sinclair regarding the purchase of one hundred diamonds?"

"I believe he approached me," answered Milton spinning another lie.

"That's funny because how would he even have known you were interested in purchasing diamonds?"

"I don't recall."

"It's not like you were a major client of his, right?"

"Yes."

"And you weren't neighbors?"

"No."

"And you don't socialize together or are members of the same social circle?"

"So?"

"Well, then tell me how, exactly, did Bart Sinclair solicit you to buy his gems?"

"He just did," responded Milton, already agitated and becoming redder by the minute.

"He just did" mocked Bo. "I'm sorry, but that's not good enough. Looks to me like you sought him out. Was he your mark?"

"Absolutely not", said a defiant Milton Rogers.

"Then tell me, Mr. Rogers, how you can sit here under oath and state truthfully that Mr. Sinclair solicited you and your wife to buy his diamonds for one hundred million dollars?"

"He just did," said Milton in a guff and rumpled voice.

"Now who's lying?" asked Bo as he slowly walked back to his seat and retrieved another file while Steve Fleishman screamed "Objection, badgering the witness."

"I'll allow it," said the judge. "I too am curious as to how Mr. Sinclair convinced Mr. Rogers to invest in diamonds."

After a moment's pause to allow the judge's comment to sit with the jury, Bo then resumed the attack.

"Mr. Rogers, you state that you lost one hundred million dollars because these fake stones—plaintiff's exhibit number one—are worthless?"

"That's correct."

"Did you get any tax benefit by having them declared worthless?"

"Not to my knowledge."

"Oh really. How about the fact that you deducted the full one hundred million dollars' loss from the gems against the profits from the sale of your publishing empire?"

"I didn't gain a penny, mister," replied Milton, now trying hard to control his temper.

"That's funny because according to your income tax return, the net tax savings for you is over twenty million dollars."

"I'm not an accountant."

"Then why state under oath that you gained nothing when in reality, you saved twenty million dollars in income taxes?"

"Listen here. I'm a businessman. I don't deal in numbers or handle tax issues. Bart Sinclair stole from me, and now he's going to go to jail for it."

Bo remained silent. Milton's temper clearly had gotten the best of him, and his true colors were starting to show. Now was as good a time as any to really get him, thought Bo.

"Mr. Rogers, did you ever visit a jeweler in Utah to purchase his synthetic jewelry company?"

Milton's face turned a few shades of white, and he mumbled something.

"What did you say?" asked Bo.

"No."

"Are you sure?"

"Hell yes."

"Then as defense exhibit number six, I have an affidavit that Mr. Rogers attempted to purchase a synthetic diamonds business of a noted Salt Lake City, Utah, businessman."

"He's lying," retorted Milton.

"Why would he lie?" countered Bo.

By now, Steve Fleishman was standing and requesting the judge for a moment in chambers.

Judge West entertained his request, and soon the parties were led into the large and cluttered judicial chambers.

"What's your problem, Steve?" asked Judge West.

"We weren't made aware of any of this in discovery, your Honor."

"So?"

"Well we aren't prepared to counter the allegations."

"It is not an allegation, but a fact," said Bo.

"It's not fair, Judge."

"Mr. Fleishman, I believe that it is extremely relevant to the case at hand. Mr. Martin is simply trying to put a doubt in the mind of the jury. If your main witness had nothing to hide, then Mr. Martin's questions will not hurt his case. But if he's correct, your client's credibility is seriously suffering."

When they returned from chambers, Bo went right for the jugular.

"Did you or did you not contact a Salt Lake City businessman to purchase synthetic diamonds?"

"Not really."

"Go on," prodded Bo.

"In Palm Beach there is a lot of theft, and so quite often you wear fake jewelry and leave the real stuff at home in the safe."

"But, Mr. Rogers, we're not talking jewelry, we're talking loose diamonds. Who are you trying to kid? Plus when you contacted the businessman in Utah, you hadn't even purchased any diamonds."

"I was getting ready to."

"So, you had already decided to buy loose diamonds?"

"Yes."

"Then how could Mr. Sinclair have convinced you to buy the stones, since you had already made up your mind as to what you wanted?"

"I don't recall."

"How convenient," said an exasperated Bo.

After a few moments of complete silence, Bo then asked.

"Mr. Rogers, do you know a man named Brad Penny?"

"Objection," shouted Steve Fleishman. "Relevant, your Honor?"

"I'll allow it, but, Mr. Martin, I hope you know that you're treading a fine line here."

Milton looked clearly frightened now. He took his time before responding.

"No."

"Are you sure?"

"Yes."

"Have you ever been to Gainesville, Florida?"

"Not that I recall."

"And have you ever visited a warehouse located in Alachua County?"

"No."

"Okay, let me get this straight. You have never met a Brad Penny; have never visited Gainesville; and have never visited any warehouse in Alachua? Is that all correct, Mr. Rogers?"

"Yes it is correct."

"Then as defendant's exhibit number seven, I want to introduce this composite drawing of the alleged perpetrator of murder and arson of the synthetic diamond manufacturer by the name of Brad Penny in Alachua County, Gainesville, Florida."

The gasps among the jurors were loud.

"That's it. In my chambers," yelled Judge West. The attorney's marched in behind the infuriated judge.

"What is going on here, may I ask?" demanded Judge West.

"Well, you honor, this composite was just sent to me yesterday. Brad Penny developed a technique to manufacture colorless diamonds. Shortly after he had finished his first batch of one hundred flawless diamonds for his mysterious client, he was murdered and his manufacturing facility destroyed," said Bo.

"Are you saying that Milton Rogers did it?" asked Steve incredulously.

"Not really. What I'm alleging is that someone purchased the fake diamonds in order to switch them with real stones.

"That's bullshit," said Steve.

"Mr. Fleishman, I'll have none of that language in my chambers."

"Your Honor, he's got nothing."

"Well, Mr. Fleishman, this composite certainly nails Mr. Rogers dead on. I believe I have to allow it.

"We'll appeal."

"Go ahead. That's the government's constitutional right. But I'm warning you, Mr. Martin if you so much as accuse Mr. Rogers of the crime of murder, I'll declare a mistrial."

"I understand."

When they returned to the courtroom, everyone was wide awake, even the jury. As the jurors passed the composite among themselves, they each stared directly at Milton Rogers. Milton was now perspiring and was extremely agitated. His mind was reeling. How could Bo know. How?

After the courtroom had settled down, Bo next offered into evidence, as exhibit number eight, Stacey's diamond necklace.

Against the fierce objection by Steve Fleishman, the judge allowed the synthetic diamond into evidence. The diamond was identical to the other synthetic diamonds found in plaintiff's exhibit number one. A perfect match!

All Bo needed to do was tie Milton to Brad Penny to nail the coffin shut.

Unfortunately, Milton had done an exemplary job of leaving absolutely no strings to Brad Penny. Nobody could produce one shred of evidence. Nobody except Stacy.

"Mr. Rogers on the tenth day of May where were you?"

"I have no idea."

"How about we try to refresh your memory."

"Okay," said Milton, slightly trembling as he reached for his glass of water.

"Were you and your wife in Tallahassee, Florida for a dinner with the governor?"

"Oh, yes. That's exactly where we were," said Milton, now gaining confidence that he had an airtight alibi.

"And did you rent a car?"

"Yes, a Lincoln, I believe."

"And did you drive it very far?"

"No."

"What was that?"

"No. We barely used it."

"Are you sure?"

"Yes."

"And was the car in your possession the entire time?"

"Yes. So?"

"Well, as defendant's exhibit number nine, I have here the mileage report from your Lincoln rental. You will note that Mr. Rogers traveled four hundred-sixty miles in all for his one-day rental."

"Do you remember how many miles away Gainesville is from Tallahassee?"

"No."

"Well, it's officially two hundred ten miles."

"So?"

"On the day in which your rental car recorded four hundred fifty miles, Brad Penny was murdered and his synthetic manufacturing diamond warehouse was burned down by an arsonist."

"How dare you?" yelled Milton as he totally lost control of himself and attempted to storm off the witness podium.

"Order, order," yelled Judge Walter West while pounding his gavel. Milton had to be physically placed back into the witness chair. Once settled, Judge West decided to call it a day.

Chapter
Seventy-Six

A s the lawyers were packing their briefcases, Steve Fleishman called Bo over for a chat.

"Bo, would your client like to plead to a lesser charge?" he whispered.

"What do you have in mind?"

"Six years in a federal prison followed by three years' probation."

"That's a far cry from the sixty-plus years he was looking at. What are you afraid of Steve?"

"Nothing. I just thought your client may want to settle. This is going to get ugly before it's all over with."

"Oh, Steve, we haven't begun to fight. Wait till I get ahold of you and Milton and Jim and Mae's little financial arrangement. You receive cash, Mae gets her juicy story, and together you manipulate the criminal justice system."

Steve turned ghostly white and said, "You wouldn't?"

"I will. And you had better watch your back, Mr. US Attorney," said Bo as he finished packing his briefcase and left the courtroom.

"What is Bo talking about," asked Nick Long.

Steve was speechless. Nick was perplexed.

Although Bo would have loved to continue grilling Milton on the witness stand, the team, namely Don, Paul, and now Bo, realized he had inflicted enough damage to completely destroy any credibility Milton Rogers had. The following morning Bo told the court he had no further questions at this time but would like the opportunity to recall Mr. Rogers at a later date. The judge allowed it and a much less confident and more subdued Milton was able to leave the witness podium.

The US attorneys did not want to put Brenda Rogers through a cross-examination like the one Milton recently experienced. Nevertheless, they needed her testimony regarding the date of the purchases.

Brenda came across as a sweet, plump, and elderly woman. She did not possess Milton's air of confidence and answered all the questions posed to her simply and to the point.

Steve Fleishman brought to light the gemology classes and tried to bring out all the damaging information on his direct examination. Even Bo found himself believing every word Brenda had to say. Bo was faced with the difficult task of attacking her credibility without alienating the jury.

On cross, Bo was able to extract several damaging aspects to the US attorneys' case. First, Brenda confessed that it was she and her husband that decided to invest in gems, rather than being enticed by Bart Sinclair, as Milton had alleged under oath, and as the prosecution had stated in their opening statement. Second, she confessed that Milton was not on any medication that would cause Sinclair's fraud and that he really hadn't even been to see a doctor. Third, she stated that it was the Rogers's civil attorney, Jim McDonald, who first suggested to them that they could deduct the jewelry loss against the capital gain from the sale of their publishing empire. Their accountant simply confirmed it.

At the tail end of her cross-examination, Bo tried to catch her off guard.

"Mrs. Rogers, have you recently been to Belgium to inspect any jewelry?"

"Um. Yes." Brenda didn't know exactly what to say, and she looked directly at Jim McDonald for some sort of help.

"And when was that?"

"Several weeks ago. I went with my daughter-in-law, Annie to examine a jewelry collection."

"Whose jewelry collection was it?"

Steve Fleishman and Nick Long had no idea where Bo was going or how this line of questioning had anything to do with the case, but they both sat and listened.

"A man by the name of Jean Valhomme," blurted Brenda but winced the minute she said his name instantly realizing her mistake.

Immediately both Steve and Nick asked for a ten-minute recess in chambers with the judge. By now Bo knew the judge's chambers inside and out.

Moments later in chambers, Steve took the first shot.

"Do you know who Jean Valhomme is?"

"Yes I do," said Bo.

"And then I guess you know that he was recently busted while trying to launder over fifty million dollars in US currency. He's presently in custody awaiting possible extradition to the United States."

Bo fired back at Steve, "Do you know he's one of the biggest drug dealers in Europe?"

"Now, how would you know that?" asked a surprised Steve.

"I've got my resources," said Bo.

"So what's the connection here?" inquired the judge.

Bo didn't want to tip his hand, but at the same time, he wanted to put the heat back on the US attorneys.

"Okay, here's our theory. Milton and Brenda bought the real gems from Bart Sinclair, switched them with the synthetic diamonds from Brad Penny, and then sold the real gems to Jean Valhomme in exchange for Ecstasy tablets."

"That's preposterous," uttered Steve.

"Oh, is it? You'll soon learn that Brenda visited Jean in Belgium, and that Jean then made a visit to the United States and met with both of them. All this activity means there is a definite connection. Further, Milton and Brenda have no other business pursuits with Jean so their visits most likely involved jewelry or drugs."

Judge West tried to absorb all the information and although he felt there existed some nexus he forbade Bo to further pursue that line of questioning.

After the break, Bo concluded with just two questions. "Mrs. Rogers, are you aware that neither Jean Valhomme nor any of his companies engage in the purchase or sale of jewelry?"

"No."

"And are you aware that he was recently apprehended and charged with several federal crimes including money laundering and drug smuggling?"

"No, I was not aware of that."

"No more questions, your Honor."

Bo had made his point and placed a seed of doubt in the minds of the jury as it pertained to Brenda and her relationship with a drug smuggler. Judge West called it a day.

The following morning, the prosecution called their jewelry expert. Bo's crew had anticipated the US attorneys' selection and were ready to address it head on.

The jewelry expert retained by the government was clearly one of the most knowledgeable and respected gemologists in the country.

Bo agreed to judicially notice the fact that Dr. Walters was an expert in the field of gemology. He didn't want to bore the jury by having them listen to the doctor's qualifications.

Dr. Walters proceeded to explain in layman's terms everything from the historical origin of diamonds to the latest technology involved in manufacturing synthetic diamonds. After several boring hours, the prosecution finally ended its direct when Dr. Walters clearly concluded that the ninety-nine diamonds (since one was missing from the inventory and was in fact in Bo's possession) were synthetic. He also determined their value to be in the vicinity of six million dollars.

Since Dr. Walters's testimony was primarily dull and boring and Bo could sense the jury was not too stimulated, he asked to be allowed to start his cross-examination the following day.

At 2:00 p.m. the judge closed the court proceedings for the day.

Little did Bo know that Milton was meeting in a seedy bar in downtown West Palm Beach on Banyan Street with Ed Garrett. Ed Garrett was the master jewelry craftsman that Bart Sinclair had hired over the holidays to create the jewelry arrangements for the Rogers.

Ed was a ghostly looking redhead. He was skinny as a rail and white as a ghost. He performed his work competently, but over the years and after several divorces, he had slowly succumbed to the bottle. He considered himself a functioning alcoholic.

"Now what do you want from me?" said Ed, nursing his third vodka and tonic.

"I know you're hurting financially."

"So?"

"Well, I've got a proposition for you."

"Okay. Shoot."

"I want you to testify against Bart Sinclair.

"No way. He was my boss."

"How about for one hundred thousand dollars?"

"That's a lot of money. What exactly do you want me to do?"

"All you basically have to say is that Bart Sinclair instructed you to switch out the real diamonds with fakes."

"When?"

"Back in November and again in December."

"What's the catch?" asked Ed curiously.

"There is no catch."

"You mean to tell me that all I have to do is say that he told me to switch fake diamonds for the real diamonds."

"That's it," grinned Milton.

"I don't trust you. So when do I have to testify."

"Soon."

"And when do I get my money?"

"Half up front and half after testifying."

"I don't want cash."

"You what?" asked Milton incredulously.

"Nope. You wire the money to my account. Let me write my number, bank, and full name on the account for you."

"Are you nuts?" asked Milton.

"No. If the money is wired today, I'll say whatever you want."

"You'll have to call the US attorneys directly."

"Heck for one hundred G's, I'll walk over there myself."

By the end of Ed's fifth vodka tonic, Ed had joined Milton's camp. Before 5:00 p.m., the money from an offshore account had been wired to his account. The following morning Ed was added to the prosecution's witness list and his name was emailed to Paul's office.

Bo was the first one to question the addition of another witness. After conferring with Bart and Dana Sinclair, Bo learned that Ed Garrett was their former master gem setter. Bart knew Ed's address and even his social security number. This information was conveyed to the crew and less than an hour later the computers were humming in an effort to uncover all the dirt on Garrett. Even Hank had directed his computer expert to shake the trees and research the man.

Chapter
Seventy-Seven

When Bo approached Dr. Walters, he wanted to keep his cross-examination short and to the point. In no way did he want to alienate the esteemed gemologist.

"Dr. Walters, you've previously testified that the diamonds are fake?"

"Yes."

"And yet you placed a value on them of six million dollars. Tell me a little about these fakes that make them worth so much."

"That's an excellent question one which I wish had been asked of me earlier," said the doctor, staring directly at the US attorneys' table.

"These fakes are the greatest synthetic diamonds I have ever seen."

"Please go on," nodded Bo.

"Normally, the standard production process of synthetic diamonds permits nitrogen to escape, which in turn causes the yellowing of the stones. Yellow synthetic diamonds are still exquisite and in many cases, the naked eye can't tell an original yellow diamond from a fake yellow diamond."

"I see."

"Well, these synthetic diamonds before me are absolutely incredible. I've never in my entire lifetime examined anything like them."

Bo was enjoying every moment and the jury even seemed enthralled.

"Tell me, Dr. Walters where would Bart Sinclair have allegedly purchased these fakes?"

"I don't know. They are perfect fakes. I'm familiar with all the synthetic manufacturers in the world, and no one can match these gems."

"Did you confer with any other experts regarding these manufactured gems?"

"Absolutely."

By now Steve and Nick were squirming in their seats. An older distinguished gentleman sitting in the back row was smiling ear-to-ear.

"And."

"And nobody, and I mean *nobody*, knows of any manufacturer who could have produced these diamonds. But . . ."

"But what, Doctor?"

"There is a Russian scientist who has developed an unconventionally slow manufacturing process that has created the closest match to these gems."

"How would you know that?"

"I and several of my colleagues visited Belgium this past year and personally observed the Russian's manufacturing process and also examined his stones."

"Any chance this Russian scientist would be of any assistance to us here?"

"Not a chance."

"Why is that?"

"Because an American by the name of Brad Penny was his apprentice, and rumor has it that this young man stole his ideas and further refined the manufacturing process further."

The courtroom was by now completely mesmerized, and it was eerily quiet.

"Doctor, have you had a chance to examine the defendant's exhibit number eight containing the synthetic diamond."

"As a matter of fact, I have."

"And what have you discovered?" asked Bo, hoping to hear the desired answer. Bo had already broken the cardinal rule of never asking a question of an expert witness to which you don't already know the answer, but Bo needed to know.

"Well, based on my expertise, the diamond in the defendant's exhibit is identical in composition to the ones found in the prosecution's exhibit."

"And?"

"And my conclusion is that they were manufactured by the same process."

"Well, Dr. Walters if I were to introduce into evidence and show you the workbook of Brad Penny, would that help you?"

"Oh, yes," said Dr. Walters excitedly.

"As defendant's exhibit number ten, I'd like to place into evidence Brad Penny's working papers."

The prosecutors leaped out of their seats. "Objection, your Honor."

"On what grounds?"

"Hearsay."

"Denied."

"The defense can't just spring this on us at this point in time?"

"Mr. Fleishman, why not?" inquired Judge West.

"Surprise. It wasn't included in the discovery."

"Your Honor if I may, I just received this information, and because it is so relevant to the testimony of Dr. Walters, I believe he should be allowed to review the materials. and as the expert called by the government, be allowed to inform the jury as to his conclusions."

"Very well, then. I'm going to allow the examination of the papers by Dr. Walters. Let's take an hour recess and then see what he has to say. Doctor is that sufficient time for you?"

"Yes, your Honor. I can't wait to examine the notes."

"Very well, then. The court is adjourned for the next hour or so."

As Bo was collecting his belongings, out of the corner of his eye he caught his father in the back row. *Well I'll be. Hopefully, I can still make him proud*, thought Bo.

Chapter
Seventy-Eight

"**M**y son, you were very good!" said the elderly attorney.

"You think so?" said Bo, looking like an eager puppy dog and shocked by the compliment.

"I'm proud of you. You know I always knew you would have made a great trial attorney, but you only seemed to enjoy numbers and tax codes. I never could understand it. Still don't."

"When did you get in?"

"Yesterday. We drove down with your dogs. Total pains in the butt! You know, I don't know what you and Ruby see in them."

"Dad!" said Bo with that "aw shucks" grin.

"Okay. They are cute, but traveling almost thirty hours in the car is not their idea of a good time. You seem to be doing a good job. I spoke with your criminal attorney, Lee Smith, and he personally feels that if you are successful in defending Bart Sinclair, then there's a good chance the government will dismiss its case against you."

"I know, Father. That's why I've put everything I have into this case. My life is definitely riding on the outcome."

"So I've also checked with Ms. Everett, and she says that your clients are all leaving in droves."

"I know that. Three or four have asked for their files each day. When I see neighbors or even lawyers out and about it, they try and avoid me like the plague."

"Now you listen to me, son. Your mother and I love you! Anything you need, anything at all, just ask, and it will be provided."

"Thanks, Dad."

"We're all going to get through this ordeal. Thank goodness you have that sweet Ruby. That girl is the best thing that ever happened to you!"

"Don't I know it!"

"Well, I've got some business to take care of. Keep up the good work."

"I'll try. You know I will," smiled Bo.

Chapter

Seventy-Nine

The one-hour recess that the judge had granted turned into over three hours. The time passed slowly for everyone. Bo was extremely anxious to hear what the doctor had concluded.

When Dr. Walters emerged from his unknown examination spot, he looked over to Bo and nodded to the young attorney. Bo said a silent prayer. The US attorneys said nothing. All eyes in the courtroom were on Dr. Walters.

"Please resume," bellowed the judge.

"Dr. Walters, have you now had an opportunity to examine the workbook of Brad Penny?" asked Bo.

"Yes, I have."

"Can you tell us about your findings?" Bo hated to ask such an open-ended question, especially since he did not know the answer, but he had no other choice.

"Well, based upon my knowledge, experience, and belief after having recently reviewed the notebook, I have concluded that Brad Penny manufactured all these artificial diamonds. Only he, and nobody else in the world that I'm aware of could have manufactured the synthetic diamonds. After examining the workbooks, the evidence is quite clear that Brad manufactured the one hundred plus diamonds. According to his calculations, he could have manufactured thousands more, but his employer specifically prohibited it."

"And do you find that weird?"

"Absolutely. You see if I was a retail jeweler, I would want you to manufacture as many diamonds as possible."

"Mr. Martin, the cost of the machinery to manufacture the diamonds exceeded two million dollars."

"Two million dollars?" asked Bo incredulously.

"Yes, and the notes specifically precluded Brad from making any further diamonds. That's the part I don't understand at all."

"What is?" asked Bo.

"Well if I was Bart Sinclair and had just spent over two million dollars on machinery, not to mention all the weekly cash payments to Brad and the employees he hired, I would manufacture a slew of diamonds. Brad had the production capacity and manpower to create thousands of diamonds."

"But his mystery financial backer specifically forbade him to create any more than one hundred?" asked Bo.

"That's correct, and that's why I say that Bart Sinclair did not request the production of the diamonds. Nor do I believe that he ever even met Brad Penny."

"Objection, your Honor. This is pure speculation," shouted Steve Fleishman.

"Your Honor if I may continue," said Dr. Walters, "the notes specifically refer to an elderly wealthy gentleman."

"Objection, your Honor," said Steve Fleishman boldly.

"Sustained. Dr. Walters, please limit your answers to the questions asked. You are not here to hypothesize."

"I'm sorry, Judge, but I know a little about Bart Sinclair. He's an average jeweler at best and knows little if anything about synthetic diamonds."

"And how would you know this?" asked Bo.

"Because I personally know the owner of the company where Bart Sinclair buys his synthetic stones."

"And?" asked Bo somewhat perplexed.

"And, this proprietor told me that Sinclair rarely purchased fake stones and that Sinclair probably wouldn't know a fake from a real diamond."

"Objection, hearsay."

"Sustained. The jury will disregard the last narration by Dr. Walters," exclaimed the judge.

"Anything else, Doctor?" asked Bo.

"Not that I can think of, except that I would like to photocopy the workbook. It's worth millions."

"Thank you. No further questions."

Steve Fleishman asked several more follow-up questions but failed to s often the damage caused by the doctor.

The two federal prosecutors were shell-shocked by their own expert's statements. Their case was going down the tubes fast. In a desperate move, Steve Fleishman announced that their next witness would be Ed Garret and requested that his testimony begin first thing in the morning. The judge agreed and called it a day.

Jim McDonald called Milton Rogers immediately upon leaving the courtroom. "What the hell is going on, Milton?"

"What are you talking about?"

"The fakes were too good?"

"Too good?"

"Yes, the expert, Dr. Walters, just got finished testifying and he concluded by stating that Sinclair didn't buy the fake diamonds, nor was he involved in their creation."

"Based upon what?"

"Brad Penny's workbook."

"He had a workbook? God damn him to hell," hollered Milton.

"What did you just say?" asked an incredulous Jim.

"Nothing. Nothing at all."

"Milton, the evidence is pointing towards you. First the composite, now a workbook, followed by the expert testimony. I'm pretty convinced that Sinclair is going to be acquitted. He could win and you, my friend, could end up losing. Based upon what I've seen, the civil case may be pure crap. Heck, you may even be sued. And if so, I'm out my contingency fee, so from now on I want to be paid hourly with a bonus."

"Can you ever think of someone else but yourself?" chimed Milton.

"Not when I'm dealing with crooks like you," countered Jim. "Well, Ed Garrett's up tomorrow. He better be good."

"He will. Trust me, he will." As Milton placed the phone back on the receiver, there was a look of pain etched across his forehead.

Chapter

Eighty

ater that evening, Ed Garrett sat in the US Attorneys' office overlooking downtown West Palm Beach and listened to the coaching of Steve Fleishman and Nick Long. Both Steve and Nick were clearly desperate, and Ed's testimony as to switching the stones could possibly change the tide in their favor.

Ed was on his best behavior. Although he had poured himself just one vodka earlier that day, he was functioning, alert, and responsive. As always, Steve and Nick were optimistic. Ed was opportunistic.

It wasn't until near midnight when Hank telephoned Bo.

"How you doing?" asked Hank sounding as if he was exhausted.

"Fine," answered Bo. "Sorry it took me so long to get back with you, but trust me, what I have is worth the wait."

"Why's that?"

"Fifty thousand dollars was recently wired to Ed Garrett's personal checking account."

"No way."

"Yes. But it gets better. The wire transfer got screwed up."

"And?"

"Well, normally wire transfers from offshore banks are so secretive that you are unable to obtain any information on the sender."

"Yes."

"Well in this case because of a mess-up, the sender's name and more importantly, mailing address, were disclosed. You'll never guess who it is?"

"Milton Rogers?" exclaimed Bo.

"You almost got it. In actuality, it was a company called Four L's, but Milton Rogers is listed as the registered agent."

"That is terrific. Have you got copies?"

"They were emailed to Paul Schwartz directly. But I'm also bringing a set with me to court tomorrow. I want to see the look on the faces of the federal prosecutors when you hit them with this information. Those government pricks."

"So do I. Hey, get some sleep, my friend," demanded Bo.

"You too."

The anticipation kept Bo awake all night long.

The next morning Steve Fleishman called Ed Garret to the stand.

Ed appeared very apprehensive and looked completely out of his element up on the witness podium.

After spending about thirty minutes on Ed's background and occupation, Steve proceeded to specifically inquire about his employment with Bart Sinclair.

Ed explained how he was hired during the holiday rush and paid quite handsomely for his efforts.

Ed informed the jury what his job entailed and stated that Sinclair instructed him to create the settings exactly as they were shown in the Rogers's illustrations.

"Anything else?" asked Steve.

"Well yes. He instructed me to switch out the real diamonds with the fake ones that he provided me."

The jury gasped at his statement.

"You mean to tell me and this entire courtroom that Bart Sinclair instructed you to replace the real diamonds with fake diamonds that he supplied you?" asked Steve incredulously.

"Yes."

"And did you do as instructed?"

"Of course I did. He was paying me."

"Do you know what Mr. Sinclair did with the original gems?"

"Certainly. He put the real ones back in his safe."

"Are you positive?"

"As positive as the fact that I'm sitting here before you," said Ed with a smug grin.

"No more questions," said a very confident Steve Fleishman.

Now it was Bo's turn. Bo slowly rose to address the jury.

"Mr. Garrett, have you received anything for your testimony today?"

"No."

"You mean to tell us that you didn't receive immunity for your testimony?"

"Well yes," said Ed begrudgingly.

"Doesn't that mean you will not go to jail for your alleged stone switching?"

"I guess so."

"Does it or does it not?" asked Bo sternly.

"It does."

"So for testifying to the fact that you personally switched the diamonds, you are free from any criminal prosecution?"

"Yes that's correct."

"And do you understand that you are under oath today."

"Yes."

"And are you aware that your immunity does not extend to lying before this court today?"

"Uh huh," answered Ed nervously.

"And if you do lie, you know that you would be committing perjury, and for that, you can be punished up to several years in jail because you have no immunity for lying to the Court?"

"I guess so, shrugged Ed."

"Well then tell me, honestly this time, have you received any money for your testimony today?"

"No. I have not"

"Are you certain of that fact?"

"Yes."

"Very well, then, as defendant's exhibit number eleven, I would like to introduce Mr. Ed Garrett's checking account statement."

"Objection," yelled Steve and Nick in unison as they immediately jumped up.

"Overruled. This is pretty interesting," said the Judge. "Continue."

"Please explain this recent fifty-thousand-dollar deposit," asked Bo.

"I won the lotto."

"By wire transfer?"

"It was an inheritance."

"Mr. Garret, I cannot emphasize enough the seriousness of lying before this court. Let me tell you that I will personally press for perjury charges if you lie to this Court. Please now, you must speak the truth."

Ed Garrett looked around the courtroom rather sheepishly and uttered, "I take the Fifth."

Bo was ready for this tactic.

"I figured as much, and that's why I'd like to present as defendant's exhibit number twelve the identity of the sender of the wire transfer and its address. Bo then read out loud the name of Four L's Inc. The jury didn't grasp the importance until Bo read that the company's registered agent is Milton Rogers. He let the jury and this new information sink in for a few moments. There was utter silence in the courtroom. Bo seized upon the moment.

"Your Honor, this gentleman was paid to lie. He was paid by Milton Rogers indirectly through one of his companies. We have now spent several weeks on this trial, and the evidence clearly shows that my client is innocent. I know it's rather premature, but I'm asking for a directed verdict. Unless the prosecution has any more surprise witnesses up its sleeve, nothing they can present will, beyond a reasonable doubt, implicate my client."

Steve Fleishman and Nick Long sat tongue-tied.

"Your Honor, we have a long list of witnesses that we plan to call. This trial could last several more weeks," said Steve somewhat meekly.

The judge looked down from his perch and slowly peeled off his glasses.

"Do you have any better witnesses that can either place Bart Sinclair purchasing the fake gems or selling them to the Rogers family?"

"Well."

"Yes or no?" demanded the judge.

"Not really."

"Then I'm granting the defendant's directed verdict. The defendant is NOT GUILTY! Mr. Sinclair you're free to go. The jury is dismissed with our thanks for their service. Mr. Martin, I'd like to see you in my chambers—now."

Bart and Dana Sinclair and all their friends hugged and started crying. The jurors sat somewhat stunned, and the press clattered among themselves. Unfortunately, Bo was too concerned about what the judge wanted with him in chambers to discuss that he held his jubilation inside. *What now?* thought Bo.

Chapter
Eighty-One

As soon as Bo sat down, Judge West handed him a facsimile. It was from the Florida Bar. It read: "Effective today, Bo Martin is hereby suspended from the practice of law, pending a full evidentiary hearing." It was signed by the Chief Judge of the Florida Supreme Court.

Bo sat speechless.

"I received the fax this morning. However, I was so pleased with your courtroom cross-examinations that I allowed you to finish. Off the record, someone very important and high up has it in for you, I'm afraid."

"What do I do now?"

"Well for starters enjoy your victory, son. You were very impressive, and it takes a lot to impress me. I am sorry to be the bearer of bad news, but you should fight to clear your name because where there is smoke, there is fire!"

When Bo emerged in the hallway, Dana and Bart immediately knew something was wrong. Dana's smile quickly evaporated as she wrapped her arms around the young attorney.

Bo said in a soft voice, "I've been suspended by the Florida Bar."

"How?"

"Here's the fax."

After glancing at the one-paragraph letter, Dana tossed it aside and said, "That was before your victory. As soon as they hear about the trial and the judge's directed verdict, they will reinstate you."

"I hope you're right."

"Come on party pooper, we have a celebration to go to tonight. Paul Schwartz's throwing the victory party at the Sailfish Club, and everyone's going to enjoy themselves—even you, buster."

"I've got to go back to the office and catch up on a few tax returns. Would you mind dropping me off?"

"Honey, it's going to work out. How on earth could they proceed against you for money laundering and wire fraud when the alleged wrongdoer is innocent?"

"I guess you're right," said Bo, trying his best to shake off the terrible sense of dread.

When Bo made it back to his office, he could immediately sense something was very wrong.

"Ms. Everett, Ms. Everett where is everyone?"

"Oh, Bo. Congratulations. I knew you would win. And just in the nick of time. I'm afraid."

"Why's that? What's going on?"

"Well, sit down, Bo."

"Okay. It seems that your associates and paralegals were all hired by two of the largest law firms in Florida, Fitz and Rawlings and some other one. I believe they packed up their belongings last night and left their forwarding addresses for you."

"Did they take everything?"

"I'm afraid so. Laptops, discs, files, original wills and trusts. Someone must have had access to the master key."

"Looks like they picked me clean," said Bo incredulously.

"That it does. What's worse is the letter they sent out to all your clients."

"Don't tell me."

"Here it is." Bo took a moment to read the letter.

"Oh my God. This makes me out to be incompetent, guilty, immoral, and a thief."

"You should sue."

"And what? Read all about the sordid details in the *Palm Beach Times*. I'm sure it would make for some nice reading to the over half a million subscribers. Do I have any clients left?"

"A few."

"That's all?"

"Well, Bo after all, you were indicted, and the newspaper articles were vicious."

"I'm ruined."

"Now don't say that. We—me and you—are going to rise above this. Time cures all ills. You just wait and see."

"It gets worse," said Bo.

"How?"

"I was suspended by the Florida Bar."

"Oh my poor boy. That's not fair!"

"Fair or not, I can't practice law, and I am in desperate need of an attorney to help me. I can perform the work, but a licensed attorney is necessary to sign the documents. Who is going to work for me?"

"I know just the person," smiled Ms. Everett.

"On yeah, who?"

"He's in your office."

"Now?"

"Go ahead. It's a pleasant surprise."

"Dad?"

"Hey there, Son."

"What are you doing here?"

"I'm coming back to help you. Even though I retired, I still retained my license to practice law in Florida and have paid all the annual dues."

"Are you sure?"

"Never more so in my life."

"Well, thanks for saving what remains of my career."

"Don't be so down. Together, we'll get through this. Plus, I'm sure the Florida Bar will lift the suspension once they read about Sinclair's acquittal. Congratulations! That was a big victory."

"I sure hope so."

"Have some faith, Son."

The two men spent several hours discussing Bo's practice, his remaining loyal clients, and how to address the mutiny of virtually all his employees. They completely lost track of time, and it wasn't until Ruby's phone call that they learned they were running so late.

The quickly planned celebration party at the Sailfish Club was wonderful. The seafood buffet offered something for everyone. Alcohol was flowing freely and all the revelers enjoyed themselves.

After everyone had sated themselves with the food and drinks, Paul Schwartz stood to make a toast.

"To my friend, and one of the best courtroom performances I have ever seen, I'd like to make a toast to Bo Martin."

Everyone joined in.

It was now Bo's time to stand and say a few words. "Well, I'd first like to thank the team," he said and proceeded to name every single person who contributed to the defense. "Without these wonderful people, we most likely would have been unsuccessful. So to you, I offer this toast."

Bart Sinclair, flanked by his wife Dana, spoke last. With watering eyes, he thanked everyone for their support, herculean efforts, and undying allegiance. And in two separate envelopes, he presented Bo and Paul their legal fees.

Bo's check was for a staggering two million dollars, and Paul Schwartz was paid an additional one million dollars.

Bo hadn't really paid much attention to all the hours he had spent working on the case. He knew that Hank wouldn't accept any money for his efforts. *I'll just have to buy him special and unique gifts*, thought Bo.

Fortunately, the money would definitely come in handy. With the virtual loss of his practice and the suspension of his legal license, he and Ruby would be set financially for at least a couple of years. Thank God for that.

It was odd, but Bo was finally starting to like Bart Sinclair despite all his faults and major character flaws. His wife, Dana, was also a dear, sweet person.

Later that night at home, Bo and Ruby shared a wonderful, peaceful, and romantic night. The dogs settled at the foot of the king-sized bed.

Most of the local television stations had reported extensively on the surprising directed verdict, and even Bart Sinclair made a brief statement. Bo went to sleep believing the *Palm Beach Times* would report the favorable decision as well.

Unfortunately, the next morning's paper headlines read, "Bo Martin suspended by The Florida Bar." Very little was said about the directed verdict, and of course, the government was already working on an appeal.

Once again, the newspaper article made Bo sick to his stomach. *That damn Mae McReynolds*, thought Bo. *She'll have her day soon, very soon!*

When Bo arrived at his office that morning, two West Palm Beach police officers were in the lobby.

"Can I help you?" asked Bo.

"Sure, we need a few minutes of your time."

"Fine. Come on back to my office. Can I get you anything?"

"No, we're fine," said the older, heavyset one.

"Very well, then. How can I help you?"

"Tell us about Ed Garrett?"

"What do you want to know?"

"Well, rumor has it he took the Fifth yesterday and then died of alcohol poisoning early this morning."

"How does an alcoholic die from alcohol poisoning?" asked Bo rather innocuously.

"He was so drunk. It was almost like he was injected with the stuff. Early medical reports show his blood alcohol to be point seventy-two. Nine times the legal limit. Know anything about that?"

"No. Why would I?"

"They said you had some pretty damaging evidence against him that you brought out at trial."

"Yes. I guess I did cause him some anguish."

"Well where did you get the information?"

"From various sources."

"Such as?"

"Such as none of your business," said Bo in his most defensive voice.

"Well, we'll see about that."

"Go ahead. Make my day."

"Do you have an alibi for your whereabouts last evening?"

"Of course. But why are you asking me? Shouldn't you be interrogating Milton Rogers? After all, he paid the man to lie on the witness stand," said Bo, now getting madder by the second.

"We may. One more question."

"All right."

"What are you doing working when your license is suspended?" said the smaller officer with a smirk.

"None of your goddamn business. Please leave," yelled Bo. "Now."

Slowly the officers made their way out of the office before almost colliding with Bye Martin. After the officers were gone, Bye asked, "What was that about?"

"Ed Garrett died last night of alcohol poisoning."

"So?"

"They think I might have some involvement regarding his death."

"When it rains, it pours. Sorry about the article, Son. Pretty bad."

"It doesn't get much worse. Think the government has a valid appeal?"

"I don't know, Bo. But you know how much they hate to lose and how the system is slanted towards the US attorneys."

"I know."

"Well, I'm ready to get started. I've never had a paralegal who knows more law than I do. Let's start with a simple will and go from there."

After an exhausting day spent educating his father and returning a few phone calls, Bo headed home. Bo had deposited the Sinclair check in his law firm's account and was informed that the check was good and that the funds would be available in three business days.

Bo had seen extremely large inheritance checks made payable to the IRS, but the large check payable to Martin and Martin, P.A. definitely put a smile on his face.

When he arrived home, Ruby had left a message on the answering machine that she was at her restaurant. Something about a pipe bursting.

The red dogs were restless, and Bo took them down to the beach for a short run followed by a refreshing swim. Bo couldn't remember when he last had enjoyed an early afternoon with the red dogs.

On their way back, Bart Sinclair was waiting in the driveway for Bo.

"How's my favorite attorney today?"

"After an invigorating run and ocean swim, I have to say I feel pretty good."

"Hey Bo, sorry about that article in the paper today. I, myself, was hoping for huge headlines proclaiming my innocence."

"Me too."

"So what are we going to do now?"

"We?" asked Bo incredulously.

"Yes I need a new trust lawyer. You evidently can't serve as my trustee, and I'd like to designate a new one."

"Bart, you simply can't do that. I'm innocent of any criminal wrongdoing, and I'm certainly not going to resign if that's what you're implying."

"I want to put all this behind me and go forward with a clean slate."

"You what?"

"You know, start fresh."

"After everything I've been through to save your ass, you want me removed as trustee?"

"Bo, I paid you more than enough money. I thought you'd be delighted."

"Don't get me wrong, Bart. The attorney fee check was certainly unexpected, but in light of your facing a possible life in prison, it was rather reasonable."

"Well, I'll give you a week. Then I want the original trust, the money, account information, and all the papers associated with it."

"Bart, you can't be serious."

"If I don't have them, I'll sue you. And I know you don't need any more negative publicity."

"I was appointed by Joe Marx. I have risked my life—and certainly my reputation—in upholding the terms of the Trust. I will not resign, nor will I allow you to remove me," said Bo rather indignantly.

"Paul says he will represent me in the removal action."

"Hire whoever you want. I will fight you tooth and nail. What's worse, Bart, is that as Trustee, I'll be spending your trust money fighting against you."

"I don't care about the money, Bo. I have lots of cash from my recent sale."

"Your recent sale?"

"You didn't really think I'd leave all those precious stones in my safe for long, did you?"

"Don't tell me you sold them," shouted Bo.

"Of course I did."

"You idiot. Those stones were for your protection and mine."

"Well, since I'm a free man, I didn't need them anymore."

"What about me?"

"What about you? You are up to your ears in legal problems. Face it, Bo—you're a disgraced suspended attorney."

"And you're an ass," yelled Bo.

"Touché, my former attorney. I guess I'll be seeing you in court. And by the way, it's illegal to have those mutts on the beach without a leash. I'll make sure that you're ticketed next time."

Bo was so furious that he felt like actually hitting the pompous ass. *After all I've done for him to be dismissed just like an ugly stepchild*, thought Bo.

Thankfully, Ruby was home when Bo and the red dogs arrived back. Bo's red face immediately told her that something was wrong.

"Honey, you look out of breath or something."

"Guess who I ran into a while ago?"

"Who?"

"Bart, the asshole, Sinclair."

"What?"

"He tried to fire me as the Trustee of the Marx trust. He even threatened to remove me in a court proceeding.

"You've got to be kidding?"

"And to make matters worse, he sold the original stones. Those stones were our ace in the hole."

"That's incredible."

"You know, he really played me for a fool."

"He played all of us. Heck, Sophia and I even went so far last night to ask Dana to join the Palm Beach Junior League."

"I knew he was a dirty low down, dishonest person. But to do this to me. It hurts. It hurts like hell."

"Don't worry, honey. You're probably better off this way."

"I won't resign immediately. I'll wait to see if he actually proceeds with a civil lawsuit for removal action."

"Sounds sort of risky to me. You may want to ask your dad about it?"

"No. I've had enough father-son interaction today to last me a long time. He's stubborn and asks way too many questions."

"Sounds like someone else I know," smiled Ruby.

"Oh, real funny!"

Ruby had finally gotten Bo to smile and at least temporarily forget about Bart Sinclair.

Chapter
Eighty-Two

The Rogers's mansion was bustling with activity. Milton hadn't slept since the directed verdict and was eager to meet with his children and formulate some sort of plan to get back at Bo Martin. Thank God, Mae was able to keep out all the damaging evidence against him from her column. He loved the fact that virtually nothing derogatory was mentioned about him.

Milton was pleased that he had friends in high places. The suspension of Bo Martin's legal license had taken too much time and money for his liking. If only he had been suspended immediately upon his Indictment.

Thankfully, Steve Fleishman was working with the federal prosecutors on the appeal of the directed verdict and was also proceeding along with the prosecution against Bo Martin.

"That ought to keep Bo on his heels until I come up with another brilliant plan. This time, he won't be so fortunate!" vowed Milton.

Chapter
Eighty-Three

The following day, the federal government filed its appeal of Judge Walter West's ruling. They cited numerous breaches of ethics and judicial error in admitting several of the defendant's exhibits. It was a quick appeal that lacked real legal authority. The Federal Appellate Court in the Eleventh Circuit was not prone to overturning or reversing its lower court rulings. So, it was somewhat surprising that an appeal was even filed.

Paul Schwartz telephoned Bo, nevertheless after he had been emailed a courtesy copy of the document and had emailed it directly to Bo's office.

"Well, Bo, have you read the appeal?"

"Yes, I have. I'm not too knowledgeable in the appellate area, especially in the federal criminal arena, but I fail to see where the government's cited legal authority calls for a retrial."

"You hit it on the head. Very insightful. In my extensive experience, it would take a miracle for the court to overrule or reverse Judge West."

"When will we know for sure?" asked Bo half knowing the answer.

"Well, we have thirty days to file our response. Don't worry yourself. I'll be filing the brief, but I do want your participation."

"No problem. I'll do whatever I can."

"One more thing."

"Yes."

"I spoke with Bart today. He wants to fire you as trustee. He said you two had words."

"That's an understatement, Paul. However, I'm not going to resign. Not after everything I've gone through."

"I understand completely. I'll do what I can to try and convince him otherwise."

"You realize I know a little too much about Bart if you understand what I mean," answered Bo coyly.

"I do. Trust me. I personally will decline to file any suit against you. You have my word."

Yes, thought Bo. *That and fifty cents will buy you a cup of coffee.*

"Well after I prepare the response brief, I'm planning on taking a long vacation."

"That's great. You deserve it, Paul."

"So do you, Bo. So do you."

"I'll keep in touch. Take care."

Bo knew he couldn't trust Paul any more than he could throw him, but after the trial, Bo figured he had at least earned his respect.

The following day's headline read "Palm Beach Attorney's Breaches of Ethics Lead to Appeal."

Once again, it slammed Bo and his behavior throughout the entire article. Nothing was mentioned as to the merits of the actual appeal. It was yet again another butchering of Bo's ever-shrinking credibility.

All Bo could think of was that he still was a very lucky man. A beautiful wife, a loving family, two great dogs, and truly wonderful friends. "I'll get through this ordeal somehow," reiterated Bo to himself.

Chapter
Eighty-Four

The following week Bo received a rather disturbing phone call from Steve Fleishman on his cell phone.

"Bo Martin."

"Yes, speaking."

"It's me, Steve Fleishman."

"I know who you are. What do you want?"

"We'd like to schedule a meeting with you and your attorney."

"About what?"

"About your money laundering activities."

"Go to hell," snapped Bo.

"Listen up. The meeting allows you an opportunity to speak with full immunity. We call it 'King for the Day.' Nothing you say can or will be used against you. We feel the session could be very productive."

"I'm sure you do. But since I'm innocent, what do I have to gain?"

"We could reach an agreement."

"Listen, Steve, I know all about your financial agreement with Milton Rogers, Jim McDonald, and Mae McReynolds. I have been blasted in the *Palm Beach Times* on numerous occasions, and I think I will continue to be chastised in the press as long as Milton Rogers remains a free man."

Steve completely ignored what Bo was saying. "We'd like to meet this Friday. Talk to your attorney. Then call me by Thursday." Click.

Bo was shaking as he crammed the phone back in his front pocket. Bye just happened to be walking past the door and looked in on his son.

"Hey, Dad, I just got a call from Steve Fleishman. It seems he wants to meet this Friday. A 'King for the Day,' he called it."

"I'm going with you, Son."

"You think I should tell Lee Smith?"

"No. I'll be your attorney."

"You will? I know what they say about having yourself for a client, but what do they say about having your father?" smiled Bo.

"They say that you are a genius."

"I'll bet," laughed Bo.

"What have you got to lose?"

"Really nothing."

"Call him tomorrow and schedule a time after lunch."

"Okay. I sure hope you know what you're doing."

"So do I, Son, so do I."

Chapter
Eighty-Five

The rest of the week passed quickly enough. Bo was still diligently working as a paralegal and basically doing everything as he had before the suspension, but he was unable to sign or affix his name to anything. Bye was doing his best to understand Bo's estate and trusts practice, but in actuality he was tired and extremely confused. Bye knew it was time to retire again but continued on in support of his son.

On Friday afternoon, Bo and Bye waltzed into the foyer of the United States Attorneys' office. There was a metal detector, an armed guard, and a steel-proof door. The men were forced to sit for over half an hour. The lower floors of the building housed the FBI and the CIA. *Too much bureaucracy and machismo for me*, thought Bo.

Bye was also fidgety. He hated waiting and knew that the meeting would be useless and a waste of time. But there always existed the possibility that the Feds would drop the case against Bo, and he could then retire and go back to his tranquil life.

Finally, Steve Fleishman came through the metal door. "Sorry for the wait."

I'll bet, thought the Martin men independently.

"Mr. Bye Martin, I don't think we've met. Let me introduce myself. I'm Steve Fleishman, and this is my partner, Nick Long."

"I know who you are. I watched the end of Sinclair's trial. You appear much more at ease in your metal confines than in the courtroom."

"Touché," said Bo.

"Listen, we're not here to argue or cast aspersions. We want to possibly settle the case against Bo. So please follow me and hear us out."

The meeting room consisted of a cheap imitation-wood conference table with fourteen heavy metal chairs. The US Department of Justice seal was displayed prominently on the wall. Several boxes of files or documents were stacked in all four corners, giving the room a look of shoddiness. The windows overlooked the Intracoastal Waterway. The sky was bright blue, but in the distance there were large dark clouds. *It could rain*, thought Bye.

"Let's first begin by saying that you, Bo Martin, are not our main target. Bart Sinclair is, and will remain, our primary target. However, as a lawyer, you are held to a much higher standard of care. We feel that you've violated the law and must be punished.

"We've now seen your performance in the courtroom and know that you are a worthy opponent. But you were very lucky. The US Attorneys' office in Palm Beach County has a ninety-eight percent conviction rate. We're good, and we know how to get our man. Normally, we don't offer defendants a 'King for the Day' unless we can use you and your cooperation."

"I'm not a snitch," interjected Bo firmly.

"You have information we feel that can help us get a bigger target."

"And who might that be?" interjected Bye.

"Bart Sinclair, of course."

"You've got to be kidding. Get out your first-year law books, and read the section on attorney-client privilege. Also, fiduciary duty and ethics while you're at it."

"Very funny. Seriously if you can give us some information on Sinclair, we will go light on you."

Bye couldn't believe Steve's audacity.

"Light? For Christ's sake, you're pursuing money laundering and wire fraud against Bo. Both carry long sentences if convicted, and both are felonies under the law. A conviction ruins Bo's legal career and exposes him to jail time. Under no circumstance will we ever plead guilty. A plea agreement is out of the question."

"Well if that's your position, then there is no need to discuss this matter any further," retorted Steve.

"Fine then. Bo, let's go," said Bye quietly.

"See you in court," yelled Nick.

"I can't wait to see you both get your asses kicked again by a Martin," proclaimed Bye as he and his son stormed out of the office.

At the third floor, their elevator mysteriously stopped and opened up directly into another set of elevator doors. Standing in the entranceway were three FBI agents with their guns raised.

"Bo and Bye Martin, please step this way."

Both men were startled and alarmed.

"What's going on?" asked Bye.

"Please just follow us."

The Martin men were led through a long and winding maze of offices, files, and computers until they finally entered a small but cozy conference room. There were no windows and only six chairs set around an oval conference table. The room contained no pictures, and there was not a single piece of paper in the small room.

Bo and Bye took their seats together at the far end of the table facing the door. One of the agents asked if they wanted water or a soda. Both declined, and the door was shut behind the agent. The Martin men were left alone.

"Dad, what's going on?"

"Heck if I know. But we'll shortly find out."

About ten minutes later two men entered the room, each carrying some files and yellow legal pads. From the bulges in their navy-blue jackets, it was obvious the men were armed.

"You don't know us, and we're not going to introduce ourselves. Let's just say that we work for one of our country's intelligence agencies. We're sorry for the method we used to get you here, but we're glad to meet you."

Bo stared at both men. One was about six feet tall, slightly shorter than Bo. He was of medium build with pockmarks on his face. He had large brown eyes, small hands, and dark-brown graying hair. The other man was much shorter, no more than five foot seven inches with completely gray hair, blue eyes, and manicured nails. He obviously was the supervisor.

He stared intently at Bo.

"The meeting you just had was orchestrated by our department. Neither Steve nor Nick were in on it though. As you know, they have a bone to pick with you. It's not often they are trounced in federal court."

"That's an understatement," said Bo. "You know if you investigated further into Steve Fleishman's personal finances, you would find that he's in Milton Rogers's hip pocket."

"We already know that."

"Well, why don't you do something about it?"

"We will. Trust me."

"Could have fooled me," said Bye looking sternly.

"I clearly understand your animosity. From our own investigation, it's clear that Bo is innocent and has done nothing wrong. He eventually will be cleared of all the charges pending against him."

"He will?" asked Bye cautiously. Bo couldn't believe his ears!

"Yes, the Indictment will slowly go away."

"What about the suspension from the Florida Bar?" asked Bo.

"In due time. Give us a break. Bureaucracies work very slowly, and we happen to be one of them."

"So what do you want with my son?"

"In the Sinclair trial, Brenda Rogers brought up the name Jean Valhomme."

"So?" asked Bye, not having a clue about the matter.

"Well, you also learned that he was arrested for trying to launder sixty million in cash."

"Yes," answered Bo.

"Well, the Europeans just released him."

"He's free?" asked Bo skeptically.

"Yes, he used his influence, power, and money to beat the charges."

"That doesn't surprise me at all," said Bye.

"Well, it substantially hurt our investigation. You see, Jean Valhomme has been under intense surveillance and monitoring. We believe he's the largest producer of illegal drugs in the modern world. His conglomeration of companies manufactures more than seventy-five percent of all the illegal tablets made including Ecstasy, Quaaludes, Fentanyl, and opioids.

"We know that he delivered a large shipment to the Port of Palm Beach for Milton Rogers. It was a very large shipment. Somehow our wires got crossed, and before we could disrupt the delivery, the containers were moved off the docks. Milton Rogers and his four sons then sold the pills to several unscrupulous middlemen. They made a lot of money, we believe. But then Milton Rogers made a huge mistake."

"And what was that?" asked Bye. Bo sat silent knowing full well everything that transpired but waiting to hear what the feds had uncovered.

"He screwed Jean."

"How?"

"We believe he shortchanged the man and ultimately paid him in cash."

"And that cash is what he was attempting to launder when he was caught?" inquired Bo, already knowing the entire story.

"Correct. How did you know that?" asked the short man.

"Where is he now?" asked Bo, dismissing completely the previous question.

"We think he's en route to Palm Beach to get even with Milton."

Bo's skin crawled. He knew what was coming.

"Now, we also believe Milton is out to get Bo here. Bo has undermined the Rogers's plot, and we feel Bo's his next target."

Bo understood completely that Milton would turn Jean on to Bo. He would attempt to persuade Jean to enact his revenge on Bo, rather than Milton.

"Based on Bo's artful cross-examinations at the Sinclair trial, we feel Bo is the next target. What we don't know is why?"

"Why what?" answered Bo rather sheepishly, trying to act completely innocent.

"We feel there is something that you're not telling us. We think that somehow you were able to financially hurt Milton. And, we aim to find out."

"I really don't know what you're talking about or why on earth you think I outsmarted Milton Rogers."

"We know all about the Trust. You've got it well hidden, I'll give you that. But there's more to the story and why you've risked your career and basically your life to this Trust."

"Just doing my job, I guess," said Bo nonchalantly.

"Well if you're not going to tell us, you might as well be on your way. If you ever feel like talking, here's my number," said the gray-haired man as he handed Bo his card. No name, just a number.

I'm sure we'll be seeing each other again."

"Oh, I hope not," replied Bo.

After they exited the building bye turned to Bo and spoke, "Son, I realize you know more than you're leading on. Did you in any way screw Milton Rogers?"

"Yes, yes I did."

"Okay. Well then we should get some security around your house and maybe even ours. If this Jean fellow is in Palm Beach, you can bet he's armed and dangerous."

"That sounds good with me."

"And one other thing, Son, whatever you did, I'm proud of you. I don't even want to know what you did to Milton, but he definitely deserved it as he is a real son of a bitch."

"Thanks, Dad!" When Bo and Bye returned back to the office, they found their wives, Ruby and Teresa, waiting impatiently for them.

"How'd it go?" asked Teresa.

"Not bad, Mom."

"What's that mean, sweetheart?" chimed Ruby.

"It means he's still under Indictment, but there may not be a quick trial or further prosecution. Bo has several things he has to work out first."

"Such as?"

"For starters, we need to get some security around here and at our homes."

"Why?" asked Teresa.

"There could be trouble brewing. That's all."

"What's that supposed to mean?" asked Ruby, staring directly at Bo and closely monitoring his body movements. Ruby could sense that Bo was worried and that he and Bye were not telling the girls everything.

Bye originally wanted to pack up and return back to Nantucket but realized that Florida was the place to be. If something was going to happen, it might as well take place in the friendly confines of Palm Beach County, Florida.

"We're going to hire guards for both of our houses, the office, and even Ruby's business."

"Do you really think that's really necessary?" asked Teresa.

"Yes, we do," answered Bye."

"For at least the next month or so, we will have twenty-four-hour security. Does anyone have a problem with that?"

Everyone shook their head no.

"With that settled, I'll make some calls, and we'll immediately have the extra security," said Bye to himself.

Chapter
Eighty-Six

ilton was in one of his foul moods. He was sick of listening to Brenda's nonstop nitpicking and being reminded time and time again how he should never have underestimated Bo Martin. Brenda was relentless and constantly harped on her husband. All she ever wanted was for her sons to be set up financially. She also could not imagine her husband being outwitted by anyone. She knew Milton would concoct another scheme to get back at Bo Martin. She just prayed that this time her husband would succeed.

Milton had learned through the grapevine that Jean Valhomme was successful in having the criminal charges against him dismissed. Milton didn't believe that Jean would leave his home and travel to Palm Beach again. No way, thought Milton, and dismissed the idea.

The entire Rogers family had gathered at the massive dining-room table enjoying their weekly Sunday night feast. Brenda enjoyed family dinner night so much that she personally did all the cooking, cleaning, and shopping.

Milton and Brenda were now totally supporting all their children and their expensive habits and tastes because Milton's master plan had backfired. Their sons and daughters-in-law were on their best behavior. Not one was personally employed, and the winter social season in Palm Beach was already upon them. The table talk centered on the extravagant costume ball for the American Cancer Society. It was the first social event of the season and the Rogers entire clan couldn't wait to attend.

Of course, I'll contribute generously again this year plus pay the fifteen hundred dollars per person for tickets for everyone, thought Milton. However, he was still preoccupied with trying to design a plan to retaliate against Bo Martin.

Right before dessert and after everyone had consumed substantial amounts of alcohol, there was a small explosion outside in the circular driveway. It jolted their family gathering and shook the house. Disoriented, the entire Rogers clan scrambled to open the front door only to find Milton's convertible Rolls Royce engulfed in flames.

"Oh my God," yelled Milton. "Oh my God."

As the entire family stood dumbstruck, Milton hollered, "call 9-1-1, call 9-1-1."

Before Brenda could reach the phone, she stared directly into the glaring eyes of Jean Valhomme. Jean and his three cronies must have entered through the back French doors by the pool, surmised Brenda. The fire was simply a diversionary tactic that captured the attention of the entire Rogers clan. Pretty ingenious, thought Milton.

"Did you call 9-1-1 Brenda?" yelled Milton before noticing Jean and his men all carrying semiautomatic weapons.

Several of the girls screamed and everyone was clearly terrified.

"Please come inside. Shut the door and be seated. Everyone. Now!" said Jean calmly.

"What the hell is this, Jean?" swore Milton.

"My friend, Milton Rogers. You didn't think you were rid of me now, did you? Especially after you shortchanged me twenty million dollars. Yes, twenty million. And to make matters worse. I'm sure you are aware that I ran into some problems getting rid of the cash, were you not?"

"I had heard," shrugged Milton.

"Hmm. Had heard. Well, guess what I heard? I heard that your lovely wife mentioned my name at a recent criminal trial." Jean rubbed the barrel of his gun across Brenda's face, causing her to tremble.

"So I did some research. And you'll never guess what I found out?"

"What's that?" said Lee, the oldest Rogers son, trying to act bold in an effort to conceal his fear.

"Your dear old dad pulled two switcheroos. First, he exchanged fake stones for real stones and tried to screw your local jeweler, Bart Sinclair. Then, he switched the real for fake stones again before they were delivered to me. I had already entered a contract to sell the diamonds, but no, I couldn't sell them because they were marbles. Do you realize you made me out to be a fool? Nobody makes me out a fool! Nobody!"

"But to make matters worse when I and my friends here came to visit and receive my rightful share, you stiffed me for twenty million dollars. To add insult to injury, the eighty million in cash was rather difficult to launder, and I was caught red handed. Fortunately, through my contacts, I was able to extricate myself from this situation. But it cost me another ten million in bribes."

"But what's even worse is that I've had to shut down all my manufacturing activities. The CIA, the DEA, FBI interpol, Scotland Yard, and probably the IRS in addition to my own taxing authorities have me under surveillance. I'm a marked man, and it's all because of you, Milton Rogers!"

"Okay, enough of the theatrics," cried Milton. "What exactly do you want from us?"

"What do I want?" yelled Jean. "Well let's see. I want my one hundred million dollars."

"That's ridiculous," said Larry incredulously a second before Jean smashed him with his gun.

Moments later, Larry, sitting closest to Jean, was sprawled out on the ground bleeding profusely out of his shattered nose and busted lip. "You think this is a laughing matter?" asked Jean.

"No I don't!" shouted Milton.

"My God, Milton, do something," yelled Brenda.

"Please, Jean. I've been duped and I'm terribly sorry for everything."

"Oh, you haven't felt sorry in your entire pathetic life. You think that with all your wealth you can ruin people's lives. What in fact did this Bart Sinclair ever do to you?"

"Nothing, really," replied Milton.

"That's the first honest words I've heard from you, Milton. Now back to my money."

Milton was thinking hard. He still hadn't devised a plan of revenge for Bo Martin but his mind was reeling. All at once he came up with a plan.

"Jean, I know who is possession of the real diamonds. I think with your help, we can retrieve the diamonds and pay you all the money that you are owed."

"Let's hear it," said Jean, "I'm all ears."

"I believe one or two people are in possession of the stones," professed Milton.

"And who might they be?"

"Either Bart Sinclair or his attorney, Bo Martin."

"Do you know which one it is for sure?"

"At this moment, the answer is no."

"But, there is a huge costume party this Saturday night and Bart Sinclair will be there. Behind our masks we can apprehend him and force him to return the stones. And if he's not the one in possession, then it's got to be the attorney." Secretly, Milton hoped that Jean would kill Bo Martin slowly.

"Where will you be staying, Jean?" asked Milton.

"That's none of your business. Let me tell you this once and only once. If you so much as contact the police or attempt to screw me again, I will kill you and your entire family. Have you got that? Has everyone got that?" shouted Jean, pointing his weapon at the heads of each and every one of them.

"We do," said Milton, still shaking.

"Well then, my friends and I will be here on Saturday. We will be dressed and ready to enact business."

Jean then pulled out a small mobile phone and spoke in French. Minutes later a horn blew, and Jean and his three associates exited the front door into a waiting dark limousine.

Milton ran to the door but was unable to catch the license plate. A black limousine on the island of Palm Beach was an all too common sight. He then momentarily glared at the remains of his prized Rolls Royce. Someone must have extinguished the fire because white powder covered the entire blackened car.

Brenda was attending to Lee, who was in a state of shock and clearly in pain when Milton walked back into the house.

A broken nose, big deal, thought Milton as he placed his hand on Lee's sweaty shoulder. "It will be alright, Son."

"I hope you're happy now, Milton," shouted Brenda.

"Listen up. I got us into this fiasco, and I'll get us out. Understood?" Everyone nodded their heads.

"Let's stick together; don't panic, and we'll end this matter once and for all."

"Dad, I want to get a gun," said Luke.

"Don't be stupid. These guys are experts. They kill for fun. If you so much as move unexpectedly, they'll kill you in a heartbeat. So no stupid mistakes. You all will do nothing. Got that? Okay. Now let's get Lee to the hospital. The story is he tripped on the marble stairs, okay?"

Later that night Brenda stared into the eyes of her beloved husband. "I'm really scared, honey."

"I know you are."

"This whole thing has been a nightmare, and I feel it's all my fault. I know I spoiled the children, and I know you devised the plan at my insistence to help the boys financially. I never imagined things getting this out of hand. My God, Milton, people have been killed."

"Honey, we're out over a hundred twenty five million dollars. I'm going to get our stones back."

"Our stones?"

"Yes. Don't worry about Jean, I've got an idea."

"Oh Milton, don't be a fool. I don't know what I'd do without you. Even with this financial loss, we're still financially secure, and so are the children. Please tell me you won't do anything rash."

"Now don't you worry. I'll win. You'll see." Milton already figured he could recover the diamonds and additional jewelry from Sinclair's safe, which would be more than enough to compensate him and pay off Jean.

Chapter
Eighty-Seven

The annual Palm Beach Masquerade Ball, held at the Breakers Beach Club and benefitting the American Cancer Society, was the first major society event of the season. Everyone among the in-crowd and "Who's Who" in Palm Beach planned on attending. The ladies would be dressed in their finest costumes. Diamonds and rare stones would literally be dripping from their wrists, fingers, necks, and ears. And what's most ironic is that all would be wearing masks, thereby disguising their very identities they were trying so hard to flaunt in the first place.

The men would be dressed in their Armani, Polo, or Bill Blass tuxedos, and the bulk of their conversations would focus on football or the stock market. Their masks would also help to hide their true identities.

The event started at seven o'clock, but the fashionably late would begin to arrive after eight o'clock.

Two large black limousines pulled into the Rogers's driveway around 7:30 p.m. Jean, accompanied by one of his henchmen, exited the first limo, and out of the trailing vehicle emerged one lone gunman. All three men were dressed in black tuxedos and identical masks, even the two drivers wore tuxedos and masks.

The entire Rogers clan had gathered at the mansion around 6:30 p.m. The daughters-in-law looked elegant, as usual, and all the Rogers men, who had evidently gained a few extra pounds over the past year sported tuxes that appeared a little too tight. Obesity was a Rogers gene that none were too enthralled with but all were unwilling to do much about.

"Please, Jean, come inside for a drink."

"Certainly," said Jean, flanked by his two compatriots. The drivers stayed beside their automobiles.

"To what should we toast?" questioned Milton.

"How about to your good health. May we be successful this evening so that your lifespan is not terrifyingly cut short."

"Touché, my friend," said Milton as he raised his glass and took a gulp of his finest Scotch.

"So, Milton, what is the plan?" said Jean, getting right to the point.

"Well, Jean, it goes like this: Bart Sinclair and his wife, Dana, will be rather easy to pick out. Dana will literally be dripping in diamonds. She will stay gossiping with a group of two or three anorexic-looking women with bronze tans and dyed blond hair. Bart will most likely hang out by the outside bar smoking a Cuban cigar. He'll soon become loud and obnoxious after he starts hitting the bottle. I would say that we should make the abduction at exactly ten p.m."

The Rogers men glanced at their large presidential gold Rolexes in order to synchronize their watches. Jean and his two friends also adjusted their watches to be in sync with the others.

"Bart Sinclair's jewelry store is located on Worth Avenue. which is about a ten-minute drive from the Breakers. We should only take one car to his store. We don't want to arouse any suspicion from the Palm Beach police with the presence of two limos."

"I figure the real diamonds are in his main safe. At least they were when he originally sold them to me. The safe is gigantic and it opens by combination only. The store also has numerous videotape monitors. So we must all keep our masks on the entire time. I'm unsure where the actual videotape recorder is located."

"No problem," interrupted Jean. "My men have already cased the store and there will be no obstacle with either the security or surveillance cameras."

"That's great. That's about all I have thought out."

"Well, good. I've planned out the rest."

"We're waiting. Tell us," demanded Milton.

"Oh no. The rest is a surprise. For me to know and for you to find out only when the time is right. Milton, you and Brenda will ride with me. The rest of your family will stay with my men."

"What do you mean stay?" asked Larry rather boldly.

"Just what I said, you spoiled rotten fat brats. None of you will step foot in the Breakers. You are my insurance. If your father so much as attempts to double-cross me again or thwarts any of my actions, you will be wiped out. And remember both of my men are heavily armed just in case you get a birdbrain idea to attempt to overpower them. But don't you worry, there is plenty of food and drink in the limo to keep you all very comfortable."

Milton had not planned on Jean's kidnapping his boys and their wives, and he was most displeased.

"That's not fair, Jean. If they fail to show up, people will talk."

"So let them."

Milton was clearly pissed. He hoped to use his sons to help extricate the jewels out of Jean's possession once they were obtained. Now, he'd just have to do it himself. Fortunately, confidence was not a concern. His ego was too large.

Brenda was still shaking in the limo as they arrived at the magnificent entrance of the Breakers. Milton joined by Brenda and flanked by Jean and his colleague proceeded into the grand hotel.

The Breakers Beach Club was a separate building from the grand hotel. It was situated directly facing the Atlantic Ocean. At the center of the room was a rather large odd-shaped swimming pool. There were four separate bars and one grand buffet area. All the tables were ornately decorated with native flowers with bright tropical colors. Fortunately, the night was cool and the outside bar and patio area were open as well.

Bart could easily be abducted from the patio and escorted around back to the side of the building where the hired help and delivery trucks were located, thought Milton and Jean.

All Brenda could think was, "Please God, don't hurt my babies. Please."

The room was packed with over five hundred of Palm Beach's finest. The decorative masks made it virtually impossible to locate anyone. But, as luck would have it, Bart Sinclair was indeed out on the patio drinking heavily while his wife was gossiping with several string-bean-looking women.

Not once in the half hour that Jean observed Dana, did she so much as look over or search to find her husband. In addition, the three drinks she had consumed had made her slightly tipsy. Jean winked at the waitress as she dropped some clear solution into Dana's drink prior to handing it to her. As she walked away, Jean was given the thumbs up sign. *There won't be any problem with Dana now*, thought Jean.

Jean and his cohort slowly made their way to the outside bar where, sure enough, Bart Sinclair was knocking back the drinks and acting obnoxious. Bart was carrying on a rather loud conversation with two men, who both appeared to be trying to escape from their situation, but to no avail.

Sure enough, several minutes later Bart found himself alone with only Jean and his companion.

"Nice masks," slurred Bart. "Since they're identical, I take it you're a couple?" joked Bart.

"You could say that," answered Jean.

"Oh, European. I've heard how most of Europe is very liberal. Down here in Palm Beach, Florida, we tolerate gays, but you'll probably be happier in South Beach with more of your own kind."

"I thank you for your valuable insight."

"No problem."

"So what type of business are you in if I may be so bold to ask?" said Jean, feigning interest.

"Oh, I'm a jeweler. Actually, I've sold most of the jewels that the women are wearing here tonight," said Bart boasting.

"Then you must be pretty successful."

"Oh, yes, very."

"That's great. You know my friend and I are involved in the import-export business."

"Is it lucrative?" asked Bart.

"At times, yes."

"I'm thinking of venturing out into another line of business."

"Really?"

"Yes, I've had a tough year, and I'm looking into maybe something more hands-off and less time consuming."

Jean glanced at his watch. It read 9:55 p.m.

"Oh, don't look at your watch. It's much too early to be a party pooper! Plus, the drinks are flowing. My treat," proclaimed Bart.

Bart downed another drink and was planning on ordering another when the stun gun that Jean was carrying immediately paralyzed him in the blink of an eye.

In a matter of seconds, Jean and his partner had immobilized Bart and were slowly carrying him around the side of the building and into the waiting limousine. Milton was already in the car.

"So far so good," exclaimed Milton. "How long will he be out?"

"Give or take ten minutes. I gave him only a short jolt."

Chapter
Eight-Five

By the time the limousine had arrived at the back of Bart's Worth Avenue store, Bart was awake, groggy and very frightened.

"Who are you, and what the hell do you want?"

"Shut up and say nothing, as we're going to exit the car and enter your store."

"Why?"

"You'll know once we're safe and sound inside your store."

Bart was trying to process everything. *I've been abducted by men—a foreigner, his friend, a limo driver, and an overweight older man. We're at my store. Thank God I have videotaping monitors and super security. The police will come soon enough.*

Once they were inside the store, Jean's companion quickly disengaged all the monitoring devices, the security alarm, and every piece of high-tech electronic security. In addition, the automatic hurricane shutters were activated, completely shutting off the store windows to the outside street. Further, no light inside could be seen from Worth Avenue.

Bart immediately sensed that he was working with professionals. He was now more frightened than ever.

Milton was impressed as well.

"Open up your safe," demanded Jean.

"Fuck you," retorted Bart.

Quickly, the back of the handgun struck Bart flush across his face. Blood gushed out his nose and his freshly opened cheek.

"You will do everything you're told. Is that a problem?"

"Not anymore," said Bart, trying to gauge how seriously he was injured. His hands were shaking so much that he had a very difficult time working the combination lock.

After several unsuccessful attempts, Bart was finally able to get the correct combination, and the huge vault slowly opened.

As Bart stood staring at the men behind their masks, he began to vaguely recognize the older heavyset man who had not spoken a word.

"Hey, I know you, you're Milton Rogers. God damn you! Your ass is mine, you got that, old man?"

Milton was certainly flustered and caught off guard. So he said nothing and acted like he knew nothing as well.

Jean took the time to examine all the various jewelry items and stones before yelling at Bart.

"Where the hell are the one hundred original diamonds?"

"What are you talking about?"

"You know the diamonds you stole back from Milton Rogers."

"Now why would I have his stones? That's absurd!" In the blink of an eye, Bart received another serious blow. This time the jolt to his right ribs was delivered by Milton, and Bart crumbled to the ground.

Jean now stood over the shaking jeweler. "I will kill you this moment unless you tell me where my stones are."

"Your stones? Who the hell are you?" questioned Bart, still grimacing in pain.

Another swift kick delivered by the older man knocked the wind out of Bart.

"It's me, Milton Rogers. These men want my original stones."

"You asshole. I don't know who or what you are talking about," retorted Bart.

"You stole the original diamonds in Antwerp from my wife. These gentlemen want what's rightfully theirs. If you don't cooperate, you're a dead man."

"I told you once and I'll tell you one thousand times more, I don't know anything about switching stones. I've been in trial, and all my thoughts and energies have been focused on saving my life, no thanks to you, old man. You screwed me, and now you're telling these men that I screwed you. Don't insult my intelligence or theirs."

That last comment earned Bart another vicious round of kicks from Milton Rogers. Bart knew he was hurt pretty badly. If he didn't think of something pretty quick, he was a dead man. Bart still had the tiny handgun he kept strapped to his right ankle. Somehow, he'd have to regain his strength in order to reach and grab the weapon. However with a few more blows, he would soon become incapacitated so he had to act immediately.

"All right. All right. I'll tell you. But please stop beating me."

Jean nodded and his cohort helped Bart up onto the chair beside the safe.

"Listen here. The jewels inside this safe are worth at least fifty million. I do not have your stones. If I did, they would be in this safe. Please don't hit me again, and please believe me," said Bart, now pleading for his life. "I've got several kids and a loving wife, who all depend on me. Go ahead rob my safe, but leave me alone."

"I don't want the stones in your safe. I only want my diamonds," demanded Jean. "And unless I hear what I want to hear, you're a dead man in fifteen seconds, fourteen, thirteen, twelve, . . .

In an instant Bart confessed. "Okay, okay."

"For a moment there I thought you were a goner," snickered Jean.

"The stones are with my attorney, Bo Martin. He has a safe in his house and he arranged the switch with the taxi cab driver and Milton's wife. Bo's a genius, and he was the one who figured out that Milton had originally set me up. Of course, I went along with it. However, he kept the real diamonds in his possession as insurance should I be convicted or he indicted."

Jean let Bart's statements sink in for several moments before actually believing him.

Bart hoped they would accept his story, hook, line, and sinker. He knew that he was setting up Bo Martin. *But so what,* thought Bart. *Better him than me!*

Milton spoke next, "Well, I believe him. That Martin is a real prick."

"Or," said Jean, "a very smart and cool operator. Fortunately, I've also canvassed his home, and we're prepared to deal with him later."

"But first, let's take all these stones and jewelry pieces."

The thought of these men robbing him was too much for Bart to take. Summoning all his strength, he reached down and pulled out his small handgun. He fired it, hitting Jean's companion directly in the chest. As he aimed next for Milton, Jean lunged at Bart with a previously concealed knife. Immediately, the knife wound made Bart drop to the ground releasing his weapon. The pain was intense. There was nothing Sinclair could do, and he soon realized he was dying. He couldn't even speak his last thoughts, but if he had, it would have been, "I'm sorry, Bo."

Milton stood horrified. Jean quickly tried to attend to his friend, who unfortunately was already dead.

"What do we do now?" asked Milton.

"We need to make it look like a robbery. Take most of the gems with us. But leave a few," hollered Jean.

"I'll contact Henri," said Jean. Jean pulled out his cell phone and spoke to the other man in the limo. Henri, the driver, entered the store moments later. The two men carefully removed their fallen compatriot's body and placed his corpse in the trunk of the car.

Despite the gunshot, all was calm and peaceful on Worth Avenue. *Thank goodness*, thought Milton as he brought the bag of stolen jewelry with him.

After wiping down the crime scene and making sure that nobody touched any other surfaces or objects, the men then emerged from the jewelry store and proceeded to the Martin residence on the north side of the island.

Milton was feeling the rush of excitement. He had no moral problems whatsoever with the death of Bart and the European henchman. In fact, Milton felt nearly invincible. He roughly calculated that the items of jewelry stolen from Sinclair's store were worth at least thirty to forty million wholesale. With his connections, Milton could get up to fifty million for the entire contents.

What's even better, thought Milton, *is that Bart Sinclair is now out of the picture*. One less human to possibly testify against Milton or cause any future problems.

Now on to Bo Martin. With Bo dead, Milton could see no additional impediments to his plan to recover all of his original money as well as increase it. Milton's greed was simply enormous.

Milton also felt confident as he touched the thirty-eight special in his jacket pocket. He didn't believe that Jean or any of his men had noticed the bulge at all. From what Milton could perceive, Jean was armed with only a switchblade knife that evidently he knew how to use. The one remaining bodyguard had a small Uzi machine gun and knew how to use it.

Milton just hoped that Bo was home, as the limousine cruised to the Martin residence.

Chapter
Eighty-Eight

o Martin had declined to attend the Palm Beach gala event. After the recent scandalous articles, Bo had become even more of a hermit. The last thing he wanted to do was attend a huge social event wearing a tuxedo and mask and carrying on idle conversations with people he couldn't care less about.

Ruby had understood completely. In fact, she had planned a girls' night out. Ruby and Sophia, Hank's wife, and several other women had rented a limousine and were going out for ladies' night.

Bo was in full support of Ruby's ladies' night, and he and Hank had made plans of their own. A long run, followed by a swim in the pool with the red dogs, Domino's Pizza, and a few beers afterward was their idea of a perfect Saturday night.

Bo and Hank were recovering from their run with a swim in the pool accompanied by the red dogs when the black limousine appeared in the driveway.

Almost immediately, Max, the male Vizsla, froze at attention and the hairs on his wet back stood upright. The female dog continued to jump in and out of the pool, oblivious to the male's concern.

Bo sensed the dog's presence of danger and slowly emerged from the pool and crept along the side of the Bougainvilla hedge. When Bo saw the limousine, he just figured the girls had returned home for a brief pit stop. However when he saw a European male holding an Uzi, Bo tensed up.

Bo had to think quickly. Clad only in his running shorts and dripping wet, he racked his mind to think of any possible weapons. Fortunately for him, the side door to the garage was open. Although it was almost pitch black, Bo knew exactly what he was looking for. In a matter seconds Bo exited the garage with two spear guns, a bang stick, and his diver's knife, which he strapped to his right calf.

Hank was still in the pool with Bella when Bo joined by Max dove back into the pool. Bo had just switched off the pool lights prior to that.

"Hey what's the big idea with turning out the lights," asked Hank.

When Bo put his finger to his pouting lips, Hank realized something was up. Slowly under water Bo handed Hank a loaded spear gun.

Whispering, Hank asked, "What do I do with this?"

"Just aim and pull the trigger."

"Got it. Hey Bo, what's up?"

"Could be big trouble. Let's just hang tight and see what happens."

"Gotcha, buddy."

Both men were clearly frightened.

Moments later, Jean, Milton, and the other European appeared before them, having come around the side of the house.

Since the pool itself was unlit but the patio and porch area were well illuminated, the men couldn't see Bo and Hank's weapons under the dark water.

Milton spoke first, surprising the red dogs.

"Martin, get the hell out of the pool and if your dogs so much as sniff me, consider them dead."

"Bella, Max," shouted Bo, "come here. Now."

Begrudgingly, the red dogs swam over to where Bo was standing waist deep in the pool. Bo's hands were still under the water, clutching the spear gun. Bo had placed the bang stick on the first step of the pool.

Hank was just steps away from Bo holding his weapon beneath the water as well.

"What's the big idea of trespassing on my property?" asked Bo.

"Now, get this point loud and clear, you son of a bitch. We're here to collect."

"Collect what?"

"You know what," demanded Milton.

"No, I don't," said Bo slowly inching his way toward the steps.

"Stay right where you are. Both of you," shouted Jean.

"I have to say I'm an admirer of yours," said Jean smiling.

"For what?" asked Bo.

"Seems to me you got the best of Milton Rogers, and he has a little score to settle with you."

"I don't even know the man. How could I have tricked him?"

"Don't be stupid, Mr. Attorney. I know you're not. You have something of mine, and I want it, and I want it right now," demanded Jean.

"What is that exactly?"

"The diamonds. My diamonds."

"I don't have a clue what you're talking about," replied Bo.

"Don't act so dumb. Bart Sinclair told us you have his diamonds," shouted Milton, now pointing his gun at Bo.

"Where'd you get that gun?" asked an astonished Jean.

"This is my show, and I'm running it, Jean. This man has ruined my life, and I'm not about to sit here and listen to any more of his lies."

"Jean?" asked Bo. "Jean Valhomme?"

Jean nodded.

"So you're the man that Brenda Rogers mentioned on cross-examination." Bo continued. "I don't know what you're doing with Milton Rogers, but he's a lying dirt bag. Did you know that he murdered a young genius after he had the man manufacture synthetic gems? Did you know that he framed Bart Sinclair and then tried to sue the man for his alleged loss? Did you know that he's also a liar and cheat who pays off the US Attorney and the *Palm Beach Times*?"

"Enough of that," shouted Milton.

"Mr. Valhomme, I don't have your diamonds. I've never had your diamonds, and you can search my house, my office, or anywhere else you want. I have nothing to hide."

"Bart Sinclair says you do."

"That's funny. Sinclair would say anything to save his skin. When did he allegedly tell you this?" inquired Bo.

"Shut up," yelled Milton.

"Where are the diamonds?"

"Not here, you prick," said Bo coldly. Both red dogs were now standing on the steps staring intently at Milton Rogers and were ready to attack.

"Jean, I tell you, Martin has your diamonds. They must be in his house in a safe or something. Believe me with a little coercion, he'll cry like a baby," exclaimed Milton.

"You want a piece of me, old man. That's fine. But trying to frame me for something I have no idea about is a yellow-bellied way of doing things. I would have thought someone of your stature and devious mind could think of something more imaginative."

Before Bo could move, Milton pulled the trigger firing the gun. Bo felt a searing pain throughout his left shoulder area. *Thank God it's not my dominant right arm*, thought Bo immediately.

Bo collapsed under the surface of the water momentarily and placed both hands on his weapon. When Bo pushed up off the bottom propelling himself into the air, he aimed and fired the spear gun in Milton's direction.

The spear hit Milton directly in his right quadriceps. Milton cried out in pain and immediately dropped his gun and fell on the pool deck shouting, "Oh my God, oh my God."

The dogs leaped at the European sidekick who had moved toward them knocking him into the pool and rendering his weapon virtually unusable. The dogs leapt in after him.

The man struck out viciously against the red dogs with his right hand which now contained a small knife. The yelping of Bella spurred Bo to act quickly.

In less than a second Bo slid under water and grabbed the bang stick. The bang stick acted virtually like a gun. The tip of the stick contained a thirty-eight caliber bullet, and on impact, the bullet was discharged.

Bo pushed off the wall and streamlined the weapon directly into the midsection of the European, who was busy flailing away with his knife at the unrelenting red dogs.

Upon impact, the man instantly went into convulsions, blood erupted from the hole in his stomach, and within a few seconds, he was floating face down in the reddened swimming pool.

During all this time, Hank aimed his spear gun directly at Jean.

Jean knew that if he so much as moved or attempted to help his fellow friend or Milton, the spear gun would be fired. Jean didn't want to experience the writhing pain that had incapacitated Milton and laid him out crying on the deck like a baby.

"If you so much as move, I'll kill you," said Hank coldly. "One look at Milton over there, and you have an idea what pain this spear gun can inflict."

"So what's it going to be?" asked Hank.

"I have no weapon, and I will not move from this spot, mon ami."

Both Hank and Jean watched Bo assist his bleeding dogs out of the pool. Each dog had several stab wounds, and there was blood everywhere in the pool and on the deck.

When Bo exited the pool, he picked up Milton's gun that lay a few feet away from the old man. Milton looked like he was going into shock, but Bo couldn't care less. The bullet hole in his left shoulder was now bleeding profusely, and the pain throughout his left arm was excruciating.

Hank soon followed Bo out of the pool and quickly patted down Jean and forced him to lie face down on the deck. In searching his body, Hank found the switchblade knife and the mobile phone. The voice mode was activated, causing Hank some alarm.

"Hey Bo, there may be more of this man's friends somewhere. This type of phone operates like a walkie-talkie. Whoever is at the receiving end most likely heard everything. It's probably only a matter of time before reinforcements arrive."

"Well, then we must act fast. The dogs have to get to the vet immediately. They saved our lives."

"I know. What do you propose?"

"Well let's take the limousine to my vet's office. We can call ahead from the car. He lives above his office and kennel, and I just hope like hell he's home."

"We'll bring Jean with us."

"Do you think you can make it with that bullet wound of yours?" asked a very concerned Hank.

"I'm okay. I don't think it hit anything major. Can you tell if it came out?"

When Bo turned around, Hank could see that the bullet had indeed exited out his back.

"It came out but left a pretty big hole."

"I know. We'll just put a bandage on both the front and back, and it will have to do for now."

"Let's tie up Jean and put him in the back on the floor. I'll put the dogs on the seat."

"Grab some towels and blankets," yelled Bo. "There's going to be blood everywhere."

"But it's not our car," said Hank.

Less than ten minutes later, Hank was speeding the large black limo toward the vet's office. Luckily, the doctor was in and available. Bo was in the back seat comforting the whimpering and injured dogs while at the same time trying to keep from passing out.

Jean was tied up and lying on the floor and looking up at Bo.

"Tell me, Mr. Martin, do you have the gems?"

"No I don't. If in fact there was a switch, which I'm not aware of, I was not a party to it."

Jean stared directly into Bo's eyes before speaking. "I am an excellent judge of character and can always tell when someone is lying. You are not lying. I believe you."

"Well that's good, but you're in a hell of a lot of trouble."

"I am very rich and powerful. If you let me go, I promise you that I can enable you to retire now. No more practice of law. No more long, grueling hours at the office."

"Sounds great, but how do I know you won't just try and kill me. And by the way where's Sinclair?"

"You are a quick study. I'll give you that. Trust me. If you help me, I'll help you."

"We'll see about that," was all Bo said.

Chapter
Eighty-Nine

Unfortunately, little did they know that less than a quarter mile behind them, the other black limousine followed closely.

Hank and Bo had barely eluded capture. Not more than twenty seconds after they pulled out of Bo's driveway, the second limousine rounded the bend only to reveal their brake lights.

By the time they arrived at the vet's office and were met by the good doctor and his wife, Bo had completely lost the use of his left arm. Try as he may, he couldn't even carry one dog. Fortunately after examining the animals' wounds, the doctor informed Bo and Hank that both dogs would recover and be just fine.

"You're going to have to leave them here with us for a few days. However once I stitch them up, they will be as good as new. I don't even want to know what happened, but from the looks of Bo, you're in serious danger. While I'm not an MD, I do know that unless you get him to a hospital, Bo could lose that arm, or worse, even die."

No sooner had he spoken when Bo collapsed onto the floor.

When Bo awoke, he was on a Gurney being wheeled into the operating room at Good Samaritan Hospital. "Don't worry, my good friend. You're going to be just fine," were the last spoken words that Bo heard.

Several hours later, Bo awoke in a hospital bed surrounded by familiar faces. Hank, Ruby, Sophia, and several other women were all crowded around his bed. Bo tried to rise, but the surgery, pain killers, and anesthesia caused him to become nauseous with his sudden movement.

Ruby spoke first. "Honey, you nearly scared us to death. We all were so worried when Hank called us. The good news is that the surgery went really well, and nothing major was damaged. You probably won't be hugging me right away, but you're going to have to be on your best behavior in order to make it up to me."

Sophia chimed in next. "Our ladies' night out didn't even last through dinner and ended up here in the hospital. It's going to be tough to top this night," she said jokingly.

"Hey, good buddy," said Hank. "Doc says you'll be up and running in no time. You lost a good amount of blood though."

"How are the dogs?" asked Bo, deeply concerned.

"Honey, they are just fine. I've been on the phone with the vet, and in a few days they will be able to come home. Together, all three of you will have to do everything I say as you all recover from your injuries."

"Hey, Bo," said Hank interrupting, "the police are outside and they seem really anxious to speak with you and me. I haven't said a word, but you and I should probably talk."

"I know what you mean."

Ruby interjected, "My God, you two almost got killed and now you are still playing James Bond. Wake up! This is serious. I don't want to lose either one of you," said Ruby, now in tears. "I've never been so frightened."

"Now, now. It's going to be okay. Everything will work out," said Bo trying to reassure her and himself.

The girls soon left, leaving the two men to themselves. Hank began the discussion.

"A couple of weird things have happened tonight, or should I say this morning. First Jean escaped with the limo."

"He was tied up, and I had the keys in my pocket. Somehow, someone must have untied him because once you went into surgery, I came out to check him, but the car was gone. I'm thinking it must have been his associates at the other end of his cell phone."

"That's probably correct."

"There's more, Bo."

"Go on."

"From what I've found out so far, a little after ten-fifteen p.m., Bart Sinclair was found dead in his store. His safe was left wide open, and all the contents were emptied. Based on the amount of blood, it looks like he shot one of the intruders, but no other body was found."

"That's so terrible," said Bo unable to find the words to express his grief. Bo was immediately concerned about the welfare of Bart's wife, Dana, and all the kids. Fortunately, Bart's own personal estate plan was prepared by Bo and Dana and the children would never have to sacrifice financially. Although no amount of money could bring Bart Sinclair back again.

"Any witnesses?"

"Nothing so far. Most of Palm Beach was at the Breakers Charity Ball. But, Bo."

"Yes."

"The bag of jewels that we found in the limo and left unknowingly behind at the vet's office was turned over by your veterinarian to the police. Looks like the Palm Beach Police think that we might actually have robbed Sinclair."

"What? That's preposterous!" uttered Bo rather incredulously.

"Exactly what I'm thinking."

"We know it was Milton Rogers and Jean. By the way where is Milton?"

"Word has it that he checked into the emergency room at St. Mary's Hospital around ten thirty p.m. He had gone into shock but was recovering well."

"Why don't the police question him?" asked Bo, trying to comprehend the total situation.

"Seems like they have. His children and their wives all confirm the same story. The entire Rogers clan went to the Breakers, found the event boring, and left. Afterward, they state the entire family went out on their yacht for a pleasure cruise."

"What does their captain and mate say?" said Bo thinking quickly.

"Well, it seems only the family went out on the boat. They didn't want to bother the hired help."

"I'll bet," said Bo, rather disgusted.

"While working down below in the engine room, it appears that Milton fell, causing the spear gun to discharge into his thigh."

"You can't be serious."

"Oh I am. What's worse is that all the family members corroborate his story."

"Where was Brenda in all of this?"

"I don't know," answered Hank. Her whereabouts hadn't even entered his mind.

"She's the key. If I'm correct, she was still at the charity ball. She'll prove they are all lying. But, Hank, what about my house? I killed a man last night."

"Are you okay with everything?"

"I will be fine. It hasn't sunk in yet. "

"Your pool is crystal clear. The deck was even cleaned with muriatic acid and there was no trace that anyone had ever been to your house."

"How about the stab wounds to the dogs?"

"They, the police, don't have an answer for that one. But, based on what they do have, you and I are the primary suspects in Sinclair's murder!"

"I just can't believe it," said Bo, trying to sit up and get in a comfortable position but to no avail.

"There's one more troubling item," Hank noted.

"What's that?" exclaimed Bo.

"It appears that the gun that shot you was beside Bart's body when the police found him."

"This is bad. Real bad! You and I are the only two who can refute everything, and yet we're the ones being accused."

"I'm scared," said Hank.

That makes two of us, thought Bo.

The Palm Beach police detectives Frank Brady and Jake Adams had waited patiently for Hank to emerge from the hospital room. They were extremely upset when they caught Hank trying to leave the hospital room.

"Trying to get your stories straight?" asked Frank.

"No, officer. Trying to comfort my best friend," retorted Hank.

"Then why send the women home?"

"Because they are tired. Their evening was a complete bust, and hospitals aren't a fun place to hang out."

"I don't know; I sort of like this antiseptic environment," countered Jake.

"Is he up to speaking?"

"Bo's on a lot of pain medication and is very groggy, but I guess he'll talk to you."

"Very well then, let's get this over with," said Frank.

Bo was still unable to find a comfortable position when the two officers, trailed by Hank, entered the room.

"Mr. Martin. My name is Frank Brady, and this is Officer Jake Adams."

"Hello," said Bo rather feebly.

"Are you up to answering a few questions?"

"Sure. I guess so."

"First let me tell you that you have the right to an attorney if you so desire."

"I am an attorney, and although I probably should have one present, I'm able to answer your questions." Bo knew in his heart that he should be represented by legal counsel but he was tired and loopy from the medication and surgery and wanted this over with.

"Both you and your friend Hank were attired in wet running shorts when you were brought here to the hospital. Now your friend, Hank, has told us his version of your evening's events, and we'd like to hear yours."

Bo spent almost thirty minutes detailing with specificity, his and Hank's entire evening.

Frank and Jake took notes and nodded their heads at various times throughout Bo's statement.

When he was finished, Frank spoke first. "That's pretty good. Almost identical with what your pal Hank has said."

"It should be exactly the same since we experienced it together," countered Bo roughly.

"Well let me bring several pieces of information to your attention. First, why did you have stolen jewels in your possession at the vet's office? Second where did you rent the limousine? Third, why is there no evidence of any struggle or gunfight at your home? And fourth, why is the gun found at the side of Bart Sinclair similar to the one that caused your gunshot wound? We are waiting on a ballistics report."

"We also have an eyewitness who saw a black limousine parked in the rear of Bart Sinclair's store," added Officer Adams.

"Of course you would," said Hank interrupting. "The men who tried to kill us first went to Sinclair's store."

"Who's to say that you two didn't drive the limousine over there?"

"What in our running shorts?" exclaimed Bo.

"Hell if I know."

"Tell me something, Detective. How many people did your witness see exiting the limousine?" inquired Bo, still struggling to sit upright.

"Well, she's an old lady, and she was pretty far away."

"How many?" pressed Bo again.

"She said there were four men who got out of the limousine."

"What about the driver?"

"The driver would make five."

"Aha. That means it was Milton Rogers, Jean Valhomme, his companion and Bart Sinclair," said Bo directly to Hank.

"Did she say they were all in tuxedos?" asked Bo.

"She just said they were dressed in black."

"And we're in shorts," interjected Hank.

"Now why again do you think it was Milton Rogers and this Jean fellow?" asked Officer Brady.

"Because Milton Rogers pulled a switcheroo on Jean and the man wanted his money back. Rogers knew Sinclair had a lot of valuable merchandise in his store safe, and this was the only way to pay off Jean."

"But why kill Sinclair?" asked Officer Adams.

"Maybe Sinclair fought back. He probably didn't like being robbed."

"Well, we know he fired a gun because we found lots of blood on the floor. Ballistics is now testing to confirm whether or not Sinclair did in fact fire a weapon."

"I take it you are also testing the blood samples?"

"Well," said Bo, "I have a rather rare blood type. If in fact, I was there at the store, then my blood would be found on the carpeting. Would it not?"

"Well, yes."

"You're not going to find any of my blood anywhere at the store because I was never there," exclaimed Bo.

"We'll see about that."

"Now let's get back to the alleged episode at your home," steered Frank.

"Okay," replied Bo.

"You say that Milton Rogers shot you and that you in return shot him with a spear gun in his right thigh."

"Absolutely! How would I know that he was injured and exactly where his injury was if I did not see it happen?" exclaimed Bo. Hank stood nodding his head.

"You have a point there," said Jake, writing it down.

"And your dogs were stabbed by another assailant?"

"Yes, the dogs attacked Jean's companion. They knocked him into the pool, and then I killed the man with a bang stick."

"Well, how come we don't have any evidence of this event taking place at your home?" asked Officer Adams.

"Because either Milton Rogers or Jean Valhomme were able to hire people to clean it up."

"And why again would they do that?"

"Because Milton Rogers killed Bart Sinclair and then attempted to kill me," said Bo coldly. "Did you speak to my vet? He saw us, he saw the dogs and the towels and the mess in the back seat of the car. He also saw Jean Valhomme tied up on the floor of the limousine."

"He mentioned that he saw a man lying on the floor."

"And did he state what time it was?"

"Yes, yes he did."

"But that wasn't until sometime after Sinclair's death."

"There had to be any number of people who saw Hank and me running together last night."

"So far, nobody recalls seeing the two of you running in Palm Beach."

"Well, heck we saw lots of people," said Hank.

"Find me just one."

"Oh trust me, we will," said Hank again.

"I have a question," interjected Bo. "Did you ever find the limousine?"

"We're still looking."

"Well, the plate on the car was DLV 133, Florida. That should help you some. You'll find that neither I nor Hank rented the limo. How in the world would we have even acquired the limo unless it was rented by Jean or Milton Rogers?"

"But where is the car now?" questioned Frank.

"We told you. It was driven away by Jean and probably one of his henchmen."

"How convenient," countered Officer Adams.

"It's the truth."

"We'll see about that."

Frank and Jake were about out of questions and were greatly perturbed by Hank and Bo's immediate answers and insightful questions. Their story held water and Frank and Jake were doing their best to poke holes into their story but to little or no avail.

"We will be in touch. Don't go anywhere."

"Do I look like I could?" answered Bo, now unable to remain in a sitting position.

When the men were gone, Bo and Hank looked at each other and in unison declared, "We need Sean Heese to investigate and round up witnesses."

Chapter
Ninety

It was agreed that Hank would drive to Sean's residence and personally hire him. Time was of the essence because witnesses often forgot everything unless confronted immediately. It was early in the morning when Hank left the hospital.

The morning *Palm Beach Times* contained a devastating article headlined: "Bart Sinclair murdered—Bo Martin the lead suspect."

Ruby was in tears when she read the defamatory article, which basically proclaimed Bo Martin the murderer and Hank his co-conspirator. She rushed over to the hospital to find her husband still sleeping. *Thank goodness, he hasn't read the paper,* thought Ruby. *I'll make sure that he misses it entirely.*

Bye and Teresa Martin arrived at the hospital shortly after Ruby. Of course, they were also extremely concerned not only for Bo's health but also because of the dreadful newspaper headline and article.

"We will sue," shouted Bye. "So help me God."

"Calm down, honey. There has to be an explanation."

Ruby in tears, embraced the elder Martins and informed them to the best of her limited knowledge what had actually transpired that evening. After listening to her story, a very relieved Bye and Teresa offered Ruby a breakfast invitation to the hospital cafeteria.

Unfortunately, as soon as they entered the food court they were mobbed by the press. Representatives from *People, USA Today, Time, National Enquirer,* and *The Star* were all there, hoping to get a lead on the alleged murderous attorney, Bo Martin.

For the next two days, a police officer guarded Bo's hospital room. The press was constantly trying to sneak into the room, and several had even donned medical scrubs in a misguided attempt to gain entry.

The *Palm Beach Times* articles by Mae McReynolds were so slanderous and one-sided that Ruby had even stopped her subscription. Of course, Bo devoured every word. It made him incensed, and he vowed to seek revenge against Mae. Somehow, some way, he would prevail.

Her latest article had put the final nail in the coffin regarding the law firm of Martin and Martin. What few clients that had remained with Bo after the first set of articles and the federal indictment, now found other estate planning lawyers and retrieved their files. There was nothing Bye could do to convince them to stay, and he was tired of trying to fight what seemed like the incoming tide.

Fortunately for Bo, each day he gained more strength and had considerably less pain. The bullet hole was healing really well, but Bo's spirits were at an all time low!

The Palm Beach Police Department had not yet charged Bo or Hank with any crime, although after reading the newspaper articles, Bo and Hank were already guilty and a conviction was imminent.

Frank Brady and Jake Adams were diligently working to make the case against the two men for murder, grand theft, robbery, and larceny. Even the federal prosecutors, namely Steve Fleishman, had already contacted the detectives and tried to push them into making an early arrest.

The ballistic reports and blood samples taken from Sinclair's store did support the fact that Bart Sinclair fired a gun, but fortunately the blood did not match Bo's blood type. It was clear that Sinclair shot someone, just not Bo.

The medical reports from St. Mary's Hospital confirmed that Milton Rogers's injury was the result of a spear gun, but what the reports demonstrated was that the gun had to be fired from a distance of at least ten feet. So, Milton's story that he fell, causing the spear to engage, was a lie. The detectives also found it odd that Brenda Rogers remained at the Breakers Beach Club and did not accompany her family on the yacht. Finally, nobody remembered seeing any of the Rogers's children or their spouses at the Breakers. In fact, their tickets were never even registered in the drawing for the Jaguar convertible indicating they had never set foot at the Breakers.

The old woman's testimony that she saw four men exit the limousine and enter the jewelry store at around nine-ten was holding up to rather intense scrutiny. She was wearing her glasses, she had nothing to drink that evening, she knew the exact time because her favorite TV show had ended at nine p.m., and she was fairly close to the limousine while walking her dog. She was hidden from the street by one of the canvas canopies that adorned the entrances to most stores along Worth Avenue. What's more, she also was able to describe the physical characteristics of all four men and noticed that one spoke with a European accent, and one was an older, heavyset man with white hair. Also, she never wavered about the men being dressed in black tuxedos and wearing costume masks.

Sean Heese had also provided the detectives with information that was vital in establishing Bo's and Hank's innocence. Several upstanding Palm Beach residents had seen Bo and Hank running along the Palm Beach bike path that evening. One prominent couple noted their exact time and physical location when they observed the two men running and recognized Bo immediately from the newspaper and TV coverage. They even remarked to each other how sad it was that Bo Martin was not going to the Palm Beach costume ball.

The Domino's Pizza delivery boy also was another piece of evidence corroborating Bo and Hank's story. Domino's documented a phone call around 9:10 p.m. from the Martin's home residence. Unfortunately, the pizza delivery man showed up at the Martin house around ten fifteen, thirty minutes late because of a flat tire. *Too bad*, thought Bo; *if the delivery boy had only been on time, he would have seen the melee at the Martin house.*

Another very troubling point for the police was the fact that Bo's and Hank's prints were not found on the bag or any of the stones found at the vet's office. If indeed, the men had robbed Sinclair, their prints would definitely be found all over the bag and the valuable jewelry.

The last piece of evidence involved the jewelry store itself. All the monitors worked properly, but the actual videotapes were nowhere to be found. All these things were the mark of sophisticated thieves and a lot of planning.

Hank's and Bo's stories were also identical, even down to the smallest of details. It was becoming pretty clear to both Frank and Jake that Bo and Hank could not have killed Sinclair. However, the relentless attacks in the newspaper against the men, the highly unusual offer of assistance from the federal prosecutors, and the constant meddling by the Palm Beach Chief of Police, who just so happened to be a close friend of Milton Rogers, made it very difficult for the detectives to exonerate Bo and Hank while pursuing the actual killers.

Chapter
Ninety-One

o's gunshot wound had recovered nicely, and by the third day, Bo wanted out of the hospital. He was sick and tired of being cooped up all day, having to eat the disgusting hospital food, and watch the various talk shows. Even the *Jerry Springer Show* wasn't entertaining anymore. His life was much worse than any troubles depicted on television.

Against his doctor's wishes, Bo talked Ruby into coming and picking him up. A police officer still guarded his room, but with Ruby's help, Bo was able to slide out without the officer's knowledge.

Piece of cake, thought Bo until they reached the main lobby where a handful of reporters identified him. They swarmed around the Martins like bees to honey, asking all sorts of questions.

Bo and Ruby managed to fight their way through all the reporters and were able to make it to Ruby's car. Soon they were back at their humble abode. The previous day, Ruby had picked up the red dogs from the vet's office. The red dogs injuries and all, were happy to see Bo. Although all were still recovering from their respective wounds, it made little difference as they feebly attempted to jump and play with one another. *What am I going to do with them?* thought Ruby.

Meanwhile, back at the Rogers's mansion, the scene was mostly tense. Milton was still in substantial pain and unable to think or plan his next course of attack.

The Palm Beach Police Chief had kept the Rogers clan up to date on the investigation into Bo Martin.

"Why haven't you arrested Bo Martin for the murder of Sinclair?" demanded Milton over the telephone to the police chief.

"Milton, this is an investigation. Two of my best detectives are on this case, and trust me, they are doing everything they can to nail Bo Martin."

"Then why the hell is he still a free man?"

"Investigations take time, and we want to be sure to dot our i's and cross our t's. The last thing this department needs is a messed-up case that fails to convict Martin and Miles."

"Miles?" asked Milton.

"Yes, we are going after both men. But let me tell you, Hank's testimony was pretty impressive, and he's going to make an excellent witness. He supports every single word that Bo says. It's so closely intertwined that my detectives don't know who to believe."

"That can't be," exclaimed Milton.

"Oh, but it is. Hank's back-up testimony corroborates Bo's version of the events. If, somehow, Hank was not available to confirm every little thing Bo alleged, then our case would be that much stronger. However with him, I don't believe we can even formally charge Bo. My men are now starting to rethink everything and are even following other leads."

"That's terrible," said Milton turning whiter by the second.

"Milton, the detectives want to meet with you and all your kids separately if possible."

"When?" asked Milton, sounding somewhat worried.

"Not until that injury of yours heals but sometime soon. The public is clamoring for an arrest."

My God, thought Milton. If it wasn't for Hank's testimony, Bo would already be charged.

Chapter
Ninety-Two

Later that evening, as Milton hopped around, wincing at every step, the entire Rogers family looked on. The boys and their wives were all summoned for dinner. All were quiet and deeply concerned. One thing was certain: they would do anything that Milton Rogers required of them. Anything!

After a delicious dinner prepared by Brenda, the entire family found themselves in Milton's gigantic den. After Milton had found one bug in the mouthpiece of the telephone, he immediately had the house searched from top to bottom. Several more monitoring devices were located and destroyed. Milton normally kept his den locked so after the sweep, the den was the safest spot in the house to talk. Milton had seen too many movies where outdoor conversations were taped and so he decided not to communicate outside.

Milton was still in excruciating pain. Fortunately, he had kept his mind focused immediately after the shooting incident, or else the evidence would have been located at the Martin's home and his own personal involvement unveiled.

The children all sat silently on the luxurious leather couches on pins and needles. Deep inside, they all realized this matter had gone much too far. Milton's personal vendetta against Bo Martin could now endanger their lives and their future prosperity.

"Now children, I want to thank you for your obedience and your devotion to me and the continued success of the Rogers family. Your mother and I love you very much. We are also proud of each and every one of you."

"What I'm going to say must remain secret and can never be discussed again. If there is anyone who can't keep quiet or who isn't with the program, please speak now."

Nobody responded. The den was absolutely silent.

"Good. That's great. Now what we have to do is eliminate Hank Miles."

"Hank Miles?" questioned Luke.

"Why him?" asked Larry.

"What about Bo Martin? Why not put a hit out on him and be done with it?" asked Annie.

"Questions, questions," answered Milton. "I want Bo Martin to suffer. I want him to spend the rest of his life in jail, away from his wife, family, and dogs. He must suffer. He has ruined everything."

"But why?" questioned Brenda. "You're talking about murder, Milton. Is that what you've come to now? Has this man so severely damaged you that you must risk your life and our children's lives with this personal vendetta against one man?"

"Honey, this one man can put me behind bars. Now do you want that? Does anyone want that?" screamed Milton, looking at the faces of everyone in the study.

"You know we don't, Milton, but we also don't want this thing to escalate any further," said Brenda, trying to pacify her husband.

"We are out one hundred twenty million dollars! That's thirty million dollars per child. Even with conspicuous consumption, it would take each child more than ten years to consume that amount. We also know Jean Valhomme's out there somewhere, and he still wants more money. He's a cold-blooded killer, so we all must be careful. Now, is everyone still with me?" asked Milton, hoping nobody would say a word.

When nobody spoke, Milton said, "I'm proud of all of you."

"What's your plan, Dad?" asked Lawrence.

"Hank lives in Jupiter. Every night after work he goes for a run. Once he leaves his community, he runs along a darkened sidewalk. He runs the same route almost every night, so I'm told."

"How would we kill him?" asked Larry.

"At this point in time, a rifle would work best."

"A gun?" asked Brenda. "Why?"

"Because any other murder method involves too much risk. One shot is all it takes. You'll have an excellent alibi because all of us will be here eating dinner."

"When will this take place?"

"Monday evening. That leaves us only three days to prepare. We have to act quickly. I think I'll tell the detectives that I will speak with them on Tuesday."

The kids all looked over at Lee who was by far the best shot in the family.

"Dad, I'll do it," said Lee, sternly.

"That's terrific, Son. You're who I had in mind. You have the most skill and patience. I know you can do it."

"Thanks, Dad."

"Well, I don't like it. I don't like it at all," said Annie. "What happens if he's not successful? What happens then?"

"I'll go with him," answered Larry.

"We are the two oldest, and we will not fail," professed Lee.

After it was agreed that Lee and Larry would execute the hit on Hank the rest of the clan left the two sons with their dad and went about their normal conversations. The topics were naturally about sex, money, and gossip. Palm Beach is one large gossip mill. The more scintillating the topic and potentially damaging, the better. Brenda and the girls loved hearing about the juiciest of rumors, as long as it didn't concern them.

In the den it was agreed that Lee and Larry would scout out the running course during the day to familiarize themselves with the surroundings and then spend two nights getting acclimated to the darkness. Milton also provided Lee with a high-tech rifle, which included a night scope and silencer. From a distance of fifty yards, the accuracy was incredible. Even a terrible shot would find it hard to miss at such a relatively short distance.

Lee and Larry did their homework and located the perfect spot. It was isolated and out of the way. Moreover, they could park their car without it being seen from the road or from the oncoming Hank. Like clockwork on Friday night, the boys observed Hank running his route after work. They closely monitored his running gait and the way he held his arms. Lee wanted a direct chest shot. One shot one kill.

Chapter
Ninety-Three

On Sunday afternoon, Hank paid a visit to Bo's and Ruby's house. As a prank, Hank asked Bo if he wanted to go for a run. Bo actually thought about it before Ruby interjected with a resounding no.

"For Christ's sake, your bandages still need to be changed on a daily basis. Until all the sutures have been taken out and the doctor gives you the okay, there will be no running." Ruby was adamant.

Hank and Bo graciously accepted defeat and acknowledged that it would be at least another week before they could resume their weekly runs.

Hank and Bo were also in pretty good moods. The Palm Beach detectives had verbally informed them they were no longer the prime suspects. In fact, off the record, Frank had informed Hank that he was one hundred percent convinced that Bo and Hank were innocent. However, his higher ups, namely the Chief of Police and the Mayor of Palm Beach, were still strongly forcing him to gather enough incriminating evidence to formally charge the men with murder. Frank instead was concentrating his efforts on Milton Rogers and his sons. Something told him that the Rogers family members were all lying.

There was one thing that Frank had said that deeply concerned Bo. He had informed the men that without Hank's credible corroborating testimony, charges would have been brought against Bo. Hank had responded by saying that he wasn't planning on going anywhere, but still the thought greatly concerned Bo.

After Hank had left for home, Bo picked up the phone. In his hand was the white business card the CIA/FBI white-haired man had given to Bo. Hesitantly, Bo called the number and waited for an answer.

"Hi, this is Bo Martin."

"Mr. Martin, so nice to hear from you. I was beginning to think I'd never hear from you. I'm glad you survived your little episode. You're either very lucky or very good. I would probably venture to say you're a little bit of both."

"Well, thanks I guess."

"So what's the purpose of your call, Mr. Martin?"

"I'm worried about the safety of my friend, Hank Miles."

"How come?"

"Let's just say that without Hank and his testimony, I could be charged with murder."

"But we already know you didn't do it."

"How?" asked Bo inquisitively.

"We know a lot of things. Trust me."

"I understand," said Bo, now wondering exactly how much they did know about him.

"Who would gain the most from his death?" asked the gentleman.

"Milton Rogers."

"Precisely. And why would he come after you if as you've previously stated to us, you have done nothing to harm the man?"

"Let's just say that I'm not high on his list of favorites."

"How about public enemy number one?"

"Now that's maybe pushing it a bit."

"Is it?"

"Of course."

"So what exactly did you do to Milton Rogers to incur his personal vendetta?"

"Lord only knows," replied Bo, not willing to divulge any more information.

"Promise me this, Mr. Martin: if we help you, will you help us?"

"Well yes, I guess. As long as it comes with full and complete immunity."

"That's no problem."

"Well good. Then do we have a deal?" questioned Bo.

"What exactly do you have in mind?"

"I'd like Hank and his family to have protection."

"Where is he most vulnerable?"

"If it were me, I would try and kill him somewhere dark and isolated."

"He lives in a Jupiter community with lots of families, kids, and dogs," replied the man. His knowledge of Hank caught Bo somewhat off guard.

"I know that. But he also runs every week night along Central Boulevard which is unlit and desolate."

"Is he that predictable?"

"You could set your watch by him. Every night after work he goes for a run. He runs the same route and only varies his pace."

"Okay. You've got a deal. When do you want us to start?"

"Tomorrow. Monday. Monday evening," said Bo.

"We're on it."

"Thank you."

"No, thank you. Anything else?"

"I was wondering if you've been able to locate Jean Valhomme?"

"Now why would you ask about him?"

"Well since we tied him up and threw him on the floor of the limo, I was wondering just what he was up to."

"And what may I ask is that?"

"Oh, nothing."

"No. Please do tell. You intrigue me, Mr. Martin."

"It's just that I believe he's not finished with Milton Rogers."

"Go on?"

"I believe he was cheated by Milton."

"You do! And how would you know that?" asked the man now pressing Bo for more information.

"It's just that Milton is a very rich man. If his life was ever in jeopardy, I would think that he'd be willing to pay top dollar. Or if anyone in his family was threatened, I also believe he would pay through the nose."

"So you think Milton is at risk?"

"Until he repays whatever debt he owes to Jean. Don't underestimate the foreigner. If, as you say, he was a big drug dealer, then he must have a lot of connections. Very powerful connections. He also must have numerous offshore accounts where he could easily hide a lump-sum payment. Or at least make the authorities jump through many hoops to locate the money."

"So what you're saying, Mr. Martin, is that Milton Rogers's life is in jeopardy as long as Jean Valhomme remains at large."

"That's what I'm saying."

"And when would he strike?"

"I believe when the entire Rogers clan is together. Maybe for dinner or something. The Rogers are a very high-profile Palm Beach family. They socialize all the time. They would be too tough to hit while out in the public. My guess is that the time to strike would be when the family is together at the Rogers's mansion."

"But they must have security?"

"You know, probably more than anyone, that no security system is foolproof. Jean's a pro. Don't forget that."

"Thanks for the insight, Mr. Martin. Please keep in touch."

"Hopefully, not if I can help it."

When Bo put the phone down, he turned and saw Ruby staring at him with great concern.

"Honey, you don't think Hank is in any real danger, do you?"

"It's just a gut feeling I have. The detectives said that without his testimony, I would be charged with murder. If Milton Rogers knows that, he could try and eliminate Hank. Milton has a personal vendetta against me and I don't put anything past the man."

"Who was that on the phone?"

"Either the FBI or CIA."

"You don't know?"

"Sweetheart, I don't even know his name. Remember when Dad and I left the office of the federal prosecutors, we were later forced off the elevator and met with two men. I just spoke with one of them. They definitely have the resources to watch Hank."

"But what if you're wrong? You got Hank involved in this mess, Bo. You've got to protect him."

"All right. Let me call Sean."

Moments later, Sean was on the line.

"Hey, Sean."

"Hi, Bo. How you doing? I haven't read any more negative things in the paper about you," said Sean laughing.

"Not yet," said Bo. "Are you busy?"

"For you, I always have time."

"Good, I want you to trail Hank."

"What on earth for?"

"I've got a gut feeling that his life may be in danger."

"Because of you?"

"Well, now that you put it like that, yes."

"When do you want me to start?"

"How about tomorrow. To tell you the truth, why don't you come by and pick me up, and I'll show you a couple of things. Hank is a runner, as you know, and he runs the same route every night. I think he's the most vulnerable when he's running at night alone."

"You're probably right. What time tomorrow?"

"How about five p.m."

"See you then."

"Bye."

Ruby had come and placed her arms around Bo. "Now that's better. I just hope you don't take all evening."

"I won't. But thanks. Thanks for caring."

"Always," said Ruby, kissing Bo lightly on his forehead.

Chapter

Ninety-Four

Both Ruby and Bo were hoping this nightmare would end shortly. They were at the point of thinking of selling their home, packing their belongings, and hightailing it to Nantucket. *Sure, the winters would be miserable,* they thought, *but the summers would more than make up for the four cold, windy, and blustery months.*

Someday, thought Ruby. *Someday soon.*

Sean arrived exactly on time the following day, and together he and Bo traveled north to the Town of Jupiter. In the early 1970s, Jupiter was known as a hick town. "Jupiter red necks" they were called. Burt Reynolds, flush with cash from his Smokey and the Bandit movies, even owned a large ranch in Jupiter.

However, the migration of northerners in the 1980s drastically changed the quiet Town of Jupiter. What once was farm country and marshland became one sprawling development after another. Most of the growth was westward, and Hank's community was one that abutted the main interstate, I-95. The new homes were all beautifully maintained. Kids could be seen outside playing on every street. Most of the families were young professionals, working hard to make ends meet.

Hank's home was a charming four-bedroom with three baths. Hank's touch of a green thumb, combined with numerous native plantings, made his landscaping the envy of the neighborhood.

Once outside the well-lit and efficiently designed master community, however, was Central Boulevard. It was a six-mile-long strip, which connected the two large east-west boulevards. Most times there was little or no traffic along the route. What made it a perfect running spot was the four-foot-wide asphalt sidewalk, which paralleled the road. For south Florida runners, asphalt is the surface of choice. It's much more forgiving on the joints than concrete.

Hank's total running route covered eight miles, but six of those miles were along Central Boulevard.

Bo described in minute detail, the running route since he had run it with Hank on hundreds of occasions. Bo always enjoyed a change of scenery every once in a while. Ruby thought he was nuts. What could be more beautiful than the Palm Beach running trail where you could view all the beautiful homes, gorgeous landscaping, the Atlantic Ocean, and the Florida Intracoastal? Bo figured it had to be Hank's companionship. The two men could run and talk for hours virtually about nothing. Ruby was just pleased that Bo had a best friend to talk with.

Bo and Sean covered the entire course taking visual notes of everything. When they were finished, the sun was just setting. It was getting dusk and harder to see.

"Where should I park?" asked Sean.

"How about right at Hank's turnaround spot. This way we can see him coming and going."

Sean reached into his black bag in the backseat of his old Honda Accord and withdrew two small handguns. Handing one to Bo, he said, "Just in case. You do know how to work one of these things now, don't you?" asked Sean.

"Sure," said Bo, taking the gun into his right hand. In reality Bo had really never fired a handgun. He had done some clay pigeon shooting and B-B gun hunting but had never handled a handgun. *Hopefully, I won't have to use it,* thought Bo.

A slow-moving Mercedes Benz four-door sedan caught Bo's attention. Since both Bo and Sean were still inside their car, there was no way for the driver or passenger in the Mercedes to identify them.

"Bo's hair stood on end when he saw the car's breaklights about one mile ahead of them.

"What on earth could they be stopping for?" asked Bo.

"I don't know. What's the car doing now?"

Slowly the Mercedes reversed and backed into a row of bushes totally concealing its identity.

"I don't like that one bit." Bo's heart began pounding.

"Don't worry too much Bo. It could be a rich couple pulling over for a little pre-dinner appetizer," said Sean smiling.

"Or it could be a killer," said Bo, stone-faced. "I'm going to walk the mile or so to the car. I'm afraid we might spook them if we drive by them. You stay here, and be ready if I call."

"Got you. One thing, Bo."

"What's that?"

"Try holding that gun a little tighter. It's not a toy, you know."

"Gotcha," said Bo. He had totally disregarded the weapon and was pleased that Sean was paying attention.

Bo was dressed in khaki shorts and a dark-blue polo shirt. Since it was now nighttime, his clothes made it difficult to see him. Only a handful of cars had traveled the north-south boulevard. Each time the headlights of the oncoming cars virtually blinded him.

Bo found himself walking briskly. He hadn't been able to exercise since his gunshot wound and was now perspiring profusely. He figured Ruby would frown on his physical activity. But he wasn't running, just walking fast.

Bo's eyes had adjusted well to the darkness, and he could see two good-sized men. Both were overweight and dressed all in black. From his perspective, Bo thought he saw a rifle of some kind. The gun was pointed south in the direction of the sidewalk.

Bo's gut now burned with anxiety. He was about a quarter mile away when he saw the man adjust his stance, raise his gun, and aim. Bo followed the trajectory of the barrel and in the distance observed the faint trace of a lone runner.

Oh my God, thought Bo. *This is it. The guy is going to shoot Hank.* Instantaneously, Bo did two things. He shouted at the top of his lungs, "Hank, get down!" and with his shooting hand aimed and fired at the darkened gunman. Bo heard several shots that were not fired from his own gun and immediately dropped to the ground. Two bullets imploded around him but nothing struck his body.

Enormously relieved, Bo rose from the ground to see the Mercedes tear out of the bushes, squealing its tires, and spraying dirt and stones everywhere in its wake.

Less than a minute later, Sean pulled up alongside Bo in his Honda.

"Are you okay?"

"Yeah, I'm fine."

"Go check out the runner. I think it was Hank. Hurry!" yelled Bo.

As Bo watched the Honda proceed down the road, he prayed that Hank was not hit. Bo saw the red brake lights. When he saw the passenger side door open and a man get in, he was relieved.

Bo couldn't believe what happened next. The same Mercedes that had just peeled out was now traveling north along Central Boulevard and this time it was not even speeding.

If only we could follow it, thought Bo. As Bo watched the big Mercedes sedan roll northbound, he was startled by the presence of Sean and Hank in the Honda. Sean had reversed the car for a long distance.

"Follow that car," shouted Bo, hopping into the back seat.

"What car?" asked Sean.

"Just drive, I can barely see the sedan. It's turning onto Donald Ross Road. Take a left up at the light."

With his attention focused on the highway ahead, Bo asked, "Hank, are you okay?"

"I'm fine, I guess. I got a few scrapes when I dove to the ground when I heard you yell. How'd you know?"

"Know what?"

"Just why the heck were you two out here in the first place?" demanded Hank.

"I had a hunch. Plus, I got you into my mess. It was the least I could do," said Bo rather nonchalantly.

"Hell, it looks like I owe you my life."

"No you don't. You'd have done the same for me. Probably even better."

"You look a little peaked," said Hank, straining his head to take a look at his best friend in the back seat. Bo had also scraped himself when he dove on the asphalt, and Hank thought he noticed a dark spot on his shirt where he had been previously shot.

"I'm fine. Just drive, Sean."

At the next intersection, Bo observed that the sedan entered the Interstate I-95 southbound ramp.

"He's going south on I-95. Hurry!"

Sean ran the red light almost causing a major wreck and proceeded to take the same southbound ramp.

None of the men happened to observe the white Ford Crown Victoria that also ran the red light and followed closely behind the Honda.

Sean accelerated the car to nearly ninety miles an hour before Bo saw the big Mercedes taillights about a quarter mile ahead.

"Okay. You can slow down now. No sense in getting too close."

Neither Sean nor Hank knew the black shape of the sedan that Bo was fixated on, so they just remained quiet, allowing Bo to concentrate.

They continued to travel south on the interstate for about fifteen minutes before Bo said a word.

"They are either going to exit on Palm Beach Lakes Boulevard or Okeechobee Boulevard."

Both exits enable one to travel east to Palm Beach. Bo figured the car had to belong to Milton Rogers or his family.

What he couldn't believe was how stupid they were to return back to the scene of the attempted crime.

"I think it's one of Milton Rogers's cars?"

"No way," said Sean.

"You've got to be kidding," exclaimed Hank.

"If it exits on Okeechobee and heads east, it's definitely a Rogers's vehicle. I'd bet my life on it."

Moments later the Mercedes did in fact exit on Okeechobee Boulevard and proceeded east towards Palm Beach.

All three men were quite familiar with the Rogers's residence, and when they saw the Mercedes about ten cars ahead of them traverse the middle bridge to Palm Beach, they no longer had any doubt.

The Mercedes traveled down Royal Palm Way before taking a right on Ocean Avenue and heading south again, right toward the Rogers's mansion.

"Unbelievable," said Sean.

"Now what?" asked Hank.

"Shouldn't we be calling the cops and reporting this incident?" inquired Sean.

Bo was uncertain what to do next. Their Honda slowly passed the massive gates to the Rogers's mansion just as they were closing. However, all three men were speechless as a man appeared virtually out of nowhere with an eight-foot metal pole and jammed the gate's entrance preventing it from closing.

"Keep driving," shouted Bo, noticing that Sean had just about stopped the car to watch in awe as the gate was reopened, allowing a black limo to enter the long and winding driveway.

"I'll be damned," said Hank. "It could be our old friend, Jean. That gatekeeper certainly doesn't look American and why would someone use a huge pole to disengage a privacy gate?"

"I don't know."

"Now what?" asked Sean.

"Turn the car around and let's park just outside the gate."

"Why not drive all the way to the front door?" The huge ficus hedge and natural vegetation precluded one from actually seeing the residence from the road. The entire Rogers homestead had to consist of at least two acres with over five hundred feet of oceanfront.

"No, outside is just fine. We can walk to the front door."

Since Hank was still in his running attire, he volunteered to run up to the front door.

"No. We all will walk. We're trespassing, I want you all to know," joked Bo in his most serious tone as they slipped through the open gate.

About halfway up the driveway, Hank asked, "Where's my weapon?"

"I only had two guns, and Bo and I need them," replied Sean.

"You two? Well in that case, stay close and cover me. But most of all be careful. We don't know what to expect."

Chapter
Ninety-Five

Lee and Larry came bursting into the family dinner. Their wives were pleased to see their flushed faces.

"My sons. How was your little expedition? I hope you have good news!"

"Not good, Father," responded Lee.

"Nothing," said Larry.

"What the hell do you mean by that?" questioned a deeply concerned Milton.

Larry spoke first. "We did everything that we had discussed and planned. The car was parked beautifully and we sat and waited for Hank to come. It was totally dark and just as Lee had the guy in his sights, someone yelled, 'Hank, get down!' and then started shooting at us."

"What then?"

"I returned the fire but doubt if I hit the man. So afterwards we hightailed it out of there. Some foreign car, like a Honda, must have stopped after hearing the commotion."

"Did you get a good look at these good Samaritans?" queried an upset Milton.

"No. It was really dark, and we thought it best to get the hell out of there."

"So where'd you go next?"

"We came right here."

"Right here?" shouted Milton.

"Why, yes."

"You idiots! Did you think that maybe you were followed or that someone set you up?"

"Well, no."

"What imbeciles. God forgive me for raising such imbeciles," raved Milton.

"Dad, we didn't know what else to do. But we definitely were not followed."

"How do you know that?"

"We just know. That's all."

"Great. Just great."

"Dad, who could have known we were set to ambush Hank Miles?"

"Somebody in this room," said a stone-faced Milton. "That's the only way they could have known."

"Well we sure didn't tell," chimed Lee. "It was nobody in our family."

"Oh really," yelled Milton, looking at everyone sitting around the gigantic dining room table.

Annie lowered her head and continued eating. The rest of the wives just sat dumbstruck.

Milton rose from his chair. In a flash he backhanded Annie across her face, knocking her off her chair.

"Dad, what the hell are you doing?" yelled a thoroughly scared Lee, trying to ahelp his poor bleeding wife.

"Bastard," mumbled Annie, trying to measure the extent of her facial injury. "You bastard. I have said nothing."

"That's it. I've had it," yelled a flustered Brenda. "You're ruining this family, Milton. I'm not going to stand for it or allow it to go any further. No more guns or murders or lying or cheating!"

Chapter
Ninety-Six

In the midst of the commotion and the tears, the Rogers family failed to notice Jean and his two cohorts enter the large dining room.

Jean fired his Uzi at the ceiling, and the noise caused everyone to freeze and stop their bickering.

"Greetings, everyone," said a grinning Jean. "Please sit. Now."

The entire Rogers clan returned to their seats.

"What do you want?" declared Milton.

"What I've always wanted, my friend. I want my money. Except now, it's going to cost you one hundred million dollars."

"One hundred million dollars. You've got to be kidding."

"No joke. Two of my best men are dead. Their families will need to be well provided for. Had you not double-crossed me, they would be alive to watch their children grow up. I would be in Antwerp, and you would be significantly richer. You, Milton, are nothing but a murderer and a thief."

"Well, I'm not going to pay you."

Jean walked slowly over to Milton Rogers and grabbed the older man's right hand. In the flick of an eye, Jean severed Milton's index finger with a razor-sharp knife that appeared out of nowhere.

Milton screamed, "Bloody hell!" The boys attempted to come to his aid but thought better of it as the two guards aimed their weapons directly at them.

"You goddamn madman. Look what you've done. Oh, God," said a blubbering Milton.

"I will do the same to everyone in this room, starting with your lovely wife."

Jean rushed over to Brenda and and held up her trembling right hand. Just as he was about to slice away, Milton responded.

"Okay. For Christ's sake. Leave my family alone. I'll pay you your damn money."

"I want it now."

"How?"

"This is the age of computers, my friend. You understandably have online access to your accounts. I want you to direct your funds to my offshore Cayman accounts."

"I can't do that," said a devastated Milton.

"Oh you will if you want to see your wife's ten fingers again."

"You've got exactly ten minutes."

"My—my laptop is in the den. Let me go get it. It will take me a while to boot it up and then access my accounts."

"Nine minutes."

"For God's sake, I'm going." Milton, bleeding, went over to the door of his den, unlocked it, and proceeded to upload his computer, which rested on his massive desk.

Five minutes later Milton shouted, "I'm ready."

Jean proceeded then to bark out the numbers of his designated accounts to Milton with the respective institutions routing numbers. Jean directed Milton to transfer ten million dollars into ten different accounts at several financial institutions.

The Rogers family all sat trembled in silence. Everyone was scared to death. Poor Milton was having to type with his left hand since his right hand was now covered with a napkin trying to stop the flow of blood from his severed finger. Nobody had the foresight to grab the index finger lying on the floor and put it on ice.

Bo, Sean, and Hank had entered the residence and witnessed the entire procession of events. They squatted, still as church mice, behind the four-foot wall leading into the living room. Sean had turned on his mini-tape recorder and had taped the entire course of events. Bo had set his phone on record. Next to them were the two CIA agents from the Crown Victoria that had followed the men to the Rogers's residence. Although not formally introduced, Bo and Hank were relieved to have them alongside. Not a word was spoken between them. Only hand gestures telling them to remain put and silent.

Twenty minutes later Milton, followed by Jean, emerged from the master den. Milton was sweating profusely, and his once-white napkin was now crimson red. Milton's golden tan had also turned several shades of white.

From where Bo and his group were watching if Jean and his men attempted to leave via the front door, they would definitely be seen. Bo started to panic until he watched the two CIA men assemble their arsenal of weapons.

The young operative broke the silence. "When Jean and his men start coming this way, we will surprise and apprehend them."

"You've got to be kidding," questioned Bo. "They're not going to surrender and they have machine guns," whispered Bo.

"We are the CIA. They will drop their weapons."

"Listen here. They won't give up without a fight. These men are killers. Don't try and be heroes."

"This is my call, and I'm in charge. You will do as you're told."

Bo looked at Sean and Hank. He was speechless. But as instructed, the three men moved back and crouched closer to the front door, enabling the two CIA operatives a direct view of the dining room.

Bo whispered to both Sean and Hank, "When the gun fight starts, we need to exit the front door immediately. We are no match for the firepower in this room."

Hank countered, "I'll open the door and we'll then run and hop in the bushes."

All agreed and nodded their heads accordingly and waited for the fireworks to start.

In no more than fifteen minutes' time, Jean had gotten what he had come for. One hundred million dollars wired to his numerous offshore holdings. In a few weeks' time, he would have laundered the proceeds several more times and cleaned the money without any trace. *Not bad*, thought Jean.

Slowly, Jean walked backward out of the dining room followed by his two armed men.

"Mr. Milton Rogers, I can't say it has been a pleasure working with you. It all could have been so very simple. But you failed to turn over the original diamonds you swindled out of Bart Sinclair after I delivered you the drugs."

"I have killed many men for much less. Trust me. You and your family here are extremely lucky that I'm a very generous man. But we have a history, Milton. You helped my wife and but for that, you would be dead."

"I'm satisfied now. So I bid you all a fond and final farewell. Don't try anything stupid that you will regret. Remember I know where you live."

None of the Rogers family members even attempted to rise. They were still aghast at what had transpired. Their father, the great entrepreneur Milton Rogers, had been played again. This time in addition to one hundred million dollars, he had lost his finger as well.

The boys certainly knew what those men were capable of, and not one of them wanted anything to do with them. They also were relieved that no harm had come to them or their spouses.

The somber moment was broken when the CIA operatives rose and shouted, "Freeze. Put your hands up."

In milliseconds, Jean's armed men opened fire on the CIA men, who in turn were a fraction of a second slow in responding. Their Teflon jackets evidently took several of the machine gun bullets, but a few found their mark and shortly both CIA men were down.

Fortunately, the CIA's gunfire had been accurate as well. Both of Jean's armed men were seriously hit. Jean was still in one piece and only one of the Rogers sons had been struck by the barrage of bullets.

At the first sound of gunshots, Bo, Sean, and Hank sprinted out the front door and dove into the nearby hedge. Hank and Bo were lying in the same clump of cherry hedges, and Sean was lying in the row of azalea bushes. Sean and Hank aimed their pistols at the front door. Bo was clutching his cell phone that was still recording and nursing his shoulder.

Jean next acted in self-defense when he grabbed Brenda and used her as his shield and hostage. Brenda was unscathed, but the razor sharp knife held to her throat kept everyone from rushing him.

Jean carefully observed the damage. Both of his men were clearly dead. Bullets had riddled their once rock-hard bodies. As Jean and Brenda approached the front door, he sensed that both CIA operatives were dead since neither one moved.

Jean realized time was of the essence, and he needed to leave the house immediately. He had no idea if the operatives had called for reinforcements. He only prayed that they hadn't. Once safely in the limo, he could reassess his game plan. His Lear jet was ready and waiting for him at the Palm Beach International Airport.

In fifteen minutes he would be safely in the air. Any number of possible Caribbean destinations would provide him shelter and safety. His connections, paid for with cash from his lucrative drug trade, could protect him forever.

Jean led Brenda down the marble front steps of the mansion. The limo was parked less than ten feet away. Although Jean had killed many people, he had no intention of harming Brenda. Once safely inside his limo, he would shove her out into the driveway.

Bo and Hank didn't know what to do. They knew that if they acted, Brenda would surely be killed.

Bo's mind was also filled with numbers. Bo had attempted to memorize the ten different account numbers that Jean had provided to Milton. Fortunately, he had recorded everything on his phone, just in case he forgot a digit or two.

In fact, Bo had proceeded to write them down on his arm while he and Hank lay in the hedges. Bo also identified the banks with each numbered account. Hank just shook his head at Bo's foresightedness.

Bo was about to confront Jean when Hank pulled him back. Whispering softly, Hank said, "The authorities can pick Jean up. He's either headed to a boat or the airport. Don't worry."

As planned, Jean used Brenda until he was safely in the car. With the engine running and moving slowly, Jean pushed Brenda out of the car. Brenda suffered some scrapes and bruises, but she would be just fine. The entire Rogers clan, minus Milton and Annie, were on the marble steps. The boys ran to aid their mother as they watched the limousine pull away.

"I swear, I'll kill that man," yelled Lawrence, unable to control his anger.

"You'll do no such thing. It's over, damn you. It's over," shouted Brenda, now shaking uncontrollably with tears streaming down her plump face.

Little did Bo and Hank realize it, but Sean had called 9-1-1, and moments later two Palm Beach police cars arrived at the scene, missing Jean's limo by less than sixty seconds.

The officers rushed into the house to find the horrific mess. The ambulances arrived less than five minutes later. Sean, Bo, and Hank all remained frozen and hidden. As soon as the entire crowd went back into the house, leaving the men outside in the dark night, they walked quietly back to their Honda Accord. It was impossible for them to overhear the conversations or the lame excuses that Milton would undoubtedly come up with. Not one man said a word. All of them were numb. Fortunately, they did not actually see the gruesome outcome of the gunfight, but they all sensed that Jean's men and the CIA operatives were killed in the fighting.

Hank's first words spoken in the car were, "I'm hungry. Let's go to Bo's and have Ruby cook us dinner."

"I've lost my appetite. I've had enough excitement with you two to last me a lifetime. How about I just take you both to Bo's house and call it a night," said Sean, still visibly shaken over all the violence.

"I don't ever want to be rich or go through this experience again," added Sean.

"Sean, thank you," recited Bo. "There will be another significant bundle of cash for your effort."

"I didn't do it for the money."

"I know that."

"So what are you guys going to do? I mean are you going to just let Jean get away?"

"I don't really know. If we notify the authorities they will start asking a million questions and I don't know if I'm prepared to answer them," said Bo thinking hard.

"Whatever you decide, Bo. I'm with you all the way," said Hank.

"Me too," chimed Sean.

Sean dropped the two men at Bo's house and sped away.

"He's a good guy," said Hank waving to Sean.

"So are you, my friend, so are you."

Chapter
Ninety-Seven

The red dogs and Ruby greeted the two men. From the looks of their scrapes and bruises, Ruby was not too thrilled.

"I'm afraid to even ask where you two have been, but I'm so happy you are both in one piece. I was worried sick, and after you didn't call, I grew more frightened with each passing minute. Don't worry, Hank, I'll call your wife and let her know you're okay. After dinner, Bo will take you home. I'm sure they will be relieved."

"Thanks, Ruby."

"Now let me take a good look at you, Bo." When he took off his shirt, Ruby grimaced as she noticed that Bo had ripped out some of his steel staples.

"You're bleeding but not too bad. If you had opened up all of those those sutures, we'd be on our way back to the hospital. Try and be careful in the shower. You've got cuts all over your knees, hands, and elbows."

"After copying these numbers on my arm, I will," said an obliging Bo. Later after his shower, he looked at himself in the mirror and suddenly felt old.

After showering and dressing, the two men sat down for one of Ruby's delicious vegetarian meals. When they could eat no more, Ruby got down to business.

"Tell me exactly what happened tonight. I need to know everything."

Bo and Hank began at the beginning and explained the entire unbelievable evening. Ruby couldn't even imagine the events that had taken place. After they were finished speaking, Ruby posed a few questions of her own.

"Tell me guys when do you think the CIA is going to show up here and start asking questions and demanding answers?"

No sooner had she uttered those words then the front door bell rang. The red dogs began to bark like crazy and rushed to see who it was. Two men in suits were at the door. The same men who had arranged the involuntary meeting with Bo and his father.

Ruby answered the door and was not even greeted with a hello. The two men brushed her aside and went straight to where Bo and Hank were sitting.

"You've got a lot of explaining to do. I've lost two of my very best operatives tonight. Their last communication said that they had followed you and the Mercedes Benz that fired on a lone jogger to the Milton Rogers's mansion. They didn't even ask for backup. Now tell me everything, or so help me God, you will rot in jail."

Bo and Hank turned ghost white before Bo began talking. He was entirely honest with everything until the point of entering the Rogers's mansion.

"We never set foot in the mansion. But we did see three men exit the black limousine. Two hired hands and Jean Valhomme. Your CIA men told us to wait outside and that's exactly what we did. We waited until we heard gunshots. It sounded really loud and deadly but only lasted for about thirty seconds. The next thing we knew, Jean came out the front door with Brenda in his arms. He was holding a knife to her throat. He got in the car, threw Brenda out, and drove away."

"We then called 9-1-1 and left the scene after the paramedics and police arrived, and we came right here."

"So you never even stepped inside the house?"

"Correct," said Bo and Hank in unison.

"Well, there are now four dead bodies. My two men and two Europeans."

"They were definitely Jean's associates," added Hank.

"And you never heard anything that transpired inside the house?"

"No. Nothing."

"Why?" asked Bo.

"It's just that we got a wild story from Milton Rogers, and we're now trying to get to the bottom of this."

"What did Milton Rogers say if you don't mind my nosiness?"

"Not much except that he alleges that you hired the European men to physically harm him and that you would do anything you could to hurt Milton and his family."

"And did you believe him?" spouted Ruby, listening intensely.

"Of course not. A child could tell the man was lying. But you have to hand it to him, he sure is persistent. We do know that Lee and Larry attempted to kill Hank, and were it not for your actions, Bo, they would have succeeded."

"Are you going to file charges?" inquired Hank. "After all it is my life we're talking about."

"We'll get to that in due time," responded the gray-haired man. "I'll promise you one thing, I will not stop until I get to the bottom of all this."

"Great," said Bo.

"Now, we're bound to have more questions, so stick close to home."

"Easier said than done," spoke Bo.

"What do you mean by that?"

"We have plans to go down to Miami Beach for the next two days."

"When will you be back?"

"Wednesday night."

"Okay. Thursday morning, I'd like to meet here with Bo and Hank around nine o'clock if that is good with you?"

"We'll be here."

"And I'll have coffee and doughnuts ready," chimed Ruby.

"Until Thursday, then."

"Bye."

When the men were gone, Ruby abruptly turned to Bo and asked, "What's the Miami trip all about?"

"Oh that's just a ruse. We're flying to the Caymans tomorrow."

"We're what?" asked both Ruby and Hank incredulously.

"You heard me. We're going to charter a plane and fly over there and then fly right back. Hank, you need to pay them some extra cash like before since I'm technically under an Indictment and unable to leave the country."

"I don't like it one bit," declared Ruby. "Not one bit."

Hank on the other hand, had an inkling of what Bo was up to. "Should Ruby bring her makeup kit?" asked Hank smiling.

"We're going to go shopping at Walmart tonight. We'll need hair coloring, tanning creams, facial stuff, and whatever else Ruby thinks we need to change our appearances," ordered out Bo.

"Whatever for?" inquired Ruby.

"Well, you don't want any bank cameras to see our normal beautiful faces now, do you?"

Ruby had to admit that she felt a certain rush of excitement, but deep down, she was clearly frightened.

"I place my trust in you, guys."

"Great," said Bo. "Now let's get moving. We have lots to do."

As an extra precaution, Bo phoned Sean and informed him of everything he discussed with the two suits. Sean agreed that none of them had actually entered the Rogers's mansion.

Chapter
Ninety-Eight

A t 7:30 a.m. the following morning, Ruby, Bo, and Hank boarded the chartered plane for the Cayman Islands. They had spent over two hours working on their disguises. The extra five thousand dollars cash paid for the secrecy of the passenger names on the flight manifold. By 9:15 a.m. they had safely avoided customs and were on their way to Main Street.

Bo had spent the entire flight outlining their respective roles in great detail. Everyone understood and was on the same page. Each also carried a briefcase with over fifty thousand dollars in cash. Seed capital is what Bo had called the money.

Ruby, Bo, and Hank were assigned three banks each. However before they even began to visit the banks, they had to first visit the legal office of Vincent Bargain, counselor at law. Vincent was a seedy little man with narrow black eyes, a clearly fake toupee, bird-like arms, and spindly legs.

Bo had never personally done business with the man but had heard through the grapevine that he sold shelf corporations with very little paperwork for cash. Vincent had made himself a little fortune looking the other way.

Their appointment was at ten o'clock in the morning, and Bo was hoping to be finished no later than noon. Bo did most of the talking during the first half hour, explaining exactly what they wanted and cautiously hinting about Vincent's sterling reputation, much to the man's liking.

Vincent absorbed everything and then began to speak. "For fifty thousand US dollars, I can have you as the owners of three separate offshore Cayman corporations. Not one individual name will appear in the public records, and the shareholders for each corporation will be the other two corporations. Statements will be sent to a post office box that you have provided me. There will exist no evidence of your personal involvement. Also, my annual fee will be five thousand dollars per corporation to serve as your resident agent and presiding officer. Do I make myself clear?"

Bo responded with a yes and a nod of his head.

"Very well then; let's begin the paperwork," said the delighted attorney. It shouldn't take more than thirty minutes once I receive payment."

"I want you to perform it now," said Bo. He his briefcase and laid the fifty thousand dollars on Vincent's desk.

"You mean right this minute?" Vincent asked.

"Yes, I do. We are on a tight schedule. The tax ID numbers and corporate stamps must be available before noon or the deal is off. Understood?"

"Very well then. I'll get right on it. Please make yourselves comfortable."

Hank and Ruby looked at Bo when Vincent left the office to have his assistant and secretary start preparing the documents.

"Whose names do we sign?" asked Ruby.

"I can't believe you attorneys," said Hank shaking his head and putting in a dig at Bo's profession.

"Our names are Bart Smith, Susan Smith, and Larry Smith. Okay?"

"Who's Susan?" asked Hank jokingly.

By five minutes to twelve, the papers were signed, notarized, and ready for the next stage. Fox Gate, Fox Hound, and Fox Trader were the names of these Cayman corporations.

Each person then took their corporate seal and corresponding tax ID number to their separate banks and began officially creating bank accounts. In addition, they received the bank's wiring ABA account number and processing codes. Each account was then opened with five thousand dollars' cash. Not one encountered any difficulty with the creation of the accounts. Further, their disguises worked wonderfully to hide their true identities as all the banks had numerous cameras. All three also signed signature cards so poorly that the best handwriting specialist in the world couldn't figure out their signatures.

The three met up for a light lunch at around 2:30 p.m. Their nerves were all somewhat frayed because they knew the hardest part was yet to come.

Bo had no idea whether any of Jean's ten different accounts contained photo identification or passwords to access the funds. He also was clueless whether or not Jean had a personal relationship with any of the financial institutions. Bo was just hoping Jean had no individual involvement with any banking official or any institution. He prayed that Jean's offshore accounts had been created and business conducted on an informal basis. If not, they were in for a most unpleasant surprise.

At three o'clock the gang separated and went their respective ways. By four they agreed to meet up and tackle the final institution together.

Much to their amazement, the banks were extremely cooperative and helpful. Nobody encountered any difficulties whatsoever. All were shocked at the actual monetary size of the accounts. Jean had literally stashed hundreds of millions of dollars into the various accounts. The ten-million-dollar wire transfers were rather insignificant based on the accounts balances, and Bo was extremely relieved.

When they met up precisely at four, all were wearing ear-to-ear smiles. Although nobody could get used to their respective disguises, they were satisfied with having relieved Jean of over $90 million.

Bo decided against pushing their luck and going to the final institution together. There was really no need. So by 5:00 p.m. they found themselves comfortably settled in their passenger seats traveling back to Palm Beach.

It was a long, taxing, and stressful day. Everyone was greatly relieved when they safely passed through the private passenger gates undetected and arrived at the Martin's humble abode.

It took at least an hour for them to wash out the hair coloring dyes and return back to their normal selves.

As an extra measure of protection, Bo and Ruby traveled south to Miami Beach and stayed the night at the enchanting Tides Hotel. Their romantic evening and restful morning were just what they needed. Bo had been under so much stress that it was wonderful to spend a lovely night and morning together. Bo was praying that everything would soon be over.

When Bo and Ruby arrived home the following day, Mr. CIA was parked outside their house waiting and watching. Ruby waved to him. After unpacking, the doorbell rang, and the gray-haired man stood impatiently.

"I'm sorry to interrupt you. How was your trip?" he asked.

"Relaxing," responded Ruby.

"How was the Tides?" asked Mr. CIA.

"Romantic," replied Bo, trying to hide his surprise.

"We were just making sure you didn't go anywhere you were not supposed to. You know, you're not dealing with amateurs."

"You know we didn't," said Bo sternly.

"So far at least."

"What exactly did you want? We're still on for tomorrow morning, right?"

"That's right. We've learned a lot more and have numerous questions for you. Enjoy your day."

Chapter
Ninety-Nine

o and Ruby spent a rather long day and sleepless night tossing and turning over and over again. Fortunately, they had caught up on their sleep the previous night in Miami Beach.

Hank arrived around eight forty-five in the morning. He also hadn't slept much the previous evening. Ruby was in the kitchen making healthy whole wheat muffins and brewing coffee while the two men discussed various matters. Both men were clearly worried, but naturally their conversation turned to sports and running topics they clearly knew and loved.

Like clockwork, the gray-haired CIA operative and his partner appeared at the front door at exactly 9:00 a.m. Both men seemed much more pleasant and even took turns petting the red dogs, who lapped up the attention.

After everyone had eaten Ruby's delicious muffins and savored her Kona coffee, the CIA men got down to business.

Unfortunately, each member of the Rogers family had hired an attorney, and nobody was speaking. Their attorneys had instructed them to remain silent until an immunity agreement could be worked out.

"Damn," said Hank. "They've had two days now to come up with a story."

"We realize that and wanted to hear your version before we proceed with filing any charges," replied the taller gentleman.

So from the beginning, Bo and Hank again recited the entire episode, being mindful to leave out the part of them actually entering of the mansion.

The CIA men took copious notes and never interrupted them. Even Ruby was enthralled by their story.

Bo also pointed out that it was odd that no article had appeared in the *Palm Beach Times*. Nothing. Not even an obituary. Evidently, publicity would have been highly frowned upon by Milton Rogers. Mae McReynolds knew who buttered her toast. She must have pulled quite a number of strings to have kept the shootings and deaths quiet.

"Mr. Martin, we also find the lack of publicity extremely odd. But, as you want us to believe, it certainly fits your version of facts."

"That it does," said Hank, nodding in agreement.

"Jean Valhomme is now on the FBI's Top Ten Most Wanted List. It's highly likely that he has fled the country and will become impossible to find now."

Bo, Hank, and Ruby were pleased at the rather quick work the federal authorities did declaring Jean a dangerous criminal.

Bo figured that once Jean discovered that his money was transferred out of his accounts, he would have an extremely difficult time determining who had pilfered his accounts. He could never safely step foot back in the United States to track down the culprits. First-degree murder of federal officers carries the death penalty or lifetime imprisonment. Bo figured that the risk of capture would far outweigh the $90 million Jean Valhomme lost.

"Mr. Martin, we want you to know that the federal assistant US Attorneys, Steve Fleishman and Nick Long, have been removed as the prosecutors on your case. It looks like the new prosecutor is going to drop the Indictment against you. With Sinclair deceased and the Rogers family not talking, there is not much opposition to your statements. The government really doesn't want to go through a long, lengthy, and expensive trial."

"Does that mean the Indictment has been or will be rescinded?" inquired Bo. He was having trouble imagining anything positive coming out of this ordeal.

"Although I don't have an official decree, I would say that it's ninety-nine percent concluded."

"I'll believe it when I see it," yelled Ruby from the kitchen after eavesdropping on every word spoken.

"We'd all be much better off if we could nail the Milton Rogers's family," declared the gray-haired man. "We just don't have anything real concrete at least not yet."

You will, thought Bo. *You will.*

The two men quickly ended the conversation and thanked Ruby immensely for her hospitality.

"Mr. Martin if anything unexpected comes up, please call. We'll be right over, and we sure could use a break in this matter. We'd like to nail Milton Rogers and Jean Valhomme."

"Will do," responded Bo.

When the men were gone, Ruby broke the silence.

"Now what?"

"Now we just wait."

"Wait. What for?"

"Until the Indictment is rescinded and I can seek to regain the ability to practice law again," said Bo.

"What about the Palm Beach police and the murder investigation of Bart Sinclair?" inquired Hank.

"At this point in time, it's only an investigation. No charges have been filed, and I'm just a potential suspect."

"Still you're a suspect," said Ruby nonetheless.

"I guess you've got a good point there," muttered Bo.

Chapter
One Hundred

The next few days passed without a word from anyone. Bo had spent two days in his office building. His reliable secretary, Ms. Everett, was manning the phones and dealing with the mail and the former client's files. She is a godsend, he thought. Bo was still unauthorized to practice law and Bye was willing to continue working as an attorney.

Bo retained less than a handful of old reliable clients, Dana Sinclair being one. Dana hadn't hired a new attorney since Bart's death and stated that she would not do so. Bo was concerned because he realized there was a tremendous amount of work to be done in handling the Sinclair estate. It would take him a few months to administer the estate correctly and file the proper federal estate tax returns.

Dana had insisted on an appointment the following week. Bo felt obligated to at least meet with her and recommend to her another competent estate attorney. The attorney fee for handling that estate could easily exceed one million dollars. "Not bad for eighteen months' worth of work," grumbled Bo, thinking out loud to himself.

It was after 2:00 p.m. when Bo was preparing to leave his office. Bo knew the hectic days at the office were about behind him now.

Bo also realized that with his law practice all but gone, his father could now easily sell the building and pocket top dollar.

In spite of all the stress, heartaches, and unrelenting hours, Bo did enjoy his work. It was his home away from home and he liked working on sophisticated estate plans designed to reduce the federal inheritance tax, which he believed was "double taxation". He also loved beating the IRS auditors on estate tax return audits where he had been aggressive in seeking substantial deductions or discounts to the final inheritance bill. His clients loved him, and the IRS feared him.

Deep down, Bo was also afraid. He didn't really possess any other special skills. He loved being his own boss and couldn't see himself as an employee of a large corporation or law firm. Plus, he knew he didn't want to become involved in the restaurant business after listening to Ruby's day-to-day woes and in handling her financial books.

Hank had suggested a possible career in the insurance industry, but that was the last thing Bo wanted to do.

As Bo was closing his briefcase, Ms. Everett poked her head into the office.

"You have a client in the lobby."

"A client? Who?"

"You'll have to see for yourself. Should I send him back here?"

"I'm in shorts and running shoes for goodness' sakes," stated Bo.

"I don't think he'll mind."

"Okay."

"You better be sitting down just to be on the safe side."

"Sitti—" Bo couldn't even finish his last words when in walked Joe Marx. Joe had gained a few extra pounds but otherwise looked great. Evidently, death had become him, thought Bo.

"Mr. Marx," said Bo, rising to greet him with an extended hand. Bo didn't know whether to hug the man or punch him. He felt totally awkward.

"Call me Joe."

"Okay, Joe. I must say I'm at a loss for words."

"As soon as I heard the news of your indictment and Bart's death, I had to come. I only wish I had known sooner. I could have really helped you at Bart's trial."

"You could say that," interjected Bo, smiling. "I thought you were dead."

"I had to arrange for my death or else Victor Butin would have searched for me forever. Tell me, Mr. Martin, how did you get him to back off and live to tell about it?"

Bo explained in detail the switch of the ecstasy pills at the Port of Palm Beach and the subsequent transfer of tablets to Victor. When he was finished, Joe was in awe.

"You've been unbelievably busy. You're still in one piece, which is absolutely remarkable, considering the cast of characters you've encountered."

"Not entirely in one piece," said Bo as he rolled up his shirt to show Joe the gunshot wound. "This and several broken bones have not helped my running career, I'll tell you that."

"Oh, I see. And the money?"

"Your trust is well protected in an account that is almost completely private. You know that Butin was able to trace the flow of funds to the account from the Isle of Man to Panama and ultimately, Grand Cayman."

"I can't believe it," said Joe.

"Bankers will do anything for a buck, and when their life is on the line, it's not that hard for them to disclose information."

"Do you think you've seen the last of Victor?"

"I do. He more than doubled his money with the drugs. I personally believe that he has no use for me, but you on the other hand, had better return to wherever you came from."

"No."

"No. What, are you crazy?"

"I can help you. I want to go to the United States attorney and give a statement to clear up the case against you. Then I can return home."

"It's too risky and I would forbid it."

"I'm a grown man," Joe yelled.

"I won't let you."

"I'm leaving now," said Joe as he stood to go.

"Wait. Don't be dumb. You need an attorney to protect your rights."

"Who do you suggest?"

"I don't know. But, how about staying at my house tonight? We can discuss matters over a delicious dinner."

"I don't want to be an imposition."

"Trust me. You're not."

"Okay."

"How'd you get here?"

"By Uber."

"Well, come and drive home with me."

"Oh, Ms. Everett," yelled Bo down the hallway. "This gentleman is Joe Marx."

"Pleased to meet you again," said Ms. Everett graciously moments later.

"Delighted," said Joe.

"He's here to help me."

"He's a miracle. I wish you had arrived several months ago."

"Thank you. So do I."

Chapter
One Hundred-One

When Bo and Joe arrived at home, the red dogs and Ruby rushed out to meet them. Ruby was a little taken aback when she saw that her husband was not alone.

Joe carried only a small travel bag in his right hand and placed it on the ground in order to pet the red dogs, who liked him immediately.

Bo didn't want to mention Joe's name outside, and he quickly ushered him into the house.

"I'm sorry for my lack of hospitality out there, but I didn't want to introduce you out in the public. Ruby, this is Joe Marx."

"Oh my God," exclaimed Ruby. "I'm sorry for my surprise, but I thought you were dead.

"It's certainly a pleasure to finally meet you. I've only heard wonderful things about you."

"Well, thank you," said a smiling Ruby.

"I would have come sooner had I known anything, but from where I'm living, I don't get much news. If it wasn't for a dear friend, I wouldn't even be computer literate. The internet amazes me and frightens me, all at the same time. While playing around on the computer, I ran across the *Palm Beach Times* newspaper. I was just browsing when I read the headlines that Bart Sinclair was murdered and that Bo was a prime suspect. I felt so bad for you that I had to come."

"How'd you even get here?" posed Ruby.

"Let's just say it was a rather arduous task. But well worth the trip."

"I hope we can have you leave this country as easily as you entered," spoke Bo.

"Don't worry one bit about me. I know exactly what I'm doing. So have you thought of an attorney?"

"I have given it my attention ever since I mentioned it. I'm leaning towards Paul Schwartz, though."

"That's excellent," responded Joe. "It's who I wanted, and I have my own personal reasons for his hiring."

"Let me call him now," Bo said. Bo had memorized the weasel's personal cell phone number during Sinclair's trial. Paul picked up on the third ring.

"Paul? It's me, Bo Martin."

"Oh Bo. So nice to hear from you, stranger. I hope things are as well as can be expected in light of everything."

"I'm fine. Paul, what are you doing right now and what are your plans for tomorrow afternoon?"

"Well, I'm about to go to Herbert's and pick up a fine bottle of wine and a gourmet prepared dinner for two."

"Cancel it."

"What about my date?"

"Cancel that too."

"Okay you've piqued my curiosity. My day tomorrow can be juggled around to accommodate you."

"Great. Do it."

"All right. Can you at least give me a hint?"

"You know where I live at the north end of the island?"

"Yes, I recall where you live."

"See you in an hour then."

"This must be serious."

"Trust me. It is."

"I'll be there in about an hour."

"Bye."

Ruby hastily prepared another of her masterpieces, and the aroma from the kitchen soon caught the attention of the two men.

"Ruby, may I help you with anything?" politely inquired Joe.

"No, you just keep talking with Bo."

Bo and Joe had come up with a game plan for Joe's limited testimony. All they needed was for Paul to carry it out.

Paul arrived two hours later looking somewhat disheveled. He brought a good bottle of red wine, which was all Ruby needed to top off her delicious meal.

Paul's fat jaws dropped immediately when he saw Joe Marx.

"Joe Marx, is that really you?"

"Yes, yes it is."

"We, I, everyone thought you were dead."

"I'm sure you did, Mr. Schwartz. I know you informed Victor Butin of that very fact."

"Trust me I can explain."

"No need for explanations. The past is in the past."

"We sure could have used you during Bart Sinclair's trial."

"I know that. I came as soon as I heard. I want to help Bo now."

"You could be in huge trouble. Are you aware of the risk you're taking?" asked Paul now sounding more sincere.

"Yes, and it's one I can live with."

"Paul," interrupted Bo. "Here's the game plan. You will be Joe's attorney. You will call the new US attorney and demand a meeting in your office. You will videotape the meeting with Joe and the US attorney and have Joe sign an affidavit in their presence at the conclusion of the meeting. You will imply that Joe will be available for questioning the following day. The Feds will have the videotaped meeting and Joe's affidavit. We feel that's enough evidence to exonerate me and dismiss the Indictment against me."

When Bo had finished speaking, the men anxiously looked at Paul, awaiting his answer.

"It's risky, but I think it just might work. We'll catch the US attorney off guard, and there's only a slight risk that they'll bring in the FBI to attend the meeting."

"Very well then, is it a deal?" asked Bo.

"It's a deal. I'll work on the affidavit and have it ready by one o'clock. The only hitch is whether the new US attorney can make the meeting at my office on such short notice."

"You have got to make it happen," pleaded Bo.

"I know."

Just as the men were finishing up, Ruby called, "Dinner time."

The meal was absolutely fantastic. Paul had seconds and then thirds. The conversation at the meal was light, but everyone was happy to see Paul leave.

Ruby spoke first after he left. "You know, I've never liked that man."

"Me either," countered Joe.

"That makes three of us," said Bo.

That evening, Bo had difficulty falling asleep. He went out on the patio. While sitting outside watching the stars and the ripples on the swimming pool, Joe startled Bo by placing his hand on his shoulder.

"I didn't mean to scare you, young man."

"I hope I didn't wake you up, but I couldn't sleep."

"Me either. May I join you?"

"Certainly," said Bo.

"You have a lovely home and a beautiful wife. You are a very lucky man," said Joe sincerely.

"I know that. After going through this entire ordeal, I have to say that despite everything, I am one extremely lucky guy. How are you?"

"I'm wonderful. I love where I live. I have more than enough money, and I'm finally at peace. I've had a difficult life, but I'm ready when the good Lord takes me. My wife and daughter are waiting for me."

"I want to thank you for your help. You didn't need to take this risk."

"You did."

"It's my job," answered Bo.

"That's bull, and you know it. How's the Trust?"

"I've got it broadly diversified, and even with the decline in the stock market and the economy, the money will more than protect Bart's wife, children, grandchildren, and probably great-grandchildren. I've also set up the line of trustee succession in the event of my demise or disability."

"Whatever happened to the diamond in the safe deposit box?"

"I gave it to Bart."

"You did?"

"You knew I would. In fact that was the test that convinced Bart."

"You do realize that when I arranged my disappearance, Bart said you'd keep the diamond for yourself. I bet that you wouldn't."

"Thanks for your faith in me. I appreciate it."

"You're welcome. So tell me, whatever became of the real diamonds?"

"I returned the diamonds to Bart and told him to hide them in a safe place."

"Did he do that?"

"No. He sold them against my expressed wishes and they were my ace in the hole."

"I could have told you he'd double-cross you."

"How?"

"I knew him better than he even knew himself. He was self-centered and greedy. A tough combination if you ask me."

"So what are you going to do after tomorrow?" asked Bo.

"I've made plans. Please don't worry about me. I'll be fine."

"Thank you. And if I don't get the chance to tell you, thank you again."

"Mr. Bo Martin, you are a true gentleman. Now get some sleep. It will be daylight in just a couple of hours."

Chapter
One Hundred-Two

Paul called in the morning to give Bo and Joe the good news that the US Attorneys' office agreed to a meeting at two o'clock that afternoon. The latest federal attorney assigned to the case as well as Steve Fleishman and Nick Long would be in attendance.

Bo called Sean and arranged for a rather large bouncer to be at Paul's office from two o'clock to whenever the meeting was over. At two hundred dollars per hour, Sean said he'd have the biggest and baddest character there.

Bo and Joe walked into Paul's luxurious office at one-thirty. The bouncer was already there. He graciously accepted the thousand dollars Bo handed him and vowed to protect Joe with his life. Feds or no Feds.

The conference room was all set up and the videocassette camera was tested to ensure that everyone would be taped and the sound level was correct.

Bo also handed Joe the small cassette tape of the Rogers family shooting to hand deliver to the US attorneys at the conclusion of the meeting.

Bo was nervous and his forehead shined with perspiration. Joe was calm and collected, and Paul was, just Paul. The affidavit was perfect. Bo was grateful for that.

At five before two o'clock, the new US attorney general, flanked by Steve Fleishman and Nick Long, entered the office and were quickly ushered to the conference room.

Steve Fleishman and Nick Long were definitely not pleased about this rather impromptu meeting, and the look on their faces reflected their true feelings. The new US attorney general was a heavyset gentleman about fifty-five years old from Miami. He was Hispanic and not really friendly or outgoing.

Paul immediately took control of the meeting, and when all had sat down, then, and only then, did Joe appear. He sat at the head of the table and introduced himself.

Paul laid the ground rules and began the direct examination of Joe Marx. It took about two hours before he concluded. Joe answered each and every question thoroughly.

When Paul had finished, the three US attorneys then started asking a barrage of questions. Each one was answered slowly and succinctly by Joe.

Bo just sat in amazement as Joe proved to be an incredibly strong witness for him.

At exactly 5:00 p.m. Paul's secretary poked her head into the room and carried a notary seal with her.

Joe read the four-page affidavit out loud and then signed it before her and all the men. When he was finished, Joe rose to leave.

"I'm going to visit the bathroom."

"Just make sure you don't go anywhere," said Steve Fleishman. "We want all your personal information. Although you may think this is over, it's not by a long shot. We may be filing criminal charges against you. Tax evasion, wire fraud, and conspiracy to name a few possible charges."

Joe winked at Bo when he left the room. Bo realized it would be the last time he would ever see the man again.

When about ten minutes had passed, both Steve and Nick ran to the bathroom. The only person they encountered was the massive bouncer. They were seething red when they returned.

"He's gone," shouted Nick.

"Where'd he go?" hollered Fleishman.

Both Bo and Paul just shook their heads.

Fleishman then added, "All that was left in the bathroom was a thumb drive. Do you have a computer? Call for law enforcement to look for Joe."

Moments later the men listened to the audiotape of the events that transpired at the Sinclair house. The sound was incredible and it clearly demonstrated Milton Rogers's culpability and guilt while completely exonerating Bo.

When the tape was finished, the new US attorney general spoke first.

"It's clear to me that Mr. Bo Martin is innocent of all charges. An order dismissing the Indictment and a formal statement will be issued tomorrow morning from our office. I don't know what your exact plans were, but I'm glad I had the opportunity to witness this firsthand. Mr. Martin, I and my office apologize profusely for what has happened to you. I will also facsimile the statement and dismissal to the Florida Bar Association. Hopefully, you will once again be a practicing attorney in Florida. And again, my sincerest apologies."

Steve and Nick said nothing at all. But Bo didn't expect much from them anyway. The three men then rose in unison to leave the office.

It was Paul who then posed the next question, "Are you going to indict Milton Rogers for the murders of Brad Penny and Bart Sinclair?"

"It's too premature right now for me to speculate, but undoubtedly, we will investigate this matter ad nauseam."

When the men had exited the office, Paul reached for the phone. He immediately got on the phone with the Palm Beach Chief of Police. After a good ten minutes of talking and listening, Paul hung up.

"Good news, Bo."

"What?"

"There will be no formal charges filed against you for the murder of Bart Sinclair. A statement is being prepared and will be released to the press, subsequent to the Feds' statement. A facsimile will also be sent to the Florida Bar. Hopefully, your license will be reinstated."

"That's incredible. I still find this hard to believe. We've been through so much. I wouldn't trade this experience for anything, but I'm thrilled it's about over."

"Well, Bo, what are your future plans? I hope you will continue to practice estate and trust law."

"To tell you the truth, Paul, I don't really know what I'll do. My practice is in shambles."

"Bo, I don't think it's going to be too hard to rebuild your practice from scratch. You have a recognizable name, you've been successful in clearing Bart Sinclair, you have beaten the charges against you, and you're a pretty good guy."

"Thank you, Paul. I appreciate that."

"Plus, you have the huge fee that you received for representing Sinclair," reminded Paul, smiling. "I myself will find it hard to spend all of my fee as well. At least this month," laughed Paul.

"You too, my friend, you too." Bo left the office and felt as if he was walking on air.

When Bo arrived at home, Ruby's radiant smile and the red dogs' licks immediately energized him.

"Honey, what took you so long? Joe was here, thanked me, said goodbye, and left."

"He came back here?" asked Bo incredulously.

"Yes, around five-fifteen or so."

"I never thought he would."

"He said thanks for everything and thank you for restoring his faith in mankind."

"Is that all?"

"Well, not entirely."

"What do you mean not entirely?"

"He left these for me," said Ruby opening the palm of her right hand and exposing two beautiful diamond earrings. Each earring had to be at least three carats. They were the perfect size. Not too big but large enough to impress the daylights out of everyone.

"Do you like them?" asked Ruby glowing as she placed them in her ears.

"I love them, but most of all I love you."

"I love you too, Bo. I really do."

Chapter
One Hundred-One

That night they slept like babies for the first time in what seemed like an eternity.

Bo had an appointment with the doctor to make sure that his wound had healed properly. While in the waiting area, the TV broadcast was interrupted by late breaking news. The United States Attorney General's office issued a formal statement absolving Bo Martin of any criminal activity and dismissed all federal charges filed against him. The US attorney briefly answered questions but refused to discuss details about the investigation into Milton Rogers and his family.

Bo was ecstatic and beamed with joy. *What a relief*, thought Bo.

Then moments later, the Palm Beach police chief issued its formal statement eliminating Bo Martin as a suspect in the Sinclair murder. Most interesting was the chief's statement that they were indeed investigating Milton Rogers.

Bo's doctor and nurses heard both announcements and treated Bo like a celebrity. The best news of all was that the doctor gave Bo the green light to resume running.

"I'm not saying it's not going to hurt a little with all the pounding, but you can't do it any further harm by running."

Thanks, doc. That's all I wanted to hear."

"One more thing."

"What's that?" answered Bo.

"Congratulations!"

"For what?"

"You know very well. Try and stay out of trouble now, will you?"

"I'll try."

"And one final thing."

"Yes."

"My wife will be calling to set up an appointment to renew our estate plans if that's all right with you?"

"That's great," stated a smiling Bo.

Chapter

One Hundred-Two

By the time Bo entered his office, Ms. Everett was beside herself and completely frazzled.

"The phone won't stop ringing, the fax machines are printing nonstop, and you have over a hundred emails. If you would ever check your phone, you would find that you have hundreds of text messages," exclaimed an exasperated Ms. Everett.

"It's okay, Ms. Everett."

"No, it's not. You've got lots to do around here. The first step is to hire a few new associates and get this place hopping like before. I hated being the only person in here recently. And I want a twenty percent raise and a say in all the new hires."

"You've got it," said Bo leafing through all the faxes, looking for one particular letter in earnest.

At the bottom of the stack was the facsimile he was most anxious to read. It was from the Florida Bar, and it reinstated him to active status as a licensed Florida attorney.

Bo really didn't think the day could get much better. He was still smiling ear to ear when his buddy, Hank, walked in.

"I heard the good news," said Miles, smiling.

"Yeah."

"Is that all you have to say?"

"Nope. Let's go for a run tonight. I'm cleared to resume training"

"Excellent. My clothes are in the car."

Both men were ecstatic that these past few months, which seemed like an eternity, had finally come to a pleasant end. Neither man wanted to acknowledge the huge risks they had taken. Death and imprisonment were two facets they wanted to put behind them and move forward.

"So what are you going to do now?" asked Hank.

Running and grimacing at conversation pace, Bo answered Hank honestly, "I think I'm going to try and rebuild my law practice, restore the Martin family name but limit my work weeks to no more than fifty hours."

"Dream on," laughed Hank. "Have you any clue how much work you have piled up back at your office? It would take you weeks to even catch up. Then with new clients from all your publicity, plus the return of your former clients, tell me how you're going to work less?"

"I'm going to delegate more."

"To whom?"

"It looks as if I'm going to hire some new people. Ms. Everett will help."

"Bo, you're also going to have to train them and pay them competitive wages."

"I realize that."

"And do you realize that in New York City, first year legal associates are making in excess of one hundred fifty thousand dollars?"

"That's a lot of Wills," joked Bo.

"I can't even imagine," answered Hank.

The men covered the next few miles with their conversations directed on the Miami Dolphins and Miami Hurricanes. They were oblivious to the late-model Crown Victoria that was watching their every step.

When the men had finished and were back at Bo's office, the silver-haired CIA agent and his partner were soon at the office door banging loudly.

Bo didn't want to answer the door, but at the last moment he relented and opened the office.

"Can we have a few words with you?" asked the partner.

"Sure, be my guest," countered Bo.

"Looks like I should be leaving," stated Hank.

"No, stay. We have questions to ask of you as well."

"Me?"

"Yes, you, Mr. Hank Miles. Both of you are not out of the woods yet."

Bo was tired from all the excitement of the past several weeks, plus he was anxious to put this whole ordeal behind him. The last thing he wanted was another federal bureaucrat threatening him with more federal charges.

"We've now questioned most of the Rogers family members."

"And?"

"Everyone's still pointing their fingers at you, Mr. Martin."

"I wouldn't expect anything less. The best defense is sometimes an all-out offense."

"We realize that and are trying to eliminate some of their smokescreen."

"So, how can we help you, guys?" asked Hank.

"The Rogers claim that the tape Mr. Joseph Marx left for the attorney general is bogus and doctored."

"It sure didn't sound that way to me," responded Bo.

"Well, we need more information on this Marx fellow. Like where does he live, what's his phone number, how can we get in touch with him, and why on earth would he help you?"

"I really wish I could help you, guys, but there's nothing I can say. I don't have any answers to your questions," said Bo.

"You know we could charge you with obstruction of justice. In this case alone you would be looking at three to five years in a federal prison camp."

"Camp Fed?" asked Bo.

"Not any more. The federal camps operate more like prisons now. They are filled with stringent rules and regulations over crowding, and a general absence of compassion to the inmates. At least your life won't be in danger."

"Am I supposed to be scared? Because I'm not. I've done absolutely nothing wrong."

"Funny, don't you realize how many people have died, and yet you sit here gloating like it's all a game?"

"Let me tell you something," said Bo pointing his finger at the two men and raising his voice. "I don't think for a minute that this is some game. I've been scorned every second of every day. I know Milton Rogers and his family are killers. I feel one hundred percent certain that Milton had Brad Penny and Bart Sinclair murdered. Heck, the man tried to kill me and his sons tried to murder Hank. So don't go around trying to intimidate me or insinuate that I haven't been impacted by this entire ordeal. I certainly have."

"We understand what you have gone through," said the silver-haired gentleman trying to calm the situation down.

"No, you don't. Not for one second," countered Bo.

"Just tell us why."

"Why what?"

"Why is Milton Rogers out to destroy you?"

"Because he thinks I stole the gems Milton was planning to pay Jean Valhomme with. I didn't steal the gems and I believe the only person who could have double-crossed Milton is Bart Sinclair, and Milton put an end to that, didn't he?"

"We don't know for sure."

"Well, open your eyes, and review the facts. I'm sure that if you check the most recent sales figures at Sinclair and Sons Inc. you will undoubtedly find a huge sale. More than likely that sale is from the real diamonds that Milton retained in his possession after purchasing them from Bart but that Bart somehow retrieved."

"But how? How did he do it?"

"Beats me," answered Bo. "I'm not an investigator."

"Okay. Well that's it from us. We're out of here. Just make sure that neither one of you goes anywhere."

"Don't worry, we'll call," stated Hank.

When the two CIA men had left the office building, Hank began to speak before Bo motioned him to shut up immediately. "Let's go outside," said Bo directing Hank to the door.

"Who knows if the office is bugged or not."

"Oh, I'm sorry. I forgot."

"No problem."

"Are you still worried about Milton Rogers?" asked Hank.

"Not at all. Trust me with the pressure now off me and focused on the Rogers family, it's highly unlikely we will ever hear from them again."

"I sure hope you're right."

"Of course I am," sounded a confident Bo.

"Well, tell me, what are the plans with the offshore companies?"

"Hank, you're the president of your very own company."

"So?"

"So, you can do with it whatever you want."

"Oh, right," Miles said mockingly.

"I'm dead serious."

"You mean to tell me that the thirty million dollars in that company is all mine?" asked Hank.

"Exactly."

"No way."

"Yes way."

"Bo, I couldn't."

"You can, and you will. My only recommendation is that you wait about a year or so before making any large purchases. In the meantime, just use the corporate credit card and enjoy yourself."

"Bo, I don't know about this. Have you used the credit cards yet?"

"No."

"Well, what are your plans for the money?"

"I may give the bulk to charity. The Leukemia Society could certainly use it for research for a cure."

"That sounds like a good idea."

"I still can't believe it, Bo. Thirty million dollars. My wife is going to flip."

"Just treat her right. Buy a new house, and have her quit work if she wants to."

"I just can't believe it. Never in my wildest dreams did I figure I'd ever have even one million dollars."

"You deserve it, my friend."

"But what about Jean?"

"I think it will be virtually impossible for him to even determine who transferred the money. Plus, he's wanted for murder in the USA."

"He could hire a hit squad."

"Then I'd be killed, but you'd be just fine. He's never heard of you before."

"I hope you're right."

"Trust me."

"I have, and I will. Thanks for the run."

"You too. Thanks for stopping by."

Chapter

One Hundred-Three

o went back inside his office and retrieved his cell phone and wallet before locking up. On his way home he called Ruby. No answer. That was odd, he thought as he drove toward his home at the north end of the island.

Bo clutched his cell phone tightly in his right hand. He was relieved to see Ruby's car sitting in the driveway. As he approached the front door, he felt something was amiss.

Seconds later as he opened the door, the barrel of a small handgun crashed the right side of his face. Bo went down immediately. The pain was intense, and all Bo could see were stars. He was disoriented and frightened. He heard a familiar voice but couldn't see much of anything.

The voice grew louder and louder as his hearing slowly returned. The ringing in his ears was tremendous, and his equilibrium was off keel. Blood ran down the side of his face.

Less than five minutes later, Bo started to recover. He also began assessing the situation.

Both red dogs lay motionless on the floor. Ruby was sitting in a chair with her hands tied to the armrests with what looked like a ski rope. She was white with fear and was crying.

There towering above her stood Milton Rogers. Bo tried to stand up, but the blow to his face had all but rendered him immobile.

"My, my, my. If it isn't my hero, Mr. Bo Martin," scoffed Milton.

"What have you done to my wife and dogs? You murderer!"

"Now, Mr. Martin, is that any way to treat a guest?"

"You are not now, nor ever will be, a guest in our home," countered Bo.

"Well, there's a first time for everything, and you've just been blessed. Now get up and sit in the chair beside your lovely wife."

Bo slowly did as instructed. It took all his energy to stand and walk over to the chair. Fortunately, Milton did not notice the cell phone that Bo still grasped in his hand.

When Milton walked over to where the red dogs were lying, Bo turned on the phone and punched 9-1-1 before placing it under the chair. Bo hoped and prayed that the operator would hear the conversation and send a patrol car.

Bo then yelled, "Mr. Milton Rogers, what brings you to 1200 Surf Road, home to Bo and Ruby Martin? What did you do, kill my dogs?" Bo hoped the operator picked up the vital information.

"Questions, questions. I'm in charge here, and I'll do the talking if you know what's good for you! Your precious dogs are not dead, just knocked out for a while."

"What do you want?"

"Shut up, I said. Don't talk until spoken to. I don't want to kill you immediately. Not until I make you suffer."

"Suffer?"

"You've ruined my life and the lives of my children. For that you will die a painful death. You will watch your precious wife and then your dogs suffer and die before your very own eyes. Soon thereafter pleading with me to take your pitiful life."

"Why?" asked Ruby with tears in her eyes.

"Because your husband ruined me."

"I ruined you! Let me get this straight. You purchased one hundred million dollars in jewels, then destroyed Bart Sinclair's reputation by suing him for three hundred million dollars. You then collected insurance proceeds and used the money and real gems to purchase Ecstasy pills, all of which enabled you to quadruple your original investment."

"Go on," prodded Milton.

"Then, oh let me back up first, you killed Brad Penny and a no-name enforcer before covering up the evidence. Then you next shortchanged your drug dealer, Jean Valhomme. This then caused him to travel to the USA in order to settle up the difference. Finally, you killed Sinclair attempted to kill Jean Valhomme, and did kill some of his mercenaries. Am I missing anything?"

When Milton looked down before responding to Bo's timeline of events, Bo turned off his cell phone and kicked it under the counter. He hoped like hell that the operator recorded everything.

"Not even close. But good try. Here's the real version of events. First, you arranged for the diamond switch with the taxi driver. When my wife and daughter-in-law were most vulnerable, he switched the real stones with the fake ones. Second, you then arranged for the theft of three containers of Ecstasy tablets. You left me with only one container, causing me to lose at least $250 million dollars. Third, you ridiculed and embarrassed me and my wife on the witness stand at Sinclair's criminal trial. Fourth, you thwarted our attempt on your friend and corroborator's life, and now I'm being investigated by the Feds. And fifth, but not least, you shot me with a damn spear gun."

"You shot me first," countered Bo.

"And I'll shoot you last!" cried the maniac.

"You won't get away with this. Just like you won't get away with the murders of both Brad Penny and Bart Sinclair."

"Now, I don't care. I'm ruined. At this point in time, I'm better off to my family dead than alive."

Bo knew Milton was now suicidal, and his only chance was to keep Milton talking long enough for the authorities to come. *Please God, let them come quickly*, the thought.

"Do you think I've lived the charmed life of Bo Martin?" ranted Milton.

Bo didn't say a word.

"Hell no. I've worked my way up the ladder of success through hard work. I compromised my morals and sold myself to the devil when I married Brenda. But her father had the money to lend me, and it was the only way I could grow my company. Then we had four mistakes. All four of my sons are lazy good-for-nothings. Did I tell you I'm even sleeping with Lee's wife?"

Bo just stared.

"It's pathetic, I know. But could you sleep with my fat wife? I get nightmares just trying to imagine it."

"How will killing us make your life any better?" asked Bo now feeling stronger by the minute. His bleeding had stopped, and there were no more stars in his head. Bo knew that he would have to overtake Milton in order to save Ruby's life. Bo just waited for the most opportune moment. He realized his window of opportunity was closing fast. Ruby's frightened face caused Bo's heart to pound, and he vowed to protect her no matter what.

"Well that's enough conversation. Now down to business," hollered Milton.

"What do you want from me? I'll give you anything. Just don't hurt my wife. She's completely innocent. Completely."

"That's why she's going to die first."

Then Milton turned to face Ruby and raised his gun with his left hand, since the index finger was now gone on his right hand. Bo sprang from his chair like a cat and threw himself at the man. The gun went off, narrowly missing Ruby and instead lodged in the wall.

Ruby looked on in horror as the two men rolled on the ground fighting for control of the gun.

In the melee of the struggle, the front door opened, and in barged several armed police officers followed by the two CIA agents. When Bo heard their commands to stop, he released his grip on Milton and began to stand up.

For a brief moment it appeared that Milton would surrender without a further fight. It was at the precise moment when everyone had let their guard down that Milton reached and picked up the gun.

The explosion sounded deafeningly loud in the close quarters of the Martin household. But that was nothing compared to the barrage of gunfire that returned the shot and riddled the body of Milton Rogers.

Bo crawled over to Ruby and tried to assist with untying her hands and feet. She was horrified and sobbed uncontrollably on Bo's shoulder once she was set free.

"Oh my God. Oh my God. I've never been so frightened in my entire life," sobbed Ruby.

"It's okay, sweetheart. Everything's going to be just fine," countered Bo stroking her hair gently and trying to calm both their frayed nerves.

"Are you two okay?" asked the police officers.

"I believe so," said Bo, speaking behalf of both of them.

But no sooner had Bo spoken when Ruby noticed dark red blood on her shirt. Ruby shrieked with fear. Bo looked down only to find himself bleeding from his left arm.

"You've been shot again," exclaimed Ruby.

Bo grabbed his triceps with his right hand and found the gunshot hole. Instantly, the pain hit him hard, he felt lightheaded, and nearly collapsed to the floor.

"We've got to get him to the hospital," shouted Ruby.

"Don't worry," said the silver-haired CIA agent. "It's only a flesh wound."

"Easy for you to say, Mr. Government Agent," countered Ruby.

"Excuse me for interjecting my two cents worth, but I've seen many gunshot wounds, and I can tell you that your husband is going to be fine."

"But what' will be the best news to you is that we got Milton's confession on tape. The emergency dispatcher was able to record everything from your phone. I have to hand it to you that was pretty ingenious. Not only did you notify us of your whereabouts, but Milton's confession will allow us to close this case. More importantly for you two, is that Bo Martin is no longer our concern. This concludes matters from the government's standpoint."

"Well that's a relief," cried Ruby. "Now can we do something for my husband? He's turning ghost white."

Bo went into shock and lost consciousness. When Bo awoke, he found himself once again in the hospital. Ruby, his parents, and Hank were all milling about in his hospital room. All were listening to Ruby describe the most recent events. Bo was still groggy from all the pain medication but was mostly thankful to be alive. The last words he heard before falling fast asleep were that the dogs would be just fine.

Hours later when Bo woke again only Ruby was in the hospital room. She was clearly exhausted from the day's events, but to Bo, she was more beautiful than ever.

Bo convinced her to join him on his hospital bed and she soon fell fast asleep on his good right shoulder. *Love, it doesn't get any better than this*, thought Bo as he too fell fast asleep.